Endorsements

"What makes this fictional story of end times so intriguing is how Judith Becker skillfully frames it within the Bible's own cosmology. Prophecies of astral and geophysical judgments today are usually dismissed either as code words for political upheaval or as ancient exaggerations of ordinary phenomena. This author lets biblical cosmology speak for itself with both its catastrophic natural elements and its supernatural orchestration for a story you can't put down."

Charlie Clough–BS Massachusetts Institute of Technology, MS Texas Tech University, ThM Dallas Theological Seminary, Retired Atmospheric Scientist with the US Department of Defense, President Bible Framework Ministries. Editorial writer on climate change for the Cornwall Alliance

"In writing Book 3 of The Armageddon Trilogy, The End…And a New Beginning, J. E. Becker again empresses with her grasp of Bible prophecy, and reinforces her remarkable talent as a novelist.…This book makes John the Revelator's great apocalyptic foretelling come alive in a way worthy of its majesty, power and glory.

Terry James, general editor of Rapture Ready website and author of The American Apocalypse and Last-Days Diary.

The End...
and a
New
Beginning

3 THE ARMAGEDDON TRILOGY

The End...
and a
New
Beginning

J.E. BECKER

TATE PUBLISHING
AND ENTERPRISES, LLC

The End ...and a New Beginning
Copyright © 2012 by J.E. Becker. All rights reserved.

No part of this publication may be reproduced, stored in a retrieval system or transmitted in any way by any means, electronic, mechanical, photocopy, recording or otherwise without the prior permission of the author except as provided by USA copyright law.

This novel is a work of fiction. Names, descriptions, entities, and incidents included in the story are products of the author's imagination. Any resemblance to actual persons, events, and entities is entirely coincidental.

The opinions expressed by the author are not necessarily those of Tate Publishing, LLC.

Published by Tate Publishing & Enterprises, LLC
127 E. Trade Center Terrace | Mustang, Oklahoma 73064 USA
1.888.361.9473 | www.tatepublishing.com

Tate Publishing is committed to excellence in the publishing industry. The company reflects the philosophy established by the founders, based on Psalm 68:11,
"The Lord gave the word and great was the company of those who published it."

Book design copyright © 2012 by Tate Publishing, LLC. All rights reserved.
Cover design by Blake Brasor
Interior design by James Mensidor

Published in the United States of America

ISBN: 978-1-62024-470-8
1. Fiction / Religious
2. Fiction / Suspense
12.08.28

Dedication

I dedicate this book to the awesome and all powerful Lord God who created the heavens and the earth, and who periodically changes them both (Ps. 102:25, 26). During these times one of the hosts of heaven comes down and interacts with the earth. This trilogy tells a story about the final encounter based on Bible prophecy. Modern man does not remember these encounters because the earth has been at peace with the heavens for twenty-seven centuries. When Jesus returns to rule his kingdom on earth, he will change the surface of the earth one more time. There have been six other encounters. Most people know about the flood but maybe not the others. My purpose in writing the trilogy is to show how these changes written in the book of Revelation come about through his manipulation of the heavens. Because of my background in geology, I tend to go heavy on description. I hope the reader will bear with me. I just want people to see the awesome power of God and his precise application of that power.

Acknowledgments

First, I want to thank my Lord for the miracles he performed when I lost four thousand words by copying an old file over my latest one by stupidity. (They were absolutely gone!) I pleaded in prayer. He restored every word. Then I did it again at the very end of the book. That time I was so beaten down by losing my motherboard, my vacuum cleaner, and my refrigerator all the very same week that I didn't even have the faith to ask for help. Nevertheless, he miraculously restored my work anyway.

I also want to thank my son Adam who helped me out of many a computer jam. Other major help and encouragement came from my invaluable critique team at Christian Authors Guild: Bonnie Greenwood Grant, Marcus Beavers, and Cindy Cooper. Thanks for being so tough, guys! You are the ones who saved the reader unnecessary frustration from my endless descriptions of geological matters. By forcing me to put such writing in an appendix at the back, the book is better for it!

Trilogy Characters

Americans

Rachel Lieberman—Recent graduate from Harvard; formerly employed by the Israeli Embassy in Washington, DC; moved to Israel to marry David Solomon just before the nuclear war destroyed America. Her hatred of the "Lamb of God" movement finally separated her from David when he embraced it. Then the invasion of Russia stopped the building of the temple where she worked, causing the loss of her employment. This forced her to depend on the new believers of the Lamb who lived in the unfinished temple.

Simon Lieberman—late father of Rachel Lieberman, martyred as a preacher for the "Lamb of God" movement in Washington, DC.

Dan and Sheila Lieberman—Brother and sister-in-law to Rachel.

Gerald Goldman—Nicknamed GG, a former US Air Force pilot stranded in Israel after the nuclear war destroyed the US.

Chinese

Chao Fu Zeman—Chairman of the Central Military Commission, Head of the Communist Party and Supreme leader of China.

Major General Lin Yiang Duduai—Charismatic leader gathering to himself the power over the great army of China after Zeman was killed in the overturning, now having aspirations of a world kingdom beginning in the East.

Bo Hai Dingxiang—a boyhood friend of Lin Yiang, a Colonel in the Peoples Army of China, whom Lin Yiang raised up to Brigadier General.

Lin Cho Chonglin—Also a boyhood friend from the same northern province as Lin Yiang and Bo Hai and joined the army with them. Also raised up to Brigadier General by Lin Yiang.

Pend Lee Zedong—a friend from the early days when all joined the army together, he was promoted along with Bo Hai and Lin Cho to be a Brigadier General.

Israelis

IDF-Secret Israeli Defense Force in Petra

General Shaul Shofat—Chief of General Staff of IDF, recently resigned from the IDF in Israel to join the secret army.

General Uri Saguy—head of Israeli Intelligence, AMAN, recently fled from Israel to join the secret army in Petra.

Captain David Solomon—IDF field Security Officer in Intelligence, often used to secure important missions. He set up the original secret army under the generals and is the commander. He was also engaged to Rachel Lieberman. They split over the Lamb of God; she was full of hatred against the Lamb, because he stole her papa from her.

Malcomb and Jonathon Solomon—David's brothers.

Katz, Matza, Hillman, Feldman—the last names of some of the men assigned to David as his security team.

Esther and Sarah Solomon—David's mother and sister.

Yigael—David's head electronics and communication expert.

Gil Shama—Electronic expert that accompanies Feldman as a spy on food shipments.

Israelis Serving the New Government

Adoni´ (Ad' dō ni ')—Supreme head of the new empire.

Eli Yadin—General staff of IDF under Adoni´.

Haik Ra'amon—Former Prime Minister of Israel (Labor Party); lover, sidekick, and adoring servant of Adoni´.

Johnny Leventhal—Formerly in IDF intelligence along with David. Also a former informer for Ra'amon against "Lamb of Godders."

Religious Jews opposed to Adoni´ in Israel

Jessie Solomon—Shas Party MK (minister of the Knesset), father of David Solomon, also head of a Yeshiva—married to Esther.

Rabbi Rosenfeld—Liaison between the Temple priests and the construction contractors for the temple.

Joshua Jaffe—Former High Priest, now one of two witnesses for *Yeshua* announcing God's plagues.

Zerub Able—Former prime minister of Israel when Ra'amon becomes puppet to Adoni´. Anointed earlier to be one of two witnesses for Yeshua, at his appearance on Yom Kippur.

Palestinians

Nabil Dakkah—head of the Palestinian Authority.

Iraqis

Sergeant Majid—David's friend in communications.

Jordanians

King Alahahm Hassih—original ruler of Jordan, replaced by Nabil Dakkah, former head of the Palestinians.

Egyptians

Esmat Mizraim—President of Egypt, resistant to the new leadership taking over the Middle East.

Osama Meguid—Foreign policy leader, who favors the new leadership and leads a rebellion against Mizraim.

Lebanese

J. Leucus Adoni´—Ambitious business man, who makes himself into the Messiah to the Jews and the Mahdi to the Islamic peoples.

Anslo Bedas—An electronics' expert who wires Ra'amon's image of the dragon.

Vatican

Peter II—Pope

John McCutchen—Secretary of State

Tony Cirillo—Pope's personal secretary

Kings of the Earth—the Christian kings of Europe.

Visitors to the Vatican

Cardinal Anton de Roquelaure—French Cardinal very active in cooperating with the Pope in destroying Lamb of Godders in Belgium.

Fabian Wolf—the Cardinal's nephew who acted as a Catholic lawyer condemning God's people as heretics. (both in Book 2)

Divine Characters

For Catholics—Virgin Mary, mother of Jesus.

For Jews—Messiah, called the Moschiach by the Lubavitch Jews.

For Lamb of Godders—*Yeshua*, the Lamb of God, the sacrificed Jesus

For Islam—The Mahdi, leader of a great Islamic Kingdom in the last days.

For Israeli Remnant—(*Yeshua*, The Branch, revealed to the nation on Yom Kippur)

For Dragon worshippers—Ashtor and Ashtoreth

Prologue

Much of the world lay in ruins. An Italian station, whose satellite still operated, announced a forthcoming special broadcast. They had been collecting information from around the world as it became available. A comprehensive eye-witness report of the destruction of the disaster that had recently befallen the earth was now ready. Adoni´ had his TV tuned to this network at all times, trying to keep up with what news as could be gathered. Up until now only sporadic reports had shown that civilization had been dealt a near fatal blow. Two months after the destruction, the special program promised to show a summary of what they knew. Adoni´, the newly recognized leader of the Middle East, and Ra'amon, his close associate, had been anxiously awaiting the report.

The evening of the broadcast Adoni´ relaxed in his favorite chair. One soft, calf-skin-slippered foot, rested on the chair's matching ottoman, the other on the floor. His hands rested on the skinny chrome armrests padded on top, where his fingers rippled with impatience anticipating the broadcast.

Even though he had slipped into his favorite winter "at home" comfort clothes, he still managed to look elegant. His head of dark brown hair, gleaming with highlights of red (compliments of his

Jewish mother), had been allowed to grow a bit longer since he entered politics. Now, it sported wisps of turned up *not quite* curls, instead of his sharp, close-cut style of before. It softened his face defying his early fifties age. The touches of gray at his temples along with his slender body gave him a distinguished look, making him look younger. He was in general a handsome man.

The room was small, not meant for guests. A soft-pillowed leather couch in creamy beige, with a lifting footrest on one end, flanked Adoniʹs chair to the left. Soft ceiling track lights shone down on a huge map of the eastern Mediterranean countries from the coast to Iran—a domain he hoped would soon be his. A forty-two-inch flat screen TV was mounted on the opposite wall from the couch. Adoniʹ looked around the room, admiring his handiwork while he waited for Raʹamon to come downstairs. *It is perfect, an intimate room for the two of us, a true den*, he thought—*a man's comfort room*. He was glad he went with more modern design in his Jerusalem palace. He had furnished and decorated his Beirut home himself with classical pieces of fine antiques to show off his wealth. But here comfort ruled. Neither was he sorry he had used the opulence of that house to completely seduce Raʹamon. He had proved a great comfort to his libido since then. Adoniʹ glanced over to the liquor cabinet across from him and decided to pour himself a drink.

Raʹamon came in, just as Adoniʹ clicked on the TV on his way back to his chair.

"You are almost late. Do you want a drink?"

"Maybe later. Don't worry about it. I'll get it myself." He was similarly dressed to Adoniʹ, in comfort clothes, although he never could quite match Adoniʹs flair for style. He had that crumpled comfortable look. He flopped down on the end of the couch and raised the leg rest as the commercial ended.

THE END... AND A NEW BEGINNING

The station's anchor newsman opened the program, "Good evening world, or perhaps I should say, *you* who are left of the world. This is Wendell George reporting from Rome, Italy. WRNK TV is proud to present to you, Mother Earth, an update on your condition. As you probably already know, the communications systems on earth have taken a monstrous blow. What with all the meteorites that fell, it's a wonder anything survived, especially our satellites. Because our resources are limited this cannot be as complete a report as we would like, especially since we suspect that much of our coastlands and islands washed completely away. However, we have contact with several countries, and although we cannot bring you pictures in all cases, we do have voice contact.

"First, the physical report: for that we will go to University of Applied Science in Munich, where scientists have been trying to piece together what has happened. Good evening, Professor Roberts. Are you ready, sir?" Professor Roberts appeared on the screen in the studio, which now filled the screen of those watching.

"Yes, good evening," replied the white-haired professor with horned-rim glasses, dressed in a subdued brown tweed suit with a white open-collared shirt.

"I understand you have come up with a reason for this horrendous catastrophe."

"Well, not me, but all of us here at the university. I am only the spokesman. I don't know if we have all the answers, but we do know that the geographical poles have reversed."

George frowned, a clear look of puzzlement creased his brow, then said, "What exactly does that mean to us laymen?"

"It means the earth has turned upside down. The North Pole is now the South Pole and vice versa. If you notice, the stars in the heavens are not the same anymore. We now look at the stars normally seen by the southern hemisphere.

"Is that what caused such terrible earthquakes?"

"Yes, and they affected the whole earth. Of course they were worse at the juncture of the tectonic plates."

"Tectonic plates?"

"Those are the blocks of the earth's crust that fit roughly together rather like a jigsaw puzzle. Normally they sort of float on the earth's semi-fluid elastic interior with slight movement and an occasional adjustment. That's why earthquakes are always being reported somewhere on the earth. We only hear about those that cause great destruction to civilization like those that happen near cities with massive loss of life. But this, this is entirely different. We think the new body in the sky interacted with the earth through physical laws involving gravity and electromagnetism. It slowed the earth's rotational speed at its first approach, causing a difference between the lighter crust of the earth and the heavier mantle underneath. This may have caused the lighter crust to slide over the slower-moving interior. The friction melted the bottom of the crust, and when the earth flipped over, it cracked the surface. That made the plates knock together causing added friction. Consequently, magma erupted between the plates, and we also got extensive volcanic activity where they meet."

"Is that why the Pacific Rim is all but destroyed?" asked the reporter.

"Yes, the Pacific Plate seems to have rotated slightly. Of course, cities such as those in Chile backed by the Andes were completely washed away, leaving barren coastlines. In fact, one of the hardest hit countries was the United States."

"How can you know all this?"

"The satellites that remain also followed the earth's movement. When it turned over, they went with it, still circling the earth."

The camera switched to Wendall and caught him shaking his head. "Amazing!" he said.

"As I was saying, the land mass of the United States is completely changed. The satellites show the west coast along with Baja, California, as an island. The entire western part of the country is riddled with volcanos, but the granddaddy of them all erupted over what was once Yellowstone National Park. The entire park was located over a super volcano, so when it blew it destroyed everything within a hundred miles and sent thousands of cubic tons of ash and dust over six hundred to one thousand miles of land from its core. Its center sent up a huge fire plume and is still throwing out fire bombs as we speak, as are the other volcanos. From Yellowstone west is in total destruction, but the east is part of a greater picture. The North American plate has twisted apart, allowing oceanic waters to connect from the Gulf of Mexico to the Arctic Ocean. Besides that, the entire eastern coastline of North America has crumbled because of the massive earthquake that accompanied the split." He paused, shaking his head. "You know, not only was the US nation destroyed in the war, but now also the land itself. It's almost like the great empires of the past that completely disappeared. Nineveh was so lost they thought the Assyrian Empire was a myth. With America's land split in three pieces, no one will recognize it, especially with the coasts gone."

"Is that why we can't get a response from any of the large cities next to the oceans?"

"Yes, plus the earth's motion of turning upside down. The sudden movement caused the fluid nature of the water to spill out of the ocean basins. Huge, heaping waves hundreds of feet high flushed the shorelines in their path, causing horrendous tsunamis. And not only that, but also the sudden mixing of hot and cold blocks of atmospheric air accompanied them, causing hurricanes with gales several hundred miles per hour ripping up trees on the coasts and carrying them back out to sea in the back sweep. All the great cites on the coasts are basically gone. Tornadoes even affected many of the inland areas, as you probably know."

"Yes," replied Wendell George softly, his face losing its confident look. He sat in silence, apparently speechless. Finally, he said, "Thank you, Professor, for painting so clear a picture of this disaster." Then he added with a strained and sober manner, "I wonder if this is the beginning of the 'Day of the Lord' so avidly preached by the 'Lamb of God' people?" The question was obviously not part of the script. "By the way, what happened to them anyway? We don't hear anyone saying, 'We told you so.'" He paused, his face showing puzzlement.

Adoni´ sat forward in his chair, his face distorted in anger, and shouted at the TV, "No way! It was purely the work of our Ashtor!"

Ra'amon sat nodding his head in agreement. "Reporters always seem to interject their own ideas into the news."

"When I'm in full power, I will put a stop to that!" declared Adoni´.

Turning back to his script, Wendell George said, "Now we take you to our studios where they will show you a satellite view."

Awed at the sight, Ra'amon exclaimed, "Whoa!" The pictures showed an atmosphere heavily laden with smoke from the scores of active volcanos ejecting fire and brimstone into the atmosphere. From space the whole world appeared to be burning. Pillars of smoke ringed the Pacific Ocean and several other places, especially a huge one in northwestern Wyoming over Yellowstone National Park. "Some of those volcanos in the United States have never been seen before." He shook his head and shuddered. "The 'Lambers' said the world would be destroyed by fire."

Adoni´ continued intermittently to mutter disgruntled words at the reporter's conclusions.

When the satellite scene swept west across the Pacific Ocean, he said, "Mount Fuji in Japan has all but destroyed the main island.

Actually, Japan as a political country no longer exists, nor do many of the Pacific Islands, and those remaining shifted their latitude and longitude, as you can plainly see," said George, his face filling the screen once more.

"It will certainly affect the economy of what's left in the Far East with the oil production of Indonesia destroyed," he said thoughtfully.

"Now, we turn to the East Coast, where scenes are being streamed to us live." Wendell George gasped, as the camera on the satellite zoomed in on Brazil's Rio de Janeiro. The city boasting two of the earth's largest forests on either side lay in an enormous mix of rubble, with trees, broken buildings, cars, ships, and any other trapping of civilization piled against Mount Corcovado and other peaked mountains in the area. Corcovado, now devoid of its statue of Christ, lost its individuality. The famous harbor had disappeared under the piles of jungle scraped off of Brazil's triangular-shaped bulk that jutted into the Atlantic before tapering down to Rio. The ocean water, apparently sweeping from the Amazon River south, carried the jungle with it, covering Rio and Sao Paulo as well. Farther south Buenos Aries showed the same rubble piles reminiscent of the great earthquake and tsunami of 2011 in Japan.

As the scene shifted to the north, he saw the new area of land in the United States this side of what would have been the Mississippi River. Again George added words not in his script, almost to himself rather than his audience. "The United States seems to have taken blows worse than any other country." Then he shifted in his seat and continued.

"No wonder we couldn't hear from the coastal cities," he said. "The oceans have ravaged the coasts everywhere. Civilization remains on a very limited basis worldwide. After that report from Professor Roberts we can understand why. Of course, the United

States' eastern cites were mostly destroyed in the war earlier anyway. We have no report from the rest of the western hemisphere."

Next, the scene turned to the west coast of Europe. It was obvious that England was hard hit by the tsunamis, as well as Portugal and Spain. Wendell George could only shake his head. "We can see why most of the world trade has all but stopped. The overturning must have destroyed much of the world's shipping. Thank goodness the Scheldt River Harbor was protected by England's landmass; even so, the water covers the lowlands of Holland having washed away their dyke system. We go now to our correspondent, Alexander Carras in Greece, to check out the Mediterranean area—Hello, Alex, tell us about what's happening in the Aegean region.

"Hello, Wendell," responded the Greek newsman, standing in front of a harbor. "As you can see behind me, much of our shipping has been destroyed." The picture showed ships broken and piled on the dry land. Some ships had crashed into the docks, smashing both, while others showed smaller crafts sitting deftly on top of larger vessels as if some giant hand had carefully placed them.

"We still have some ships moored in the secure harbors of the Adriatic, which are at present undergoing repairs. We hope to have a fleet seaworthy shortly. Unfortunately, the waters from the Black Sea/Marmara Sea corridor destroyed a great deal besides shipping. The geologists tell us that the huge block of rock under the Bosporus Strait (which had made it shallow compared to the depth under the Marmara Sea and the Black Sea) gave way, letting the Black Sea's deep waters spill through the straits, washing out the Bosporus and the Dardanelles completely. Now the whole area is part of the Aegean Sea. Its overflowing waters swept away much of our eastern coast.

"Because of this loss of shipping, I understand many countries, mainly in Europe, suffer from lack of fuel. The pipelines don't help either, with the oil and gas lines from Russia lying in pieces because of the earthquakes," continued Alex. "Now, they are wholly dependent upon Israel's gas lines from under the sea, but I doubt if they held either, since much of the Mediterranean dumped into the Sahara Desert."

"That will up the death toll," replied George. "Transportation and heating have really taken a blow. Even wood for heating homes is scarce in some places because of the ravages of the hurricanes we heard about from Roberts. The ferocious winds must have ripped up the trees, and the giant tsunamis swept them away. The falling meteorites lit some of the forests on fire as well. January is no time to be without fuel."

"Speaking of tsunamis, wasn't most of Istanbul destroyed by the Black Sea spill?"

"Yes, the Black Sea sweeping west of the Pontus Mountains, except for their small steep river valleys, thrust its main body of water through the Bosporus, taking out all of Istanbul except what was on very high ground," Carras said.

"I'm sure many places around the world suffered this same disaster where large bodies of water were close. Thank you, Alex," he said, turning away from the studio monitor showing the Greek reporter.

"Now turning to the political scene, one of the bright spots in the world is the developing cooperation of the nations in the Middle East. Having recovered from the catastrophe with surprisingly minimal destruction, they are genuinely working for peace.

"China is a different story, however. Their eastern coastal provinces from Beijing southwest have been torn away all the way to Taipan. What's left of Beijing is now part of the new coast of the Korean Bay, whose waters filled in the space of the great crack under sea level. The original Communist Party government perished in the disaster. Major General Lin Yiang Duduai seems to have inherited the leadership of their new government."

Adoni´ listened with satisfaction. He said to Ra'amon, "The world that's left will be carved up among the strong, and *we* are going to get *our* share. Now is the time to develop a real Global Community. What we need is one economy, one religion, and one political ruler over the whole world. We already have the religion and the leader—me." He smiled. "I feel my greatness beginning to rise."

Ra'amon looked over at Adoni´ with adoring eyes. *And I will find my place in history by your side.*

What an opportunity!" continued Adoni´. "All the earth's governments will be in disarray. Their economies ruined! Surely we can take advantage of their weaknesses and offer them some leadership. Together *we* will rebuild civilization itself!"

"Yes," shouted Ra'amon, punching the air with his right fist.

Chapter 1

The political climate in Israel had changed rapidly after the destruction of the Russian Army.[1] The people idolized Adoni´, seeing him as the fulfillment of their ancient scriptures because he predicted his god would save them. He and his god had indeed saved them from the Russians by turning the world upside down while pouring flaming meteorites on the Russian army. A popular saying was "Who can make war like the Beast?" referring to the Dragon god in the sky. Seeing Adoni´ as their Messiah was only possible because they were almost totally devoid of knowledge of the Hebrew scriptures. Popular sentiment seemed to rule.

Cautious *Yeshua* believers, seeing the trend, moved as many of their belongings into the temple as were necessary for existence. *Yeshua* had said in his word that having food and raiment they should learn to be content, and they were. They knew *Yeshua* would come and end their hardship, so having the essentials and each other they concentrated on enduring. They had cordoned off private areas for each family and reserved other areas for common use. The women took over the menial tasks together, such as feeding the group and doing the laundry, or caring for the children. The men provided the groceries from their pooled resources; most still had employment in the economy. The unemployed dug[2] a shaft, hoping to find storage rooms under the temple, which they did after digging twenty some feet straight down.

As a symbol to the outside world, Joshua, their high priest, and Zerub Abel, their former prime minister, procured black tent material, the sackcloth mentioned in the ancient Scriptures, that the women fashioned into garments for them. They were simple robes that hung to their feet. To the populace, who glimpsed them on occasion when on the Temple Mount, they looked like two black crows who spelled doom and darkness. To the former orthodox priests, who had rejected *Yeshua*, they screamed mourning as in fasting and sackcloth. It angered them because they felt condemned as priests—especially since Joshua Jaffe, their own high priest, had deserted them for a different God, "the Lamb."

After a month of adjusting the laws in the Sanhedrin and the constitution of Israel, they arranged for Adoni´ to be qualified for kingship in Israel. Then they began the preparations for his coronation. The faithful gathered on the temple porch daily to watch the spectacle unfold. First, wrecking crews had shown up to remove the wall that separated the Dome of the Rock from the Jewish Temple. Then they had begun to build a platform to the temple's right (facing east) stretching across the site of the former wall. Zerub Abel said at the time, "Is this some kind of symbolic gesture to say we are all now *united*? Not a chance!"

After they completed the five-foot-high platform and its steps, they covered it with red carpet and embellished the sides with purple velvet drapes topped with golden swags. A canopy above repeated the gold and purple. Three chairs covered with gold velvet upholstery divided the platform equally, except the center chair, slightly larger and resembling a throne, stood forward by a foot. Several rows of special seating stood in front of the coronation grandstand.

THE END... AND A NEW BEGINNING

The coronation day arrived amidst much celebration and fanfare. Jerub Abel and Joshua Jaffe, along with all the other faithful, stood on the porch to observe the ceremony. On that day, the crowds had been gathering since before noon, not wanting to miss a single minute of the ceremony. Gradually, dignitaries filled up the seats in front. Finally, the crowd hushed at the sound of trumpets. Through the eastern gate, the one called the Golden Gate, marched six men, three abreast, holding long straight silver trumpets sending out synchronized blasts at intervals as they marched. Hanging from the long trumpets were banners emblazoned with a red dragon. Behind them came a golden carriage drawn by two pure-white horses, holding Adoni´ and Ra'amon seated on tufted golden-velvet seats. Behind him came six soldiers, dressed also in white uniforms on solid black horses, each carrying rifles in the holsters mounted to the saddles.

"The sheer audacity of the man!" declared Zerub Abel. "He dares to use *our* Golden Gate, coming up *our* ramp, and crossing *our* bridge to the Temple Mount. He humiliates us Jews and debases our God on his own holy mountain."

"Be careful. You may stir up his wrath against us," said one of the priests.

"Don't worry. Our God is able to take care of us," said Joshua in a whisper.

The royal parade came to the huge painting of Ashtor, the bloody Dragon god's image erected at the corner of temple altar before the Russian invasion. They stopped momentarily to salute the image before continuing to the coronation platform. Adoni´, arrayed in a regal uniform, dismounted the carriage. He walked to an image of himself, a statue standing at the base of the painting, and pressed himself against it, then stepped back to bow low.

"Look at that!" sneered Zerub Abel. "Is he indicating that he worships himself? What blasphemy!"

Adoni´ climbed back into the carriage, and they continued to the platform. He ascended the stairs and stood proudly overlooking the crowd. He looked every bit the image of a glorious king adding the finishing touch to the setting. Arrayed in dress whites with gold epaulets on the shoulders, a satin, royal-purple band stretching diagonally across his chest, he punctuated the glory of the platform. He waited, while Ra'amon carried an ornate gold-plated box up the stairs. Then a man on the front row of dignitaries joined them on the stage.

By the arrangement of the procedures, Adoni´ apparently wanted to leave the impression that he had taken over Jehovah's territory. But it wasn't completely true. God, by his word, had measured out only the courtyard to Adoni´ and the Gentiles. The temple priests still ruled the ground to the left behind him from the altar backward and including the unfinished Jewish temple. He only held the ground from his dragon image at the corner of the altar forward into the courtyard. Part of his crowd occupied that forward ground. High government officials and dignitaries from his coalition of countries sat in the reserved seats. Supporters among the people crowded in every remaining space behind those seated.

Chapter 2

Joshua Jaffe looked with disgust at Ra'amon, the former prime minister of Israel and now known as Adoni´'s most avid supporter, as he signaled the trumpeters. "What a sycophant!" he declared.

The trumpeters stood in their smart dress uniforms, short purple capes flung over their shoulders, like flamboyant drum majors of a high school band. They stretched out at an angle, three on each side of the platform, facing the crowd but eyeing Ra'amon at the same time. They raised their trumpets, ready to sound the opening of the ceremony.

Seeing Ra'amon's signal, the trumpeters sent twelve blasts of the trumpet, each exactly four seconds in length. A newly appointed official of Adoni´'s government arose from the left-hand chair, stepped to the small lectern, and read a long description of the feats accomplished by Adoni´, especially the power unleashed by Adoni´'s god against the Russian Army. Finishing that, he went on to enumerate the reasons Israel would now be ruled by a king. As he finished, the crowd whistled and cheered their approval.

Next came the actual crowning of the king. Ra'amon carefully removed the crown from its golden box. He lifted up a magnificent piece of art with ten horn-like projections adorned in gems at the pinnacles. A huge ruby in the center of the front represented Adoni´'s god, reminiscent of the color of the dragon seen in the sky in his first appearance.

Ra'amon stepped forward with the crown held high over Adoni´'s head and said, "I crown you king over Israel as well as the king over the kings in Assyria, Lebanon, soon Egypt, and with many more to come."

A shout went up from the people, and then they began to chant, "Long live the king of Israel! Long live the king of kings!" The tumult continued until Adoni´ raised his hand to quiet them.

"I am not only your king, but also your god. Remember, I told you that Ashtor has made me his representative on this earth. Those sacrifices are for expiation of sins." He turned and pointed to the altar to his left. "I forgive you your sins. I will look after you. I and my god are one. You don't need to offer blood sacrifices to us everyday as the priests offered to *Yeshua*, who doesn't even exist. This altar will now serve the real god," he said, pointing again to the altar. "Ashtor will show us how to worship him and replace the rituals so stringently required by the old god. Just follow me, and together we will build our god a great kingdom, a utopia on the earth." Again, cheers and whistles filled the air.

Joshua Jaffe, still watching from the temple porch along with the rest of the faithful, shook his head. "How *dare* he stand here on the holy Temple Mount and make such a blasphemous statement!" Suddenly, his breath almost stopped as the indignation of the Lord rose up inside him. Turning, he pointed directly at Adoni´ with his right index finger and burst forth with a loud voice, "*You* are no god, neither is that image god. You speak blasphemy! The image you saw in the heavens was merely the instrument our great Creator, or one of his hosts used to destroy the Russian army." Then he turned to the people, again pointing his finger toward them, and said, "And

THE END... AND A NEW BEGINNING

you—you are like the people of Jeremiah and Elijah's day. You are reprobates just like them."

"Yes you are," said Zerub Able in just as loud a voice, as he stepped up beside Joshua, providing an unmistakable unity. "Therefore, you will not see rain upon your land for three and a half years, says the Lord God of Israel. You will learn who God really is, as those reprobates of old did!"

After seconds of stunned silence, the people erupted in a violent outcry. Adoniʹ watched the tumult with an unperturbed grin and then raised his hands quieting the crowd. "Don't pay any attention to them. Our god reigns. They will soon see who is god indeed." Then he motioned to Ra'amon to continue the ceremony. Following this, the kings already allied with Adoniʹ and various government officials came forward to swear fealty to the new king. At the end of the grand ceremony, the men on horseback pulled their rifles from the holsters in unison, raised them, and shot a twenty-one gun salute into the air as a tribute to the new king. The smell of gunpowder permeated the air, reminding the people that military power now backed their new leader.

—

Rachel was shocked at the spiritual power and prophetic message given by the high priest and former prime minister. *Do they believe that Adoniʹ is that infamous leader spoken of in Daniel like I do? I must go and study that again.* She had not connected the "little horn" in Daniel with the New Testament. In fact, she had avoided their study of the New Testament altogether because it spoke of the Lamb, the Christian's God, whom she hated. *Maybe I should join them just to understand their thinking. I don't have to believe like they do, just stay informed.*

All work on the temple had stopped long ago because Adoniʹ had suspended the government-subsidized finances. His excuse was that too many other things took priority since the earthquake. Much of the infrastructure of the city was in need of repair.

Because of this, Rachel found herself without any means of support, since her job was to work between the priests and the construction crews on the temple construction, overcoming language barriers. The economy had become extremely tight, and food prices were soaring. She had ridden out the catastrophe on the Temple Mount along with the rabbis and others of the faithful. Jesse was particularly warm toward her and gave her that security she had been missing. Even now in her loss as to what to do, she didn't feel as lost as she could have otherwise. She hated depending upon them for her needs, but what else could she do?

A year ago, when Rachel first joined the faithful at the temple, Jesse had told her about Ezekiel 38 and 39 that predicted the Russian invasion and ultimate destruction. She had studied that passage and seen it come to pass. Everyone rejoiced together as Jehovah fulfilled his word. Such a joy and confidence showed in these "elect" that she began to rethink her faith. Solid evidence proved that God lived again among his people. The power from the ark demonstrated that. It had become the means of heating their living quarters during the winter months. But she hadn't gone as far as to accept *Yeshua* as the *Moschiach*. No, she was not really one with them in spirit, and she felt badly about living off of them. Jesse had moved back home because of his responsibilities in the Knesset. But Rachel, having no income, had to give up her apartment and come back to the temple. She needed to contribute. But what could she do?

Chapter 3

Lt. General Shaul Shofat, chief of general staff of the Israeli Defense Force, leaned forward, his hand tracing a small award placard sitting on his desk. His mouth closed in a grimace as he shook his head. He didn't dare say what was on his mind. Some electronic ear might hear. He was proud of his past service; the award had venerated his bravery serving his country when he was younger. A knock on the door brought him out of his reverie.

"Come in, my friend. It's good to see you," he said to General Uri Saguy, as the IDF's Intelligence chief stuck his head in the doorway.

After shutting the door, Uri looked at Shaul and lifted his eyebrows as if in a question. "You don't look too busy for this overworked chief of general staff I keep hearing about."

Shaul sighed. Then he said with mock enthusiasm, "Sit, sit, my friend. I was wondering if you would like to go to lunch today. I have a special job for you. Our new king has some enemies. We need to make a special unit in Intelligence and assign it to cover this."

Again Uri looked at Shaul in a questioning manner. Shaul raised his finger to his lips. "So I thought we might as well do lunch," Shaul went on.

"I'm surprised. I—I thought everyone loved Adoní."

"Apparently not."

After the two men came out of the office laughing and joking about where to have lunch, General Shofat informed his secretary, "We may take a little extra time today. Tell anyone who calls I may not be available until three o'clock. We have some planning to do. Might as well do it over lunch," he said, as he gave her a wink. She smiled back.

After they were entirely out of the building, Shaul spoke in earnest, "We must be extra cautious. You know Adoni´ doesn't trust us, and I wouldn't put it past him to have spies everywhere—even listening devices. Don't say anything while in my car. If it has a bug, that would add to his suspicions. Don't even turn your head to see if we are being followed."

"Don't worry," said Uri, "I am aware of our situation, and I had some of my trusted and *very* talented men prepare us a device for detecting a tail while we are out."

Shaul laughed. "Leave it to Intelligence to tap into the electronic genius of the Jewish mind. How does it work?"

"It looks like a GPS screen. Actually, it's only a small digital video camera showing the rear traffic on the screen. I'll watch it closely while you drive. We can communicate with hand signals if a tail shows up. Shall we try it out?"

"That will be perfect. We can talk about this new restaurant outside the city that I heard of. It will give us an excuse to use the device." As soon as they reached Shaul's car, Uri pulled a small screen from his pocket, set it in the GPS holder on the dashboard, and turned it on. Then he said, "Just where is this new restaurant that you need an electronic device to find it?"

"He proclaimed himself…as God," exclaimed David, the commander of the hidden army in Petra. "What blasphemy!"

THE END... AND A NEW BEGINNING

"And that's not all," said David's father, Jesse, a member of the Knesset (MK) who represented the Shas Party in Israel's government body. "He also said they didn't need to offer sacrifice on the altar anymore either, because the Jewish god didn't even exist. Of course Adoni´ had already caused the priests to suspend the daily sacrifices because of the dragon image standing at the corner of the altar."

"He must be that beast defined in the book of Revelation," said David. "Remember we studied about him before we left home."

"I have some news you will be interested in," said his father. Since the work on the temple has been shut down, Rachel lost her job and had to move back in with the temple believers."

David smiled. *That was very good news indeed.* "Has she changed her mind about the Lamb?"

"Not that I know of," replied Jesse. "How did she develop such a hatred for our God? I don't believe you ever told me."

"It all started when she was a child. She was such a Jewish zealot, even then. She was persecuted by some equally zealous Christian children and very much offended. Then *Yeshua* appeared to her papa when the asteroid caused the darkness. You know, that week when we signed the peace covenant with the Palestinians. Remember, you called me in Washington."

"Yes." He paused. "Her father had a special calling from *Yeshua* himself?"

"Big time! In fact he became a famous leader in the 'Lamb' movement in Washington, D.C. and was later martyred. Rachel had been very close to her father, learning from him all about the M*eschiach* (Messiah). When he told her he had met the Messiah and he was the Lamb of God, she exploded and wouldn't have anything to do with him after that. You see, she had heard all about the Lamb of God from those children."

"Well, maybe being around the believers at the temple will change her mind."

"I hope so. I waited so long for her to come to Israel and now this. It's been really rough on me since we broke up—By the way, we haven't heard anything from our army headquarters since Adoni´ was crowned king. I wonder what is going on. Even the radio contact to base has been cut off."

"Maybe Adoni´'s blasphemy has something to do with it," said Jesse.

"Maybe." After David hung up he frowned. *What will that mean to my small hidden army?*

—

That's it, finis, Israel's head of general staff, the highest ranking officer in the IDF internalized. He had just finished copying the last disc of data from his hard drive and wiping his computer clean. For three weeks he had been taking his files that were in his cabinets home a bit at a time in his brief case. General Shofot finished shutting down his computer in his office in the newly built Kiryat Building that was now headquarters to the IDF in Jerusalem. (Hezbollah had destroyed the former Kiryat Complex in Tel Aviv with nuclear dirty bombs supplied by Iran, before they signed the peace treaty.) After leaving his resignation in a letter intended to be posted to Adoni´ the next day, he locked his office door and headed for his wife's sister's house to pick up the rest of his family. After dark, they would head to their rendezvous point at an old airfield storing discontinued helicopters for sale.

That night the IDF who opposed Adoni´, and all who knew of the secret army in Petra, gathered in various secret places to load all the equipment they had collected during the last few weeks.

Chapter 4

At dawn they approached David's secret army without any prior notice except for the announcement as they approached Petra. They flew in with several helicopters, two of which were heavy transporters, carrying fuel, supplies, and special electronic equipment needed to carry on a clandestine existence. They had even managed to include a couple of jeeps. As far as the rest of the IDF knew, they simply disappeared, taking with them many secrets of the army. The entire upper echelons of the department of Intelligence, with call letters AMAN, disappeared with them. (They had screened out those who approved of Adoni´.) Their action constituted treason, big time, and they all knew it, especially Adoni´'s government, after their disappearance was discovered.

When General Uri Saguy, head of AMAN, arrived with his department heads and their families, it sealed their secret location. Besides that, they had wiped out all records and names from their computers and cleaned out their files before they left. No one in the army outside their department knew of the secret army except General Shofat, who had just resigned as Chief of General Staff of the entire IDF. He came along also with his whole family. The operation had been carefully planned and executed.

Almost as soon as he landed, he said to David, "Adoni´ took over our government, and Ra'amon is his puppet. When I saw Adoni´ proclaim himself god, that was it! I couldn't stand it any more. First he said it, and then he posted an official decree stating that sacrifices were no longer necessary in his new government and stationed soldiers on the Temple Mount to enforce it. As if the priests could sacrifice anyway, with that hideous picture of the Dragon on the holy ground.[1] Then he took credit for the destruction of the whole Russian Army. Can you believe it? Such an act of God! The man is a colossal blasphemer."

"I couldn't serve under him and maintain a good conscience either," said General Saguy. Serving him would be like denying God. I never thought I would turn against my own country. But the people are under his spell. What can we do about it, Solomon? We *have* to do something."

"Well, sir, the first thing we will do is gather the faithful together and pray. We have discovered that God is ready to answer our every plea. I'm sure it is his will to stand against the devil's man."

"I'm sure it is," replied the general. "But what can *we do* to stop him?"

David thought for a second then replied, "I don't know, maybe join his enemies. The first thing we need to do is set up a network of communications to keep us informed. Did you bring any computers with you?"

"Does a dog have fleas?" Saguy laughed. "Of course, we brought computers as well as any other device I thought we might need. We haven't been in intelligence for years to be caught unprepared," he said. "Remember our motto—Truth prepares readiness! Every electronic device we have for gathering information came with us. Nothing but the finest for the true Israeli army."

"Absolutely!" said David. "Nevertheless, we will ask God's direction in all that we do from henceforth."

THE END... AND A NEW BEGINNING

David called the faithful to gather for prayer and asked God to answer the blasphemy of Adoni´, to preserve the saints still in Jerusalem, but most importantly to guide them in their fight against the evil working in Israel. Many of the older believers offered prayers as well. After the prayer David ordered one of his men to assign living quarters to the newly arrived. He asked his mother to speak with the women, helping them to adjust to their austere quarters. The new army brought with them tents for a whole city.

Although a regular army general was now in their midst, David remained in command in the field. General Saguy retained a senior advisory position since he commanded intelligence, not combat troops. Former Lt. General Shofat had resigned from the military and no longer held *any* rank. Yet, he too functioned as an advisor because of his revered wisdom. Both generals developed a close relationship with David.

After General Saguy had been there about a week he said to David, "I've been thinking over what you said about joining Adoni´'s enemies. You know Egypt's Mizraim has no love lost for Adoni´. In fact, he had a personal grudge against Adoni´ for taking over like he did. I'm thinking we might gain his help. I know an Egyptian general. We had some contact during Desert Storm. Even though we didn't get into the war, we were prepared to. Why don't I call him and see how things stand? Will such a call endanger our position?"

"No." said David. "Go ahead and call. Using the handheld phone through the satellite cannot reveal our location. We have an encrypted line with our own spread spectrum signal that cannot even be detected. Yigael says the signal can then be picked up by any phone system, so long as we have the proper routing. It is purely God's grace that our satellite survived the meteorites."

"Do I need to talk to Yigael to set it up?" he asked.

"Not really, if you have the numbers for a watts interface to their military phone system." replied David. "That gives me an idea. I could call some friends we made in Baghdad. We might find another ally. I was constantly hanging around the communications unit at the base while we were trying to get home from our spy trip, and I made friends with a couple of the operators and took note of how to reach them."

"But Captain," said Matza, "Those guys wouldn't still be there after the Russian takeover. And who knows what damage the meteorites might have done."

"Well, we have a number. At least we can find out who *is* there—if it even works."

Chapter 5

General Saguy made his call and reached the Egyptian general. After identifying himself he asked the general, "How are things going in Egypt these days?" He sensed a slight hesitation.

"That depends on who you think god is," he replied. "You probably already know this, but Mizraim doesn't think it's Adoni´."

Uri Saguy laughed heartily. "Neither do we."

"We?"

"Yes, a few of us in the IDF have formed a secret army to stand against Adoni´. We were wondering if you were interested in working with us."

"Sounds interesting, but we are pretty busy arming against attacks right now. He seems to think we belong under his thumb. What are you doing?"

"We are seeking ways to shut down his food shipments."

"I don't see how we could help you, but King Hassih might. I understand Adoni´ depends upon Iraq for his supplies. Jordan is much closer to Iraq. He's here, you know. Mizraim gave him asylum. How can he get in touch with you?"

"He can't. We do all the calling to keep our camp secret. Find out if he is interested in joining us. I'll call again."

When David pressed the numbers for the Iraqi base, a voice answered right away.

"Central headquarters, Sergeant Majid of Communications speaking."

Delighted to hear a familiar voice, David realized God had arranged the contact. *It had to be more than a coincidence!* He said, "Hi, Sarge. This is Captain David Solomon of the Israeli Defense Force. Remember me? You said to call you."

"Daveed. You made it through the war, I see. What's up?" he asked. Both he and David were speaking in Arabic.

"That's what I called to ask you. Are the Iranians gone?"

"Yes, but I would think you would already know that. After all, Adoni´ reorganized the whole country. He already ordered our farms to get into full operation now that the enemy has fled. You know that would not even be possible without the earthquakes."

"What do you mean?" asked David.

"Don't you remember when you were here, the rivers were mere trickles? That was because of the dams up north. The earthquake broke up the dams, and now we have plenty of water for our food production."

"I know about the food shortage and Adoni´ ordering the food production in Babylon. I'm just wondering about the political climate there. Is everyone behind Adoni´'s efforts?"

In the moment of silence, David sensed caution.

"Well, Captain, that's kind of a tough one."

"You mean there's mixed feelings?"

"You might say that."

THE END... AND A NEW BEGINNING

"I know what you mean. It's the same here."

"But I'm talking about the military. One doesn't know who to obey half the time."

"So am I. We are divided as well. Look Sarge, I'm just going to say it straight out. I'm with those who oppose Adoní. Which side are you on?" David asked, confident that his call could not be traced.

David heard a sigh of relief. "Thanks be to Allah! I was afraid to speak. The Iraqi military here have lost its control over our nation. Some only serve Adoní outwardly, to keep their jobs. I tend to side with them, but we have to be careful. Others think Adoní is almost a god."

"Sarge, do you think you could help us out by keeping your eyes open?"

"It might be dangerous. How could I get in touch with you?"

"You don't. We'll always call you. We can't afford for anyone to know our location. You just gather information, okay?"

"Like what?"

"I don't know yet. We just wanted to make a friendly contact. What are your hours on duty? Or give me your home phone if that's better."

"Let me think about that. My hours change; we rotate. You'll just have to take your chances. But I'm sure you know how to improvise if you get someone else."

"All right, we'll be in touch," said David and clicked off.

"Bingo!" said General Savoy coming into the room excited. "Adoní has stirred up a hornet's nest in Egypt. King Hassih took refuge there when the Russians came through Jordan. He's upset that Adoní's taken over his country. He said King Hassih might help us. Why don't we ask him to join us?"

Chapter 6

When the earth turned upside down, every mountain and island had moved out of its place—some small moves, others great. However, in China more than mountains moved. Riddled with fault lines, that nation's earthquake record contained five out of the ten worst earthquakes *ever* recorded. Naturally, this great movement of the whole earth hit them very hard.

Seeing their ancient Dragon god grow close to the earth, the population fled to underground caves and cities built during the Cold War. They fled to any underground haven where they could escape the falling meteorites that accompanied the close approach of the sky dragon. The high officials of the Peoples Party and the army retreated to their safety bunkers created for them and their families in case of a nuclear attack in an earlier decade. Deep underground and well supplied for survival, the two bunkers divided according to ranks. The Youquan Shan bunker just east of Beijing contained the top officials of the government including Chao Fu Zeman, the leader of China, the chairman of the Central Military Commission, and the highest echelon of generals of the two and a quarter billion standing Peoples Liberation Army of China, the largest in the world. The bunker located at Hohhot harbored lower-ranking generals of the army and their families. Fleeing from Beijing, the top officials all made it safely to their lair except the Commander of the Second Artillery Corp, General Lin Yiang Dehuai. He had taken a few days off to visit his family in Duolun in Inner Mongolia. Instead, he raced his family to the nearer bunker in Hohhot.

Those in Hohhot, after shaking from a tremendous shock wave that lasted for a seemingly interminable minute and three-quarters, looked around surprised by the little damage to their bunker. During the shake, a lighted wall map crashed to the floor, shattering glass in the silent room. A few chairs rattled, loose objects rolled off the desks, but the ceiling held.

Families still clutching each other relaxed their grip. Everyone looked around in surprise.

"We're alive!" shouted a child in their midst.

"We didn't collide with the great dragon after all," said a mother.

Major General Lin Yiang Duduai commanded the attention of the men. "Everyone to your post! We must assess our damages. Check your equipment. Communications, see if you can raise Youquan Shan bunker in the Tai Hang mountain range. Women and children, to your quarters. Children will need rest after all this tension. Kitchen crew, fix some snacks for everyone. We have lots of work ahead of us and no time for lounging at meals. Housekeeping, get that glass swept up before someone is hurt. You maintenance crews, check the air quality of the bunker. We may be here a long time."

Everyone in the room yielded to his commands even though another usually held the position of commander to this bunker. Dehuai was one of five commissioners under the supreme head of China. That made him higher in rank. Each turned to his assigned job. Soon the only sounds in the room were chairs scraping, pieces of glass being swept together, and computer noises. Careful attention had been made to the placement of the electrical power lines.

None of the lighting failed, nor their electrical equipment, but communications remained silent.

"Sir," called out Corporal Wong, "my systems here in the bunker work, but I can't raise anyone. I think the problem may be our tower up top."

Dehuai ordered the wiring crew to check the lines to the surface. Then he sent specialists in air assessment to the exit on the surface. Finding the air safe, he and General Bo Hai Dingxiang exited the bunker to check on the tower themselves. They carried binoculars with them to scout the surrounding land. They saw the problem immediately. The tower lay on its side atop the raised mound under which the bunker burrowed. The force of the fall had severed the cables. They would need a construction crew and a large crane to reset it, then the electricians could reattach it. This was their most crucial need. Fortunately, they had the equipment in their large bunker to cover such a contingency.

The hours Duduai waited for the repairs to be made, he thought about the flattened city of Hohhot he had glimpsed through the binoculars. No longer would their gaudy building lights shimmer up and down their sides or their industrial plants send out goods. Earlier, they had been voted the most prosperous city per capita with their trade with Russia and Northern China, but no more.

I wonder what else has been destroyed, he thought. *That earthquake lasted way too long. Most earthquakes only lasted a fraction of a minute. What if Beijing got it too?*

"Sir," a technician in communications suddenly shouted. "Shenyang SAC (Second Artillery Corp) headquarters reports a 9.4 earthquake has hit Beijing, Heibe, Shanxi, and maybe more provinces to the west. They also want to know if we have heard from the Chairman of the Party and his commissioners. They are waiting for instructions. But they went ahead and sent out helicopters to assess the damage."

"Tell them we'll be back in touch, when we know more." said Dehuai. *Good, they have finally broken through. We have ears now.* "Try again to contact Youquan Shan Bunker."

―

Just after the setting up of the Dragon portrait beside the altar, Joshua Jaffe and Zerub Abel had decided the ark of the covenant should not remain in its tent since service could no longer be made without the altar anyway. The portrait defiled the holy ground, situated as it was right beside the corner, so they quit offering the morning and evening sacrifices as soon as Adoni´ erected the painting. When they asked God if they should move the ark, the *Sh'khinah* glory left the ark. They took that as an answer and had some of the priests wrap it and carry it into the unfinished temple. They then proceeded to set it in what would have been the holy of holies. They hung its veil temporarily as best they could with what materials they had brought up from the tabernacle separating the holy object from the rest of the unfinished temple. As soon as the veil was securely in place, the *Shi'khinah* returned.

Joshua Jaffe and Zerub Abel had been especially called witnesses for *Yeshua*, when the Messiah appeared to the whole congregation on Yom Kippur the year before. Since Adoni´'s take over, the entire priesthood had moved their families into the unfinished temple. By bringing the ark into the temple, they had hoped to counteract the image in the courtyard. Now, it comforted them, just knowing God's presence was with them. They all felt the closeness of Lord *Yeshua* in their midst. They all worshipped, even the women and children, and prayed daily before the ark's veil. Joshua remarked, "I guess we are reduced to being messengers, since we can no longer serve the people as priests."

"Yes," said Zerub Able, "But remember *Yeshua* appointed us to be witnesses and to proclaim his word. How can we tell the people, since those remaining in Jerusalem cannot approach the altar now? Maybe he intends for us to be witnesses to that beastly man, Adoni´ and his puppet, Ra'amon—like Moses and Aaron were to Pharaoh—just like when you confronted Adoni´ at his coronation. That was absolutely God speaking!"

"Oh yes, those were the Lord's words. I felt the power of them surge within me. No way could I have kept quiet." said Joshua.

"However," continued Zerub Able, "we need to establish other accesses to our temple. I see in the book of Revelation where we are the only ones safe, having the firepower of Elijah. Our companions need to come and go unseen as we cannot accompany everyone when they move about."

"Yes, I concur. Why don't you assign some of the younger men to the task? Since we already have the shaft and ladder to the chambers under the temple, it would be wise to develop several exit points on the lower level."

Chapter 7

"Mother of God, how will we deal with this mess?" exclaimed the pope that day when the shaking was over. It was his first reaction at the time, before he saw the damage to Vatican City's buildings. Every breakable thing in the room shattered, littering the floor with fragments. But outside, the Colonnade of Bernini's precious statuary, that had lined the tops of buildings, lay fractured on the ground along with the giant obelisk.

Weeks after the overturning, one ominous reminder remained. Mt Vesuvius, in her full glory, spewed fire and brimstone upon the remnant of Pompeii and Herculean. Italy had been hit pretty hard because the two great tectonic plates, the Euro-Asian and the African, met lengthwise down the whole country. The Alps in the north had bounced, as had the Apennines, which lay upon the actual division between the plates. So naturally Rome, being just south of the mountainous spine, received a monumental shake.

Pope Peter complained to John McCutcheon, "In spite of our troubles with the shrinking Church, now we have to deal with repairing our broken buildings. I wonder why Our Lady didn't spare us this destruction. Adoni´ claims the credit for the overturning goes to his god. Can his so-called god be more powerful than Our Lady?"

"How can that be, Patissimo? Our God created the heavens and the earth. Maybe the Lambers were right. Maybe it *is* the Day of the Lord spoken of by the prophets of old."

"But," the pope argued, "if that is the case, why didn't Our Lady tell me?"

Then he remembered the incident with the captain of his Swiss Guard when he had returned from their mission in Israel. The Peace Covenant had decreed them three-and-a-half years to govern the "Old City" being a neutral force between the Israelis and the Palestinians. Their mission having been completed just the week before, Pope Peter had called in Andrea Freuna, his trusted captain, for a final report. He was anxious to get an "on the ground" assessment from one who dealt day to day on the Temple Mount and in the "Old City."

"Your Eminence," said Freuna as he bowed to kiss the ring of the pontiff.

"It's good to see you, my son. You and your fellows did a great service to the world. Now we have peace, and you have a principal part in its making."

"We only did our duty as best we could."

The pope noticed a slight wincing and a fleck of doubt in Andrea's eye. "What is it, my son? I detect some doubt of my words."

"I'm worried, Your Eminence, that the peace may not last."

The pope frowned. "Why would you say that?" asked the pope.

"At the beginning of our service it was very exciting. Joy seemed to burst forth from the Jews as they began to build their temple. Everyone worked together in harmony—even the religious parties, except for a few of the leaders in ultra-orthodox sects. But the atmosphere changed after that fellow Adoni´ began to show up more and more. He actually preached to the Jews from the top of the dividing wall when the Russian army headed toward Jerusalem.

He told them that the dragon in the sky was *God*. The next thing we knew, the government erected two giant paintings of the dragon on the Temple Mount, and people began to worship them. They put one at the corner of the altar in front of the temple. It defiled the holy ground so the priests could not offer the daily sacrifices."

"What? Did Ambassador Berelli know about this? I received no report of it?" said the pope in astonishment. "All I heard was that Jews had recognized Jesus."

"Yes, they had tremendous crowds for their festivals, a great stirring up of religious activity energized by some men dressed in white."

"Curious. Were they some kind of cult?"

"I don't know, but they wore some kind of short white robes just past their knees, and they had sandals that laced up their ankles. They appeared everywhere around the 'Old City,' preaching about salvation. They really stirred up the Jews and drew crowds wherever they went. I heard a rumor that they were some kind of 'Lamb of God' preachers," said the Swiss guard.

"What! It couldn't have been them. We wiped *them* out…or did we?" said the pope, troubled.

"I don't think you did, because some of my men helped the Israelis with security, and they said that when the Lamb appeared, the men in white disappeared when he did. After they left, their robes lay on the ground. Even their undergarments! My men helped the priests pick the garments up. The priests counted one hundred forty-four thousand robes," said Freuna.

The pope was silent. His brow formed a deep v between his eyes. After a few seconds he dismissed Freuna. *I must consult Our Lady about this.*

Chapter 8

General Lin Yiang Dehuai had leaned forward in his chair that day when he still awaited word from the main bunker, his brow wrinkled with worry. "We must reorganize and combine the army, or we will have utter chaos in the country," he said aloud to no one in particular. "Surely the commissioners will order martial law until we can assess our damages."

Since everyone in the room concentrated on his own particular job, trying to monitor the situation, he had seated himself to think through the problem. Dehuai decided that it would fall to him to lead this newly reorganized Peoples Army of China if Youquan Shan did not respond soon. It seemed obvious. If Chao Fu Zeman (chairman of the Central Military Commission) and his central committee had survived, they would be barking orders to this bunker by now.

"But how?" asked General Dingxiang, a faithful companion who had known Lin Yiang since childhood and happened to overhear his assessment. "We don't even know who has survived yet. Besides, other communication towers may be down because of the earthquake."

Lin Yiang stood up, contemplating Bo Hai's words. "Maybe some will work. Any word from Yuquan Shan bunker yet?"

"We have been trying, but it's been an hour since we repaired our lines. Their mountain could have collapsed and buried them. It must have been a big quake considering the jolt we experienced."

General Lin Chonglin, along with the technicians, had been watching the monitors showing satellite pictures. What he saw was a jagged coastline that didn't match any geographical map he knew of. Suddenly the remains of a huge city came in view. "Oh no!" he shouted. "That's Beijing, look! See there's the crumpled top of the Temple of Heaven. There's no mistaking that roof."

Everyone turned to look at the satellite pictures and began to talk at once. "How can that be Beijing?" asked one.

"Beijing is not on a coast. Where did all that water come from?" said another.

As they watched they realized the land had parted. The Korean Bay must have gushed in to fill the gap. The Tai Hang Mountain range had split in half. "That's why they never responded," said the communication's officer, Corporal Dong. "Their bunker lies underwater."

"You knew they were already gone, didn't you?" said General Bo Hai Dingxiang. "You always were way ahead of the rest of us. Will you be in charge now?"

"I believe so. I am the highest ranking man left, the only commissioner." He shook his head. "I wanted to gain a high position in the government, but not this way. There is no honor at all gaining it by default."

"You will make your own honor by what you do now. What are your orders, my honored friend and commander?"

"Set communications to work contacting every military base, division, and branch of the Peoples Army of China that we can reach. Declare Martial Law through the whole country. We need an assessment of the country at large. We must take command before chaos erupts into anarchy. Other members of the army will surely try to take advantage of the situation. We must act—now—to unify the nation.

"And Corporal," commanded Dehuai again, "Get me back SAC headquarters in Shenyang. Let's find out what their helicopters saw." Everyone jumped into immediate action. A general air of purpose spread through the room, as Dehuai's voice sounded with absolute authority.

Colonel Bo Hai Dingxiang leaned over to Colonel Lin Cho Chonglin and whispered, "It looks like our friend will get that shot at the greatness he dreamed of when we were all boys. Do you think he will be like his hero Genghis Khan?" he said, laughing.

Memories of the three of them racing over the extensive grasslands of Inner Mongolia practicing their horsemanship skills filled Bo Hai's mind. Their small town of Duolun, located just fifteen miles from the great Kubla Khan's palace, made the Khans regional heroes. At an early age they pretended to be the armies of Mongolia's greatest conqueror. Lin Yiang appointed himself Genghis Khan, while the other two played his close generals. Their fathers despaired of counseling them toward any other vocation beyond the military. They had attended one of the many military schools located north of Beijing where Lin Yiang had graduated with honors in the artillery school. Together they rose through the ranks, and now they were at the top—a dubious honor, in view of the conflict that might follow.

Lin Cho finally responded. "It might truly be. He always had that leadership quality, even when we were boys. It will be a real honor to serve under him."

Chapter 9

Mizraim, incensed with Adoni´'s takeovers, saw Adoni´ as a greater threat than the natural disasters. In spite of the fact that water from the Mediterranean had swept his coast during the overturning of the earth. the river delta had protected them. The thrust of sea water had pushed the soft delta into a diverting dam causing the main body of water to flood the Sahara Desert, washing out the sand. The mountains west of the river had prevented a backlash. But now facing the loss of sovereignty over his own land, he began to build up his army, knowing a confrontation would come eventually.

Adoni´, sensing Mizraim's attitude of rejection, consulted with the generals of Israel. He declared, "All our coalition of kings and countries here in the Middle East have united, except for Egypt. We cannot become a mighty empire until all our region unites. The Egyptians have important strategic assets, particularly the Suez Canal. Besides that, they divide us from our African brothers in Sudan and Libya, who accept me as their Mahdi. Egypt's leader, Mizraim, rebuffs my every appeal for him to join us. He opposes my leadership. He must be subdued. I fear we have no choice but to use our military."

The generals agreed heartily and began to plan and gear up for the campaign against Egypt.

Mizraim, being informed of Israel's military exercises, continued to fortify his defenses. When Israel invaded the Sinai with their superior tank force, Egypt met them in the desert. But Adoni´ could not be stopped. The dragon figure in the sky flung his meteorites down upon the Egyptians, leaving the Israeli Army untouched. The heavens seemed to support him. Meteorites fell on Mizraim's army. So rather than have his country completely destroyed, Mizraim brought Adoni´ to the conference table quickly to negotiate a peace. But it was just a ploy to gain time on the part of Mizraim. He had no intention of keeping the agreement of joining Adoni´'s coalition of nations.

After returning home from the peace table, Adoni´ turned his attention to the economic woes caused by the disasters. As leader of the empire, it fell to him to feed his people. With Egypt under his control and his political appetite satisfied for now, he discussed the problems with Ra'amon.

"We have to do something to counteract the losses our god brought upon the land to destroy our enemies. Our people will be weak if we can't feed them. Remember, I promised to take care of them."

"Have you consulted Ashtor?" asked Ra'amon.

"He hasn't been around for me to ask."

"Can't you call him?"

"I don't have his number," said Adoni´ sarcastically.

"I meant by prayer. Isn't that the way you talk to a god?"

"No, we communicate face to face like Moses did with the god of the Israelites.

"Can't you at least try?" pleaded Ra'amon.

"No, this is a human problem. What good would his munitions in the sky do in this regard?"

"Since you think we humans can solve the problem, why don't we call in agriculture experts and ask them to devise a solution?"

"Sometimes you are actually brilliant. Do you know that? That's just what we will do."

Ra'amon beamed at the compliment.

Ashtor suddenly appeared in his herculean form, much as he had when he first revealed himself to Adoni´. With muscles bulging from his short golden tunic, reaching just below his hips, golden sandals on his feet, and his scepter dangling from his hand, he spoke. "I understand you need my assistance." Adoni´ lifted his head slightly, "I believe we can handle it."

"Wait, let's hear what he has to say. After all he *is* god," said the timid Ra'amon.

Ashtor immediately took charge of the conversation, "You know, if you really want prosperity you need to learn how to worship me. Both the male and female side of me were worshiped by the ancient peoples, and I increased their fertility." "Well, if that will help us, then maybe we do need your help. How do you want the people to worship you?" asked Adoni´.

"First you must make a more permanent representation of my heavenly person."

"You mean a statue instead of a painting? I was already planning to do that."

"Yes, but you will need more than that. You will also need a garden. Some small rooms or even tents will do and an altar for burning incense and an asherah pole."

When he explained what the accessories were to be used for, both Adoni´ and Ra'amon smiled.

"That will be like opium to the people, irresistibly seductive," said Ra'amon

"Exactly," said Ashtor, "and insure their devotion to us."

"We'll do it!" Adoni´ decided. "Ra'amon, I'll tend to the political business—you handle the religious."

―

Ra'amon called in architects to draw up the plans for the garden and rooms as Ashtor had described. He invited Adoni´ to join him when called in the artists that had painted the canvas pictures of the dragon set up before the Russian invasion. He also called in some construction engineers. It was one of the engineers who said, "I don't see how we can stretch the image's form out like it is in the painting. Why don't we just coil his body like a serpent? That way we can concentrate on the heads with their horns and perhaps crown them to represent the different kings of the empire."

"Oh, I like that idea," said Adoni´. Together they drew up the design and dimensions.

Adoni´ commissioned the full-blown image of the dragon to be cast in a composite of marble powder and overlaid with a gold alloy, but he left the raising of money for the project and its construction to Ra'amon.

Ra'amon immediately went on line and on the air to promote the idea of a permanent statue to their heavenly dragon. He told the people: "Ashtor, our great god represented in the sky, has appeared to us and requested a permanent statue and a place for you to worship him. We want you to be a part of it. Will you contribute to the building of a place of worship by sending in contributions? We would like to have everything finished in time for the Easter celebration."

Evidently the people approved, because the money began to pour in.

―

While Ra'amon built the image and the garden, Adoni´ began on his agricultural project. First, he called all of the benefactors of the land he had given away earlier to a meeting in Jerusalem. The consensus of that meeting was to collect the farms together into big agriculture super farms run under the delegated heads appointed by the government. Adoni´ immediately appointed and sent officers to implement their new plans. To combine all the lands in Israel, Lebanon, and Iraq with former Syria—the new Assyria, the smaller farms of individuals had to be confiscated for the overall good of the people. To keep the good favor of those whose lands he took, he ordered the overseers to appoint former owners over the plans for planting and overseeing. Each man knew what grew best on his former land and now, with the help of the government money, he could develop it fully.

Chapter 10

Tanzin Abdul, a Syrian farmer, beamed as he realized that with government money he could plant a crop of higher value than he could normally afford. He had owned a strip of farmland in the agricultural bread basket of Syria between Hama and Alleppo. It was Syria's part of the Fertile Crescent. In fact, it was the larger part of Syria's only one-third-arable land in the whole country. Strip after strip of crops lined the main road between the two cities, each holding a different vegetable or grain. Fences or stone walls separated them. They were not wide as they fronted the road but very deep rectangle plots of individually owned enterprises. Adoni´ had combined several of these blocks to form one farm.

Tanzin convinced his former neighboring land owners they could earn higher profits if they multi-cropped. He had studied crop rotation and using cover crops to improve the soil, and now he could put some of these things into practice. They planted a cover crop of buckwheat and plowed it in. Then they planted the main crops.

After the fields turned green, they all gathered to congratulate themselves on their success. It had just rained, and the fields glistened in the sunlight that morning.

"Do you see the difference our methods make?" Tanzin said to the other five of his group.

"I see it," replied Moubedya, his closest neighbor. "The crops are growing very fine."

"Yes," said his neighbor on the other side. "They are superior to the other farms around. I'm glad we took your advice."

Others joined in the praise. Elated, Tanzin told his wife that night at dinner, "You would not believe the respect I am receiving from my neighbors. At first I thought it would be a bad thing to combine our lands, but it looks like Adoni´ knows what he is doing."

"You are a good man, my husband. Adoni´, too, is a good man. Surely he is the one prophesied to come, the great Madhi. He comes to save us from these terrible times. I bought a little statue of his god in the market place today. Do you not think we should give him worship?"

"It probably wouldn't hurt," said Tanzin.

—

The agricultural problem settled, Adoni´ turned his attentions toward Ra'amon's project of making the image of his god into a permanent stone-like image. But before they could begin on the image itself, Adoni´ decided to tear down the altar that belonged to the Jewish temple and replace that space with his idol.

When a giant crane appeared at the site with a wrecking ball suspended from its tower, along with a bulldozer and a truck, Joshua Jaffe and Zerub Abel rushed out onto the temple porch. Someone had heard the rumble of the machinery as it approached and immediately reported it. The intent was clear.

"Stop, in the name of *Yeshua*! That altar belongs to the great God of the Jews, the God who made heaven and earth."

The operator of the crane laughed. He simply pulled out his rifle and aimed it at the two witnesses.

Remembering what the book of Revelation had written about this time, Joshua Jaffe raised his arm and pointed with his finger. Fire shot out and engulfed the operator, charring him black as burned toast. The crane cab was untouched, but the operator's body left a message. His face at the moment of death froze with eyes bulged, and his mouth gaped wide open in an expression of pure horror. The other operators took one look at his tortured face and fled in terror.

Zerub Abel stared at the man in the cab then back at Joshua in wonder. "H-H-How did you do that?" he stuttered, eyes wild.

"I didn't *do that*. I just acted upon God's word. He said that the two witnesses had the power to use fire against any that would hurt them. He was about to shoot us. I didn't know what else to do."

―

Having heard the news, all the construction contractors refused to remove the altar.

"Fine," said Adoni´. "We'll just desecrate their altar so they won't want it anymore."

Ra'amon asked, "How will we do that?"

"We will sacrifice a pig or a large boar on their altar like my ancestor Antiochus IV did!"

Chapter 11

Zerub Abel commanded the temple people to keep watch on the construction, daily, recording what was done. He said, "We must keep track of what they are doing. It may become important to know what the idol is made of."

First the construction crew erected a wall of plastic tarps attached to steel scaffolding to hide the construction site, presumably from the temple priests. The construction behind the image site had already begun upon a foundation room. Daily the workmen of both came and went, occasionally casting furtive glances toward the temple as if they were doing something wrong.

After finishing the foundation, they began on the structural part of the image. First they formed the image of the body in crumpled wire mesh and welded it to engineered supports, forming the rounded coils. The necks were made from ten-inch iron pipes, cut at different angles then welded together to give them the appearance of movement. Around these, more crushed wire fleshed out the structure with sinews. Evidently, the heads would be formed separately and attached later.

At the same time a landscaping crew began to cut down and remove some of the trees on the north side of the Temple Mount over next to an Arab boys' school. This was in a section of the Temple

Mount located beyond the paving that surrounded the Dome of the Rock and the unfinished Jewish temple, a semi-garden region bisected by an east-west walkway. Facing out diagonally from the northwest corner of the mount, they planted a narrow evergreen garden around a twenty-by-forty-foot cleared rectangle. After they transplanted a five-year-old oak tree near the front of the rectangle, they built a pavilion over the rectangle, leaving three sides open. This left room for a crowd to stand on its three sides to observe the ceremony performed in it. The back wall hid a structure for holding a giant screen above the pavilion for close-up viewing by the crowd beyond the front rows.

The roof had an opening in the top toward the back, allowing a vent for the smoke to escape from a small altar for burning incense. About five feet in front of the altar stood two pieces of statuary: to the right of the altar (viewed from inside) a five-and-one-half-foot-tall obelisk, and to the left of the altar a five-and-one-half-foot-tall voluptuous image of Ashtoreth,[3] that would be presented to the people as a consort to Ashtor, their god. Across from the pavilion, on the other side of the east/west walkway, along the outside limits of the pavement to the side of the temple, large tents and partitioning hangings were being erected.

Rachel's time to watch happened on the day when the finished heads arrived. She climbed up the ladder onto the platform, wondering what interesting things she might learn today. The observation post had been set up high enough to look down over the curtained barriers set up by the workmen. The tiny window overlooked the construction site. She sat close to the wall and leaned her face against the opening. Before her the half-finished, coiled serpent with feathered scales that continued up the seven necks awaited the heads. It showed a grotesque headless array of wires dangling from the protruding pipes. "Arg," she said under her breath. She had not imagined the idol to be so ugly.

From the ground no one could see what was involved in the building because of a two-story temporary fence, mounted around the site. That was why they had to construct a peep hole up high in the temple wall to watch. She picked up the diary of recordings and entered the time and the date. She leafed back and read the entries of previous days. The observers before her had recorded the attachments of the molds to the wire skeleton and the pouring of some type of mortar-like mixture into the molds. Yesterday's entry told of the unveiling of the molds, but nothing had been done since. She could see the tops of colorful tents being set up on the other side of the short buildings that lined the pavement to the north of the image. She looked to see if the diary mentioned their activities. "*Hmm,*" she thought. "*Nothing much. I wonder what that's all about.*"

Hearing trucks arrive, Rachel laid down the diary and looked through the hole. Men lowered and carefully carried seven crates, setting them down at the base of each neck.

"Have I missed anything?" asked Sarah, a young woman who belonged to one of the priestly families, as she climbed onto the platform.

"They are just unloading some crates, probably the heads of the statue. Here, have a look."

"Ugh! What an ugly thing it is. Sorry, I'm late. What do you want me to do?"

"We can take turns looking; otherwise we'll get a crimped neck. You watch for awhile. I've already begun to write. What are they doing now?"

"Opening the crates—Oh gross!"

"What?" said Rachel.

"It's a horned dragon head with wires and some sort of box hanging out—here, see for yourself."

Rachel stood up on her knees and hobbled to the opening, as Sarah sat back on her heels out of her way. "Could be some sort of speaker. I wonder if Adoni´ intends to broadcast through the image." Sitting back down, Rachel picked up her pencil and sketched what she had seen along with her own thoughts of what it might mean.

Breaking only for lunch when the workers did, Rachel and Sarah had watched as electricians attached the wiring in the pipes to the boxes attached to the heads, confirming their suspicions. The final touch installed a red cloth cover for the speakers to match the insides the open mouths. Then they concealed them inside the hollow heads before attaching the heads to the necks. By the end of the workday, the dragon had seven heads with ten horns scattered among them.

Chapter 12

It preyed on Pope Peter's mind for days. *Could he have been wrong? What if the Lamb of God had been Jesus, like the Lambers claimed? What will happen to me? I had thousands of them killed on my orders. It had to be a false teaching, didn't it? Didn't the Holy Mother Church have the only truth? On the other hand, the promised kingdom had shrunk instead of grown as he'd expected. His prayers to the Lady seemed empty, without power. Where was she? Why didn't she answer?*

He sat in the papal chambers with his head between his hands, elbows on his knees. For once he cried out to the great heavenly Father. "Oh holy God, Father of heaven and earth, show me the truth." He had barely finished the last word of his prayer when a woman appeared in his room standing by his holy crucifix hanging on the far wall.

"I believe you wanted to see me," she said, with a toss of her head.

The pope saw a beautiful woman dressed in a costume usually associated with that of a belly dancer or a harlot, lacking any virtue or modesty. He blushed. He had never seen a more sensuously dressed female. "Who are you?" he demanded, with the voice of an incensed moral judge insulted by her lack of modesty.

"You don't like my dress?" she said. "Perhaps you would prefer this one."

At that she changed into the innocent virgin with a blue mantle over her head and a diamond-encrusted cross hanging from the rosary around her neck.

The pope gasped. He recognized her at once as his vision of Mary. "Who *are* you?" he repeated as he jumped up out of his seat.

"Well that depends upon which civilization you refer to. I have been the virgin for many hundreds of years, at least to Europe and western countries. Before that I was Isis to Egypt, Aphrodite to Greece, Diana to Rome, but Semiramis to the earliest people."

As she said each name, she changed into a recognizable figure from the pages of classical mythology; her ending appearance showed a woman crowned with a tower on her head and rows of breasts cascading down her front.

"But my Bible name is Ashtoreth, the Queen of Heaven originating in Sidon. I am also the mother goddess of the prince Nimrod—Osiris, in his Egyptian name."

"Why are you here?" he demanded.

"You asked the great God of heaven and earth for the *truth*. He sent me."

"But how could you live through all those ages—are you his daughter?"

She threw back her head and laughed in derision. "No…and neither are *you* his son."

"I…am…the…pope—*the* Vicar of Christ on the earth," he spat out in anger.

"No you are *not!* You have served the Queen of Heaven—me, all of your life! Especially lately, because through *you* I have destroyed thousands of *Yeshua's* believers. Here, look into my cup," she said, as she stuck it under his nose. "Would you like a sip?"

As the sickening smell of blood filled his nostrils, he drew back suddenly, his hand brushing the cup. Blood spilled down his vestment.

"It was delicious," she continued. "In fact, it made me drunk. But it's yours now. Wear it to your judgment." She let out a diabolical laugh as she disappeared.

The pope grasped his chest, let out a loud cry, and crumpled to the floor.

His bodyguard, hearing his cry and the thump, rushed into the room and knelt at his side. He called out an alarm to security.

"The pope is down. Call an ambulance!"

When the guard turned His Eminence over, he looked for some indication for his collapse. Seeing the blood, he quickly tore open his robe. But there was no wound.

The hideous image, when it was ready to be unveiled on Easter morning, wore six bejeweled crowns on the seven heads projecting from the coiled serpent, which in turn rested upon an empty room twenty by twenty feet square. The image itself was only fifteen feet high. A full-sized image of Adoni´ had been carved on each side of the base.

The seven heads were reminiscent of the original seven heads seen on the dragon when it first appeared. Adoni´ had imagined that the ten crowns, also seen on the original dragon in the sky, were to be his original Islamic states to fulfill the promise of the Mahdi. These were Israel, Assyria, Sudan, Libya, and now Egypt. He intended to add Iran, Afghanistan, Pakistan, Turkey, and another made up of small countries in Europe—all Moslem first, then the countries surrounding the Mediterranean Sea, at least those who survived.

At present the image was covered with part of the tarps used for concealing it while under construction. Several men in red robes stood ready to drop the cover on command. A great crowd had gathered to witness its debut and to celebrate the first real Easter in thousands of years.

Ra'amon, clad in a gauzy white robe with a wreath of flowers on his head and sandals, appeared first, coming through an opening in the tarp. He walked over to the left of the image and climbed an ornate circular stair wrapping around a pole to a platform above the crowd that had garlands of fresh flowers wrapped around the railing.

"Welcome to you all on this auspicious of all days," he greeted the crowd. "It is fitting that we unveil the image of our god on the day of this spring festival, because today we will introduce you to Lord Ashtor's consort, Ashtoreth, who together bring prosperity and fertility to our land in the spring. And now our great king Adoni´ will come and unveil our god." He swept his arm to the image behind him where Adoni´ emerged from the tarp and walked to the right where an obelisk stood whose base was surrounded with statues of alternating rabbits and ornate Easter eggs.

He officially opened the ceremony by signaling the removal of the covering with a shout. "Behold your god!" The tarps fell all around the nearly three-story-high statue.

The crowd went wild. It shouted, whistled, and clapped, roaring its approval. After a few minutes Adoni´ lowered his hands, motioning for quiet.

"At last we have a full representation of our god in the heavens. The statue part reaches fifteen feet into the air, with its heads centered over its coiled body underneath. Feathery scales protrude from the necks and body of our dragon statue just like his image, in the sky, except here he is coiled and at rest, ready to receive your worship. A bloody red hue appears at night when red floodlights light it. Isn't he magnificent?"

Again the crowd roared. During the tumult Ra'amon descended the steps. The slight breeze blew open the white gauzy robe to expose a bare leg above the knees as he walked over to join Adoni´. When the crowd quieted again, Adoni´ turned to Ra'amon saying, "I have put Ra'amon in charge of religion. He will officiate everything that pertains to the worship. So now I turn over the rest of the ceremony to him."

Ra'amon beamed at the announcement and took charge. "The world needs to revive its true festival for Easter. The Christian Easter was an upstart anyway." As Ra'amon was placing wreaths of flowers on the altar, finishing that part of the ceremony, Joshua and Zerub walked out of the temple. Ministering in the office of a priest, Ra'amon never noticed their presence. He was intent on doing the ceremony just right. An assisting priest already had a small bed of coals smoldering from a fire lit earlier. Ra'amon had both hands full of incense to put on the coals. First, he lifted both fists into the air, as he proclaimed worship to Ashtor. The attendant crowd bowed in reverence, but a loud, jarring voice interrupted their holy atmosphere.

"Adoni´ is *not* the Lord. *Neither* is this idol, god. To prove it, our God Jehovah will destroy Adoni´'s newly planted fields because you have offended him," Joshua prophesied boldly and with great determination. "It is blasphemous to offer incense on his holy altar to a false god! Besides, that altar was made for burning sacrifices, not incense."

Caught off guard, Ra'amon stared at him, at first in helpless silence, then sputtered, "Ashtor *is* Lord. The angel of the Lord has declared it. I, myself, have seen him."

"You will see who is Lord," said the former Prime Minister Abel, "when the fire falls and begins to burn up all your fields." With that, Joshua and Zerub turned and went into the temple.

Ra'amon raged within. *I'm in charge here. Adoni´ gave me the power to direct the religious activities of the people. How dare those prophets still hold to their ancient religion and oppose the power of the real god!* He turned his back on the prophets and faced the people. "Don't pay any attention to them. We have the truth. He picked up one large remaining flower wreath he had reserved, descended from the altar, and handed it to Adoni´." Turning to the people, he said, "Now if you will follow us to the gardens, I will explain to you the latest revelation from Ashtor."

The crowd followed Adoni´ and Ra'amon past the pavement and then fell in behind as they turned on to the east-west walk-way to the pavilion. After their leaders had entered, the people surrounded it. Inside the twenty- to forty-foot space, a small altar smoldered with coals on top of its red bricks. Adoni´ walked over to the left side of the altar to the Ashteroth image and held the large flower wreath in front of him.

Ra'amon, standing in front of the altar, addressed the crowd.

"As a group, you bow before the statue of Ashtor to worship as you just did, but today I am going to show you how to worship your god as an individual. First, I will demonstrate ritually as your high priest. Later, we will also appoint priestesses that will initiate young women, and priests that will initiate young men into individual worship here at this garden. But for today, only I will demonstrate." When he finished speaking, he raised his robe back over his shoulders and shrugged it off. He stood before the crowd in a very short, white tunic, tied in front, leaving a deep V open at his hairy chest. Then he walked over to a curious-looking bench with sloped ends that was built over the tree stump, with its roots still in the ground under it. In the center of the bench a four-sided, pyramidal-shaped cover stood with a painted dragon stretching around the four sides. He removed the cover to reveal a raised padded cushion surrounding a carved protrusion of the stump that resembled a highly polished Cyprus knee (the root projections that grow out of the water next to swamp cypresses), except it was only one and a half inches in diameter. It was a narrow pillar, but its top was not pointed like the obelisk but blunted with a kind of head or knob. Above the pavilion a large screen had been mounted so all could see a close-up of what went on in the ceremony. It was also being filmed.

Standing over the bench he spread his hands saying, "This bench is called a Mastaba. It is designed in such a way that you may become one with your god. This is known as the most popular ancient rite of fertility, because he brings both prosperity and great happiness when you worship this way. In this act you become the representative of Ashtoreth, but this asherah pole, he pointed to the tree stump, represents Lord Ashtor. At one time, the whole world worshiped Ashtor and Ashtoreth, his consort, in this manner. In recent times Christianity has almost destroyed their worship. We will revive it."

Most of the people looked perplexed, but some began to leer, anticipating the act of worship. Ra'amon walked over to the altar, picked up a golden container of incense and threw it on smoldering coals on the small altar. A sickening sweet smell spread through the air. Then he picked up a golden glass bottle with a crookneck stem from the altar and carried it to the bench and set it on the ground. Turning to face the altar, he raised his hands. "Oh my god, I worship you and become one with you." He carefully positioned himself, his hands holding him up and sat down upon the pole, taking it into himself. Then he began to gratify himself sexually on the electrical mechanized bench before the crowd. Afterward, he arose and poured the resulting fluid on the altar, shouting, "My offering to you, O great Ashtor."

At this, Adoni´ carried a large flower wreath over to the obelisk and lowered it around the pillar.

The crowd stirred with mixed remarks. Some said, with disgust, "That's nothing more than public masturbation!"

"No," said others, "it truly is becoming one with our god. I can't wait to worship in such a *pure* way."

Slipping his outer robe back on, Ra'amon quieted the people. "Our god can also be worshipped in a couples' fertility rite. Either take your own partner or take advantage of our priests and priestesses here at the temple. But to my way of thinking you can gain more happiness on an asherah pole. Facilities are available here in the tents across the walkway. Eventually you may build your own places to worship on the hills surrounding Jerusalem or beyond. Here at the temple you will have to make an appointment, as spaces are limited. Eventually we hope to make portable poles for home worship. After a final prayer you may go and worship. If you can't get in today, the facilities will be available every day." With that he raised his hands and prayed. "Oh great Ashtor, bless this demonstration of your union with Ashtoreth to bring spring's fertility into our lives." Then he dismissed the crowd. They pushed and shoved in their attempt to be first in line for the facilities.

Adoni´ smiled at Ra'amon, "You did an excellent job."

Ra'amon grinned and nodded. "That was great fun! I'll want to do this often!"

"I think we should keep it to a few occasions—make it special."

"But what are we going to do about those interfering prophets?"

"I don't know. Maybe Ashtor will tell us."

Ra'amon walked off, lost in his own thoughts. He was pleased at how things went this morning. He could really get into this worship stuff. That was almost better than his experiences with Adoni´, especially the exposure before the crowd. How arousing was that! When the people learned the ways of his god, they would all be under his spell. Adoni´ was into power over the people politically, but *he* would be the power over them religiously! Was it the Russians who said "Religion was the opium of the people"? He would make it so. Who could resist such a sensual way to worship?

Meanwhile, Ra'amon had video to show the people, a demonstration of the way to worship their new god, since he had the whole event recorded. After all, not everyone was here this morning.

Ra'amon had been speaking to the world about Adoni´'s calling, i.e., leading the world to a new utopian status. On occasion Adoni´ himself would speak. They had broadcast on both radio and TV networks right here from the Temple Mount. On it they proposed the New World Order a la Adoni´. Through this media, Adoni´ began to reach beyond his own kingdom.

They revealed the new statue of the Dragon, and Ra'amon explained what Ashtor was about to the rest of the world; consequently, their new faith was growing. Worshipers were springing up everywhere. Ra'amon even had a side business going—exporting little images to worship at home. Soon he would export asherah poles as well. After all, everyone had seen the image in the sky. With the devastation everywhere, people had been looking for hope. The new religion gave them that and, along with it, a chance to build a new world and a sensuous new religion to bring them happiness. Not only that, but it was much more gratifying. So-called Christianity lost its influence among the nations completely.

Chapter 13

The triple-bypass operation on the pope's heart restored him to almost his former self. All through his recovery he thought about the incident just before his collapse. He rationalized that what he had seen was brought on by the worry and stress. The devil had manufactured it to deceive and discourage him. It incensed him that Satan would imitate his precious Holy Virgin in such a derogatory way. *He would not accept it!*

Faced with still another problem, Pope Peter paced back and forth in the papal office, hands behind his back. *Just when I got the "Lambers" under control, Adoni' raises another opposition to my Kingdom. He is turning into a beast, maybe even the one in the scriptures. I should have listened to the others and realized he wants to be the head of the kingdom on earth. But he represents the devil. I'm sure of it. His influence increases daily, while the Church is losing ground all around what's left of the world.*

"Oh, Holy Virgin, reveal your will to me," he prayed out loud.

A knock on the door interrupted his plea. "Yes, come in."

John McCutchen stuck his head in the door and said, "Pattissimo Father, a courier from Egypt seeks an audience—a secret audience."

"This is highly unusual. Why must it be secret?"

"He refuses to say, Your Grace," said John.

"Very well, I will see him. Bring him here." *Perhaps it'll take my mind off my troubles,* he thought.

Mizraim, having secured the pope's alliance should Adoní come against him again, began to fortify the Sinai peninsula with ground-to-ground missiles hidden in tunnels and sunken in the rocky outcrops of the short stubby hills rounded by wind erosion scattered throughout the Sinai Desert. He was determined to stand against the arrogant Adoní. *He was not Allah, nor Jehovah. He was Satan himself despite his claims. At least in my opinion,* he thought.

Adoní received a report from his spy in Egypt. Adoní had a following there that had heard the broadcasts proclaiming him as god, but more than that he had an insider who sat at Mizraim's very table, one of Mizraim's trusted aids who reported the buildup of the Sinai to Adoní weekly.

"So, Mizraim intends to defy me again, does he? That will *not* be tolerated!" He called in his Chief of General Staff for the IDF, who led his multinational army. In doing so, it reminded him of the large departure of the Israeli army that had disappeared. *I must deal with that issue,* he reminded himself.

"General," he ordered, "Call our forces together and make ready to invade Egypt again. It seems they don't understand our force or the power of our god. No need to take our heaviest forces. They just need a 'little hand slap' to bring them into line. Ashtor will do that."

Mizraim called out to the Western nations, and they sent ships from the restored Greek Fleet armed with Tomahawk missiles. The pope had alerted NATO to be on call, telling them Adoní was a danger to the Lord's kingdom. Armed with short-range missiles, they stopped Adoni´'s forward army of tanks dead, by firing a warning a volley of strikes just in front of them.

The pope, being assessed of the war situation, sent a strong protest to Adoni´ in Jerusalem. It read:

"You have broken the Holy Covenant. I have reports that you have stopped the daily sacrifices at the Jewish temple and set up an image to a false god in the courtyard. Furthermore, you have declared yourself equal to God. This is blasphemy! This is not to be tolerated. If you do not stop immediately and return Egypt to religious freedom, the armies of Europe will be at your door, not as your allies this time, but as your enemies." This message was delivered to Adoni´ about the same time the IDF headquarters received word from the army in the field. The report from his generals came back. The sky did not come to their rescue this time to defeat Mizraim. Instead, they were stopped by the Europeans,

Adoni´ cried out to his god. "How can I rule a great empire if I can't even rule all the Arab nations. Where are you, Ashtor?" he cried in a demanding voice, not bothering to call him lord in his disgust.

Immediately the herculean figure appeared. "What's the matter? Having a little difficulty? Do I have to drop meteorites on the Egyptians again?" he said in a whiny voice.

"You said you would give me great power," demanded Adoni´. Where is it? The pope won't let me invade Egypt."

"The pope…won't…let…me…invade…Egypt," he mocked in staccato. "You didn't ask me what to do. If you had you wouldn't have made such a mistake. You know, I *could* move inside of you and make you invincible. That way you would never fail again."

"You mean inhabit my body?" Adoni´ asked in surprise.

"If you like," he said with an accommodating smile. *Or even if you don't like,* he said to himself, knowing that his man was now firmly in his control.

"Yes," he replied in a clipped voice, "I *would* like. I want more power!"

"Of course you do, it's only natural, being the angel that you are."

Chapter 14

"What do you mean?" said Adoni´, a puzzled expression creasing his brow.

"Your father never told you the circumstances of your birth?"

"Yes, he did. He told me about the great conjunction of stars on the night of my birth. It was an indication of my greatness to come," said Adoni´ lifting his head in a proud manner. "Besides, I am the last remaining heir to the Grecian Seleucid Dynasty, which according to my father will rise up again."

"That may be true, but that's *not* what I meant. Your father was sterile, but he still wanted to fulfill that great prophetic word concerning the Seleucid dynasty, but he was the last of the line. So he made a deal with me to allow one of my spiritual children (the giants of angels born to women), descended from the time after the great flood, to visit his wife at night."

"That can't be. My mother was a devout Jewess. She would never have participated."

"She never knew. He slipped her a drug to make her compliant," said Ashtor.

"Are you telling me that my bloodline goes back to angels?"

"Technically, but your blood father was what is called by your generation as a Nephilim, the word for 'giant' in the original language. You see, I chose *you* before you were born, by choosing your parents specifically. New Age people have been watching for your rise. So have the Masons, but they fowled up and began to make up their own fulfillment." He laughed. "They even picked a black man as their Osiris. But *you* are the real Osiris."

"Really," said Adoni´, his eyes widening. "I'm impressed."

"You should be. Your DNA was carefully blended with specific Nephilim DNA."

"You mean that I am a hybrid?"

"I chose the best bloodline for you—the one with the most angelic DNA, who came from angelic breeding—children's children from the original hybrid strain. In fact, we resurrected the original Nimrod, long dead, by extracting some of his DNA. Also you are destined to follow your father's illustrious ancestor, Antiochus IV, even though he was no angel, no pun intended."

"You have the power to do this?"

"Of course. We gods have much experience in crossing DNA. We corrupted the whole DNA strain of the world before the flood, except for Noah and his children at the very end. But back to our former conversation, do you want me to inhabit your body or not?"

"I already told that you that I did," he said smiling in triumph.

"As you wish," said the figure, disappearing as he took possession of Adoni´'s body.

Adoni´ felt a surge of power, a new confidence, along with a consciousness of a strong inner voice. Not a blocking of his personality—this was a cooperative cohabitation. As Adoni´'s thoughts enjoyed his new knowledge of angelic ancestry, he heard Ashtor chuckle. *This having two minds would take some getting used to.*

When Ra'amon joined Adoni´ to remind him to ask about the priests, he addressed Lord Ashtor as well.

"I thought you said Ashtor was here," burst out Ra'amon.

"I am here," said Lord Ashtor, using Adoní's mouth.

"What?" questioned Ra'amon, frowning in confusion.

"You shall no longer be weak in front of them, neither of you," Ashtor pronounced as a decree. "You too shall have an angelic spirit, Ra'amon. I will give you the spirit over fire, and he will give you power to call down fire from heaven. Set up sacrifices on their *own* altar and then call down fire to light them just like Elijah. We'll show them who has the power of god."

"Adoní?"

Then Adoní's voice sounded, "No, that was Ashtor speaking through my voice. He is inside of me now. Do what he says, and if they still won't believe, send some soldiers and have them killed. I have more important matters to tend to. I have to deal with the pope and Europe."

Ra'amon trembled. This strange new feeling came over him. Yes! It seemed like a feeling of power, confidence—something. Now he would no longer be weak and subservient to Adoní.

"Not so fast," said a voice from within. "Now, you will be servant to me."

"Who is me?" said Ra'amon, trembling.

"Appollyon, the ruler of the fire in the bottomless pit."

"And are you powerful?" asked Ra'amon.

"Very."

"Good, now I know I will be assured a place in history."

Chapter 15

The next week Adoni´ called together the leaders of his newly organized coalition of kings to take counsel against the Holy Covenant. These nations had reverted to absolute monarchies or dictators after the destruction, because it was a more efficient form of government. People looked to leaders to guide them through these bad times.

The kings of ten nations gathered in Israel's old Knesset building along with their top government officials. Adoni´'s coalition of "kings" consisted of the new Assyria (made up of the former Syria, Lebanon, and Iraq); Iran; Af-Pakistan and Turken-Ubekistan (two sets of countries combined); Saudi Arabia; Turkey; the new country that was formerly Macedonia, Greece, and Albania, now called Greco-Malbania; Pales-Jordan; and Israel. Adoni´'s territories covered almost the same land conquered by Alexander the Great, except that it had included Af- Pakistan and all the way to the southern border of Kazakhstan, the bear's foot of the Media/Persian Empire.

Standing before his coalition, Adoni´ called the meeting to order.

"Gentlemen, welcome to the first meeting of our collective Empire of the Great Islamic nations. I have brought you here today to address a problem that affects us all. As you know, most of Europe is still under the influence of the Christians. If we are to have an empire that covers the world, we must address the situation of religion. Although we know Allah has revealed himself in his final form as the supreme God of Forces, the Catholics and their puppet kings in Europe suppress our Arab brothers dwelling in their midst. We need to free them so they can worship our great Ashtor."

Many heads nodded. A murmur went through the auditorium.

"Most of you know Egypt has rebelled against our coalition, and Europe has interfered in matters that don't concern them. It has come to my attention that the pope was behind the order to stop my army. Three years ago he sent out the word to his churches that he has been appointed to lead a new kingdom of God on the earth. He monopolized the scant fleet of ships owned by Europe to refurbish Rome. The pope seems to have consolidated Christianity's power there. They have been preparing the city to rule the world.

We can't expect them to be a part of *our* empire," proclaimed Adoni´ in his best oratorical voice. "Western Europe thinks they are superior to us. They always have. If they are to respect us, we have to show them our power. Allah always promised us a great empire." he said, playing upon their Moslem aspirations. "Now, its time has come."

The whole delegation jumped to their feet, with a roaring applause amidst shouts of "Praise Allah." Adoni´ motioned for quiet, and everyone sat down.

"I say let's use our small nuclear devices against them and wipe out all their missile-launching facilities. That will keep them from retaliating."

A lone man stood up. He was the king of the one country in Europe, Greco-Malbania.

"Your Excellency, great king Adoni´, might I suggest that we don't use nuclear missiles. After all, have we not had enough suffering in the world from them already? Besides, that would add to our food problem. All we really need to do is use conventional smart bombs to take out their means to launch weapons."

"Perhaps you're right," said Adoni´. "But I want the Vatican and Rome gone, permanently! In fact, I think we should send a message by using the big bomb there. Let that be a lesson to any other imperial aspirations. I say we take it by surprise and wipe it off the map. What do you say? Are you with me?"

It only took an hour for them to agree. Several questions came up and were discussed and debated. Some of his own IDF objected to using a hydrogen bomb on Rome, because the fall out might endanger Israel being due east. In the end, they decided to use Israel's non-nuclear rockets on the missile silos and Iran's small nuclear missile on Rome.

They didn't want to destroy Europe, only shut down their capability to retaliate. So they would send only conventional weapons. But bombs required planes. Finally, it was decided that missiles sent would be the new non-nuclear warheads developed back in 2011. They would be guided by the Israeli military satellite. Without manufacturing ability, due to the disastrous meteorite bombardment having destroyed their manufacturing network, Europe would not be able to rebuild their war machines.

The countdown began. They were ready by June.

Meanwhile, the rain of fire prophesied by the priest/witnesses came upon the fields just before Pentecost and destroyed the wheat harvest in Israel. Another load of meteorites fell, along with burning sheets of naphtha and the disgusting red dust that turned everything to a bloody color, especially if it fell on water. The trees, even green crops along with the grass, burned in the falling naphtha, and the crops were destroyed as promised, which meant for those in

Israel they would only have the early barley harvest from April to sustain them for the year.

With that, the lines were drawn: on one side Jehovah, God of the Jews, and on the other, Ashtor, Adoni´'s dragon god of forces. The city of Jerusalem became a crucible of hot, conflicting powers.

The Syrian bread basket suffered from the downpour of the prophets' prophesied plague, as well as the Israeli wheat. The fields had grown more productive than ever with the government's help. The harvest was just days away. Tanzin Abdul rejoiced with all his friends, expecting the highest yields yet, until after the onslaught from the sky hit. They were forced to remain undercover until it passed by. Then they rushed to their fields.

His neighbors beat Tanzin to the fields, where they stood weeping. He had passed multiple fields before he came to theirs. He hoped against hope theirs had escaped the ravage but no such luck. When he arrived he saw the same result. The crops had burned black from the falling naphtha. They had been golden ripe and ready to harvest only days before. He too wept as he knelt to examine the soil. Even it was burnt. The oily tar-like substance must have soaked into the top layers of soil. Not only had it ruined the crop but the very soil. It might be years before anything ever grew again.

"I heard that those blasted prophets at the temple in Jerusalem caused this," said Moubedya, his neighbor, full of anger.

"But I thought Adoni´'s god was in charge of the heavens," said Tanzin. "What will we do now? Starve?"

Chapter 16

To celebrate the destruction of the Russian Army by their god nearly a year ago, Ra'amon, in obedience to Adoni´, set up sacrifices for worship to the dragon. He hired more priests from the disaffected semi-orthodox who had rejected the Lamb, to assist him. They would do the killing. (Ra'amon was not about to actually sacrifice animals himself). He ordered bundles of wood laid upon the altar. Then he invited the people to his memorial sacrifice.

First Ra'amon climbed to the top of the altar to address the crowd.

"Welcome, all you faithful worshippers of Ashtor, to our celebration. It will be a double blessing to our god. We have just received word that they have finished the cleanup of the battlefield next to the Dead Sea. Our men appointed to the task of cleansing the land of the dead bodies had been working for seven months. Finally, it is done! Not only have they cleaned up the dead, but they also have begun gathering all the wooden instruments of war, but it will more likely take *seven years* to do that. So I am authorized to announce that every Israeli citizen may gather all you want for firewood for winter."

For the special occasion, Ra'amon wore a white robe with a yoke of red and purple, encrusted with jewels. Crowned upon his head was a tall white headdress similar to the pope's MITRE. It suggested a status of a master priest. Standing on the top of the altar overlooking the crowd, he said, "These beasts of sacrifice represent the great sacrifice of our god when he killed the mighty Russian Army like sacrificial bulls, rams, lambs, and goats." Then he looked down upon the men in white below him and commanded: "Slaughter the beasts."

Lined in front of the altar were seven animals—a bull, and two rams, two lambs, and two goats. Seven priests slaughtered the animals as the crowd watched with obvious fascination. Then each priest carried his sacrifices up the ramp, except for the bullock, whose priest cut it up before the altar and had help carrying it up the ramp. They all laid their sacrifices upon the wood. Ra'amon led them back down the ramp in procession. Reaching the ground level, he faced the altar, the men in white forming a semi-circle behind him. He raised his hands shouting, "Oh great god, Ashtor, our all-powerful god of forces, show your mighty power. Light your own fire!" Mumbling to Appollyon inside, he said, "Okay do your tricks."

Suddenly the altar top burst forth with fire, falling down in a stream. It leapt in a great swishing noise and quickly consumed the sacrifices. The smell of burning fat and savory meat caused the people to salivate.

Ra'amon surged with satisfaction when fire fell at his command. Of course he had taken precautions just in case. (He had soaked the wood with olive oil).

The people were awed. They let out a great shout; the men bowed to the idol in Arab style. The TV cameras taped the spectacle, streaming it to the rest of the known world.

Jaffe and Abel appeared on the temple steps, once more protesting in loud voices. "Again you have desecrated the altar of the living God. Now the true Lord God of heaven will take away your food from the Great Sea. First, he will hurl a mountain into the

Mediterranean and turn a third of the sea red like blood, then he will make the whole sea like the blood a dead man," called out Joshua Jaffe so that all could hear.

Then Zerub Abel stepped forth and spoke, "I say again, because you worship this image, it will not rain for the rest of the three-and-a-half years I pronounced before, so there will be no…more…crops," said Zerub Abel. "This is an affront to *Yeshua*, the true God of heaven who alone sends the blessings of rain… *or* withholds it."

Ra'amon turned to his soldiers and commanded, "Shoot them." But before they could pull their triggers, fire shot out from the temple witnesses. It burned the soldiers as they dropped. He turned to others and commanded, "You, over there, kill them."

They shook their heads and said, "No way, man."

In a rage Ra'amon called down fire upon the cowards, who cried out in agony as they rolled around on the ground burning. Ra'amon nearly burst with pride. *He did it. I really do have the power to cast fire from heaven.* The worshipping crowd stood stunned. Ra'amon turned to the camera crews and said. "Strike the images of the priests and their fire. No need for the whole world to see that!"

The battle of the gods had begun. But Ra'amon stopped short of trying *his* fire power on the two prophets. He wasn't sure he could win.

"Foolish man," screamed Apollyon within.

Ra'amon cringed. After this he would try to be brave. The spirit within, after all, *was* an angel. "I will learn from you," he told him.

"Yes, *you will!*" replied Apollyon. "I spared you this time, giving you a chance to 'try your wings,' Next time *I* will make the decision. You have to understand, not only am I the god of fire, I am also Molech, *the* King, the great destroyer. It was I to whom the ancients sacrificed their children.

"And, by the way, you will soon be needing my help to get rid of those unwanted babies. Abortion doesn't excite me quite like the fire. Your practice of worshiping through sex is over-running the population. I could take them off the people's hands. By sacrificing them to me, they could gain power from me. Not only that, but I would gain power and excitement I haven't had for centuries.

"And, just so you know, the spirit in Adoní, Ashtor (not his real name), has *less* power than me."

"Then why aren't you ruling him instead of me?" asked Ra'amon, garnering more and more courage to speak up.

"Because it's *his turn* to rule over an empire. But you will defeat the prophets through me," he said.

Ra'amon surged with satisfaction. He actually had a more powerful spirit than Adoní.

Chapter 17

The reports came in from most of the provinces. Except for Beijing, Shanghai, and Hong Kong, the rest of the major cites survived, even though the damage created huge piles of broken civilization. The army took control of the local governments as ordered. Life began again as the people started to recover and rebuild.

General Lin Yiang Dehuai led as if born to the position. He inventoried his resources and discovered he was short on food and oil. With a little innovation that could be solved. Food from the northern, less damaged farmlands could be transferred to southeastern regions via coal-powered trains where rails could be restored. That was the first priority. But local transportation and heavy equipment ran on petroleum, and many of the refineries were gone. I want to check the situation in the Pacific Islands. Send out a reconnaissance plane to see what survived in the Philippines and Indonesia," ordered Lin Yiang. He remarked to his friend Bo Chai, "It's a good thing we took out America's bases in the island chains before the earth turned over, or we would have competition for the remaining meager oil supplies. Even so, petrol will have to be restricted to government business.

"Yes, it *is* a good thing you persuaded the commission to take down the American forces when we did. Of course, you knew we had the advantage and caught them when they were vulnerable, after the war with Russia."

"We still lost a lot, even so," said Lin Yiang. "It wouldn't have been possible at all without our extended missiles program. We never could have competed without taking out their carriers."

The incident Bo Chai referred to happened almost immediately after Russia destroyed the US mainland. China's Missile Launch Facilities Watch had picked up Russia's launch against the United States and alerted the High Commissioners. Lin Yiang, as the Artillery Commander of the Central Committee, persuaded the whole military command that this was their chance to break out of the box that the United States, allied with Japan, Korea, Taiwan, and the Pacific Island chains, had held them in since World War II. They had long known that in order to have a strong influence in the Western Pacific, they needed to control the Taiwan Strait, giving them free access to the South China Sea and parts west as well. Here, one third of all the maritime traffic in the world passed through the Strait of Malacca, plus *all* the hydrocarbons of the world destined for Japan, the Korean Peninsula, and northeastern China. The United States had kept it open to all nations. By putting it under China's exclusive control, they would essentially become the dominant nation in the eastern hemisphere, which was their ultimate goal. But US carrier power had held them at bay.

Lin Yiang convinced them that now was their time to move. It was their chance to take possession of their own Taiwan and open up the seaways to the whole Pacific Ocean exclusively to China. Besides, he wanted to prove their newest ship missile in real combat.

Their Anti-Ship Ballistic Missile (ASBM) was impossible to seek out and destroy on the ground, because their launching pads were carried abroad upon ever-moving trucks. The missiles had the speed of Mach 10 and range of two thousand kilometers, reaching the limits of their destination in just twelve minutes. What made them so deadly was that their course could be altered at re-entry to the atmosphere to hit a *moving* ship. Not only that, but the US defense against them was not fail proof. It could be overcome with decoys and multiple launches against a single target. One missile would eventually get through.

Without the airpower from the aircraft carriers, Chinese drones and submarines could launch smaller versions of the ASBMs, the Short Range Ballistic Missiles from a distance avoiding the deadly network of computer-coordinated, comprehensive AEGIS Systems of the US cruisers and destroyers. With these they could eliminate the remainder of the traveling naval fortresses.

As soon as the United States determined that the China's ASBM was operational, they had redistributed their Pacific navy. Taking that into account, Lin Yiang determined the strategy.

"Gentlemen, I suggest that the United States being under wholesale attack from the Russians, their command to the Pacific fleet may not be their primary concern. Of course, standing orders under such an attack will apply. Nevertheless, they may be vulnerable, where we have the advantage."

Lin Yiang convinced the Chinese Naval Commissioner that the US atomic subs would be their main obstacle. Immediately Chinese subs loaded with nuclear missiles cruising the eastern ranges of the Pacific were ordered to destroy the two US sub home-bases in the state of Washington and the carrier base in San Diego. The ships not already at sea would be sitting ducks. Land-launched ICBMs headed toward the submarine bases in Guam and Japan. Others had orders to seek out and destroy any US submarines found in the "blue water" of open sea. Russian subs were off limits. They were not the enemy. A massive ground army followed the naval attack in the battle for Japan. It surrendered right away.

At that, both Koreas surrendered also. Then the US carriers' air power came against the China mainland in this battle. But by launching their ASBMs, the Chinese took out two carriers, the Japanese home-based USS George Washington and the USS Carl Vinson and their peripheral warships in the battle. The USS Nimitz and the USS Ronald Reagan escaped to Australian waters out of range. The USS Abraham Lincoln never entered the battle. That accounted for all the carriers in the Pacific. Seeing all hope of help from the US gone, Taiwan lay down their arms. In the end, China was definitely in charge of the South China Sea.

That was over three-and-a-half years ago. Now the problems were not political, but survival itself.

Chapter 18

Fabian Wolf came to Rome with his uncle, Cardinal Anton de Roquelaure, to meet the pope. While they were discussing the deterioration of the church, Fabian stood at the window, bored as ever. With the persecution over, Fabian needed new excitement. He noticed light reflecting off something in the sky.

The Italian Army headquarters near Rome picked up a blip on the radar screen. Before they could identify the invader, it hit. Ground zero was Vatican City. In an instant, the small mushroom cloud rose up from the former seven hills. Using the precise electronic transmission capabilities of the Israeli IDF, Adoni´ had sent his nuclear bomb upon the head of the church.

Shipmen on treasure ships bound for the seaport at the mouth of the Tiber River watched Rome's mushroom cloud from miles out in the Tyrrhenian Sea, weeping bitterly as their prosperous businesses went up in smoke. An officer, suddenly feeling a rise in temperature, looked up, and gasped, "Oh my God!" Others began to scream as they saw a body so big it blocked out a whole section of sky above them. Its bloody-red color burned at its tip with white-hot incandescent heat from friction with the atmosphere. "Set a course for Gibraltar," screamed the Captain. But seconds later it extinguished their cries. Its splashdown cast water hundreds of feet into the air, like a giant rock thrown into a small pond. One third of the Mediterranean Sea's displaced waters washed over the coastlines. It even extinguished the nuclear fires still burning in Rome. Gigantic waves of red sea water (red because of the dust that accompanied the mountain) rushed on land until spent, and then retreated, taking everything in its path. One third of the Mediterranean Sea's displaced waters from the Straits of Gibraltar to the Island of Sicily turned red. Every other coast suffered a tsunami. Only the ancient Italian cities built on the mountain tops in medieval times, and those on the other side of Italy's mountainous central range, survived. Mt. Vesuvius and Mt. Etna began to rumble as the edges of the tectonic plates, which met in the mountainous spine of Italy, became fluid from the impact. The pressure of gases and liquid rock relieved itself through the ancient conduits to the surface. Great columns of yellow smoke streamed into the sky.

Adoni´ smirked over his successful launch, even though he had no sure knowledge of results yet. The news was slow to reach the Middle East since one of the major broadcasters had been in Rome. Rome was not Adoni´'s only target, however; the nuclear launch sites of the French were also targeted as well as Britain's Nuclear Naval Base at Faslane in Scotland. US and NATO bases in Germany and elsewhere were also taken out. *The "crimson whore,"* Adoni´ thought to himself about the Church (referring to the Cardinal's red coats), *and her kings will ride over our heads no more. Now I must take steps to consolidate the remainder of Europe under my control. I have only to convince the vast Arab populations in Europe that I am their Mahdi, and they will be mine! Later I will reorganize the whole kingdom and enlarge my divisions.* He smiled with satisfaction. *Adding Europe will make my kingdom greater than the Roman Empire, even greater than the ninth-century Islamic Empire.*

"Can you believe it?" exclaimed General Saguy. "Adoni´ has nuked the pope and disabled Europe. The whole continent could be turned into anarchy just like America. If *Yeshua* does not come soon, there will be no world left for Adoni´ to rule."

"Egypt will not be safe now with the pope's leadership over Europe gone. Do you think it's time we revealed our position to our friends down there?" asked David.

"We could offer King Hassih refuge. After all, this *is* his country," said the General.

"Why don't you call that friend of yours again and suggest it?" said David

When the general told King Alahad Hassid of the phone call, he had been surprised to hear that he had a friendly army awaiting him in his *own* country. After that he anxiously awaited another call from them. He had a few contacts in Amman who remained faithful to him and kept him informed, but to find out that an Israeli army was willing to give him shelter and protection in one of his country's national treasures infused him with new hope. When the general in Egypt asked him if he would like to join the Israelis, his answer was: "Oh, indeed I would. To be back home would encourage all the faithful that remain. I absolutely must go and my wife as well. But how can we accomplish it? I am sure I am watched by Mizraim's enemies. And the last thing I want to do is give away the Israelis' secret."

"Don't worry, we'll take care of everything."

Adoni´ told Ra'amon what he planned to tell Europe about the attack.

"You are going to blame Russia for sending missiles against them? Won't they know she exhausted her missile cache against the United States?"

"No, people will believe most anything if it comes through the media from a leader they admire," he said. "They wouldn't be watching for a threat from us. Use of any attack with nuclear devices would be thought unheard of since the US/Russia War. Their guard would be down. Besides, the Israeli electronic weapons took out their radar. Then again, you forget that our spiritual allies will blind their minds with deception," he said.

Ra'amon frowned.

"Didn't I tell you about them?"

"I don't think so."

"Ashtor told me that he has a whole kingdom of spirit beings that promote his ideas on the earth. They will blind the minds of the Europeans, so don't worry. Just set up the broadcast."

A day later, Ra'amon set up the broadcast to talk to the remaining world in Europe. The same message went out over the Internet to every one still online. His appeal: "Citizens of the world, we must band together. Our whole civilization is in danger of crumbling. *Russia* has bitten the hand that fed her in her death throes. We extend our condolences to you. We will do what we can to help you. Much of your leadership in Europe is gone. Your great spiritual leader is gone. Our sympathies go out to you. Come join with us. We will rebuild the world together."

But his celebration at home was short-lived because of the effects of the sea.

Simone Ben-Ami, one of the fishermen whose boat docked on the Kishon River near Haifa, was out to sea fishing when he noticed a slight odor in the air. Looking at the water, he saw a light red sheen spreading across the water. *Strange,* he thought. *I have never seen the water look like that.* The farther he went out to sea, the deeper the color became. It glimmered in the morning sun, a reddish-brown color.

The Mediterranean was not the best of places to fish anyway. Deep-water fishing was out, because the bottom was too deep, and the Levatane Basin next to Israel's shoreline was much saltier than the rest of the sea. Some species could not thrive there. Beyond that, even the surface-water fish were diminishing. Chemical plants dumped their waste into the Kishon River, and the water next to shore spoiled the fishing. Simone went farther and farther into the sea to bring home a good catch. The sea was unusually choppy today. Suddenly, a squall blew up, and the wind started blowing strongly from the west. He started to cough, his lips began to tingle, and his tongue felt strange. All at once the waves swirled with masses of dead fish. "What is going on? Could this be Red Tide?" he muttered. He had heard about it, but never, in all his days of fishing, had he encountered it. His eyes watered and his nose burned. The choppy waves seemed to thrust the fumes into the air like an aerosol. He pulled in his nets, letting what catch he had go. He didn't want to draw up poisoned fish. He shouted to his crewmen, "Turn the boat around. Let's head for home." He noticed they were in the same discomfort as he. He hoped they could outrun the menace, but the wind was blowing hard toward them. Joel, one of his older men, began to hack unmercifully. Knowing he had emphysema, he ordered him below. "And shut the cabin," he said. "Maybe that will lessen the effect."

By the time they reached their dock, the men could hardly stand they were so weakened by the ordeal. On the way back they had encountered some of the larger creatures of the sea floating belly up.

Chapter 19

News of what happened to the Mediterranean slowly trickled in. What the prophets had promised had happened. They proclaimed that the Lord God of heaven would send a burning mountain into the sea, and it would dwindle their food supply even more by destroying the creatures of the sea. The beautiful beaches of Israel's shorelines were littered, first with dead fish, and then larger sea creatures began to wash up—sharks and dolphins. The decaying mess stunk, and the cleanup became an overwhelming operation, but still the situation worsened. Adoni´ and Ra'amon went over to Caesarea to view the state of affairs. They traveled in a four-wheel-drive vehicle, with the windows closed. Adoni´'s curiosity was aroused watching as men in gas masks, operating huge front-end loaders, scooped up the rotting mess and loaded it into giant-wheeled earth-movers.

"I guess the odor from that mess must be horrendous. Is that why they're wearing gas masks?" Adoni´ asked his student driver, secured in Caesarea.

"No, although that's bad enough, but if you opened the windows, you would understand. The gas from the Red Tide stings your eyes. It's quite painful," said the student.

"What's Red Tide?" asked Ra'amon.

"It's the bloom of algae, a type of organism that releases a pungent gas into the air."

"Algae?" questioned Ra'amon. "How can that be?"

"Because of the impact of the burning mountain, the turbulence of the sea stirred up the phosphorous deposits on the bottom. After mixing them with the iron-rich dust from the mountainous object and the added heat of the burning mountain, it brought about ideal conditions for a gigantic 'bloom' of Red Tide."

"Okay, but what *is* Red Tide?" repeated Ra'amon.

"Idiot!" barked Adoni´. "He just told you it's an algae."

Ra'amon frowned at Adoni´, "I mean, why is it called a tide?"

"Because it's only noticed near the shore, I guess." Seeing an opportunity to show off his knowledge, the marine biology major explained, "Red Tide is a one-celled organism normally found in seawater that suddenly increases at an enormous rate when just the right conditions exist. During a bloom, the sea temporarily turns red due to the organism's coloring, which is in evidence because of the magnitude of increased reproduction. This multitude ties up all oxygen in the water. That asphyxiates the fish. The poisonous toxins emitted from billions of Red Tide organisms destroy the larger sea animals. Because of the sea-wide conditions of the present outbreak, the whole food chain broke down, causing the other sea life to die as well. The Mediterranean Sea is dead! Meanwhile the toxins from such a widespread bloom escaping into the air are quite fierce, stinging the eyes and throats of people on the shores working to clean it up."

"So that is why they are wearing gas masks?" said Adoni´ again.

"Yes, normally blooms were just local in scope, but this bloom eventually affected the entire sea. Thus, the Mediterranean Sea looks like the blood of a dead man. With its patches of dead sea life floating on the putrid surface, it looks like the separation of hemoglobin from plasma in a dead man."

Adoni´ recognized the phrase "blood of a dead man." The priest's prediction—he raged inside at their apparent power. Ashtor was strangely silent.

King Hassih and his wife Nicole packed several suitcases for an extended stay in Sharma El Sheikh, Egypt's resort on the Gulf of Aqaba. After a week of enjoying the beautiful waters of the Gulf, they loaded a covered jeep with their belongings and were driven by a loyal member of Mizraim's own body guard to a rendezvous in the desert with an unmarked helicopter.

David rushed under the blades before they stopped, to greet the king of Jordan as soon as the helicopter landed in Petra. "Welcome home," he said, stretching forth his hand.

The king shook it heartily. "I can't believe it," he cried as he dropped to his knees and kissed the ground. David moved back to the plane and helped Nicole down the steps, while the other IDF officers and former head of staff greeted the king. Then the king saw his own people, clothed in native garb, waiting patiently to be noticed. He stretched out his arms and greeted them. They immediately dropped to their knees and bowed their respect. He bid them rise and began speaking and mixing among them.

General Saguy spoke to the king when he finished greeting his people.

"Your highness, we have prepared a little refreshment before we take you to your hotel in Wadi Musa. We thought you might have some questions to ask about our operation. Then, too, we would like to hear of your ordeals in this conflict."

"Thank you. I was hoping for such an opportunity." They ushered the royals to the Forum Restaurant —the very best they had to offer in Petra. The king looked around, seeing the various army tents set up on the grounds. "Looks like you have turned Petra into an efficient army base."

"Yes," replied General Saguy. "It's mostly due to my man here, David Solomon. I sent him initially to set it up."

"We started small, but when the generals and their forces showed up with all the equipment, we became a real army base," said David. "Your loyal Bedouins helped a lot too." He motioned to the crowd of them following behind. Nobody thought anything of lowly Bedouins mingling with a king and high military officers. They were all one here in Petra.

Chapter 20

Adoni´ had just returned from viewing the coasts. He was sitting alone in his office thinking about what he could do. With the fishing industry dead, a significant amount of their food supply diminished. This, along with the damaged crops, caused Adoni´ to ponder the future of his kingdom. All hope of feeding his kingdom from the west vanished since Europe was still dealing with limited radiation. Of course he could import from the Red Sea or the fertile fields of Babylon. *What had he done by attacking the Christians?* It appeared that their god was still around. Or was it the god of the Jews? "No," came the fierce and dominating answer from Ashtor within. "It was *my* work consolidating *my* power on earth. We had to get rid of the contenders anyway."

"Of course," Adoni´ said in agreement with himself (that is Ashtor). Thinking it over, they came up with a brilliant idea. "I will issue food passes and ration the food. *But* I will require my followers to bow down and worship me in order to receive their pass. The rest can starve." *Talk about consolidating power.*

He smiled in response to his own cleverness. It would also separate the true followers from the false. They would need a design for their pass and a foolproof way to implement the system. "We must talk to Anslo about this. I want the latest technology I can get for this project. I'll put Ra'amon in charge and put the project under religion."

—

Anslo Bedas was the electronics specialist who set up the computer network connecting Adoni´'s banks. Adoni´ sent Ra'amon to Beirut to speak with him. Ra'amon, having been briefed by Adoni´, told him what he expected as a result, then asked, "How can we do this?"

"Do I understand you correctly?" said Bedas. "You want a completely cashless society?"

"Yes, as means of regulating trade, especially of food items because of the shortage."

"Okay, the first thing that comes to mind is the two dimensional 2-D bar code technology. It's not necessarily a new technology, but it keeps getting improved upon, and it is extremely efficient. We could print it on a plastic card or even tattoo it on flesh, say on the hand or on the forehead of each recipient. A scan over the mark would bring up the images and numbers on a high-density digital TV screen right at the counter. That way a central computer, where the person's wages are on file, could tally the trips and amount of food sold to each individual. When an individual has reached his limit either of his wages or his ration, the screen would report it. Tattooing on skin, which cannot be transferred or stolen, would be foolproof. Even cards would be useless if stolen."

"But why couldn't cards be stolen and used by someone else?"

"Because we'd imprint them with a picture of the individual in the code or a retina scan or both."

"You can put a picture in a bar code?" asked Ra'amon, surprised.

"Sure, it's not really a bar code in the sense you are thinking, like in grocery pricing. This is nonlinear. These consist of a multitude of dots like in computer pixels, because it's digitized. We could design it with a logo of the bank or anything else you want on it, like personal data, blood type, etc."

"I want to be selective in who receives the code, so I want it connected to Lord Ashtor, our god. Make it a reward for our faithful followers," Adoní said.

"You can put anything on it you want," said Bedas. "For example, we could take the motif of the dragon image and place the individual's picture in the center of the dragon and the numbers underneath. We can use Adoní's 666 number of the bank to activate the scanner, followed by an individual number for each person and a closing number to indicate the end of the bar code. Like I said earlier, it would be foolproof. You could update the individual's picture every four years like drivers' licenses. The changes would be slight so the alteration would be slight also. Of course, the retina print would never change unless the person developed diabetes or some other eye-disabling disease. You could also collect information on each individual in a central data base and keep tabs on his movements through his purchases. Of course that means that all banks would have to be affiliated."

"That's already in the works. But how can you put that on a hand or forehead?" asked Ra'amon "And what would it look like?"

"Tattooed on the surface of the skin, it would just appear to be a small rectangle of black pixels, squares, and lines—a permanent mark, that's all."

"Can a scanner pick it up off of skin?"

"Oh yes, in fact the data stamped upon a 2-D bar code is so redundant even a poor scan can pick it up," replied Bedas. "All you need is a CCD scanner such as they use in many manufacturing concerns. I would recommend the PDF-417 because it can decode any symbolism you could design."

"Excellent idea," said Ra'amon, not having the faintest notion of what he meant. "How about developing it for me? How long do you think it will take?"

"Not long to set up the computers and other devices. The biggest problem will be setting up the machinery for getting the people tattooed. Issuing cards doesn't take long at all, once you have the design."

"Work on an idea to separate the believers from the unbelievers. Then come to Jerusalem and set it up. We'll pioneer the system first in Israel. Then if it works, we'll expand to the other countries," said Ra'amon. "Let me know as soon as you have something."

Chapter 21

Bedas, Adoni´'s electronic specialist who had been working on the requested system, was ready to report his ideas. The food issue had grown worse daily. Adoni´ tried to control prices, but a black market developed, and he was anxious to clamp down even harder with control. Bedas came directly to the palace. Adoni´ welcomed Bedas warmly.

"Finally you have something to show us?" He called for Ra'amon to join them.

"Mr. Bedas!" exclaimed Ra'amon. "I've been waiting to hear from you. What have you got for us?"

"If I may set up a few pieces of equipment." He brought in an ordinary high density TV monitor and a scanner along with some sort of camera-like devices from his car.

"What are those?" asked Adoni´, pointing to the small devices.

"These are your eyes and ears," he said, laughing.

"I don't understand," replied Adoni´, puzzled.

"Ra'amon said you wanted me to devise a way to separate *your* sheep from the goats. So, I've decided to give your dragon image real eyes and ears. We can even give him a mouth, too, if you like."

"How do you propose to do that?"

"With these little jewels," he said, pointing to the strange objects on the table. "See these lens-like objects? They are really miniature HD digital video cameras called CCD cameras, operated by a tiny chip. We will place them in tandem for the eyes of the image, making seven pairs of eyes that can see from every angle all around the image. Each pair of eyes will send one signal across a laser beam to a HD video screen in a building across the valley, where we will record it. Of course, sensitive microphones will pick up the audio at the same time. A computer operator can print out a picture of any dissenters who refuse to worship your image and pass them along to your card-dispensing stations for identification."

"Marvelous, simply marvelous," remarked Adoní, and Ra'amon agreed. "What do you need to set it up?"

"I'll need access to the image. It is hollow, isn't it?"

"Yes, I set it upon a twenty-by-twenty-foot empty cubicle with access to the necks, anticipating sound equipment," said Ra'amon.

"Then I can wire it up, and we'll be ready to go. You might want to enclose it in something to hide our activities if you want to keep our alterations secret."

"Yes, yes, you're right. I'll order a barricade built. We don't want those nosy priests poking around."

When Bedas demonstrated the 2-D bar code with a sample card, Adoní looked on with satisfaction. Finally, *he* would be in control of everyone's very existence. After Bedas left, Ashtor manipulated Adoní's mouth into a smile and said out loud, "Now they will worship me or else."

Chapter 22

David had appointed several members to his staff of advisors: the two generals, his communications expert, Yigael, his former intelligence team, plus GG, his brothers, and King Hassih. He needed the king's contacts to help set up circumstances beyond their valley. He called them together to set up their hijacking scheme. They all crowded in David's office, converted from the Petra museum's original office. Chairs brought over from the restaurant filled all the empty space.

"Now that we are all here," said David, "let's open in prayer." With bowed head he said, "Our great God and Father, endow us with thy wisdom as we seek to follow your directions. Your people all grow hungry. Your enemy Adoni´ demands loyalty to him before we can eat. Father, show us how to circumvent his plans to feed your people. In *Yeshua's* name we ask. Omen." A chorus of Omens followed.

During the past year, David and his little army had made the caves more habitable and had greatly fortified their defenses. God Himself had regulated the heat in their little caves supernaturally. The local Bedouins exchanged meat, cheese, and occasionally grain traded from other native communities in exchange for money from the secret army, but food grew more and more critical. David, who regularly gleaned information from his friend Sergeant Majid, heard that Adoni´ intended to use Babylon as headquarters for his food project. The information that Adoni´ had created a regular route for food trucks coming from Iraq was good news.

"Daveed," said Sarge, the last time they talked. "We have recruited a small group of dissenters to join our cause. In fact, one of our new recruits joined himself to the unit loading the food convoys. He has exact information on their scheduling. How about that!"

"God is good!" answered David. "Great work, Sarge."

"This gives us a way to fight against Adoni´," said General Savoy when he heard the news. "Once we get our plans finalized we can begin hijacking Adoni´'s food and starve his people. Perhaps they will rebel against him."

"And we can use the food to support the faithful both to God and to the Jordanian king's faithful here in Jordan," said David.

"Well, it sounds good. But it's only so much talk if we can't *do* anything about it," said the King of Jordan disparagingly. "We have such a small army."

"You're forgetting Jewish resourcefulness. We have helicopters, horses, and light weaponry. We can do a lot with that—Katz," said David as he motioned to him. "Bring us in some maps of Jordan and Iraq from the other room. What's the best way to ship food from Babylon to Israel?" he asked the king.

"Well, there's no rail line between our two countries, so they will have to ship by truck or fly it in. I guess the main road from Baghdad to Ammon is the best bet."

Looking at the map, David saw another possibility. "They could send it down the rail to the Persian Gulf and ship it to Eilat by sea. But they would still have to truck it to Jerusalem. I don't see how we could affect planes, but trucks we might stop."

"Trucks are more economical than planes. I think he would use trucks," said General Shofat.

"I think we could handle trucks. Now all we need to know is the time table of the train, and we can make some plans. Then I'll call Majid and see what he can find out."

"Train?" asked General Shofat?

"How else will we get the cargo from north Jordan to here?"

"Oh, of course," replied the general.

David reported his findings to the rest at their next meeting.

"Majid says the shipping orders are reported to Israel via our communication satellite. They are using computers. Yigeal, get on this right away, and see if you can access it."

"But even if we know the schedule, how would we handle the trucks?" said the General.

"That's the problem we have to solve," replied David. "I talked to Sargeant Majid yesterday. He says the trucks are shipping food back to Israel on a regular basis now. They leave Babylon at six a.m. every Monday, Wednesday, and Friday morning. Your Highness, how long would it take them to get to Amman?"

"Hmm, let's see." He pondered. "I know it's over eight hundred kilometers."

GG spoke up, "Could you put that in miles for an uneducated American as far as the metric system goes?"

"Jonathan, go to the computer and look it up," ordered David. "I should have looked it up myself before the meeting."

General Shofat interrupted, "I wouldn't think three shipments a week would be enough."

Jonathan, looking up from David's personal computer, said, "It's nine hundred and nine kilometers or five hundred sixty-five miles."

"What is the speed limit here in Jordan?" said David again, looking to the king.

"It depends on the road," said the king. "The road to Baghdad is excellent, and I believe the trucks would easily do sixty to seventy miles per hour, maybe more. Did the Sarge say how many trucks come a day?"

"You're right, General, that doesn't make sense. I should have clarified that. I'll have to call him back."

"What difference does it make?" said the king. "We are almost twice that distance away from Route 10."

"So?" said Malcolm.

"Well, even if we could hijack a truck, what would we do with the food —and how would we get rid of the trucks?"

"We'll figure it out," said David.

General Shofat leaned over to General Saguy and whispered. "I like this guy's spirit. We did well to choose him."

"I know," said Saguy.

David addressed the king again. "Your Highness, do you have any loyal citizens in contact with you? With a little outside help we might just pull this off."

The king thought for a minute and finally spoke. "I had a few businessmen, loyal friends who decried Adoni´'s taking over my country. They came to me in Egypt and offered help. In fact, they insisted that they would help any way they could. They left me their phone numbers, but I didn't see how they could do anything."

"What kind of business?"

"One is an officer high up in the Hejaz Railway. Another owns a fuel oil company. Now he might help us by supplying gas for your helicopters."

"And what is the name of the rail from Amman down to Ma'am?" asked David.

The king jumped up all excited. "Why, it's the Hajaz!"

"Exactly."

"You already knew that, didn't you?" The king looked at David with admiration.

"I was just hoping. I've been asking *Yeshua* to give us a connection with the railroad."

"I volunteer for the hijacking," said Matza.

Katz echoed, "Me, too."

"I'll fly a helicopter," said GG.

"Don't leave me out!" cried Jonathan, all excited.

"Let's not get ahead of ourselves. An operation like this will take some precise planning. Plus we still need more information. King Hassih, get in touch with your friends and see if the offer still stands. Jonathan, you and Malcomb get on the computer, see if Google Earth still works, and find the best place on Route 10 to hijack the trucks. Find out all you can about your spot. That we can do now."

"We helicopter pilots can be thinking about what planes to use and how to equip them," said GG. "We'll also figure the poundage we can carry and the gas it will take."

"We'll need experienced truck drivers," said the generals, almost in concert.

"Two great minds think alike," said General Saguy, laughing gaily. "I don't know how long it's been since I had this much fun."

Chapter 23

Lin Yiang saw the end of his civilization coming. If China was to sustain their present level of development, they had to have oil. They had plenty of coal to make electricity, run trains and ships. But unless they developed electric cars and electric war weaponry, they would be back to horses just like the Russians. And he was sure it was oil that the Russians were after in the Middle East when they invaded, a prize he now eyed. The comet defeated the Russians. He had heard through the news that Jerusalem had totally escaped the Russian assault.

The Russian Army had defeated itself under the comet's bombardment from above. He would not let it defeat him. Genghis Khan was relentless and swift. His methods worked because of his unswervingly strict discipline in training his men. Knowing he had no other recourse, he got out his history books and began studying Genghis Khan and his strategies in earnest.

Meanwhile, he ordered Lin Cho Conglin, his other boyhood friend and second only to himself in horsemanship, to begin commandeering and breeding sturdy ponies for combat. It became a national effort. He spoke to the youth of the northern steppes of lower Mongolia to excel in their skills. Such skills could earn great glory for China. Although each soldier would be issued a rifle and a hand gun, he sponsored contests in ancient weaponry—spears, bows, javelin, and swords. He put blacksmiths to forging well-balanced swords, both curved and two-edged, like a Roman warrior's, and steel bows.

Young men and youths flocked to his new military schools. The romanticism of an ancient age appealed to them. Even the countryside flourished economically as the farmers raised food for the growing army. Cowhide became premium, becoming the choice for armor, being layered with hard-fired, thin ceramic plate because it was lightweight. A whole industry flourished around the new national passion of equipping their army.

Lin Yiang himself inspired their worship, as he enthralled the young army with tales of Genghis Khan when he visited their camps. On occasion he wowed them with his own skills as a horseman. They hung on every word he said. He became their hero.

As each unit of a hundred soldiers completed their training, each soldier was issued four horses. When enough for a full company of three units developed, Lin Yiang addressed them.

"Today you will begin a new phase of your training. Up to now we have concentrated on your riding and fighting skills. That you *must* know to fight the kind of war we will wage. But today you will begin training in survival skills. Each of you has been issued four horses. Your *life* depends on your horses surviving. And that depends on you.

"First, you will learn what plants are good for foraging from the land, both for yourself and your horses, because we will be traveling fast without hay or oats. You will carry only beef jerky and a small bag of meal for emergency. When that is gone, you will each have a small extraction syringe to draw blood from your horses to drink. You will learn how much you may withdraw without injury to them.

"You will also learn to rotate the loads of your horses, you being the heaviest load they will carry at any one time. We will basically live off the land. We will confiscate the stores of the people we conquer on the way to our destination, even replace our lost horses when necessary. However, if you properly care for our sturdy Chinese breed, they are better than replacements. The goal is to capture the oil production of the Middle East, not just territory. China's future depends on it. Remember that. Do not stop to collect trinkets on the way. That will slow us down.

"I will permit rape of conquered women as a reward after the battle is won locally on our way. I know you have been deprived of women because of the practice of aborting girl babies. Many of you might even bring home a wife. However, until we are victorious and have the prize in hand, you will only indulge in sexual activity when allowed by your officers. Disobedience carries the death penalty."

Chapter 24

Joshua Jaffe and Zerub Abel stood before the veil in front of the ark of the covenant asking *Yeshua* about their next announcement of God's plans. "I could not even imagine what Revelation meant when it talked about the sea becoming like a dead man's blood, but that's exactly what they said it looked like. God's word means what it says," said Joshua Jaffe.

"This next plague is just as puzzling," said Zerub Abel. "How can a falling star fall upon a third part of the rivers and fountains? And it looks like we will have to add the third vial judgment to it as well, since it's working out that each vial follows right behind each trumpet judgment."

"I know," said Joshua. "But at least we'll know when to announce it."

"You mean because of the martyr's blood connected with it?"

"Yes. It may be time for the beheading to start." Their fellow temple dwellers had begun meeting daily to study the book of Revelation in the New Testament. Joshua had discovered the passage concerning the appointing of two witnesses and surmised that it referred to Zerub Abel and himself. In studying the trumpet judgments they had discovered what the Lord planned to do.

God spelled it all out in his word for them, all but *when* to deliver the messages.

When the believers realized that God's next assault on the Beast (whom they identified as Adoní) would come against the drinking water, they began to store water in closed vessels.

Rachel participated with the others in their study of Revelation. Interested in the part about the false ruler and his prophet, she reasoned that if Adoní was the false ruler, then Ra'amon must be his prophet. But when she read the whole book, she saw mention of the Lamb several times. She hated to admit it, but it did look like everything was coming to pass just like the New Testament said. She could not deny what had already happened exactly as the book prophesied. After all, a mountain-sized object had just fallen into the sea. They had all watched it fall. *Were the Rebbes of her upbringing wrong? Could the Lamb be the Moschiach after all?*

She decided to talk to Joshua Jaffe. She couldn't find him inside the temple, so she went outside on the porch. He stood with a small group looking at the activity in the courtyard. Workmen were erecting that same curtained wall they had put up during the construction of it.

"What's going on?" asked Rachel as she approached the group.

"Looks like they are going to work on the image some more, and they don't want us to see," replied Joshua.

"Doesn't it say something about that in the Revelation?" asked Rachel. "About the image being able to talk and cause those who would not worship it to be killed?"

"I think you are right, Rachel. Let's go take a look at that."

"Your Honor, could I talk to you about something that is bothering me?"

"Of course, but first come along and we'll look that up that passage you mentioned." On the way he asked, "What is it that troubles you, my dear?"

"Well, I can't deny what is happening, and it all seems to be written in the New Testament."

"Yes, this has been a surprise to us all. We have denied that the Christians had any truth, and now we discover we've only had half of it. I suppose one reason is their treatment of us, but part of it stems from a curse Jehovah put on our ancestors because they rejected his Word and his ways. Our eyes could not see the truth because our minds were blinded."

"Is that what happened to me?" Rachel asked thoughtfully.

"Perhaps. It's not easy to admit that something you believe in so completely is wrong."

"I guess I'm going to have to admit I'm wrong about the Lamb. But could you show me from the Tanakh where that Lamb is the *Moschiach?* I'm the kind of person who has to be shown *why* something is true."

"You know the passages concerning the Messiah as king?"

"Yes. Show me where he is a sacrifice. That's the part I don't understand."

When they reached the room that had been set up as a kind of library and study with reference books, he pulled out a New Testament. "Where did you see that reference to the image? Do you remember? We'll look it up first before we forget."

"It's in the part about the false prophet," said Rachel, turning to the thirteenth chapter of Revelation.

"Ah yes, the part about the mark for buying and selling. We've been expecting that. It definitely has something to do with the image. They're probably setting it up right now. If the image determines who will receive the mark by whether they worship the image or not, there must be some technical way for it to tell. Cameras maybe? That's probably what they are doing."

"But Your Honor, surely the people are not so ignorant they can't figure out that the statue cannot see or hear."

"Oh, I don't know about that. They seem to be mesmerized by anything Adoni´ tells them. It's like he speaks to them as a god. We'd better warn our people to get food while they still can. Also, tell them they will be damned if they receive the mark."

"But, Your Honor, how will they eat?" Rachel said, deeply concerned.

"We will all have to depend upon God, now won't we? The book of Revelation makes it clear that he curses those to damnation who worship the Beast.

Now let's talk about *Yeshua* as the Lamb."

Chapter 25

Joshua Jaffe began in Genesis and explained to Rachel why the Lamb had to come to put away the sins of mankind. "Starting in the Garden of Eden," he said, "God clothed Adam and Eve with the coats of animals to cover their nakedness, which spoke of their absence of righteousness caused by their disobedience. Those animals died as a substitute for Adam and Eve's sin. But being merely animals, their blood could not satisfy God's absolute justice, nor could it take away the guilt conscientiousness of man. But they looked forward to the day when a man, the woman's seed promised to Eve, would take away the sins of the world and fulfill every sacrifice."

"You mean all the sacrifices of the Torah speak of *Yeshua's* one death?" asked Rachel incredulously.

"Yes. We don't understand quite all the symbolism yet, but when I stood on the steps on the Day of Atonement, I saw quite clearly that the Passover lamb was a picture of *Yeshua* dying for our families and the kid of the goats for our nation. Each sacrifice defined a certain beneficiary ever widening until *Yeshua* paid for the sins of the whole world. All the sacrifices pointed to his one death. When we saw him it was only to acknowledge his death two thousand years ago. The scapegoat portrayed his carrying away of our sins. After we accepted him, we all experienced a cleansing of our consciences.

You see, it's a question of worth. One man is worth more than all the animals *ever* sacrificed, therefore animal sacrifices could never satisfy true justice. But *Yeshua*, being God himself and of infinite worth, because he lives forever, was worth more than every man that *ever* lived. He, being in the form of a man, was a perfect substitute."

"But where does it say that *Moschiach* has to die?"

"*Yesha'yahu* (Isaiah) tells of him exposing himself to death and being numbered with sinners. Daniel talks about the Messiah being cut off. King David speaks of his anguish on the cross in Psalm 22. Then in Psalm 16, he told of God's holy one not seeing corruption, showing his early resurrection. So you see, it was there in your Tanakh all along, but you didn't see it that way because of blinded eyes, just like the rest of us. Some rabbis even thought prophecy indicated two Messiahs, Ben Joseph the suffering one and Ben David the ruling one. Instead, there was one Messiah who comes to the earth twice. He came once to die for the sins of mankind and then will come again to triumph over his enemies in judgment, just before he takes over as king. We are seeing the judgment right now. Soon we will see him as king."

"What do I have to do to experience the cleansing of my sins?"

"Be satisfied fully that he is who he says he is and repent of your sins and rejection of him. Let him become your sacrifice to God. When you do, his Holy Spirit will enter into you and help you, so that you know you are accepted."

"I will be able to *know* I'm accepted?"

"Yes, when the Holy Spirit takes up residence inside you, he brings an awareness of a cleared conscience—a clean feeling and an unspeakable joy. It's a completely inner experience, but by it *you know that you know* everything is all right between you and God."

"I will study this further," said Rachel thoughtfully. After all her vehemence against the Lamb, she wanted to be alone to sort out her emotions. She needed to think things through. "One more question. Do you think *Yeshua* will forgive me after all the railing I have done against him?"

"Of course, my dear, we all did the same. You were a bit more passionate perhaps. The New Testament says that the natural man is an enemy of God. We all needed to repent. That's why when *Yeshua* came to us showing himself as our sacrifice, we had a mourning. We all had to adjust our thinking, and it was a painful process. You are just a little behind the rest of us."

"And a long way behind my papa," she said, tears filling her eyes. "He was one of the preachers you know. David saw him at the tent that day."

"That's right, I remember you said how persuasive he was the day I met you. You poor child, you have suffered enough. Let *Yeshua* heal your wounds," he said as he drew her into his arms to comfort her.

Rachel retreated to her room. She understood fully now. All that remained was her surrender, but it came hard because of her pride. She had worn it as an armor against the assault of the Christians she had encountered from her adolescence on. She struggled with her emotions. She had grown to hate the "Lamb of God." Now she must bow to him. What else could she do?

In thinking about her life, her past flashed before her. She fell down on her knees and began pouring out her confession. "I am so sorry," she said, sobbing as the true nature of her rebellion confronted her. She repented of her stubbornness, her anger, and yes, her treatment of her papa and David, as she saw herself from their point of view. "Oh Lamb, forgive me. *Yeshua* save me from myself," she pleaded. "I believe, I believe, be my sacrifice." Suddenly a feeling of love engulfed her, consuming her. When she arose, she felt clean and forgiven as a wonderful peace settled over her. "The Holy Spirit," she whispered. "It's true. It's really true. You *can* feel him."

Chapter 26

It had taken six weeks to set up the equipment in the idol, the processing, and the tattoo stations. During that time the temple believers pooled their money and went into a frenzied buying spree while the food was still available without a mark. They stored it, mostly dry staples, within the temple structure. The believers living in the economy did the same.

It didn't go unnoticed. Ra'amon had overseen the setup of the equipment in the image. He complained to Adoni´. "The 'Lambers' are stockpiling food in the temple. How do you think they knew?"

"Maybe their 'Lamb' told them. Don't worry. What food they have can't last long. Then where will they buy more?" he said, laughing.

Finally in October, when they were ready, Adoni´ made a declaration on TV. "My fellow citizens of the world, time has come to make a change in our monetary system. We have devised what we think is a foolproof way to conduct our business by eliminating fraud, even the black market, and also introduce a means of rationing our food supply fairly. We will try this in Israel first. After we see if it works here, we will expand it to the rest of the kingdom. Haik Ra'amon, Minister of Religion, has also been appointed

Chairman of Commerce. I'll let him tell you the details." He turned to Haik. "Mr. Ra'amon."

"Thank you, King Adoni´," he said, smiling into the camera in his winsome way. "It will work like this: each person will receive a tattoo on their right hand or forehead, whichever is your choice. In the tattoo will be a picture of you, an imprint of your retina, and a special number issued to identify you as a purchaser. When you purchase an item—anything—the clerk will scan your mark with an electronic device, and it will pick up your picture and number on a screen right at the counter.

"This will record your purchase by sending it directly to a central computer at the bank. There, a computer will automatically deduct the purchase from your account. We will no longer accept currency as legal tender. Instead, we will register your wages at our central bank. All transactions will be cashless and accurate. By this, we will eliminate all theft and black market activities.

"There is only one requirement. You must acknowledge your allegiance to our kingdom by your bowing to the god who saved us from the Russians and continues to work through our great leader King Julius Leucus Adoni´. You will do this by kneeling and worshipping the Great Dragon image. The marking will begin on the Temple Mount next week. We will start with the Alephs and work our way straight through the alphabet," he said, referring to Hebrew.

"You will receive a notice in the mail telling you when to come," continued Ra'amon.

"In addition to individual numbers and transactions, we will also have a number for corporate businesses for purchase in the wholesale market. These will be special bankcards stamped with the name or number of the image depending upon which kind of business. The food business cards will have the name and picture of Adoni´ on it. All other business transaction cards will be stamped

THE END... AND A NEW BEGINNING

with the number of his bank. We have to make separate cards to ration and regulate the food for wholesalers and retailers. These too require bowing before the image before they can be issued. At a separate tent on the mount, you can register your business and pick up your card.

Fellow citizens, this is the way we can show our gratitude to our glorious leader. I personally intend to be the first to get my mark, and I will be proud to wear it right in the middle of my forehead."

With that he smiled, and the announcer came on saying: "Stay tuned. We will have a discussion about the new system with Mr. Ra'amon and King Adoni´ after this commercial."

Then a panel of reporters discussed the new monetary system with Adoni´ and Ra'amon answering questions. The most asked question and least understood answer was: "Why must the mark be tattooed to the skin? Why can't we all have cards like the businesses?"

Finally, Adoni´ answered them himself plainly and with firmness, yet in a soft and persuasive tone. "*All* individuals will have a skin tattoo, even the business people. This is necessary because cards can be stolen, and faces can be altered. With a tattoo showing your face *and* a retina scan, no one can falsely misrepresent himself. Besides, business people have to present both their cards and their skin tattoo to buy wholesale. This assures a theft-proof and fair system for all. Not only that, but it also marks you as a loyal citizen of the kingdom and a worshipper of our god." The session ended by soliciting volunteers for implementing the system.

While Ra'amon got the monetary system going, Adoni´ set up trade routes and trucking to transport food. He had concentrated on the Tigris/Euphrates Valley because he had staunch devotees there. It made good sense because of the already fertile soil, and they had an abundance of water from the two rivers (an essential element because the prophets had successfully stopped the rain in Israel). His people in Iraq would flourish exceedingly, assuring loyalty.

—

They did flourish. So much so, they began to refurbish the ancient city of Babylon, partially restored by Saddam Hussein earlier. Besides, it was nearest to their growing fields south of Baghdad. Adoni´, pleased with their efforts, made Babylon the main depot for his trucks. Thus, Babylon became the mouth for feeding his kingdom and a great commercial city. Adoni´ also refurbished the palace built by Saddam in the outskirts of the city, intending to rule from there eventually.

Chapter 27

Government workers took down the temporary barrier around the image and emptied some of the worship tents that stood along the boys' school on the far side of the Temple Mount to the north. They used these tents to provide a place for tattooing the people.

The city's hotels filled with those from out of town whose names began with the first letter of the alphabet, whether Hebrew or Arabic. They directed the crowd first to the area surrounding the image that was roped off to hold limited numbers. Special officers of Religious Affairs regulated the entering and exiting. The officers admitted one hundred people at a time to allow enough room for bowing before the image, Muslim style, in/around the obelisk and the round stairs. (Adoni´ had told both the Jews and the Arabs the reason God forbade bowing down to an image in the past was because it was reserved for the present time for this final revelation of God). The officers had already received their marks on their foreheads.

As each allotment stood before the image, it spoke, commanding their allegiance. Bedas had outdone himself in making the image realistic. By focusing several cameras on the image he had superimposed a holographic image upon one of the mouths, but the sound actually emanated from one of the short horns above it. It was very effective. Unbeknownst to the worshipers, they photographed each response, and it relayed ahead to the exit station. Those who had remained standing were weeded out and sent to a separate tent for questioning. If they still refused to bow down, they denied the mark to them. Instead, they recorded their names and addresses.

The faithful watched from the temple porch. They had no intention of complying. Zerub Abel, absent from the "Alephs," appeared conspicuous. This was brought to the attention of Ra'amon and brought prompt action. Officers approached the temple steps demanding an audience.

Appearing on the porch of the temple, Zerub Abel said, "What is it you want?"

"Ra'amon sends word that if you do not bow to the image and receive your mark, as an example to the people, you will be executed."

"Let Ra'amon come and tell me himself," replied Zerub Abel.

Taking more authority than they were given, the incensed officers drug two of the "refuseniks" from their line, stood them before the temple porch, and shot them. The people gasped in fear, but they blamed Abel for the victim's deaths, yelling their disapproval.

In answer, Abel addressed the onlookers. "You see what a bloodthirsty god you serve. We will *never* serve Adoni´'s god." With that, he turned and went back into the temple. The angry crowd advanced toward the temple steps, but fire shot out from his finger and dropped the two foremost of the protesters. That stopped the crowd, but the hatred for the faithful increased. They shook their fists and blasphemed the old God of the priests.

Ra'amon took the incident to Adoni´. "What can we do with those in the temple?" he asked. "No one can approach them because of the fire."

"Have you used your fire against them?" asked Adoni´ sternly.

THE END... AND A NEW BEGINNING

Ra'amon hesitated. "No," he said.

"Why not?" snapped Adoni´.

"I was afraid their fire might be stronger," he said with his head down.

"Than the power of *Ashtor*?" he demanded in a loud voice. "Nonsense. But maybe there's a better way than direct confrontation. We have the names of those who have not applied for their mark, do we not?"

"Yes, of course."

"Then select someone prominent among them and execute him. Do we have any MKs that have not applied for their mark?"

"I'll check," he said as he sat down in front of his terminal with access to the main computer. He sorted according to occupation. "Yes!" Ra'amon shouted. "He's perfect."

"Is it anyone I know?"

"Do you know Jesse Solomon?"

"Captain Solomon's father?"

"Yes."

"You're right. He *is* perfect. Maybe executing his father will bring him out of hiding."

Ra'amon remarked, "I was greatly disappointed when David defected."

"That reminds me," said Adoni´, "what have we found out about the army personnel that disappeared?"

"We're pretty sure they went to Egypt."

"Don't you know?" he asked angrily.

"No," he said lamely. "I've been concentrating on the new technology. I'll have to check with the army."

"Well, then do so," he snapped. "Meanwhile, I think we should round up those refusers who are not living in the temple along with Solomon. We need to make a public announcement with executions. Line up several chop blocks in front of the image and have some large medieval type axes forged and sharpened. I want this to be a graphic example. We'll see who still refuses to fall down before the image. I personally will be present and offer them a choice."

Chapter 28

Ra'amon found two hundred and fifty-two names listed that had refused. After they had the instruments of execution prepared, he ordered the first fifty-two arrested. That week Ra'amon placed ten eighteen-inch-square wooden blocks to the side of the image facing south. He wanted the temple people to be able to see what was happening. Several chairs were set up fifteen feet out from the image facing the blocks. A mere fifteen feet beyond the blocks was a fence to confine the people.

On December 25, Adoni´ and Ra'amon, followed by several MKs, entered the Temple Mount from the Arab side marching in step with six drummers, three preceding them and three behind. The drummers and the dignitaries entered from the east. The dignitaries filed in front of the seats and sat down, while the drummers stood three to each side of the chairs and blocks. Ten large men wearing black Keffiyens over their heads, with only slits as openings for their eyes, entered and stood at each block. (The traditional Arab headdresses were to protect the identity of the executioners). Next, ten prisoners marched in with their hands cuffed behind them, flanked on each side by Adoni´'s special police. These were lined up in front of the blocks.

Adoni´ rose and addressed them: "It has been brought to our attention that you have not received your mark. Perhaps you did not understand that this is the only way we can make commerce fair for all our citizens. I give you another chance to join in our great kingdom by falling down now and worshipping the image of our great society."

Out of the first ten, one saw the axes, the blocks, and the masked men, then fell down and worshipped, eyes widened in fear.

"A very wise decision," declared Adoni´. "Unshackle him and take him to the marking tent." He was led around behind the chairs and on to the marking tent. "Now, what about the rest of you?" asked Adoni´.

They stood there silent and motionless, faces resolute.

Adoni´ motioned to the executioners, who in turn forced the other nine to their knees and laid their cheeks flat on the blocks. "Merry Christmas!" smirked Adoni´ sarcastically. Then he nodded to the head drummer standing to his right. He in turn signaled the rest. They began a drum roll. The executioners lifted their axes in unison and brought them down when the drums stopped. The heads rolled in all directions from the block, while the headless trunks convulsed like chickens with their heads cut off, spurting blood that covered the block and ran down the sides. A prearranged crew dressed in white coveralls and long commercial rubber gloves came and gathered up the bodies, loading them onto a cart hitched to a jeep. They drove it to the east side and lined up behind it, their bloody suits and gloves testifying to their task.

Then they brought the next round before the blocks. The men stared wild-eyed at the blood-stained blocks and the hooded executioners, seeing their imminent fate.

The drum roll had attracted the attention of the temple dwellers. They crowded on to the porch to see what was going on. They

THE END... AND A NEW BEGINNING

gasped as they realized some of the faithful were being executed. "Why does not God send his fire upon Adoni´ and the rest like he did before?" asked one of the wives.

"He only sent death to them when they came after us here in the temple," replied Joshua quietly. "Remember the Revelation said those who would hurt us would be destroyed by fire. These are evidently those also spoken of in the Revelation who are to be beheaded as martyrs."

"Who are they? Can anyone see?" asked Rachel.

"No, they are obscured by their guards," replied another.

Another drum roll sounded. The ten refused and ten heads rolled. Adoni´'s faithful crowd, who had been invited to witness the "rebels'" judgment at the temple, looked on, fascinated. They shoved and pushed for a better view. This was not some special effect in a movie. This was pure gore.

Finally, after they loaded the second group on the cart, Adoni´ ordered the area cleared of all but one lone executioner. Then they brought forth a special prisoner. Those on the porch all began to whisper among themselves. Rachel said, "Who is it?" and pushed her way to the front at the steps.

"No, no, noooooo," she screamed as she recognized Jesse, her words lost in the drum roll. The ax came down with a thud.

Rachel fainted.

Chapter 29

"Take her inside," said Joshua, as the men gently gathered her up. "I think it is time for another judgment announcement," he said to Zerub Abel. "The Revelation says God gives them blood to drink after they have killed his saints and prophets. That's exactly what the third trumpet and vial judgment calls for."

Rachel roused as some of the women fussed over her, wiping her face with a cold cloth. Rachel came awake with a start. "What happened?" she asked, pushing away the cloth.

"You fainted when you saw Jesse…" said one of the ladies softly, unable to finish her sentence.

"Oh, now I remember." She sobbed, tears streaming down her cheeks. "Oh, why did it have to be Jesse? Why is it everyone who is dear to me has to die?" she cried. "Oh, *Yeshua*, why do you allow it?"

"We cannot question God, my dear," said Joshua Jaffe's wife Anna. "Remember, *Yeshua* said we would have to go through the fire. It won't be long before he comes and destroys Adoni´. Then we will all see our loved ones again. Be comforted with that thought."

"Yes," she said, "and I will tell Papa how sorry I am that I did not believe him." But silently she uttered this prayer. *Yeshua, please don't take David. At least let him live.*

Joshua Jaffe motioned to Zerub Abel, and they walked to the bottom of the steps and called out to Adoni´.

"Ah, finally we evoke a response from our adversaries," said Adoni´, smiling. "Be ready to use your fire," he muttered under his breath. Ra'amon nodded.

The crowd parted and left a clear path between them, fully aware of the firepower of the temple group. "You see what happens to those who oppose me," said Adoni´ fearlessly.

"I see that you are heaping up judgment from a righteous God," replied Joshua. "Since you like blood so much, Almighty God who made heaven and earth will send you blood to drink. Your whole kingdom will be given a bloody bitter gall to drink, and many of your subjects shall die because you have killed God's precious faithful believers."

"Now," said Adoni´ to Ra'amon.

He raised his hand and pointed it toward the two prophets. Fire fell from heaven all around them and licked the dust where they stood, but it didn't touch the high priest, the former premier, or their garments. They simply turned and walked up the steps. Once at the top, Joshua pointed back at Adoni´, who had stepped beyond the altar toward the porch of the temple.

"You are standing on God's holy ground."

Fire engulfed him and he dropped to the ground and rolled in agony, his clothes burning. The people gasped. Words filtered through the crowd, repeated as they traveled. "They have assassinated our leader, our Messiah."

But seconds later he rolled past the altar, extinguishing the flames as he rolled. He sprang to his feet like a phoenix, completely restored except for his clothes. Then he lifted his hands in triumph. "See, I live!" he shouted, as he turned around for all to see. Holding his hands high in the air, he said, "By the power of Lord Ashtor and

THE END... AND A NEW BEGINNING

the decree of heaven, I live! Right now the ark is protecting them, but soon we will discover the magic of its power. Then we shall see whose god is more powerful. See, I was dead like the celebrated Jesus. But now I am alive, and it didn't take three days. See, my powers are greater than his." He shook his fist toward heaven. "There is no god up there except mine. No saints, no other resurrected ones. No trinity, only Ashtor. Are you my faithful believers?" he asked, working the crowd to a fever. A roar of approval went up. The cameras were filming the whole affair. "I have decided that I will worship Ashtor today in thanksgiving for my life. You are invited to watch if you like." Many followed him to the garden.

■

Lin Yiang Dehuai had consolidated power among the Southeast Pacific nations just as Adoni´ had done in the Middle East. Dehuai, however, lacked the subtle negotiating skills of Adoni´. Instead, he used the huge military inventory acquired by China in the early nineties to persuade them. Most of the countries in the region had internal squabbles because of the chaos and upheaval caused by the overturning, which gendered weak governments. In the disarray due to the many upheavals, it was easy for China to take over. No other nations would come to the victim's aid. Who was left to object? The UN no longer existed, and the West was occupied with its own problems.

After having conquered all the nations south and west of China with the exception of India, Dehuai had run out of gas, and his vast war machine on the ground came to a halt. Only his nuclear navy remained.

Mass destruction from the earthquakes and tidal waves had shut down manufacturing, sometimes for the want of a single part, like what happened in the early nineties when a factory burned that produced the silicon for making microchips. It affected manufacture of computers around the world and sent the costs soaring. Post-catastrophe manufacturing multiplied that problem several times over as the delicate network between corporations collapsed.

But even more significant than that, oil production had stopped completely. China produced its own needs until the nineties, when their double-digit economy's demand caused more than six hundred thousand barrels a day deficit. However, now with her refining plants shut down and the oil source in the Pacific destroyed, all petrol-run engines stopped. The few ships that survived the ravages of the sea were in the process of being retrofitted to coal burning, but until they were finished, the army was landlocked, except for a few nuclear ships. The subs were worthless for transporting troops.

The land vehicles were left where they stopped, and modern civilization of the Far East died. With the loss of fuel, warriors were once again reduced to horses, but of course Lin Yiang had anticipated this and he was ready. China possessed the greatest number of horses in the present world. (The United States formerly held that title, but they were mostly pleasure horses). China had the biggest population to feed and took full advantage of the situation. Her vast, newly trained army began to move west, her horses outnumbering the men four to one. Since the west had used up most of their modern armament on Russia, Lin Yiang's mounted warriors with steel-forged bows and swords, who had trained in ancient warfare, especially archery, now had the advantage. Taking his cue from Genghis Khan, Duduai made sure his archers were deadly, even riding at full speed. Another tactic borrowed from Khan was psychological. He turned cruelty into a weapon of fear, butchering all who opposed him even slightly, so that the next conquest came easier as the enemies gave up rather than fight.

Chapter 30

The new world order had begun. Adoni´, apparently burned by the prophets of God, had risen up as a phoenix from the ashes of his burning while the world watched. Just like Jesus, he had been resurrected, or so their delusions told them. Actually, he believed Ashtor protected him, but in truth God was not through using him yet. It deluded the wicked into thinking it was a miracle. Watching his act of worship bonded him even more closely to the people who had adopted the worship act completely and heaped shame upon themselves as they practiced it more and more.

Rachel had recovered through the tender attentions of the women. When Joshua came in to check on her, she assured him that she was all right and asked, "How are we going to get word to David and his mother?"

"I've already been thinking about that. Since this crackdown with the mark, we are so restricted that no one can leave the temple without bringing death upon himself." *If we only had a way to communicate,* thought Joshua. Then he continued. "Jesse was our contact with David through his military phone. I wonder what happened to it? But on second thought it might not do us any good. I believe you have to dial in a special code to reach the military satellite. If only we had both the phone and the code, we could stay in touch."

"Jesse used to have it in his car. He showed me where he had it hidden. Surely the code would be with it," said Rachel excitedly. "Maybe it's still there. We could mark my head with ink to simulate a mark. Who would know the difference? I could try to get it."

"You would have to walk. Your mark would not work for a taxi or a bus, remember."

"How about if we borrow someone's bicycle?"

"You mean steal it? No, too dangerous. Suppose you got caught? Besides it's too hilly. It might be worse than walking, having to push the bike."

"Well, then I'll just have to walk. I could spend the night. I still have a key from when I lived with them. Or if someone here can tell me how to hotwire the car, I could drive Jesse's car back."

"Might work, but I'd never let you go alone," said Joshua. He thought for a minute, then said, "I could send my son with you. He knows enough about cars. He used to tinker with them all the time."

Joshua called for his eighteen-year-old son Jeremiah to report to him. When he showed up, his mother, who had been standing next to Rachel, walked over to Joshua and put her hand on Joshua's chest. Looking deeply into his eyes she said, "Are you sure you want to do this?"

Joshua raised both eyebrows when he looked into his wife's eyes.

"What else do you suggest we do? We need that phone, and no one else here at the temple can hotwire a car."

By the look on her face he could discern her thoughts. He drew her to him and whispered in her ear. "I have the same concerns as you, but we will have to trust him into *Yeshua's* care. Can you do this, my dearest?" She nodded. He knew the reason for her anxiety. Jeremiah was their only son.

THE END... AND A NEW BEGINNING

Joshua introduced him to Rachel. After some deliberation they set about marking both their foreheads with ink—Anna marking Rachel and Joshua marking Jeremiah.

"Good thing it's cold. Sweat could make our marks run," Jeremiah joked, game for the adventure. Rachel set out with Jeremiah just after dark.

The temple residents had not been idle all during the last year while being cooped up in the temple because of the attitude of the people. They spent much of their time digging tunnels. When the temple construction began, and the walls were up to hide the interior, the priests had brought in archeologists hoping to dig down and explore the regions under the mount. Earlier, by using radar and sounding equipment, they had already determined that a large vault existed on the east side of the western wall, but because of Arab occupation of the mount, they had been unable to excavate until recently. After the temple construction ceased, they had sunk a shaft and penetrated the ceiling of a vast underground complex evidently used for storage by the priests of Herod's day.

The Western Wall Tunnel, originally dug by Israel's Ministry of Religious Affairs for tourism, was on the other side of the subterranean wall where they dug. But when Adoni´ caused the daily sacrifice to cease by his dragon image and further instituted his religion in place of Judaism, he had ordered the Wailing Wall plaza and the underground complex given over to shop keepers for a bazaar. Many more tunnels had been dug in the latter part of the second decade after the year two thousand to connect various underground diggings for tourism. The whole complex became a virtual underground city.

Chapter 31

After digging their own exit tunnels under the mount, the believers had tunneled north, eventually intersecting the large quarry cave called Zedekiah's cave, located under the city between Herod's Gate and Damascus Gate to the Old City. From there, they had made another exit to the east side of the city wall between the corner and Steven's Gate.

Climbing down the ladder, Rachel and Jeremiah made their way to one of the exits and hurried out into the streets.

"How far do you think it is to their house?" asked Jeremiah.

"Far enough," said Rachel. "We will have to hurry along to make it before daylight. Too bad we can't take a bus."

"Hey, do you think we could hitch a ride?"

"I don't know," said Rachel, frowning with caution. "Could be dangerous."

"Come on, let's be resourceful," Jeremiah said with the exuberance of youth. Besides, he was thinking of his feet. He walked over to a truck that had stopped for a traffic light and asked, "Say, could you give us a lift over to the Bukharian Quarter? My sister and I have a low balance in our account and can't afford to take the bus."

"What have you got that you will trade me for it?" asked the driver, not at all surprised by the request, because a healthy barter system had sprung up among the poorer people in order to make ends meet.

Rachel pulled a fancy calculator out of her purse and said, "How about this?"

"Sure, hop in."

Rachel and Jeremiah told him where they wanted to go, giving an address a block away from the Solomon's. "This is our first attempt at bartering," said Rachel.

"Oh yeah?" asked the driver. "It works out pretty well most of the time. Some people have whole rooms full of stuff. Others come to them instead of going to the stores. They'd rather not have all their purchases recorded."

"Where do they get the things to barter with?" asked Rachel, amazed.

"Nobody knows for sure, but we suspect most of it comes from houses of those who have been arrested."

"What kind of items are in demand?"

"Your calculator was a good choice."

"Really, why?" asked Rachel.

"Because in the bartering stores they set certain values on things, and we need calculators to balance them out. I tell you it's downright awful how the government has its fingers into everything now. We had to do something. Everything is regulated." They continued their discussion, Rachel and Jeremiah both sympathizing with their new friend, until they reached their destination. After they thanked him and said their *mazel tov's*, he drove off down the street. Rachel said, "Jeremiah, you're a jewel. Now let's move quickly before he comes back this way and sees we didn't go in one of these houses."

"Why not cut through here to the next street?" He pointed to a darkened alley.

"*B'seder.*"

Chapter 32

David's normally mild temper flared when he heard the news about his father. "Those bastards!" he cried, smashing his fist down on the table used as a makeshift desk. "I can't believe the evil Adoni´ is capable of. He must be inhabited by the devil himself."

Everyone in the room looked at David. Never had they seen him really mad or use bad language. "What's happened?" asked Katz in shock.

"They've started killing off the believers, my *abba* included," he said, as his voice broke. "Go find General Saguy." Turning his ear back to the phone he said, "Sorry, everyone wanted to know what happened."

"Naturally," replied Joshua Jaffe. "Say, I need to tell you we announced the destruction of the water mentioned in Revelation chapter 8, so be careful to cover and store what you need to drink. Also, I have to tell you the food supplies are running out for those who fled to the caves. They have been stealing what they needed, but that is getting dangerous since Adoni´ started putting guards around all food dealers."

"Do you know where they are? We may be able to help them."

"Some of them are in the caves under Herodium. Some of their group belonged to the Ministry of Religion and had a key to the underground refuge, but most of them are down around Ein Gedi and farther south in the Hever caves."

"How do you keep in touch?"

"Spies. We copy the mark on the forehead with ink so our people can move about undetected."

"How do you communicate? By the way, how did you reach us?"

"Rachel and Jeremiah, my son, went to Jesse's and got the mobile phone you gave him out of his car."

"Rachel has come back to the temple?" asked David, his voice rising. "I'd given up on her. *Abba* told me she left after the war scare."

"Yes, but I have even better news. Rachel has accepted *Yeshua* as her Lord."

Tears came to David's eyes as he broke into "Praise the Lord!"

"Changing the subject, is there any way you could secure a military phone for those in the caves?"

David thought for a minute. "Maybe. We have extra encrypting devices brought in by the defecting intelligence team, perhaps extra phones as well. That's what we need to do. I'll get Yigael working on it right away. Is there any way I can talk to Rachel?"

"I'll have her call you back. She's out right now."

"Out of the temple?" David nearly shouted. His heart stopped momentarily.

"Yes. She's become quite adept at securing our needs in the barter system. It helps her to feel useful."

"But how do you go in and out undetected?"

"We dug down inside the temple and connected to one of the tunnels the earlier priests had dug under the mount. We have a ladder we can pull up if we have to. There are several outlets to the tunnels. We keep them all guarded."

"*Asita hayil* (Well done)," said David. "God is good! Tell Rachel to call as soon as she returns." With that he clicked off. But the phone call never happened, because she kept missing David and he kept missing her.

—

"What's happening? I hear they are killing our people," said General Savoy, then softly to David, "Sorry to hear about your abba."

"I'm going to have to take the bad news to the family. Meanwhile, see if the king's people are ready. Our people grow short of food. We need to start raiding food trucks, now!"

David found Esther in the restaurant kitchen, helping with the noon meal. He asked her to step outside on the shade-covered verandah of the restaurant.

"What is it, David? We're awfully rushed right now," she protested.

"Mama, it's *Abba*," he said gently. "You'd better sit down."

Catching his mood, she became alarmed. "What's happened?" she asked slowly, as she eased herself into a chair at a table.

"That beast, Adoni´, has had him executed."

"Not Jesse! Why?" she demanded angrily as she jumped up. "What did he do?"

"Adoni´ has issued a mark, a tattoo for the people to use in buying and selling. Remember, we studied about it in the Revelation. Of course, father refused to worship his image. Joshua Jaffe believes Adoni´ intended to make an example of him since he was an MK. Nineteen others were beheaded along with him."

"Beheaded," she said aghast. "How beastly! Jesse's become one of those mentioned in the Book, hasn't he?" she said slowly, more of a statement than a question. Her eyes turned glassy in a shocked daze. David took her into his arms, and they cried on each other's shoulders. Then she said, "We need to tell the children."

Chapter 33

More determined than ever to strike back, David finalized the hijacking plans. Malcomb and Jonathan researched the road to Baghdad and found a spot, where the road passed through a mountainous wilderness. It even had a side road that diverted for a short distance from the main road—probably part of the old road, before straightening it.

After determining the time on the day for the operation, the next day the helicopters took off with twenty men at dawn. They took two medium helicopter transports, a Blackhawk UH—60A and an Iroquois UH—1, (each with a capacity of carrying 14 men). They also took road barriers for roadblocks to aid in their deception for stopping the trucks. Each man wore a Jordanian military uniform and carried an Ak-47.

After they reached the section of road they had chosen for the hijack, the helicopter went in low to check it out. Malcomb, who was in charge of the operation, radioed the other helicopter.

"Jordan, set your helicopter down and set up the first road block position in the middle of the road toward Al Mafrak. We can't have any traffic coming on us during the hijack." This was the town in northern Jordan near the Syrian border where they intended to drop off their cargo to the train.

Jordan landed the helicopter l out of sight, around the mountain well beyond the hijack point Three uniformed men jumped out and removed the road barriers from the plane and set up the roadblock. They informed the stopped vehicles they had to turn around because a land slide had occurred, damaging some trucks. Roadmen were working to get them back on the road, but the road behind them was impassable. Since the soldiers were in Jordanian uniforms, no one questioned their authority.

Meanwhile, Malcomb ordered GG to take them to a high altitude to scout the road to Baghdad, looking for the food convoy. He didn't want to attract attention by appearing to be something other than an army helicopter heading for Baghdad.

"Not too much traffic on the road today," GG commented.

"That's a good thing," replied Malcomb. "It would simplify things if the convoy was alone without other traffic within sight."

"I believe that's it ahead," said GG

"Appears to be," said Malcomb, looking through his small telescope. "Let's go on up the road and check out any traffic close by."

Seeing the next car ahead, GG said, "There's the next. Looks to be about five miles between them."

"That's good enough."

GG's helicopter raced back to the other roadblock location to drop off the roadblock crew to stop the car behind the convoy and any others. By now the convoy had passed and they had to be in position before it got to the hijack spot. They had time since helicopters were faster than trucks.

Meanwhile, the trucks were stopped at the hijack site with still another road block. Malcomb, dressed in an officer's uniform, stepped up to the driver of the guard truck. "We are sorry to stop you, but there's been a hijacking this morning, so we are checking identities. Will you and your passenger please step down out of the cab. May I see your credentials?"

"Where was the hijacking?" asked the driver.

"I don't know. We were just ordered to check all trucks. Sergeant, get all those men out of the back of the vehicle and check their identities," ordered Malcomb with authority, speaking in Arabic.

Katz walked around to the back and motioned with his gun. He turned and said to the other soldiers, "Help me check these guys. Let's get this over with."

The guard soldiers complied. While everyone was digging out their IDs, the hijackers raised their weapons. Malcomb said, "Drop your weapons along with your IDs. Just follow orders and no one will get hurt. Sergeant, have your men gather up their weapons and throw them in the back of the truck."

"Let me guess. This *is* the hijacking," said the officer of the soldiers.

Matza and the rest of the Jordanians joined them, bringing up the food truck drivers. They herded the captives to the helicopter farther up the road. Katz and Matza tied them up while others stood guard, then loaded them into the Blackhawk, Katz securing them in their seats while Matza climbed in behind them in the cargo area with his gun. Then Katz climbed into the co-pilot's seat to ride shotgun. GG took off going northeast away from curious eyes on down the road.

Three Jordanian truck drivers in civilian clothes climbed into the trucks and drove them to just beyond where the cut-off road came back to the new road and stopped. Jonathon and Hillman set off two small charges that brought a cascade of dirt and rocks to just cover the pavement, enough to block the road but doing little damage to the roadbed. Jonathon and Hillman jumped into the back of the guard truck with the rest of their Jordanian soldiers, and the three trucks took off. When thy reached the next road block they were waved through.

The roadblock unit loaded up their helicopter leaving behind a "road closed" notice. They radioed Malcomb, who was riding shotgun in the guard truck. "Did everything go okay?"

"Like clockwork."

Then they went back to pick up the lookouts, place the "road closed" sign, and inform the backed-up traffic of the land slide.

Malcomb radioed food truck one. "Did you remember to disable their communications?" he asked.

"Roger," came the reply. He heard the same from truck two.

"Good, we've completed step one. I will report our progress to base."

David waited anxiously. "They should be about through with phase one."

"Yes," said the generals who had both helped plan the timing. The king was with them also.

"Red Shoe," came Malcomb's voice on their receiver.

"Yes, yes, come in. We read you."

"Phase one complete. No problems, out."

The generals cheered. David shouted, "Hallelujah! Thank you, *Yeshua!*"

"Well, they certainly didn't say much," said the king.

"Those were their orders," said General Saguy.

"Oh, of course," said Hassih. He would wait until they reached the warehouse in Ma'an before he celebrated.

GG, Katz, and Matza took their prisoners across the border into Syria. GG set the helicopter down about a mile from a small village and helped their prisoners out. They threw a small knife about a hundred feet away and said, "Cut your way to freedom and walk in that direction for about a mile. There's a village." The helicopter took off heading north until out of sight of the prisoners, then due east before turning south back to Amman.

━

The other helicopter flew to a small airport in Al Mafraq, where the king's friend in the fuel-oil business had ordered a truckload of fifty-five gallon tanks of airline fuel to be loaded onto a truck to be picked up that afternoon.

They were told that the driver would be dropped off by helicopter. It was designated for the King of Jordan's personal use. It was assumed to be the present king of Jordan, Nabil Dakkah. The driver showed his papers and proceeded to drive his loaded truck to the railway station in Al Mafraq. Here he would be joined by the food trucks and all the cargo loaded into three boxcars destined for a warehouse just north of Ma'an, twenty miles from Petra. The oil-truck driver would drive the empty, fuel-oil delivery truck to the Heqaz rail spur in Queen Alia Airport after he picked up the drivers of the food trucks.

The plan was to find a supermarket and hide the food trucks in plain sight toward the back of its parking lot. They left the keys in the ignition, hoping some enterprising truck drivers would seize the opportunity to acquire a truck of their own. The drivers called in their location to the Jordanian driver of the fuel oil truck, who picked them up and drove all three of them to meet the train at the airport.

Chapter 34

Adoni´ screamed into the phone, "What do you mean two food trucks have disappeared?"

"We lost contact with the drivers at noon today, so we sent out a search party, but all we found was a landslide."

"What about the military escort?"

"Gone as well."

Adoni´ let out a stream of curses in Jehovah's name at the thieves! "What were the trucks carrying?"

"According to the transport order, one truck had mostly staples such as grains and beans, and the other had fresh vegetables from the greenhouses."

"Send out an all points and find those trucks!"

The believers hiding in the caves sent messengers to the Temple Mount to relay their desperate needs. Upon hearing of David's raid, they had Joshua call Petra. The general took the call.

"Operation Red Shoe."

"Temple calling," said Joshua. "We have some of the cave dwellers here, and they are desperate for food and supplies."

"Give us the exact location of the caves, and we can drop in with a load."

"Here, I will put them on," said Joshua, handing the phone to Uri Samak, the leader from the Ein Gedi general area.

"Uri Samak here," he said.

"Uri, the first thing we need you to do is get some communication for your people for each separate location. When we bring the food, I'll leave you a means to communicate directly with us. In the meantime, mark a landing place for us tomorrow morning at daybreak using brightly colored blankets or clothes. Pick a nearly level spot that is at least 22.86 meters square needed to land the sixty-foot UH 60A Blackhawk."

"We'll be ready," he said and clicked off.

Malcomb caught up with David just as he left headquarters.

"Hey David, we got trouble from the sky again."

"What now?"

"I've been looking at the comet every night through my telescope, and last night I just happened to see something else heading toward the earth.

"It is probably something to put blood in the waters that the prophets are predicting. We'd better alert the people to stay under cover. I'll order more water stored and work out something for the horses—maybe put them in the Siq. With its narrow opening at the top, they should be protected from most of what falls from the sky. Afterward we can bring them over to the Forum Restaurant and let them drink from the water lines there."

Lin Yiang Duduai's army struck terror in the hearts of his enemies that lay in the path ahead. The few who escaped spread the word as they fled that he spared no quarter and was devoid of mercy of any kind. This led to some easy victories but did not spare the mothers and daughters of the conquered. The farther the army went toward their goal, the more ruthless they became. However, the closer he got to the Middle East, the more Duduai became affected by missiles from the sky. His army feared no human army, but falling stars were another matter.

In fact, as a major star approached, many of his men scattered looking for shelter, especially those who still had their horses. He consulted with General Pen Lee Zedong. "How can we overcome this fear? I can't fault their bravery against men, but this exact fear destroyed the Russians. That's why they failed to take the oil fields. We can't let it happen to us."

"Why don't we work *with* their fear."

"What do you mean?"

"Agree with them that it is a danger and appoint lookouts to study the sky. There is usually some prior warning. If we have a plan in place, some shelter designated, and a specific meeting place after the threat passes, we can keep them together and prevent panic."

"You are absolutely right. We need scouts to spy out places for shelter from heavenly assaults, especially for our horses. Caves or natural rock formations would be best, rock overhangs, maybe narrow ravines—any place that affords some protection," said Duduai.

"But what about our foot soldiers? We now have a whole division of them, due to the loss of horses. They might not be able to reach the shelters in time. We need to come up with a plan for them," said Pen Lee.

Duduai thought for a moment, "I remember a tactic that the Roman soldiers used in battle. It was called the 'testudo (tortoise) formation.'" They huddled together in groups using their long shields to protect the whole group. The front row dropped to their knees behind their wall of shields resting upon the ground and held upright in front of them. The row behind raised their shields over the first row's heads, laying the front of the leading edge of their shields on top the front shields. The third row held their shields upright on the ground for supporting the back of the second row's shield, and the front of the fourth row's overhead shields and so on. The sides and rears did as the front. Some covered their heads, some covered their sides, but together they covered the whole group.

"Of course, the Romans' shields protected them from arrows and spears, lightweight compared to meteorites. But I read where they were strong enough to make bridges over ravines for horses and chariots to cross. Perhaps we could form a protection like that from the small stone missiles from the sky." They began to experiment. Some knelt down for the upright supports, and others overlapped their shields over their heads, forward and sideways as well. Those holding an overhead shield turned perpendicular to the rows next to them so they could stand closer to one another to overlap the shields on the sides as well as front to back. They kept working until they perfected a tight shielding over twelve men. The result was truly like a tortoise shell. Duduai drew his horse close to the manmade tank and climbed upon it, walking over his men underneath. It was strong, perhaps as strong as was said. It wouldn't protect from huge stones, but it might protect from small stones and fire falls. Soon each man knowing each of the positions could form the armored umbrella, quickly filling any position that was lacking.

When the star finally exploded beyond the atmosphere, the foot soldiers formed their shells quickly and deflected many falling stones and much red dust. Fire was not an issue in this assault.

Chapter 35

Panic gripped the city. They saw what appeared to be a star coming straight for the earth. It shone so bright it could be seen in the daytime. The falling star looked like it headed right for Jerusalem, but actually it looked the same to the whole Middle East. Where would it hit? How could they survive?

But to everyone's surprise, it exploded with a deafening sound of hundreds of cannons, shortly before hitting the earth's atmosphere. The whole earth must have shuddered from the force of the explosion, because the ground bounced with the shock of it. The sky fell as the air filled with millions of smaller stones from the exploding bolleride. Thick red dust rained down upon all open water from the millions of fragments of the star. It colored everything red, especially the water.

The galling spray of rocks and dust covered one third of the earth's surface, centering over the Middle East. Many died of the rock falls, but others, desperate for something to drink, drank the bitter waters and died from their gall.

One of Adoni´'s regional officers, Ali Gantz, was ruling over the city of Afula and commented to his subordinates, "How are we to cope with this latest hardship? This cursed, bitter red dust is everywhere. It's settled into the soil, and it is so soluble it has poisoned our coastal aquifer. Even the Sea of Galilee, Israel's drinking water supply, is contaminated. They didn't get the pumps turned off in time. Has anyone tried drinking this stuff?"

"My wife has tried filtering it," said one of his older workers.

"Did you drink it?" asked Ali.

"No," he replied. "It dissolved into the water itself. In fact, it dyed the cloth she used to strain it and ruined the dress she was wearing."

"How about the rest of you? What are you drinking?"

"Milk," replied one. "My kids won't drink water anymore. They just spit it out, because it's so bitter."

"Good suggestion. That's one we can pass along as a suggestion to our citizens."

"We have a water distiller," said one of the younger men. "My wife is a health food nut. She insisted we drink pure water, and am I glad! Otherwise we would not have been prepared. Say, I have heard that some have died from drinking it."

"My granddaughter got sick and died," replied his bitter municipal water officer, Shaul. "Damn those prophets. They are to blame. I wonder if the believers in *Yeshua* are having trouble finding water?"

"We need to look into that," said Ali. "If they have a supply we'll find out." Then he ordered Shaul to look into it.

Several days later Shaul reported, "The believers all have plenty of water. They saved it up in closed vessels."

"Good, tell our fine citizens of Afula to raid their houses. Let them die of thirst. It's their prophets who have brought this on us."

The believers scattered throughout Israel had pure water to drink, and those on city water drank the water from the tanks until it was contaminated. But even that was severely rationed. All baths were prohibited. The waterworks in Jerusalem eventually found a way to filter the dust out and neutralize the bitterness, but many died before they perfected their process. But a few enterprising business men got rich by mining the ice under the glaciers on Mt. Hermon.

When Adoni´ found out that the believers had water to drink, he ordered those on record as having not received their mark to be rounded up and executed. Several families were executed before the believers realized the danger. Then they fled south to the caves.

If the bitter water were not bad enough, the exploding star had yet another effect. Because it was so large, it had exerted a force against the earth, shoving it slightly out of its stabilized more circular orbit and into an elliptical one. Scientists, aware of this, predicted that six months later the earth would begin to rotate at a greater speed because of it closer proximity to the sun.

In March Joshua Jaffe had posters printed (by hand) to tell the public of the next plague of God coming upon them. He said: "You have debased yourselves even greater in the sight of God by sacrificing your babies to the god of fire. If you thought the bloody water bad, wait until God sends the next plague. He says, 'You will feel my fire burn *your f*lesh' and you will know it is God's doing because he will remove eight hours (one third) out of the day."

These were tacked up around the city during the night. The people raged when they saw them. They feared more fire falls. Many still carried burn scars from the earlier meteor falls on the fields, which also dropped burning droplets of naphtha upon the skin of the people. The sores caused by the burns took weeks to heal. They blamed the prophets for all their troubles. They stormed in mass to Adoni´'s new palace built on the Mount of Destruction in place of the United Nations building, which had fallen in the first earthquake during the darkness. They demanded that he do something about the prophets and the food supply.

Adoni´ sent Ra'amon to the Temple Mount to address the people.

"Our loyal worshippers, there is no fire coming from heaven that is not mine. My god is the god of fire. He is the same god of fire you sacrifice your babies to in the garden below Silwan village. He will destroy these enemies. But it has to be in his time. Bear with me. We shall win in the end. As to the food, our trucks are being hijacked by thieves. You must all help us identify them and bring them to justice."

After he returned to the palace, he said to Adoni´, "We have to get the hijackers. They are taking more and more food trucks, one out of every five. How do they know when to intercept them? There must be a leak in our security in Iraq. They even seem to know about the tracking devices. The trucks just disappear."

"If it truly is Jordanians like they say, they would be taking the trucks south. Why not set up some observers along the Desert Highway?"

Adoni´ frowned, "Somehow I don't think it's them. I suspect the defecting Israeli generals. This operation smacks of military planning. I don't think the Jordanians are quite that clever. But where is this army? They appear to be coming out of Syria, but why can't we find them? And what are they doing with all those trucks?"

"Well, whoever it is must be supplying the food to those without the mark."

"How do you know?" asked Adoni´.

"Have you heard of any dying of starvation?"

"No."

"What we need is someone to infiltrate the temple compound and find out what is going on."

"Like who? They wouldn't accept anyone with a mark."

"True, we'd have to find a way to disguise it," said Ra'amon.

"Say, isn't Rachel Lieberman still in Jerusalem? She was engaged to Solomon, remember? He may be involved in this hijacking. She would know what's going on. Let's try and pick her up."

THE END... AND A NEW BEGINNING

Adoni´ put out special agents to track down Rachel. They found she had given up her apartment. When they questioned her old roommate, they got their first clue.

"She spent the time of the invasion at the temple, but when she came back she didn't have a job anymore so she couldn't stay here. I ran into her not long ago, but she didn't tell me where she was staying. When she left the apartment she left with an older man. Maybe she shacked up somewhere."

It was a dead end. Or was it? Could the older man have been David's father? But before they could pursue that line of investigation, the great heat predicted by the prophets began, and people simply stayed inside, many underground in whatever cool spot they could find. The raids on the trucks had stopped anyway because of the heat.

Chapter 36

By August, days had grown shorter and shorter until they lasted only sixteen hours instead of twenty-four per revolution. From daylight to dark, a mere eight hours and twenty minutes passed. Time flew by as one third of a day was eliminated. They could tell that the orbital path had changed as well because the sun was quite a bit larger in the sky and hot! Boy, was it hot! The mercury soared to 140 or more degrees in the daytime and dropped only to 110 at night. The heat continued into October when by a regular calendar it should have cooled off.

The faithful, still in the economy, moved back into the temple with increased numbers. Those in the temple expanded to the underground, even though the *Shi'kinah* glory in the ark moderated the entire space. David and the army in exile were cooled by God under a supernatural cloud, "a shadow from the heat." People in Jerusalem moved into the dry cisterns or archeological digs under certain houses. Much of Jerusalem was underground because of their interest in archaeology. Businesses took up spaces underground at the western wall, making the plaza a main commercial center. Eventually, buying and selling had to take place at night, so they slept in the daylight hours if they could.

The skin of those who ventured out during the day blackened and blistered. Everyone chafed and complained and blamed the prophets in the temple. They blasphemed the God of the Jews who sent the plague of heat, for they realized now that the burning spoken of by the prophets did not mean flaming fire but scorching heat.

Electrical brownouts occurred frequently as air conditioning overloaded the power supply. The people groaned under the extreme heat. Daily it took its toll in people dying of heat prostration, mostly the elderly and the young. If it weren't for the shorter days, no man or animal could survive.

Adoni´ and Ra'amon were strangely silent, but the people blamed the Hebrew God.

When Lin Yiang reached the shores of the Ural Sea, he met his first real obstacle in his conquest. Since that star exploded over the Middle East, the weather began to change. It was hot. And it was not a local weather pattern. This took a great toll on his army, especially the horses, as they began to die from the exposure all the way back to China. This greatly reduced his power. He expelled the locals from their shelters as the army dug in for the duration. He had to wait for reinforcements from China and from the local countryside throughout the conquered territory behind him, before he could go on anyway.

After three months the earth moved on past the sun, and the temperatures began to cool off to normal. Then the people began to worry about the weather at the earth's apogee. It was obvious that the earth's path around the sun had become elliptical. If heat happened at its nearest approach to the sun, what would it be at the farthest extent from the sun? An ice age? With bitter cold and non-stop snow?

Men had always taken for granted the ideal conditions of weather afforded by a near circular orbit and a slight tilt giving changing seasons. How could mankind survive such drastic changes? Fear ruled the world.

By contrast, the believers took comfort in the Bible. It was all written. They knew what to expect. They also knew when it would end. They could endure anything believing in *Yeshua's* promise. They knew Adoni´ was limited to twelve hundred and ninety days of power from a scripture in Daniel. The day count had begun on the day he erected the Dragon portrait, effectively stopping the daily sacrifice.

Adoni´ had his astronomers working on a new calendar. In the end they decided the earth now had 368.52 days in a year and 30.71 days in a month, but the hours in a day began to stretch out longer as the earth moved away from the sun. Those same astronomers determined that the earth's closeness to the sun, with its gravitational pull, had whipped the earth around, causing the faster spin. In like manner, the earth would slow when it reached the other end of its orbit, and days would be longer. The scientists made regular announcements on the order of Adoni´ to calm the people. Adoni´ always appeared with them to have the last word.

"The earth is undergoing a thorough cleansing. I know it is hard for you to endure, but if we are truly to have a new world, these things must happen to cleanse our world of curses. They are all natural things, not the work of some ancient god of the heavens. Ashtor is behind all of it making us a new world. The magnetism of the sun has the earth in its grip."

After the broadcast, Joshua said to the believers, "He's right about God making us a new world. He just has the wrong god. And the scientists are right about the magnetic field of the sun also. God told Job that the daystar would take hold of the 'wings' of the earth and shake the wicked out of it. Earth's magnetic fields could easily describe her wings."

When the scientists announced that as the cause of earth's troubles, the people put away their fears that the Hebrew god was causing it, but it was still hard to bear.

The sun boiling down on the desert lands of the Middle East caused the hot dry air to rise rapidly, creating whirlwinds filled with sand. The Pacific Ocean heated up several degrees because of the volcanic activity around the ring of fire, and the additional heat absorbed by the earth gave rise to a severe El Niño in the western hemisphere that affected the whole world's weather. The Atlantic Ocean bred hurricanes one right after another. The western hemisphere drowned in torrential rains; the eastern hemisphere, more particularly, the Middle East, baked or swirled with sand devils.

A sound came out of the sky, a moaning, trembling type of sound, almost ghostly, saying "Woe, Woooe, Wooooooe." Was it a warning—a promise of worse things to come? Didn't earth have enough troubles? But at least the sun began to cool. A few in other parts of the earth heard the words and began searching for the true God of heaven. But none of the beast-worshippers could distinguish the voice from the rest of the din.

The faithful rejoiced to see God's power. For they alone knew those words were already recorded in Revelation to be spoken from the heavens. Nothing surprised them, for it had been *all* written in his Word. One of their favorite songs was Psalm 46, for it described exactly what was happening to the earth.

> God is our refuge and stronghold,
> a help in trouble, very near.

THE END... AND A NEW BEGINNING

  Therefore we are not afraid
 though the earth reels,
  though the mountains topple into the sea---
its waters rage and foam; in its swell
  mountains quake. Selah.
  ...Nations rage, kingdoms topple;
 at the sound of His thunder the earth dissolves.
  The Lord of hosts is with us;
 the God of Jacob is our haven.
   Come and see what the Lord has done,
   How he has wrought desolation on the earth....

Chapter 37

"It's time for another announcement," said Zerub Abel. "Already they forget the power of God, ever since it cooled down. Their spiritual darkness just keeps on thickening."

"Shall we announce the next plague to show them their darkness? We know what it will be even if we don't know when it will strike," replied Joshua.

"How do you want to announce this one?"

"Putting up posters would be too dangerous this time. The people all hate us. They might kill those hanging them up."

"Let's get David to call the TV station and let them announce it over the air. He can contact the station directly. They can't trace his call."

By now it appeared entirely evident that the trumpet judgments spoken of in Revelation chapter eight and the bowl judgments of Revelation chapter sixteen were vitally connected. The bowl judgments were the final end of the trumpet judgments, which added a greater measure of God's wrath. The first judgment of hail, fire, and blood had also dropped burning oil droplets upon the worshippers of the Beast, burning blisters and causing ulcers that took weeks to heal.

After that, the mountain-size meteorite dropped into a third of the Mediterranean Sea, from Gibraltar to the island of Sicily, turning it red. Then, the situation escalated into the outbreak of Red Tide, making the whole sea like the blood of a dead man. By the time the falling star exploded over the land, spraying it with the thick red dust and affecting the springs and drinking water of one third of the earth, the pattern was fully established. Therefore, they could predict the coming darkness to be the result of a great star falling into the soft interior of the earth, an actual collision with a major object from space, boiling up dust and smoke from the impact.

This star would not explode in the air like the former star, but would plunge deep into the earth, opening up the crust and hell itself. Out of the abyss, riding on the thick black smoke and emerging from within would come a new species of insect, presumably inhabitants of the star. These insects would ascend from the pit along with innumerable hitchhiking spirits from hell that were limited by commandment to plague only the subjects of the Beast who carried his mark.

"I think we should just announce about the star and the darkness. Let the insects be a surprise," said Zerub Abel.

"No!" argued Joshua. "Be specific, so that they know that the Lord has decreed it. Especially since they will only attack the Beast's followers. Remember, God did the same thing to Pharaoh."

"What do you mean?"

"He sent hail and darkness on the Egyptians, but not on the Israelites, making the difference very clear."

Yigael, the electronic specialist in Petra, called in a press release from the prophets addressed to the people. The message said:

Now that the earth is cool again, you return to your idolatrous worship. You forget the power of Jehovah, but he will continue to judge your sins by sending three more woes, each greater than the last. In the first woe, our great Hebrew God has already launched a heavenly body that will collide with the earth. As a result, great clouds of smoke will billow from the point of impact, and the ash of the explosion will fill the air with clouds darkening the sky for days. It will be as in the days of Egypt, a darkness that can be felt. Out of the darkness will fly locust-like creatures that will be attracted only to you who have Adoni´'s mark. They have great carnivorous teeth that can bite and tear, but worse than that, they have tails like scorpions that can sting. Although their sting is not deadly, it will be very painful. You would rather die than suffer it, because its effects will last for five months. You won't die, but you will wish you could.

It wasn't until two days after the announcement reached the TV station that the news reported it. The Temple crowd had waited anxiously to see how it would be received. When it failed to be reported the first day, Joshua called Petra. "Did Yigael send the announcement to the station yet?"

"I believe so, but let me make sure." said General Shofat, who took the call. He turned to David and asked, "Didn't Yigael already send the announcement to the TV station?"

"Yes, we sent it out as soon as we got it. Why?"

"Joshua was wondering why they didn't respond today."

"Maybe Adoni´ refused to let it be reported," replied David. "We will wait another day and resend it."

But they didn't have to resend it, because it appeared on the news the next mourning as the headline. The anchorman, seated behind his studio desk, began his report thus: "Those evil prophets of the ancient Hebrew God are at it again. This time they are predicting a great collision to occur between a possible asteroid-like body with the earth. They say the collision will send up so much smoke it will darken the earth for days like the days of Moses in Egypt. As if we could believe that! Falling meteorites and space debris, maybe, but a collision? I don't think so!" Deriding their message even further, he scoffed, "And get this, they say some sort of insect will come out of the smoke to bite and sting those of us who have the king's mark. How ridiculous! Everybody knows there's no life on those barren rocks in space." He didn't even bother to mention that this plague was only the first of three woes.

—

Rachel was on her way to the barter store when she ran into Francie, her old roommate.

"Rachel, How are you?" she said "I haven't seen you for at least a year or two."

"I guess it *has* been that long. I'm really doing well," said Rachel. "Are you still working for the Post?"

"Yes, it's so exciting these days." Touching Rachel's hair, Francie said, "You've let your hair grow long. It's quite beautiful. You know, you have the looks to qualify for being a priestess. Have you thought about applying?" asked Francie.

Rachel frowned. "What are you talking about?" (The temple people were unaware of what went on in the garden or the chambers).

"You don't know about the new worship in the garden? How can that be? It's all the rage! It's sooo exciting, especially the asherah pole. I'm saving up so I can worship at home before my very own image and altar. They can be a little pricey, depending on the type of wood your bench is made of," said Francie, with a twinkle in her eye. "A whole new industry has started making them for home use. And, of course, they keep adding more at the temple site."

"Do you use them to kneel on?" asked Rachel.

"Oh no," Francie let out giggle. "It's a ritual where you have sex with Ashtor."

Rachel was incensed. "That's pure wickedness! Don't you know that worshipping idols is against the laws of God, and to do it in that way is an abomination!"

Francie laughed. "Oh Rachel, you were always such a prude. Worshipping Astor is so exciting, better even than having sex with a man. Besides that old Jewish God doesn't exist."

"Oh yes he does! He's the one causing all the earth's plagues."

"No, even the plagues are part of Ashtor's plan to cleanse the earth. He is making a place for Adoni"'s Utopia."

Rachel shook her head, "You are completely deceived."

"I am *not!*" Francie retorted, raising her chin and walking off in a huff.

Chapter 38

Rachel sought out Anna, the high priest's wife, to ask her about the asherah pole. She told her what Francie said about the new worship.

"I can't imagine such a thing! I'll ask Joshua if there's anything about it in the writings connected with idol worship in the past."

"One thing I have noticed, men seem to have little respect for women these days. I had a man grope me on Ben Yahuda Street near Zion Square the other day in broad daylight."

"How awful. What did you do?" asked Anna.

"I laid him out."

"What do you mean?" she asked, frowning.

"I used my martial arts skills. I used to practice tae kwan do when I was in America. Before I came to the temple to live, when I still had an income, I took a refresher course. Am I glad I did."

"Was he a little man?"

"Not particularly," said Rachel. "If you know the right moves, even a woman can take down a man."

"Amazing," said Anna.

Anna sought out her husband, Joshua, to ask him about the asherah pole. After listening to her report, he said, "I have been suspecting something of that nature was going on, after witnessing the Easter celebration with its emphasis on fertility. Seeing the whole crowd follow Adoni´ and Ra'amon to their new garden, they probably led them in a demonstration.

"Wickedness has come full circle. They have reverted to the days of the ancient prophets when the false gods were worshiped by sex acts of every abomination. That must be the purpose of their colorful tents. As to their asherah pole, it could be a reference to the pillar or grove mentioned in the histories of the wicked kings of Israel's past. They were wooden, because they could be burned. Josiah cleansed the land of this wicked worship, but Israel quickly reverted to it after his death."

―

The raids on the trucks began again immediately after the weather cooled. Adoni´'s search for Rachel began as well. Adoni´ had issued a description of her and set up watchers surrounding the temple compound, the most likely place to encounter her. But it was fruitless until the 29th day of March.

Slipping down before daybreak, she stepped into the wall tunnel along the western wall. From there, she entered the Wailing Wall plaza. Once outside she blended with the morning shoppers entering the stores. She was on her way to the barter store when one of the watchers identified her. Calling to his companions on his cell phone, he said, "Target sighted." After indicating his victim, they grabbed her before she could use her skills. She protested but to no avail. On orders to bring her directly to Adoni´ no matter what time, they rushed their prize to his palace.

Since it was still early, Adoni´ appeared dressed in a rich silk robe, a silk scarf tucked around his neck. Though he had just arisen, he looked impeccably dressed as always.

"Well, well, what have we here?" asked Adoni´, feigning surprise.

"Why have I been brought here?" demanded Rachel, showing her inflammatory temper. "I haven't broken any laws."

"Aw, Miss Lieberman, we had lost track of you, and we can't seem to find David either."

"Are you in the habit of tracking everyone? What happened to our free society?" she demanded, unimpressed with his position.

"Oh come now, Miss Lieberman. May I call you Rachel?" he went on, not giving her a chance to answer. "Surely you wouldn't deprive us of your beautiful self. I have need of your services."

"Which are?" she asked, narrowing her eyes in distrust.

"We need to get in touch with David."

"Oh," she laughed, "so that's it. Well, you're out of luck. I broke my engagement to him when he joined the Lambers. You should know how I feel about them. Johnny worked hard informing on them for you. He knew how I felt."

"Johnny Leventhal?"

"Yes," she snapped.

"Well, is that so? I didn't know. But of course, he's another one that is missing," he said, shaking his head. "I can't understand why anyone should turn against me. All I'm trying to do is keep everyone alive through this terrible cleansing of the earth."

"Not *quite* everyone," said Rachel, roiling with sarcasm.

"Desperate times require desperate measures, my dear. Without firm control we would have anarchy like the rest of the world. I feel I've been called to bring back order and lead us into the new world after the physical purging is over. Like Noah, I intend to replenish the earth."

"Only God can bring order out of this chaos. Do you make yourself equal to him?" she asked, astonished at his audacity.

He smiled, "Of course, how else could I command such a large segment of civilization? At least ideologically."

"Why do you want David?"

"I need his expertise in rounding up the hijackers. He's a valuable man I could give a high position if he would come forth. You don't know where he is?"

"No, but even if I could tell you, I doubt if he would help you since you killed his father."

"Ah yes, I'd forgotten about that. Perhaps not." he hesitated a second and then suddenly asked. "I see you have your mark. Why is your number not in our computers?"

"I...I don't know," she stammered.

"Bring me a wet cloth," he ordered one of his servants. "We'll just see how permanent this mark is."

Rachel stepped back, "Hold her," he ordered the servant. He dabbed at the mark causing it to run. "Aha, just as I thought. They are moving among us with false marks. And I suppose the hijackers are feeding you?"

Rachel remained silent.

"So, you hate the Lambers, eh? How come you eat their food? And stay in their temple?"

Still Rachel said nothing.

"Lock her up in the green suite upstairs and set a guard at her door."

Roughly, one of Adoni´'s men took Rachel up the marble stairs and through a long, lavishly furnished hall. Small crystalline sconces lighted it. Brocade papered panels edged with molding lined the walls, and the carpeted floor felt soft as she walked on its thick, pale green pile. Silently they walked to the end and turned to the right wing. Finally, reaching the end door, he opened it to reveal a luxurious sitting room of a suite decorated in varying shades of subdued green, coordinated with the bedroom and bath beyond. The French doors of the sitting room led to the balcony overlooking the city to the west. Under different circumstances, Rachel might have enjoyed her surroundings, but turning to her captor, she asked, "What am I supposed to do here?"

"Be a guest of King Adoni´," he replied and locked the door.

Rachel went to the French doors and tried them. "Locked, of course," she cried in disgust. Rachel wondered what they would do with her. Even if they tortured her, she couldn't tell them anything, because she didn't know where David was. Thank God she didn't! David showed wisdom in not telling those at the temple where he was. Would she be executed like the rest? What happened to the women? They had only seen men executed.

She checked out the bedroom. Her eyes were filled with luxury such as she had never seen. "Too bad he's the enemy," she said out loud. "I could get used to this." *Maybe that is their plan, to soften me up and turn me to their side,* she thought.

Several hours later a maid came tapping on the door. "The key is on your side," sneered Rachel.

The young girl entered, a big, ugly mark set squarely in her forehead, spoiling her otherwise lovely face. "Here are some clothes the king ordered. I hope they fit." She dropped two rich, silk, lounging suits, and a soft lace negligee and gown set onto the sofa along with various silk undergarments. "Lunch will be sent up shortly. I'll collect your present clothing at that time."

As she went out, Rachel caught a glimpse of the guard as he shut the door. He wasn't particularly muscular; she wondered if she could render him unconscious with her tae kwon do skills. "Great," she said defiantly, her hands on her hips, "now what do I do?"

Chapter 39

When Rachel didn't return by evening, Joshua Jaffe became alarmed. Usually she managed to return just before the shops closed. She had not come in her regular exit, nor had she used any of the others.

Joshua called David's personal cell phone, reaching him in his living quarters.

"Rachel's missing. She didn't come back tonight."

"Oh no, I feared something like that would happen. What do they do with the women and children? You only mentioned men being killed."

"We heard that they are being sold as slaves. Some of the children have been sold to the Greeks and shipped away. We've also heard they're using them in barter, trading girls for wine and boys for harlots."

"Bastards! So you don't think she will be killed?"

"Probably not, with her looks."

David groaned. He knew what that meant. Finally, he said, "Let me know if you hear anything…anything at all." He hung up, sat down, and dropped his head into his hands as he cried out to God. "Oh my God, my God, my pure and innocent Rachel. *Yeshua, Yeshua,*" he groaned in his anguish, "Protect her and shield her."

After several minutes, he raised his head and ran his fingers through his hair. Somehow he felt at peace. Had his prayer been answered? He placed her in the hands of the Almighty. What else could he do?

Johnny Leventhal made the rounds in the barter stores. He had become quite adroit at meeting his needs in this manner. Gradually, he became acquainted with the regulars, including those at the Temple Mount. This particular day Yusef Dajher, an Arab believer who had attached himself to the temple faithful, asked Johnny if he had seen one Rachel Lieberman in his travels around the city.

"No," said Johnny. "I know who you mean. She's a friend of mine. But I've lost touch with her lately. Is something wrong?"

"Yes, she's disappeared."

"Was she one of us?" he asked cautiously. "The last time I talked to Rachel she was violently anti-Lamb."

"But she's changed her mind. She's accepted *Yeshua*," said Yusef.

"Remarkable," he said, almost unbelieving. "Listen, I move in many circles in my business. Although I'm no longer in the military, I still have friends there. I'll keep my eyes open. Maybe I can find out something. Where shall I contact you?"

"I'll be back here on Friday."

"Good enough. Shall we say ten o'clock?" said Johnny, and he went his way.

Yusef returned to the temple encouraged. Perhaps they would learn what happened to her. He told Joshua his hopes.

Friday morning he met Johnny back at the barter store. "Did you find out anything?" he asked hopefully.

"Yes, four men picked her up just outside the Basement shop on the Wailing Wall Plaza."

"How do you know?"

"I asked around, describing her appearance. Lots of people remember her because she's so beautiful."

"Where did they take her?"

"Someone overheard one of the men say they were going directly to Adoniʹs palace, even if it was early in the morning."

"I wonder if she's still there."

"I could nose around the servants and see what I can find out. I used to know some of them," offered Johnny. "Servants know everything that goes on in a great house."

"Yes, I suppose they would. The high priest would be eternally grateful. He thinks a lot of Rachel. He's afraid she might fall into the hands of wicked men who would use her body."

"No need to worry if Adoniʹ has her. He's a homosexual, you know."

"No, I didn't know, but nothing about that man would shock me," said Yusef.

"I'll go now. Meet me again tomorrow, and I'll tell you what I find out. If she's there, perhaps we can rescue her."

"Same time?"

"Yes." With that, Johnny completed his business in the store and left.

The next day Johnny returned with the information. After hearing where Rachel was, Yusef said, "I think you need to talk to Joshua Jaffe. You know how to contact him, don't you?"

Johnny hesitated, then replied, "My affiliation is with the others."

"You mean the believers in the caves or David and his men?"

"Those in the caves."

"Oh, then you haven't been to the Temple Mount?"

"No, my job was to shop the barter stores."

"All right then. Come along, I will take you in."

Yusef took Johnny to the entrance that connected from an East wall opening into an old quarry called Zedekiah's Cave, where they twisted and turned through what appeared to be a maze. At some points they had to crawl because of the small opening. Eventually, they arrived at the main complex and the ladder ascending to the temple. Johnny marveled at the extensive passageways they had. He said, "I am really impressed with the work you have done."

"Well, we didn't do it all. Some of these chambers have been here for many centuries. Others have been added, mostly just to connect the various entrances. We had little more to work with than a compass and some digging tools left by the construction crews. But the limestone under the mount is soft, which makes it possible in the first place."

"You have more than one entrance then?"

"Yes, but I only know this one. We might have had more, but at one point we ran into some sort of moat filled with debris. These tunnels go every which way. If you're not careful you can get lost. Some say you could go all the way to the Kidron Valley through the natural caves. But I wouldn't want to try that. You could get lost and wander around for days or maybe until death."

"Why do you know only one entrance?"

"It's a safeguard to keep security tight," Yusef lied since this was Johnny's first trip in. They had to be careful with first-timers. Unbeknownst to Johnny, he had doubled him back several times before he came to the main tunnel. He would have to be a genius to remember every turn since the tunnels intersected in many places.

Chapter 40

Looking up the ladder to the top, Johnny estimated it must be twenty feet. He climbed up behind Yusef where Joshua Jaffe himself greeted him at the top.

"This is Johnny Leventhal, a friend of Rachel's. He has news of her and wants to work with us to rescue her," said Yusef, also introducing the high priest.

"Welcome, my son," said Joshua, "Do you think it is possible to get her out?"

"Yes, I think so, if you will give me a hand. I have a friend that works for Adoni´. He will help us too, being on the inside."

"Praise the Almighty," said Jaffe. "What do you want us to do?"

"Once he takes her out he will have to have safe passage away, because his life would be in danger."

"Of course, I'm sure he would be welcome with the army."

—

The maid tapped on the door and then entered. "Tonight the king wishes you to dine with him and Mr. Ra'amon," she announced and deposited a dinner dress. "You will be ready at half past seven, and I will take you down."

"Just you?"

"No, the guard will go with us, so don't think you can run away," she said. "I don't understand why he keeps you anyway. You could be sold for quite a price. Or maybe used in one of the snuff films—he certainly has no use for you."

"What do you mean 'snuff films'?" asked Rachel.

"They been known to use the wives and grown daughters of the beheaded in sex films where the women are killed. There seems to be a demand for them among some types of men, but like I said, he is not personally attracted to women."

With that she turned and walked out.

Rachel made a face at her retreating back, thinking, *And how glad I am of that*!

"Snuff films," she said, "how much more evil can they get?"

Rachel held up the dress, a sleeveless, emerald-green, silk shantung softly draped at the shoulders with a sprinkle of sequins only on the drape. "Hmmn, looks expensive," she said, as she held it to her shoulders in front of the mirror. Then she tried it on. The bodice hugged her slim waist, and the skirt hung straight from there. "At least he has good taste," she murmured as she turned her back to the mirror to see the fit.

"It would be so good to get out of this room after having been cooped up for two weeks having nothing to do but watch TV."

At first she had luxuriated in the bath. They could not spare water in the temple for more than the barest bathing. The bathtub seemed sent from heaven. But then how many baths can you take? *They are going to try to pump me*, she thought. *But maybe I can turn the tables on them and get information myself. It could be useful, if I ever get out of here.*

Chapter 41

Promptly at seven thirty the maid returned. Rachel was waiting. The maid led Rachel down to the main floor with the guard bringing up the rear. Finally, they came to a small sitting room next to the formal dining room. A small table had been lavishly set in one corner. Evidently it would be an intimate supper for just the three of them. Both Adoni´ and Ra'amon arose from their seats as Rachel was ushered in.

"How lovely you look, my dear," said Adoni´ as he took her hand and led her to the table.

"Yes, yes, I must concur," agreed Ra'amon. "How nice to see you again."

Rachel merely nodded in response. Adoni´ seated her. He motioned to the servants as he seated himself and the waiter brought in the appetizer.

"Well now, how have you been these last two weeks? Is everything to your liking?"

"One could not fault the accommodations of this prison, but it is totally boring watching TV all day," she replied as civilly as she could manage. *I must be careful not to show antagonism*, she reminded herself.

"Aw, forgive me. I must remember that I'm dealing with an extremely intelligent woman here. Perhaps you would like to choose some books from my library. I have an excellent library you know—books in many languages, in fact."

"I'm sure you do, but I don't plan on staying indefinitely," she smiled an overly sweet smile. "What is it you want with me anyway?"

"For now, just your company. Haik and I don't have much female company. It's rather nice for a change, especially one as lovely and intelligent as you."

Haik smiled at her, "He's right, you know. Most of the women who work with us simply haven't got it up here," he said pointing to his head. "Not to mention being as easy on the eyes."

"But I understood you…." She stopped, suddenly embarrassed.

"Are lovers," finished Adoni´. "Quite right, my dear. But that doesn't mean we don't appreciate beauty and intelligence or female company. Besides, I think you may be able to help us after all."

Rachel frowned. "I don't see how. I really *don't* know where David is. Nobody does."

"You mean he's not in contact with the Temple Mount?"

"I don't know what all goes on at the top. All I did was shop around for our needs. That was my job."

"How can you shop without a mark?"

"Oh, surely you know a huge barter system has developed to go around your mark. People basically don't want you knowing all their business. What difference is it to you anyway? Remember, you are just trying to save us all with fair food allotments," she said, again displaying her overly sweet smile.

"Oh, you *are* entertaining," said Adoni´ laughing, enjoying the challenge. Their waiter brought in a savory Middle Eastern dish Rachel did not recognize. Its pungent smell of garlic filled the room.

"Yum, smells good!" remarked Rachel, anxious to change the subject. "What is it?"

"Lamb—it's fixed by my own special chef from Lebanon. The vegetables are from the greenhouses in the Negev. Praise Ashtor, the hijackers haven't stopped them from coming in from there. We had to reroute the shipments from Iraq. They took them out as fast as we could send them."

"Do you know who is hijacking your food?" Rachel asked innocently as she lifted a delectable bite to her mouth. She had heard about it on TV.

"Don't you?"

"I told you I don't know anything from the top level. The hijackers may be feeding the barter stores, but we still had to trade for any food I picked up."

"What have you got to trade?"

"The ladies at the temple make fine embroidery and such." Rachel noticed that Adoni´ told her very little. *How can I get him to open up more? Does he know David is behind the hijackings or not?* "I heard a rumor that the Jordanians were raiding your trucks."

"That's what you'd like me to believe, isn't it?"

"It's not true?" she asked, feigning innocence.

"The raids are too well planned. I think it is a military operation."

"Have you put your intelligence men on it?"

"Of course, my dear, but most of the military intelligence flew the coop. And what's worse, they took all their records with them. But, not to worry, we have replaced them. The defectors are out there in the desert somewhere and probably behind the hijacking, but *we will* find them."

Ra'amon had remained silent for quite a while listening to the banter between Rachel and Adoni´. "I hated it when David left," he said, finally entering the conversation, "but an even greater blow came when Johnny deserted me as well. We had become quite close during the 'Lambers' hunt.

"Johnny doesn't work for you any more?" asked Rachel, surprised. "He and David used to be good friends, but they split when David returned from Kahzakstan. That's when David and I began to have trouble, too."

"Well, they must have made up since then. He left us when the military defected."

The waiter brought in dessert, a spiced fruit of some kind with whipped cream.

Wiping her mouth delicately with the linen napkin, Rachel said, "I've enjoyed this meal very much. Thank you for having me. I think I'll take you up on the offer to choose from your library after all."

Adoní arose and pulled out her chair. "The pleasure was all ours," he returned. Then he led her to his vast library.

After Rachel returned to her room with several English translations of classics, she went over the conversation of the evening. *Now what was that all about?* They certainly didn't learn anything from me.

Chapter 42

Yigael called David into the HQ and said, "The shipments have been changed. They are now shipping from the Iraqi port at Umm Qasr in the Persian Gulf, so that means they will come by ship to Eilat or Al Aqabah.

We'll have to send spotters to watch the ports. There's plenty of food in our warehouse right now, but we need to be ready for when the stores get low. Katz, tell the General Saguy to come to headquarters and call the king."

After they arrived, David apprised them of the situation. Jordan's king said, "We have a container port and you don't. I would think that they would ship food via containers rather than any other way. They will probably use Al Aqabah and then transfer the cargo back to Israel from there. It doesn't make sense for them to come up the Desert Highway."

"True, unless some trucks go to Amman," mused David. "This will be a different situation entirely from our other operations. We'll need a spy in the shipyard immediately, and I would prefer two, one with electronic abilities. They may put GPS devices on these trucks like they did on that last raid in Jordan. That was so close it was scary."

"Yigael would know which of our men would qualify for that," said General Saguy. "He would also know if we could jam their signals. Besides, they will probably put the army in charge of the convoy and keep in touch with Jerusalem. It's going to be complicated. By the way, shouldn't Yigael be here?"

"Yes," said David, "Katz, go call him. And the convoy will be heavily armed, no doubt," said David, shaking his head at a seemingly impossible task.

"We can't drive the trucks away as easily either," lamented Malcomb, "because the road in the Dead Sea Valley is not as remote as the road from Baghdad. We'll have more traffic to contend with."

"We need to study the maps before we make any plans," said David, realizing even more the complexity of this hijack.

Johnny had been back to the Temple Mount several times, but no one had let him near the communication equipment. He bartered himself a cellular and asked to have it set up on their system so he could keep in touch outside the Temple Mount, but he found out they were not on the local system. He just happened to be there when the report came in that a shipment was due from the port of Al Aqabah.

The one assigned to communications called Jaffe in to talk to David.

"Okay, we'll make arrangements with them. One of their men is here today. Oh, and David, he's going to try and get Rachel out of Adoni´'s. Do you want us to send her to you?"

"You know I do. How and when?" David brightened visibly by that bit of news.

"He has a friend among the servants. He will leave with them. They have it set up for the first Friday in May. It's the servant's day off. Where can they meet you?"

"That's three weeks off. They'll be driving, right?"

"Yes."

"Then have them take her to Ein Yahav. We'll meet them there." After returning back to where Johnny was, and reporting, "From now on we will have to get our food through the caves believers. They've stopped shipping by truck from Iraq and are bringing food in by sea. David's men will jump them as soon as they come up the highway from Eilat, and the Hever people will unload them and carry the cargo back to their place."

Joshua finished. Johnny asked, "Where is David?"

"Nobody knows. All we know is that they have a base somewhere in the desert."

"Then how can you communicate with him?"

"They set up the communications through the army intelligence experts."

"We send via satellite. I don't know how they send. But it is all encrypted through this device."

"Neat," replied Johnny, smiling to himself.

A couple of days later, Malcomb went to the HQ looking for David. Motioning him aside, he said, "You'd better have Yigael get on the Internet and find out what he can about the comet."

"Now what?" replied David, coming to appreciate Malcomb's interest in the sky.

"I thought I caught a glimpse of something. I can't tell much with my little lens, and the haze in the air seems to keep thickening, but it seems like a new star, asteroid, meteor, or something heading toward us. Maybe it's nothing, but I think you should check it out."

"I'll get Yigael to look into it. Meanwhile, maybe I'd better talk with Jaffe—could be the 'star' predicted in the Revelation, the one that plunges all the way through the crust. We already sent the announcement to Channel 2 back in November."

Chapter 43

Rachel was surprised to have a man delivering her food trays. On the second day he casually asked her if she knew a man named Johnny Leventhal.

"Why yes," replied Rachel, suddenly wary. "Why do you ask?"

"He has been asking me about you."

"How do you know Johnny?"

"We used to be in the same school when we were young. But he's one of us now."

"Us?"

"Believers."

"Johnny?"

"Yes, he accepted *Yeshua* and is working with those at the temple."

"How do you know this?"

"I'm a plant from the Ein Gedi believers to keep up with Adoni´'s moves. Here, look," he said as he went into the bathroom and dabbed a wet rag at his mark making it run at the corner. "I'm going to get you out of here, and Johnny is going to help."

"Really?" exclaimed Rachel, unable to believe the good news.

"Yes."

"Oh, hallelujah! When do we leave?"

"Not until my day off, Friday after next." He drew a pen from his pocket and, looking in the bathroom mirror, repaired the damage to his mark.

"What has Johnny to do with us leaving?" she asked, a little dubious.

"He's going to take you to David. And by the way, my name is Raol."

Rachel smiled, "I'm glad to make your acquaintance."

After Raol left Rachel could hardly contain her excitement. *I'm going to see David at last.* A frown suddenly darkened her visage. Would Diedrienne be there to spoil the reunion? Did David belong to her now? The last time she saw David, her old rival was sitting next to him in a restaurant. If he belongs to her I have no one to blame but myself. "Dear Father, I leave it in your hands," she prayed. "Your way is the best way." She just wouldn't worry about it. She heard the key scrape in the lock. Raol already took her dishes. *Who would be coming now?* The door opened to reveal the guard. He slipped inside.

Rachel stood up, placed her hands on her hips, and demanded, "What do *you* want?"

"Oh, I just decided that since neither Adoní nor Ra'amon has much use for you, I would entertain you."

"Oh, really?" Rachel watched for her chance.

"Oh, yes," he said with a leering look.

"And you were sure I would welcome your advances?"

"Doesn't matter, since you are not a follower of Adoní, you're fair game."

She smiled her sickening sweet smile at him and said, "I don't think so."

When he reached for her shoulders, she whirled around and slammed her foot into his right knee. He screamed as it jammed the kneecap backwards. But when he bent to grab it, Rachel brought her knee up hard under his chin, knocking him on his back. One last hard kick to his head, and he was out. Then she took him by his arms and began dragging him back out into the hall. This was the hard part. He must weigh at least a hundred and sixty pounds. *Why couldn't I have maneuvered him closer to the door?* She stopped tugging and tried rolling him. Almost through sheer determination she used all kinds of moves to get him outside her door. Finally outside, she removed the key and locked the door from her side. *I hope he has a good explanation for this in the morning.* Then she began to laugh. Maybe there will be a change of guards tomorrow. She rubbed her back. She hoped she didn't pull a muscle in her struggle to move him.

When the guard came to he groaned. He could tell his knee was ruined. He tried to get up, but it hurt too much. "Damn that woman!" he muttered. Why had he thought she was a weak little kitten? At least she spared his balls. He glanced over at the door and realized the key was missing. He picked up his communicator and called the head servant. "Yacov, I'm in a little trouble."

"Yeah, what's wrong?"

"I tripped and fell on my knee, and I can't get up. Can you send someone up to get me? I must have twisted it as I fell. It hurts pretty bad."

"Okay, hang in there."

Yacov was suspicious. He had heard that Petrie had been bragging about how he would pluck the flower under his guard. Yacov warned him that Adoni´ had a special use for her. He was more worried about Rachel. His orders were to meet all her needs beautifully but keep her safely under lock and key.

He didn't send anyone else but went to see the situation for himself. When he arrived Petrie was on the floor moaning and rubbing his knee.

"Let's have a look at that," he said, squatting down to examine it.

The knee had swollen and had taken on the color of a nasty bruise. When Yacov touched it, Petrie yelled. About that time, another servant showed up with a wheelchair. After they lifted Petrie into the chair, Yacov asked for the key.

"Isn't it in the door?" asked Petrie.

"No," he said, as he tried the door. "It's locked."

Yacov knocked gently on the door and called, "Rachel."

She responded by unlocking the door and removing the key. When he opened the door, she was standing there holding out the key to him with a big smile on her face.

"So, you tripped, did you. I was wondering how you could do that much damage on this soft carpet. Are you into martial arts, young lady?" he asked.

Rachel nodded.

"Bitch!" muttered Petrie.

After looking over the maps of the Ein Gedi and the Nahal Hever region, David decided he could not make a plan good enough for the hijacking without some "on the ground" reconnaissance. He called Uri Samak, head of the Hever Caves group. After he came to the phone, David asked, "When would be a good time to come to your compound? We need information in order to plan our next hijack."

"I'll be here tomorrow."

"Good, the sooner we can plan the basics of this, the better. When we know the actual circumstances, we'll adjust what we have to. I'm going to need your help."

"We'll do what we can."

"Where is the best place to land the helicopter and maintain security?"

"The same place you land your helicopters when you deliver food," said Uri.

"Of course," said David, laughing at his foolish question. "How will we see if it is dark?"

"We will have to outline the landing spot with lamps."

"That would work. I'll be there early tomorrow," he said as he clicked off.

The next day, David had GG fly him to the top of the Cave of the Letters. GG had dropped many a load on top of this mountain above the caves. David had heard of this place, but he had never visited it. It was located just 2.5 Kilometers south of the Ein Gedi caves in the Hever Nahal (river) Canyon, nearly a thousand feet up from the canyon floor. The cave was famous for housing the followers of the Bar Kochba Rebellion. The cave was absolutely huge, more than three hundred yards deep, with extensive tunnels and three separate entrances. It was also nearly inaccessible, but the believers had improved the ancient trails reaching it. They actually occupied another cave as well, called the Cave of Horrors, where archeologists had found many skeletons of the Bar Kochba rebels when they excavated in the fifties.

Uri greeted David as he exited the helicopter.

"Good to finally meet you face to face," said Uri, a man of moderate height in khakis and a jacket. The wind blew briskly even though the sun shone.

David, in his army uniform, reached out and grasped his hand. "Yes, it surely is. Your name is well-known among us."

David shook his head. "I never realized what a lofty place this is. It's a good thing I came to see the situation. This hijacking is going to prove challenging."

"Yes, but won't you bring the supplies in the same way as you normally do?" asked Uri.

"Of course, but we will require much labor to unload the trucks quickly. Would you have a place to unload the trucks that is out of sight of the main road. Is that possible?"

"Actually, yes," replied Uri. "The people in the Ein Gedi Kibbutz are all believers. We could pull the trucks into their compound onto the roads to the back of their fields. But it could still be risky. What if the helicopters were noticed when they were landing or taking off to bring the cargo to the top of our mountain? Wouldn't it be better to unload the trucks somewhere else and simply fly the food shipment in? Could you spare four helicopters to bring in the supplies to the heights above our caves—two for the caves in the Hever canyon and two for the ones in Nahal David? We have a pulley system set up from the top of the mountain to lower our supplies through a shaft into the cave."

"Well, that would simplify things. Some of the supplies could still be sent to the Ein Gedi Kibbutz, for the store there. With the helicopters alternating, it shouldn't take long if every one helps."

As soon as David stepped into the helicopter for the return trip, he said to GG, "Let's take a short detour on our way back to base. I want to look over the possibility of unloading the trucks at Masada. I know the Tourism Commission shut it down when the tourism industry died, and it's back away from the main road."

Chapter 44

The world watched as the new menace approached the earth. They knew what to expect, at least in Adoni´'s kingdom—darkness from an asteroid collision. The prophets had proclaimed it. The fearful remembered the theory that such an occurrence supposedly made the dinosaurs extinct. The prudent believed them. They made preparations to stay inside when the impact was imminent. Others, growing used to such disasters, went about their daily concerns as usual. No one paid much attention to the prediction of insects. After all, how could *that* be?

The whole earth shuddered at the impact, causing earthquakes to ripple around the planet. The "star" plunged through the juncture of the European/Asian tectonic plates in the Apennine Mountains just north of what was formerly Rome. Coming in at an angle from east to west, the heavenly missile lightened the atmosphere to near incandescence for hundreds of miles across the sky, blinding men's eyes, scorching the ground beneath its path, and boiling the Mediterranean Sea.

But coming at an angle lengthened its course through the crust, doing more than just poking a hole. It angled the thrust of material coming out directly toward Adoni´'s kingdom. Following the collision, billows of thick, black smoke mixed with a choking ash thrust upward and outward from the vast opening of at least a hundred miles across. The farther it spread the wider it got. Eventually the whole Middle East was enveloped in its discharge.

Rachel, engrossed in her reading, suddenly felt a jolt. She had been expecting the first woe, knowing it had been announced. "Uh-oh. The next plague must be coming. I hope the darkness doesn't last until my escape day," said Rachel out loud as the windows rattled, and she felt the slight tremors from the impact. She jumped up so quickly that she dropped her book. "I wonder where it hit?" She went around to all the windows to make sure they were shut. At the last window, she watched as the air darkened and the street lights came on, then disappeared as the darkness thickened. She left the window, feeling her way to turn on the lights. Then she heard a roar she couldn't quite identify. It was a squeaking, no… grating, no, that was not it either. It was a whirring, like one might imagine chariots' wheels along with thundering hooves to sound in some ancient battle. She heard a buzzing noise up close outside and slight tapping against the window. She went back to investigate. "Locusts?" she questioned. "No, scorpions with wings." Three of them crawled on the window, probably attracted by the light. She bent down to examine them closer. The "locusts" looked back at her.

"Why, they have faces!" she exclaimed. The locusts met each other face to face and appeared to confer with one another. They were about three and a half to four inches in length, fully armored, like horses dressed for a medieval battle. But their heads were like miniature women with long streaming hair—ugly women! When they opened their mouths to communicate, they displayed strong, sharp eyeteeth like carnivores. Rachel shuddered. She studied the razor-sharp stinger on the upraised tail. She moved away from the windows and returned to her reading, unconcerned. She remembered enough from the scriptures to know they would not attack believers but only those with the mark.

After seeing the impressive "star" streak across the sky, the believers retreated into their homes to await the impact.

"Make sure all the windows are shut," called Zev to his wife Yael. "It's coming."

But his voice was drowned out by someone hammering on the door. When Zev opened the door, two government employees confronted him.

"GGS officers working for Religious Affairs," said a burly officer in uniform. "You are under arrest for black-marketing food." Zev and Yael had a food storehouse for the believers and had been distributing food to the faithful still living among the people. Fortunately, no one else was there other than the man and his wife who ran the "store," because all the believers were inside their own homes awaiting the darkness to come.

Just as the officers clamped the handcuffs on them and led them to the street, they stumbled because of the impact of the asteroid, and then the darkness began to swirl in.

"*Holy Bopkess* (goat shit), what's going on?" asked one of the officers as he pushed Lev along toward a large van.

"Must be the darkness predicted by those accursed prophets," replied the other. "Move along *Hazzer* (swine)!" he said to Yael, the man's wife. Suddenly, they were engulfed in a thick, congesting smoke mixed with ash. Everyone began coughing and choking and gagging. The arresting officers tightened their grip on their victims. Then they heard it, the weird whirring sound.

"What's…(cough, cough)…that?" He screamed and began beating and swatting the unseen menaces, his companion doing the same. "Leave them, let's get in the van." But the van had disappeared in the darkness. They felt their way, heading in the general direction they knew. This slowed them down, allowing more bites and stings. Once in the van, they shut the doors and turned on the lights.

"Oowee, just look at that sucker!" said one as he swatted at a large insect. He knocked it to the floor and stepped on it, grinding it under the sole of his shoe. Then he screamed as two more attacked the back of his neck, biting and stinging. "Get 'em off me!" he cried, writhing in pain as his companion tried to brush them off, but they had grabbed hold tenaciously with their teeth. When he finally dislodged them, they took chunks of flesh with them, causing his companion to howl, "Oww!" Then it was the other man's time to scream.

They spent the next half hour destroying the rest of the "locusts" that had entered the van with them. Not an easy task, since the insects seemed to be armor plated, tough to kill, and intelligent enough to hide. Finally, they nursed their pains in the welcomed quiet. The buzzing had nearly driven them crazy, not knowing when to expect another sting.

With the lights on in the van they could see swarms of "the little monsters" on the windows. "Turn on the headlights. Let's get out of here! Maybe we can slough them off by moving. Otherwise, we are trapped in here." But suddenly they became aware of the effects of the stings.

"Aieeeee," cried the driver, "look at how the stings swell, and my whole body is on fire." Then he grabbed his throat in a panic. "My throat is closing. I'm going to suffocate!"

His companion began furiously scratching the stings, crying out, "My legs are going numb!" Then he discovered an open wound from a bite, where blood streamed down his cheek and mingled with mucus pouring from his nose.

The driver turned on the headlights and nothing happened. Just a small, dim glow lighted up black particles swirling in front of the headlights and completely diffusing the beams. With a sinking feeling, they realized they were trapped. They cursed the God of the Jews with every other breath as they scratched the swelling patches. "We should have paid attention to the part of the prophecy about the insects. How long will we be trapped? Do you remember how long the darkness is supposed to last?" asked the companion, still scratching. One thing was certain, he thought, *We will not walk!*

"I don't…" The driver gagged, then spewed his dinner all over the dashboard.

Chapter 45

Lin Yiang had just restored his army, and they were on the move again when they sighted a great, dark cloud on the horizon arising from the southwest. "Now what?" he said. "It doesn't look like storm clouds. Too black. It looks like we will have to encounter that raging darkness sometime after we turn south at Rasht."

"Yes," said General Bo Chai Dinxiang, who was currently riding by his side. "But remember, it is all happening to the people we wish to conquer. That will weaken them further. Besides, by the time we get there it may have dissipated."

"You're right. It may all be to our advantage."

Zev and Yael groped for each other when their captors released them because of the attacking insects. Zev felt a tap on his shoulder and heard a voice say, "Come."

Zev felt for his wife. "Yael? Is that you?" he shouted above the buzzing noises and coughed intermittently. Suddenly, he realized his hands were free.

"Here I am," she shouted back, groping toward his voice. Reaching him, she clasped his hand. The buzzing all around them made it impossible to converse. Then a hand took hold of Zev's other hand and led them to the safety of a tunnel to the Temple Mount. Yael followed along Zev's unhesitating and sure direction. Once inside of the tunnel, Zev picked up a flashlight at the entrance.

"How did you know where to go?" she asked.

"Someone took my hand and guided me straight here."

"Where is he?"

"He dropped my hand just as we entered the tunnel."

"Awesome! It must have been an angel!"

They rushed through the tunnels till they reached the ladder. Once upstairs they related their story to the others. All rejoiced until Joshua said, "How did they find out about you?"

"I don't know," said Zev. "I've been worrying about that all the way here. We've been very careful."

"Could be we've been infiltrated."

"A traitor in our midst?" asked Zev incredulously.

"It was bound to happen. According to the scriptures, Zerub Abel and I will be overcome by the 'Beast.' I think everyone needs to evacuate the temple while you still can, while it's dark. The locusts will not harm you. Yael and Zev have proven that. *Yeshua* can lead you out just as he led Zev and Yael in."

"But where could we go?"

"He will take you where he wants you."

After partaking of their last meal together and embracing the prophets, the believers packed up bare necessities.

Both Joshua and Zerub drew their wives aside to say their last goodbyes.

"I want to stay with you," said Anna.

"No, my dearest," said Joshua. "I could not bear the worry of what could happen to you. We know we shall be killed. Nothing can change that. Please honor me and go with the others. Remember, in only a matter of days *Yeshua* will return. According to the Revelation, Adoni´ will only have thirty more days to rule after our deaths." He embraced her one last time and said, "Go with God, mine own heart."

She acquiesced, as did Zerub's wife. Then, they joined the others and descended the ladder last, clinging to their husband's hands before slipping away. The group headed for a single exit. Above all things, the believers wanted to stay together. If no hand was there to take them, at least they would have each other. They chose the shortest route to the outside.

Knowing what to expect, Zev and Yael headed the procession. As soon as Zev stepped outside the tunnel exit, it happened.

The whole crowd found themselves in a lighted room full of people.

"What the …"

"Where are we?" questioned Zev, completely disorientated.

Everyone buzzed with excitement. David, recognizing some of the believers and realizing what had happened, climbed onto a table in the restaurant and shushed the crowd. "You have just witnessed a great miracle. These are the temple believers. Someone come up here and tell the rest of us what happened."

The newcomers pressed Zev forward. He told his story to the rest, especially the part about the "locusts."

"Yes," said David, "we've seen them. They look ferocious. I wouldn't want to be a Beast worshipper."

"We may have been betrayed. We must be really careful from now on," said Zev.

"Well, you're safe now. No one knows where *we* are."

The darkness lasted for four days, and then the ash began to settle. It was nearly a foot thick in places. Even as the light returned, the sun did not. At first it was barely light enough to see the ground, a sort of deep twilight. Gradually it got lighter.

Slowly the populace came out of the darkness. Since the insects' normal food supply from their home in space did not exist here, they died. The people were in an ugly mood. Everyone had multiple reminders of the plague. Those who by chance had escaped the insect attack had members of their families who were stung and bitten. They blasphemed the God of heaven who brought the plague and refused to stop their worship of the dragon and forsake their idols. By now everyone had a small replica of the dragon in either wood or alabaster. It was becoming popular to fall down and worship them in their own houses instead of at the temple courtyard, especially if they had their own asherah poles.

Every clinic jammed with patients. Doctors dispensed their limited antibiotics as long as they lasted. But the efforts to kill the bacteria carried by the "locusts" were futile, since they hailed from a different world. The stings seemed to have no antidote at all. Doctors just shook their heads. Besides the bites, every sting had provoked an allergic reaction, and those affected swelled up and appeared to double their weight. But the itching that accompanied it was a thousand times more aggravating than the initial pain of the sting. Many wished for death. Some even tried taking overdoses of narcotics. But nothing worked. The chemical substance in the stings evidently counteracted everything. At least that was the popular explanation. The sores from the insect bites festered and refused to heal.

Hadassah in Ein Kerem, the hospital that dealt with the worst cases challenging medicine in Israel, determined that the allergies caused by the stings affected the body's central nervous system. This caused the brain to order the release of certain chemicals into the body that resembled allergic reactions that caused severe swelling of the tissues and constant itching. They had no apparent antidote, and the sores spread rapidly inwardly and laterally. Finally, they used the old-fashioned remedy of introducing maggots to the wound to destroy the putrid infected flesh. However, with the multitude of hatching insects, where the isolation of the victims was necessary for treatment, the cure was a little slice of hell in itself.

Chapter 46

The people's hatred of the prophets grew daily. They blamed them totally for their suffering. They demanded that Adoni´ do something about the despised men. After days of protesting before his palace in great numbers, Adoni´ appeared on his balcony.

"It's time," said Adoni´ through a small microphone, which was hurriedly set before him, "for my god to show his power. But for him to be able to overcome the firepower of the ark, he needs your help. You will have to agree with me in prayer. Let us all pray together. Only united will we see the end of these prophets. As we speak, officers are on their way to arrest them."

The crowd in front of the palace, now placated, knelt and prayed, repeating the words after Adoni´ phrase by phrase: "Oh great God and Lord Ashtor, hear us…We seek to end the power of the prophets, help us!…Grant your power to the officers and protect them from harm. Overcome their god and show your power."

Rachel saw the crowd, but she could not hear what was being said, since her balcony doors were locked. She caught a word now and then. "Lord Ashtor…prophets…power…" They must be praying against the prophets. She felt so cut off. *What had happened in the dark?* Her TV had been removed after her complaint. *Were the people angry because of the "locusts?" Oh well, I'll know soon enough. Just three more days and I'm outta here. I can't wait!*

—

Joshua heard them coming up the ladder and motioned Zerub into the next room. The first two men to emerge from the ladder shaft were completely covered in clothing such as those used by firefighting crews: leather and Kevlar helmets and gloves with turn-out jackets and pants. Each climbed up awkwardly, armed with a small pistol tucked in his waistband. Cautiously, the first man stuck his head up to eye level to survey the room. Finding it empty, he stepped off the ladder, scanning the empty room. Then he motioned the others to come quickly while he covered the door with his pistol.

Joshua and Zerub waited in the next room, both seated. There would be no dramatic rescue this time, and they knew it. The *Sh'khinah* had gone out of the ark. Their twelve hundred and sixty days of protection, mentioned in the book of Revelation, were up. Knowing they would eventually have the victory over Adoni´ kept them calm. Soon, they would see *Yeshua* again. The trial by fire was almost over for Israel. According to Daniel, Adoni´ had only thirty days left to rule, then he would be history. *Yeshua* would come and take over the kingdom for himself.

The two in protective suits entered first. "You are under arrest," they said, nervously pointing their guns.

"Do not be afraid," said Joshua. "We will come quietly. Our time has come. Tell the others they can come in. No harm will come to them." They stood up and walked toward the porch to the courtyard.

The suited men stayed right behind them, and the rest hung back, apparently afraid to trust the prophet's word. Someone in the back called Adoni´ on a cell phone.

"We have them and they came quietly."

THE END... AND A NEW BEGINNING

"What about the others?"

"What others? There was no one else here."

"Hold them there on the steps until I get there." Then he turned to the crowd below and made an announcement.

"Your prayers worked. We have them in custody right this minute."

A huge roar went up from the crowd.

Quieting them, Adoni´ added, "If you want to see them executed follow me to the Temple Mount." Then he turned to Ra'amon and said, "Call all the news agencies. They will want to record this for the whole world to see. I don't want to wait for any ceremonies. Let's strike while we can."

He ordered his limousine. He was infused with extra power and had been ever since the darkness fell. He had not been bitten or stung nor had any in his household, who were inside during the whole four days. But he had seen the terrible pictures on TV news reports; many incidents, showing the jammed hospitals and the interviews with doctors with close-ups of the damaged flesh. He was elated beyond measure. Victory, at long last! Soon he would know exactly where David and the secret army hid. He had an informer who had worked out wonderfully. He put his army on alert. In three days we will attack and wipe out the stubborn resistance, and then the kingdom will be secure. The stubborn holdouts would succumb or die. "Yes!" he shouted out loud, startling his driver. Ra'amon, seated at his side, picked up his hand and lifted it up as a sign of victory.

Chapter 47

The two prophets stood before Adoni´ and Ra'amon, calm and silent.

"Well, have you nothing to say now?" Adoni´ mocked. "Your latest predictions perhaps? Come, come, we are waiting to hear. Has your god abandoned you? Or were our prayers too strong for him, huh?"

"Our God reigns," said Joshua.

"Where? In the heavens? No such place. Gabriel, Michael—all ancient appearances of Lord Ashtor. Misunderstood by ignorant ancient men. There are no angels, no Jehovah, no *Yeshua*. These are all distortions of Lord Ashtor, the powerful God of Forces. The plagues are cleansing the earth for his kingdom of which I have been chosen to rule," said Adoni´ in an oratorical mode.

The people cheered him on, roaring, "Kill them!"

"Not yet. The media is not ready, and the world must see our triumph," he said. "Also, we are waiting for rifles from the army for the firing squad. It's the quickest way. The chop blocks and axes are in storage. Besides, they're messy. I want this over with—fast!"

While they waited, they bound the priests' hands behind their backs, and left them standing in front of the temple altar. Within the hour every remaining network with correspondents in Jerusalem had cameramen on the scene. He did not blindfold his prisoners in an act of mercy, because he wanted the media and the world to recognize them. He commanded his firing squad to line up. Only then did Adoni´ give the order. "Shoot them." The men raised their rifles and fired. The two prophets dropped.

A roar went up in the crowd. As soon as it quieted Adoni´ said, "Take them to the wall and throw them over. We will not suffer them to be buried. Let the vermin finish them."

"No!" exclaimed Ra'amon. "Let them be left on display. Let everyone come and see that they are really dead and our troubles finally over. We need to celebrate. Put them in the middle of Zion Square. Let everyone that gathers there or passes by see them. Put them on television for the world to see."

"Yes, declare a great holiday. Let us rejoice now that the plagues are over," shouted some of the foremost of the crowd that overheard Ra'amon.

Then Ra'amon whispered, "Let's use their deaths to consolidate our power."

"Well, you see to it," snapped Adoni´. "I have other work to complete before we can truly celebrate." He was thinking of David.

Adoni´ called a meeting of the joint chiefs in the *Cor Zahal* (Israel's underground Defense Force headquarters). "*Rabotai* (Gentlemen), I want an army of considerable size to go in and wipe out the hijackers. It is just a matter of hours before we know their location. This is the moment we have all been waiting for."

"We've been trying to work out the sequence of the spread spectrum code on their phone for weeks, but so far haven't hit it. How can *you* find out in hours?" said the new intelligence chief.

"We have an informer who is close to getting the information. What will we need?"

"We have several armored vehicles plus four hundred men, one hundred of them paratroopers, just in case their base is hard to access. I have them waiting for instant call up. We only await your signal as to where to go," said Yadin, the IDF chief.

"Wouldn't helicopters be a better way to transport men in a desert area?" asked Adoní.

"We can do that, too. We are prepared for any contingency."

"Good. I expect this to be the last great barrier to our new civilization. Once we get the food under control, the people in opposition will die or surrender. Surely this purging of the earth can't last much longer."

David called in the king of Jordan. "The temple group was betrayed, and the Herodian believers have been arrested. We need to think of defending our position. It would be nice if we had some allies."

"What about Mizraim? He's been itching to get back at Adoní. Do you want me to see what he's up to?"

"Yes, no doubt a showdown is coming. I'll leave that to you and the general. Meanwhile I'll beef up our fortifications here. That's the advantage of being in Petra. It is easy to defend. After that I need to finish the hijack plan for when the ships come in. Adoní has raided some of our barter stores, and our people grow hungry," said David, ever mindful of the plight of the people.

Adoní was still in the war room when word reached him that Egypt was mobilizing against him and had invaded southern Israel from the Sinai. After studying the reports, the generals suggested a plan of action. Adoni´ immediately ordered his northern army of Lebanese/Syrian troops to join the Israeli Army. He called for the Sudanese to attack Egypt from the south, and Libya to attack from the west.

Adoni´'s northern army pushed the Egyptian Army back to the Sinai. The battle raged for two days. The battle was won, however, when Adoni´ brought in the Lebanese/Syrian troops by the two remaining ships in the eastern Mediterranean to the Suez Canal. It had already been secured by the Libyans. Landing the troops behind the lines at the canal, they cut off the main Egyptian army still in the Sinai.

New leadership in Sudan had sided with Adoni´ after the Russian invasion. They attacked Egypt from the south, landing in the southern region of the Sinai. Their destination was Sharma El Sheikh on the east side of the Sinai Peninsula. The Egyptians had shut down the Straits of Tiran by fortifying it with big guns aimed at the shipping lanes. They had stopped the first ship to make it through after the darkness and one of the few still operating in the Persian Gulf. It sat idle at the entrance to the Gulf of Aqaba. Therefore, it was crucial for Adoni´'s forces to get that ship to the Jordan port of Al Aqabah. A unit of Adoni´'s Israeli commandos landed at Etzion near Eliat, an old Israeli air base dating back to their occupation of the Sinai. They attacked from the north. Between the squeeze of the two forces, Sharma el Sheikh fell within hours.

On the Sinai front, the main Egyptian army was crushed between the Israeli army moving south and the Lebanese/Syrian moving north from the Gulf of Suez and the Canal. A follower of the dragon in Mizraim's own household assassinated the Egyptian leader as he tried to escape, leaving the country in confusion. Adoni´'s army overran Egypt. Converging with his other allies, the

THE END... AND A NEW BEGINNING

Sudanese and the Libyans, he stripped the country of all remaining wealth. Elated at eliminating the Egyptian Army in just three days, Adoni´ returned home, leaving behind a substantial force to rule, until he could finish off David.

Chapter 48

As Rachel waited impatiently for Raol, she worried about her clothes. These silk loungers would never do out in public, too conspicuous, but she would need her underwear and nightgown, so she wrapped everything in her nightgown to take with her. Shortly someone knocked on the door. As it opened she heard Raol say to the guard, "*L'Azazel!* He *would* ask me to do this. I have to get her down before I leave. My day off, you know."

"Isn't that the way it always goes? Will you be bringing her back?"

"I hope not. I've got plans for the day. Besides, she may not be coming back," he winked at the guard.

"Good, I hope she gets what's coming to her!" said the guard, looking at Rachel full of hatred. "Mazel tov, have a good one," the guard said as he limped to shut the door.

Rachel followed Raol down the carpeted hall. They turned and went down a back stair. Raol motioned for her to stay back as he looked into the bottom hallway. "Okay, come on," he said as he headed for a service entrance. He opened a cleaning closet and said, "See that bag? In it are some boys' clothes and a cap. Put it on and pile your hair up under the cap. We will try to pass you off as a boy. Then wait in here until I see if Johnny is here yet."

"*B'seder* (okay)."

"I will only be a minute, so hurry."

After dressing, Rachel put all her other clothes in the bag. Raol returned shortly to find Rachel ready. "Let's go. Johnny's in the garage waiting for us."

When they reached the garage Johnny said, "Yo, Rachel?"

"Johnny?"

"In the flesh."

"You've put on a good deal of weight since I saw you. I wouldn't have recognized you."

"Good to see you, *too*," he said sarcastically. "And *you* make a fetching boy," he laughed, opening the back door to the car. "Get down on the floor until we get away from here." Raol got in the front seat, and Johnny backed out and turned toward the street. After they turned several corners, Raol said, "You can get up now, Rachel."

"Do you know where David is?" she asked.

"No, but his men are going to meet us in Ein Yahav. He's probably in the desert nearby."

While Adoni's armies were fighting in the south, Ra'amon had led the people in a wild celebration that bordered on an orgy. After displaying the prophets in the street for nearly three whole days, they had moved them back to the Temple Mount. Ra'amon had his men place the bodies of Joshua Jaffe and Zerub Abel on the temple altar beside the image. The people, such as were able, danced around the altar, even climbing onto the ledges and poking the bodies in desecration. Although they still hurt and itched from the latest plague, they rejoiced that the plagues were over. They refused to believe that the prophets had merely announced God's plans. Mob psychology had conditioned them to believe in magic, especially after Ra'amon taught them how to access the spiritual realm through incantations before their idols. They saw the prophets as *causing* the plagues, using magic through the ark.

Ra'amon had declared this event the beginning of a new holiday, replacing the Christmas of the Christian god. The people responded by sending gifts to one another and feasting for three days in celebration. After Adoni´ returned, they intended to burn the bodies as human sacrifices to Lord Ashtor.

When Adoni´ returned from his battlefield on Friday morning, he immediately called the communications unit at the *Cor Zahal*.

"Any word from our informer?"

"Not yet."

"Well, sound the *azakah* (alarm) as soon as you hear. I have an army waiting."

The burning was set for noon that day. Ra'amon dressed himself in the rich vestments of Jehovah's high priest taken from the temple, with the exception of the miter, because it was inscribed with "Holiness to the Lord," and he didn't want to give glory to the Jewish god. Instead, he wore his white pontifical head covering. He paraded back and forth before the bodies.

Adoni´, to indicate his victory over Jehovah God, sat upon the holy ark of the covenant on the temple porch to observe the burnings. Dressed in extravagant robes of royal purple, he proclaimed himself victor over the forces of the prophets and made himself god of all. Ra'amon mounted the steps to the porch, carrying a small, handheld microphone and said, "Let us worship our God!" Then he turned and fell down before Adoni´. The people responded in like manner. After a few moments Ra'amon raised himself and shouted. "Our god reigns!"

Adoni´ smiled at the adulation, but Ashtor said within, "At last, my rightful place."

The people responded with a roar.

"Light the fires," Ra'amon commanded.

"Light it yourself." Ashtor's voice emanated from Adoni´.

Ra'amon pointed his finger at the bodies, but nothing happened. Ra'amon turned red at the failure but motioned to his men, who came forth with butane lighters and set fire to the petrol-soaked wood. Flames leaped almost instantly in a ring around the bodies. The people roared in approval until they discerned movement on the altar. Both Jaffe and Abel stirred. Then they sat up and finally stood to their feet, unscorched. The crowd, hushed with astonishment and fear, stood gaping at the spectacle before them. These men had been dead for *three* days. Standing in the fire, the prophets looked around at their persecutors. Then a loud noise—no a voice commanding for all to hear, said, "Come up here!"

The prophets slowly began to rise, up…up…up as they ascended into heaven, clearly visible to the crowd. They watched until they were mere white specks showing against a deeply overcast sky. Adoni´ left in disgust. *Where* was Lord Ashtor when he needed him? Ashtor within remained silent.

Shaking their heads in awestruck wonder, the crowd murmured among themselves. Was Adoni´ wrong? Did Jehovah God live in his heaven after all? Fear fell upon all.

Chapter 49

The clouds began to break up, and the sky beyond revealed another wonder in the making. The dragon star approached the earth once more, again accompanied by a vast army of warriors as he had when he came against Russia's coalition armies. His entourage appeared way off in a distance as they often had after the comet was born. As the dragon star veered away, the army neared the earth like the end of a children's "crack the whip" line. The horsemen filled the sky—millions of them. They replaced drab clouds with dreamlike images splashed with Technicolor hues of orange and blue like some bizarre cartoon on a sky-wide screen. As they came closer, the earthlings saw that they wore armament, both the warriors and their steeds. The crowd dispersed in alarm.

Within the hour, before all the people could reach their homes, came a great shaking. The tallest hotels swayed and buckled. Every tower in the city fell. The fairly new settlements crumpled as well as the houses of antiquity in the "Old City." But the worst of it fell upon the tenth of the city containing the Temple Mount and surroundings. The unfinished temple structure was leveled and collapsed into the underground excavations. The stately marble columns of the Dome of the Rock buckled and dropped as well. The intricate mosaic ceiling and walls shattered and came raining down, crashing and breaking in ruin. The dragon image on the mount shed most of its heads, exposing the wiring inside. The wires stood out like grotesque, disheveled hair from the necks, some retaining the tiny cameras looking like bare eyeballs that dangled and bounced from the earth's motion. The buildings and the trees of the garden were leveled.

When the dust settled and they began to dig out, it was determined days later that seven thousand people in Jerusalem lost their lives within a few seconds. Coming on the heel of the prophets' resurrection, no one doubted that it was the wrath of the Hebrew God that had flattened the city. Some tried to change their minds and give him glory, hoping he would pardon their misplaced loyalty.

Angry with his defeat but determined to take his revenge on the remaining believers, Adoni´ had rushed to the underground headquarters as soon as the prophets disappeared, to see if the report had come in.

Johnny took Route 1 out of Jerusalem and headed down toward Jericho in the Dead Sea Valley. "Probably be less traffic this way than going through Hebron," he said.

"Where are we going?" asked Rachel

"About a two-hour drive from here to an aqua-culture village by the name of Ein Yahav."

"Is there any news of our friends?" asked Rachel. "I've been out of touch."

"Yeah," said Johnny. "Adoni´ is cracking down on the barter stores. Several believers have been raided and killed."

"Oh no, the *Hazzer* (swine)," spat Rachel. "Anyone I know?"

"Did you know the Rubins?"

"No."

"They were over in the Beit Israel neighborhood," said Raol.

"I never shopped that far away from the temple. Say, something happened a few days ago I'm very curious about. A mob of people showed up at Adoni´'s palace. Actually, they showed up a couple a days. I heard them praying on that last day. What was that all about?"

"They were trying to overthrow the priests at the temple because of the darkness and the locusts," said Johnny, suddenly reaching down and scratching his leg.

"Oh, they'll never do that because of the ark. It protects them."

"Not anymore, I'm afraid. They killed the two prophets three days ago."

"How is this possible? Are you sure?" gasped Rachel in shock. But then she remembered the scriptures. *Of course it had to be*, she thought.

"Have they been resurrected yet?" she asked.

"No, they are dead, dead. I saw them lying dead in the street myself at Zion Square," said Johnny, almost with satisfaction.

Rachel grew still. *What is it about him that bothers me? His size? He was always so trim and muscular like David. Now he is grotesquely bloated...with fat or what?*

The two men talked in the front seat and left Rachel to her thoughts. After an hour or so Johnny said to them both, "Shall we stop at Ein Gedi for an early lunch? Ein Yahav is such a small village. There may not be facilities there. And besides, who knows when David's men will show up."

All during lunch Rachel was distracted by Johnny's scratching. Finally, she said, "Johnny, what is the matter with you? You can't stop digging at yourself. You're turning red."

"I've had an allergic reaction to something I ate. The doctors don't know what to do for it."

"I never heard of a food reaction that was that violent, apart from the ones that kill."

"It's a rare thing, but I've been assured it's temporary," he replied.

They arrived at Ein Yahav shortly before one. "Nobody told us where to be. I guess they will find us. Shall we just walk around the center of the village?" said Johnny after he parked the car. As they walked along, Rachel began to notice that the people of the village were all bloated just like Johnny and scratching as well. She grew suspicious. Was that the result of the insects, the locusts? She grabbed his arm as they walked along, but he winced with pain and drew back.

"An mitzta'er (I'm sorry)," she said. "Have you hurt your arm?"

"It's nothing just part of my *tzoress* (troubles)," he said with a frown.

Suddenly, Rachel understood why Adoni´ had invited her to dinner. She had been set up. Johnny hadn't defected at all but was in fact being led straight to David through *her*. She couldn't let that happen. But what could she do to stop them? Warn the others when they showed up? David's location must be protected at all costs. *Even at the cost of her own life.*

Chapter 50

General Lin Yiang Dehuai's army had slaughtered its way from China above the Himalayan Mountain ranges farther south, an easier trail for horsemen, then through the mountain passes of Kazakhstan. From there they crossed over Uzbekistan, skirting the southern edge of the Karkum Desert, and then passing across Turkmenistan. From that country they followed the coast of the Caspian Sea through northern Iran where they met little resistance. They planned to turn south at Rasht, taking the most direct route to the border, passing through Islamabad.

But as Dehuai approached the turn off to Tehran, he gathered his officers to plan their strategies. "We have come to the first of our real challenges," he said. "This country still has oil, how much we don't know. Their oil may be limited, since they depend upon others for its refinement. That means they may have a mechanized army. At some point they will resist us. We are fairly protected at present by the mountains between Tehran and us. I believe they would have the advantage if they waited until we hit the great plateau."

"What can we do? We are not strong enough to take on a mechanized army head on," said General Bo Hai Dingxiang.

"We wait until we are stronger. First, send messages to triple the troops coming to replenish our lines. In the meantime, we will raid their arms depots and rearm ourselves with conventional weapons, perhaps even a few vehicles."

Behind Dehuai's lead army, newly trained armies were moving swiftly to join them, stopping in occupied territory only long enough to rest their horses. That way, fresh troops were constantly reinforcing the whole line. Sometimes the new troops took up the occupation of lands as the rested troops moved on. Messengers maintained a constant communication all the way back to China. They used modern technology whenever possible, primitive when necessary. China seemed to have unlimited manpower to keep up the line as it lengthened. They also augmented their ranks by pressing young men from their conquered peoples to join them.

Lin Cho Chonglin, Dehuai's childhood friend, had remained in China to train new soldiers to provide both soldiers and rulers for their conquered peoples. Once subdued, the people were ruled strictly but kindly, so the line maintained order the whole way.

Bo Hai sent ten men to take the message back to the line. Meanwhile Dehuai pulled his troops into easily defended narrow mountain valleys, where his type of warfare would have the advantage, to wait for reinforcements.

Hillman, Katz, and Matza had come over to Ein Yahav with GG in a helicopter before noon and landed north of the village out of sight. GG stayed with the helicopter while the other three, dressed in native clothes instead of their uniforms, went into the village to meet Rachel.

"There'll be a wedding soon, I predict. Didn't I tell you back in Washington?" said Katz to Matza.

"Yes, you did," said Matza.

"I can't wait to dance at his wedding," said Katz gaily.

"Think we'll ever find a bride like that?" asked Hillman.

THE END... AND A NEW BEGINNING

"*Halevai of unz* (May we be so blessed)!" said Katz, noticing that Matza wasn't joining in their jocular mood. "What's the matter, Matza? Why are you being so serious?"

"I was just thinking. Maybe we should take some precautions. What if this is some kind of trap with Rachel as bait, a ploy to find out our location."

"How can that be?" asked Katz. "Jaffe said Johnny is one of us now."

"I don't know, but I remember he used to work closely with Ra'amon. Besides that, David believes he thinks Adoni´ is the messiah. I think we should separate. Let me come behind you as 'back up' just in case something goes wrong."

Hillman nodded. "Wouldn't hurt."

After they agreed, Hillman and Katz walked on while Matza dropped back.

After searching the main part of the village, Katz called Matza on his small field radio with the mouthpiece attached to his ear hidden under his head covering. "It doesn't look like they have arrived yet. Find a place in the shade to wait."

"Okay, but I'm still going to stay back. Call me if you spot them," said Matza, stepping under an awning to wait.

Katz and Hillman settled in the shade of a building with a view of the only street in the village.

Katz was first to recognize Rachel even in her boyish outfit. She had taken off the cap, letting down her hair and making it easier. "There they come," he said. "Call Matza."

"*Oy vavoi!* Is that Johnny with her?" questioned Hillman. "What's happened to him?"

"I don't know. He looks like a lot of other people in this village," remarked Katz. The believers had been shielded and did not know about the effects of the locusts. They let Rachel and her two companions walk on past then rose up and fell in behind them.

"*Shalom*, Rachel," said Katz.

She whirled around at the sound of her name. "Katz!" she cried with delight as she clasped him by the shoulders, giving him a hug. Whispering low in his ear she said, "Don't tell them anything. They're traitors."

Johnny caught the surprised look on Katz's face and drew his gun. He had surmised that Rachel was onto them because of his condition. He grabbed Rachel, holding the gun to her head. "So, you figured it out, did you?" Looking at Katz, he demanded, "Tell me where David is or I'll shoot her."

"Let him shoot. Don't tell them," she cried.

"Aw, Johnny," said Katz, starting toward him. Without hesitation Johnny shot him through the heart. He dropped with an expression of surprise frozen on his face.

Rachel screamed, "You fiendish devil!" and began to struggle in his grip.

Johnny tightened his hold even more as he said to Hillman, "You'd better tell me. I'd hate to damage this merchandise. She'd bring a pretty penny on the slave market."

"You wouldn't dare!" cried Rachel through clenched teeth.

"Oh, wouldn't I?"

Hillman didn't fear for his own life because Matza would be there shortly. He said, "He's in Jordan."

"Jordan, where?

"Petra."

"Why did you tell him?" Rachel cried, as Johnny began dragging her away.

Suddenly, the ground began to shake. Everyone looked around them in surprise. Rachel took advantage of the moment. Placing her thumb with its sharp nail between her fingers on her free hand, she used a powerful karate jab to Johnny's sore arm to set herself free.

THE END... AND A NEW BEGINNING

He yelled, dropping her in pain. She bolted. The wall of the building they stood beside buckled inward, and the top of the wall came down, crushing Johnny beneath. Raol fled in the confusion. Rachel dropped to her hands and knees to check for a pulse on Katz, but it was no use—he was gone. Her eyes filled with tears—oh, why did another person she was close to have to die?

After the shaking stopped, Matza came running up. He dropped beside them,

"No, nooooo!" he cried, beating the ground with his fist. He didn't need to find a pulse. The glazed eyes told the story. "Who did this?" he demanded between sobs.

"Johnny," replied Rachel, "he was the traitor." Then she spoke in anguish, "Oh, no! Raol got away, and he knows where David is. We've got to stop him!"

"Who?" asked Matza.

"Raol. I suppose he was the servant friend of Johnny's," said Hillman.

"Yes," replied Rachel. "They were very clever. They had me completely fooled until we got here. Then I began to suspect Johnny's condition was due to the locusts because so many of the townspeople had the same condition. I knew a believer would not be affected."

"Let's get out of here," said Matza. "Hillman, help me lift Katz's body to my shoulder."

"I'll help you carry him."

"*Lo, b'aleph* (flat no)," said Matza firmly. "With no one will I share this task," his voice breaking.

"What about Raol?" cried Rachel.

"We'd never find him in this confusion." The villagers were starting to come out of the rubble. "I'm glad we put the helicopter outside of the village. Let's go."

When they reached the edge of the buildings, they heard the helicopter rotors beating the air close by.

"GG must be looking for us," said Hillman, and he started to wave. Rachel joined him. GG saw them and descended.

Rachel and Hillman climbed into the open door of the helicopter, pulling Katz's body in, out of the arms of Matza. "Somebody hit?" called GG from the cockpit.

"Johnny killed Katz," said Hillman. "Killed him in cold blood."

"Oh, no, not Katz! We went all the way to Kazakhstan and back together without a scratch," he said, shaking his head, eyes watering. "Not fun-loving Katz," he murmured.

The helicopter took off, winding its way upward then turning southeast toward Petra. Matza sprawled next to the body with his back against the wall. He sat for the rest of the journey staring into space, tears streaming down his cheeks.

After the great earthquake, an army gathered in the sky once more. However, this army was bigger and covered the whole heaven. "Here comes our greatest test," said Lin Yiang to his men. "This is what defeated the Russian Army."

Chapter 51

Once airborne GG called headquarters, "Red Shoe, this is GG. Do you read me?"

"This is Red Shoe. Go ahead, GG."

"We've got the merchandise, but we took a hit."

"Do you need medics?"

"No, Katz is dead. Tell David. Over and out."

The news hit David pretty hard. "Not Katz, not on such a harmless mission. It must have been the earthquake," he said, tears coming to his eyes. Katz had been special. He was more than one of his team. He was a good friend. How he would miss his good-natured humor and his loyalty. But the blow was balanced by the anticipation of seeing Rachel. He was waiting when the helicopter came down.

He ran in under the swooshing blades before they stopped. Rachel dropped into his waiting arms. "*Hamoodah* (Darling)," he cried as he crushed her to him, kissing her forehead, her cheeks, and finally her lips unashamedly in the presence of his men.

When he released her, she cried, "Oh David, Johnny killed Katz in cold blood. He was trying to reason with him, and he just shot him dead."

"Johnny?" he asked, full of shock.

"Yes, he was the informer and the traitor. He's the one who got me out of Adoni''s palace."

David's eyes flashed with anger. "The devil himself must have gotten into him. I knew he had changed but to sell us out…and to kill Katz, an old friend. Well, that makes him wicked beyond measure. Just wait until I get my hands on him."

"He's already dead. A wall fell on him when the earthquake hit. "Oh," he said, almost sorry. "God has saved me the trouble. But I must admit I think I could have enjoyed killing such a snake." Then he murmured, quietly quoting scripture, "Vengeance is mine says the Lord." *God has kept me from blood-guiltiness.*

"How was it here during the earthquake?" asked Rachel.

"It just shook for a few seconds. Remember, we're almost solid rock here." He turned to Matza, who was unloading Katz's body. Matza wouldn't let anyone help him, not even David. He carried the body to the restaurant where it would be made ready for burial. It was a strange sight, Matza being so short, and he almost dragging Katz's lanky body. David and Rachel walked behind in silence.

After they left Katz's body to the women for preparation for burial, David took Rachel on a tour of the grounds close to the restaurant.

Suddenly, Rachel remembered Roal. "Oh, David, Roal got away. He knows where you are. You have to get ready for an attack!"

"We're always ready," replied David calmly as he continued showing her around. "Did you hear what happened to the Jaffe and Abel?"

"Yes, Johnny told me they were killed."

"That's all he told you?"

"Yes, why?"

"That's probably all he knew. It must have happened after he went to get you."

"*What* happened?"

"They were getting ready to burn their bodies on the altar at the temple when *Yeshua* resurrected them right before their eyes."

"Really! How do you know?"

"We have a TV. It was televised."

"Just like it says in the Revelation—David, did you hear? I have accepted *Yeshua* and believe like you do now?"

"Yes, I know. Jaffe told me about you. It was the best news I ever had."

"Oh David, I'm sorry for all the grief I've caused you. I know it's no excuse, but if you only knew how I suffered as a child from the Christian Goyim. You have no idea of the bitterness I held toward their God. I just didn't understand. I know now that same happiness and joy that Papa felt. I can't wait to tell him. It won't be long until I see him again. Do you know it's only a month until *Yeshua* comes back?"

"Oh Rachel, *Hamoodah*, It's so good to have you back," he said as he squeezed her shoulder.

Rachel stopped for a minute and looked at him. "Is it?"

"Is it what?" he asked, confused.

"Diedrienne is not waiting somewhere to claim you?"

"You are talking about that time you saw us together?"

"Yes."

"That was completely innocent. We had worked late and were simply eating together. It was not a date. She's not even here. As far as I know she never accepted *Yeshua*. But you...I see you didn't lose any time studying the New Testament."

"We had classes every day at the temple. Mostly we studied the Revelation. I hope you have Bibles here. I didn't have access to one at Adoni˝'s, and I missed it terribly."

"We have lots. Funniest thing. Someone found a whole cache of Bibles and literature hidden in one of the caves. The Christians must have anticipated our coming here. I'll get you one and get my mother to find you living space among the women," said David. "Now I want to talk to Matza. He's been hit pretty hard with Katz's death. Maybe we can console one another. I'm really going to miss Katz. He could always lighten up any situation."

—

Adoni´ had hurried to the *Cor Zahal* before the earthquake hit. Ashtor would take care of the armies in the sky; he wanted to see if word had come from the informer. He joined the others gathered in the pit, the war room, which had two story walls of maps all around the room. The generals clustered over a mock-up of the land of Israel where aids would move around little figures representing the various divisions once they moved out and reported back their positions.

The building shuddered. "Earthquake?" they murmured to each other, faces filled with fright as they steadied themselves by holding onto the mock-up table. Two of the lighted glass-fronted wall maps fell crashing to the floor, glass shattering. The crashing noises from outside penetrated even their sunken lair. But it was well built and safely withstood the shake. Riding out the quake in the underground room unscathed, Adoni´ ordered the cleanup of the city left to civilians, even though the IDF wanted to dispense soldiers to guard against looting in commercial areas.

"*L'Zazel!* Leave it for another day!" he cried in fury, driven by mad revenge. "I want every available man to attack the stronghold of our greatest enemy. Get helicopters on alert! Put the air force on alert, and get armored divisions ready to roll," he commanded the heads of his armies. "Send out surveillance planes over every inch of the Judean Desert, the Paran wilderness, the Negev, and even into the western regions of Jordan. Comb the areas and find them!"

"But Mr. Adoni´, sir, how can we know the damage on our bases? Surely that is more important than coming against the hijackers. They too will wait for another day," suggested General Sorrukh.

Adoni´, remembering an incident that he heard of in Iraq many years ago when Saddam was opposed, slowly and with deliberation removed a revolver from one of the officers' holsters and shot the general through the heart, dropping him before the stunned eyes of his officers. "Any more suggestions?" he asked coldly as he laid the gun aside. The group slowly shook their heads.

Communications brought a note to one of the generals. "We have their location. Can you believe it? They have been hiding out in Petra all along."

"Get in touch with surveillance. Have them photograph Petra. I'll get the army moving. You can tell us of their fortifications as we go," said Adoni´, who went out to lead his army in person.

"But Premier, what about the trouble in the sky, those armies?"

"Don't worry about them. Remember, our god fights for *us*."

Chapter 52

David had hoped to keep their position a secret, but now it seemed inevitable that they would come under attack. With Petra being a valley rimmed with high canyon walls and isolated peaks, it would almost have to be an air attack. With the narrow Siq, the only way in on top of an escarpment and the wadis, the only way to climb it from the Arabah, both were easily guarded. By the time an army entered the Siq's narrow crack, thrust apart by ancient tectonic forces, it would become a killing field. Snipers hidden on the top of the walls up to six hundred feet high would make mincemeat of them, for there was no cover between the walls, just a barren, sandy path interspersed with uncovered patches of Roman cobblestones. It was almost as bad if they tried to climb the wadis.

David had put gun implements at intervals in the caves and up every wadi in Petra, but especially on the west-facing rock wall that extended from the Siq. The northern approach to the valley was the most open. Because it was so wide, he had to put a line of guns facing both ways in the center of the valley at the old Byzantine and North walls, telling them both to only shoot *after* the planes passed over them to protect their locations. He stationed a lookout watch on top of Umm al-Biyara, formerly believed to be the Mt.

Sela of the Old Testament. This was the highest point around, and it took nearly three hours to make the climb to the top. Of course they set it up the easy way by helicopter. The post included an alarm with loud speakers hidden in the shadows of the cliffs to call all personnel to their battle stations. The post also included three heavy machine gun placements, one facing north and the other two facing east, set in some ancient cisterns that had been camouflaged on top to match the surrounding rock.

Since David expected an air attack, the guns on Umm al-Biyara were paired with two sets on two other high places. One set on the hill to the north across from Umm al Biryara, which would catch any plane coming east between the two hills in a crossfire. He placed two on the hill of the High Place of Sacrifice and another high up on the cliff face high over the garden tomb, which would do the same to any plane going south. Still another was in the rock face above the Roman Amphitheater to guard the valley to the Siq. Al Habis, a smaller hill that rose from the valley floor slightly northeast of the first two gun positions on Umm al-Biyara, had caves on its western face. The gun implements here would augment the rest, with the other two sets firing straight on. On the top of Al Habis three more were located near the old Crusader castle. Two pointed northeast, and one at the southern most tip augmented the gun positions on the southern approach.

Thinking the enemy might bomb the Forum Restaurant expecting it to house the command post, they had opted for the museum at the base of Al-Habis instead. Being so close to the rock mountain, it would be harder to hit.

He set the helicopters under camouflage in the canyon below that opened to the Arabah, where the horses were. He would only use them against an army on foot. After all, he was only defending, not taking up an offense. He didn't want to risk losing his helicopters.

Even so, the helicopters were armed, and he left a small force in the canyon to man them. Fortunately, he had anticipated having to defend his fortress when he first set up the secret army post. He had planned his defense then. Each gun emplacement had adequate rounds of ammunitions for a heavy attack.

The women and children, plus the Bedouins not enlisted to fight, were split between the Monastery and the Treasury, both having large rooms carved from solid rock. Once inside they would be safe. Each was assigned and knew exactly what to do, for David insisted on doing escape drills. Those taken to the Monastery required the helicopters because of its location. Although safely away from the valley fortress, it was a thousand steps high with intermittent, sloped paths. Thus it required more notice to implement.

Chapter 53

Spotting a plane on the horizon that evening, the lookouts sounded the alarm for everyone to get out of sight, all, that is, except the Bedouins. All the army tents had already been taken down and stashed. All guns were pulled back out of sight awaiting the attack signal. David counted on remaining undetected if possible.

That night the generals in the pit looked over the reconnaissance pictures of Petra. "Why, there's nothing there except a few Bedouins and their goats," said one.

"But even if they are there, according to this aerial photograph, you can't get a regular army in there anyway, except from the top side. Although there's a steep trail up from the Arabah, you could never take an army up that safely if it's fortified. It will have to be paratroopers," said another.

"I wouldn't drop paratroopers in there—too much chance for ambush. Why not just send a fighter squadron in on a strafing mission? If they're there they'll shoot back. Then we can plan from that."

"That would probably work. It could be as innocent as it looks anyway. Our informer may have received a false report," said General Eli Yadin, head of general staff.

"The sky looks bad. What if we get another meteor attack?"

"Premier Adoni´ says the meteorites are for our enemies. Don't worry about them."

Petra was an impregnable fortress in ancient times, and time had not changed that, because every avenue open to the attacker gave the defender the advantage. If they came up from the Arabah, a few of David's men could hold them at bay, since there were only a few wadis they could climb. If they dropped paratroopers in one of the wadis on top, they would have to face guns in the caves with little or no cover. It was impossible to come through the guarded Siq. So even with modern warfare, the fortress was still formidable.

"They know we should be here. They're looking for us," said David.

"They shouldn't see anything to give us away. Even the gun emplacements at the walls are completely covered," said General Saguy. "You have done a marvelous job planning your defense, David. I certainly picked the right man for the job."

"We'll see," said David. "If Johnny's friend gave them the word, they won't stop with just reconnaissance. They'll send planes. I would. Call in the Umm al-Biyara team. Since it's such a long, hard climb on foot and we can't take them up with helicopter in a battle, let them all bivouac in readiness until the battle or at least for a week. We'll do the same with the other gun emplacements." Basic army bivouac supplies stored in each gun emplacement made the order possible.

"Captain, what about the shelters for the women and children? Shouldn't we stock them with food and water?" asked Hillman.

THE END... AND A NEW BEGINNING

"Supplies are already in place, but let's put everyone on alert and move them in now. I don't want people running to shelters or battle stations under an air attack, especially that long haul up to the Monastery. Besides, it looks like we're are going to get another bombardment from the sky. Everyone needs to stay undercover anyway. Hillman, you see to the shelters for civilians, and arm the Bedouins with rifles to protect the women and children."

The camp bustled as everyone hurried to carry out the orders. The king placed his Jordanian ground troops. Their one vulnerable spot was the banks of solar panels on top of the Forum Restaurant. But these would have to stay where they were. They supplied power for their electronic equipment. The batteries were fully charged at the moment, but if the panels were damaged, it would knock out their satellite communications once the batteries went down. But then again, they were only crucial to the hijacking and might never be used again anyway. Who else was left to talk to? Egypt was gone. The temple group had moved in with them. The only radios that mattered now were the small-powered field radios for communication between units and headquarters, and some of them were solar powered.

Malcomb was in charge of the lookout station. He had spent many a relaxed night on watch gazing through his telescope, but not anymore. They all needed their rest. They would come in daylight when they came.

The set orders were to refrain from firing on the first pass and keep radio silence. If they could maintain the illusion that only Bedouins dwelt there, so much the better. There would be time enough to shoot if they were discovered.

They didn't have to wait long. At dawn the alarm sounded.

"Here they come," said Malcomb. "Six F-16s. Good choice in these close quarters. The Phantoms would be hard to maneuver."

They swooped down low. flying in from the northwest right over top of the monastery crew. Then they dropped down over the valley and turned north over the wide part of the valley where they came in range of the Jordanian troops waiting in the caves. One man raised his rifle and fired.

"Eagle five to squadron leader, I've been fired upon."

"*B'seder*, I read you. Machine gun?"

"No, single shot. Could be just a Bedouin."

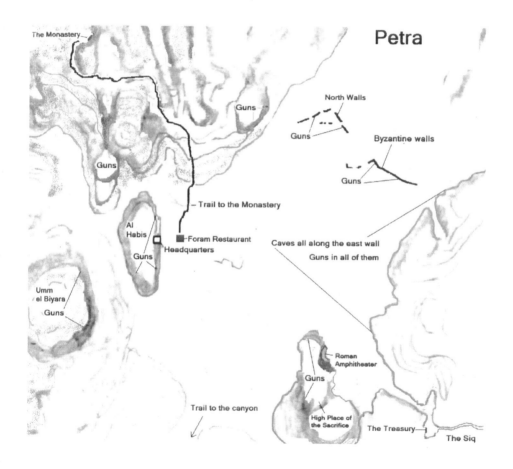

Chapter 54

"Let's make another run the opposite direction, only this time Eagle three and four take the right canyon and Eagle five and six take the left. We'll take the middle. Take a few shots and see if you can flush anything. But look sharp—an army could be hidden in those caves."

The Israeli generals in the pit were listening to the pilots. "This run should tell us something," said the chief of general staff.

The F-16s descended again, roaring back through the valley two abreast. The central pair began strafing around the colonnaded street and Nabateans baths in the central ruins and met no response. But the four in the other two canyons met with fire.

Malcomb broke radio silence.

"They're splitting up. Two are ours. Two are yours. Showtime," he said, speaking to the amphitheater gunners.

The guns rat-a-tatted in staccato. The two F-16s heading west burst into flames almost simultaneously after being riddled with bullets from both sides of the narrow four-hundred-and-ten-foot canyon. As Eagle four and five veered to the east in a wide turn, they came abreast of the Palace Tombs, which were filled with guns. They blazed away barely two hundred feet from the planes. One losing control crashed into rock face above the amphitheater, scattering wreckage and fire for hundreds of feet. The other climbed out just in time but with several bullet holes streaked across his fuselage.

"I'm hit! I'm hit!" cried Eagle six.

"Eagle three and four bought it!" shouted Eagle two, "and I heard a crash to the left!"

The generals in the pit listened in dismay. Three F-16s gone. How was it possible? Well, at least they knew they were there.

"Squadron leader to Eagle five, come in."

"It's no use Squadron Leader, Eagle five hit the wall."

"Eagle six, where are you?'

"Above and to your right."

"Did you see anything?"

"No, they must all be inside the caves."

"Stay out of the narrow canyons and try to hit those caves on the east wall. They're full of guns."

"They're turning and coming back from the south," said Malcomb.

"Hold your fire until they are abreast of you," David ordered.

"Here they come!"

The guns caught them in their crossfire between Umm el-Biyara and the High Place as they came in almost at the same elevation.

"I'm hit!" cried Eagle six.

"Eject! eject!"

"Too low, I…"

"Scratch four," called Malcomb as he watched the fourth plane hit the valley floor in a fireball.

"Climb!" ordered the squadron leader to the remaining plane. "Let's go home and study those pictures."

"Report," called the general in the museum headquarters to the gun positions in the caves.

"No casualties," was the return from each station.

"They'll be back. Only this time they'll be wise to our defenses. They'll bring missiles. Let's make some changes," said David.

He thought about moving the gun crews from the east caves, the Royal Tombs, to the craggy heights above them using a helicopter to lower them and their guns into natural crevices. The caves were safer against bullets, but he knew they were on to that location and would hit them there with missiles or smart bombs. Better to be exposed and have the element of surprise than to wait for a bomb in relative safety.

But as he started to give the order, he had a troubling in his spirit. Was the Lord trying to tell him something? He turned to the rest in the command center and said, "We've won the first battle. It would be dangerous to get cocky and think we've won the war. I think we need to take time for prayer and see what the Lord wants us to do next. Take out the next few minutes and each of you seek the Lord. Let's see if he will speak to us."

David wandered off by himself and found a secluded place at the base of Al Habis. He lay down prostrate on the ground and cried out unto the Lord. "My God and my Savior. You and You alone have put me in charge of these people. Now, oh *Yeshua*, show me your will. Make me to know how to lead them and what to do to save them." Quieting his mind to listen, he suddenly *knew*, not thought, but knew for sure the plans of the enemy. He rushed back to headquarters. It had to be a visitation from the Holy Spirit, for David knew he would have doubts if it were only his own mind. But he didn't have doubts. H*e knew*. Was this what the scripture called "a word of knowledge?" He didn't know…but now he knew what to do.

Chapter 55

Lin Yiang approached Iraq with intent to cross the Tigris and Euphrates Rivers at Baghdad where both rivers would have wide bridges for his army on horses. Otherwise, the rivers would provide a formidable barrier, especially since the earthquakes accompanying the week of darkness were bound to have destroyed some of the dams in Turkey and Syria. The waters of the Euphrates had nearly dried up south of Baghdad earlier, but now it would be back to its full measure. Besides, that's where the bread basket of the Middle Eastern empire lay. They could refill the bellies of the army before they went on.

The pilots were debriefed as soon as they returned. "It's a regular killing field, sir. Gun emplacements were everywhere. You can't go in low, because they get you in a crossfire. There's no way to strafe most of the caves in the narrow valley, because our guns are mounted forward. The caves are perpendicular. You can't maneuver," said the squadron leader to the brass.

"Show us the gun emplacements where you know the guns are."

"Well, we were going for the caves on the east side because that's where they got the first plane. There's no way to know where they are in that west canyon, probably both sides, but they are well camouflaged. We didn't see anything."

"Best thing would be to stay high out of gun range and send in missiles."

"But it would destroy all of Petra. The only way you would get them all would be to destroy every cave. There's at least a hundred. No, there's got to be a better way," said another.

Just then Adoni´ came into headquarters, back from the field army, which had halted in Arad when they heard the reconnaissance report.

"Bring me up to date," he demanded. After listening to their disparaging report, he said, "What about chemical warfare? Isn't there some kind of nerve gas that kills instantly and then dissipates, leaving the terrain undamaged? Who is left to complain about human rights? Both Iraq and Iran have gases if you Israelis don't."

"That may be the only answer."

"See to it," he commanded.

David got on the field radio, "Listen up, all gun crews. Pack up all your guns and as much ammo as you can carry and head toward the Treasury at the Siq. You on high ground, be ready for pick up with the helicopters." He turned to Yigael and said, "Contact the helicopters and get them all up here on the double. Do we have any horses up here?"

"Yes," said Jonathan, "The Bedouins used them earlier this week to bring in supplies from our warehouse."

"Good. We don't have enough time to bring those up from the canyon. Bring what we have to the Treasury at the Siq. We have to evacuate the whole valley. Send a helicopter to the Monastery and start them moving back. Bring out mothers and small ones in the helicopters first. Go ahead and take them to the warehouse at the railroad."

"But David, why?" questioned the general, shocked at David's sure, clipped commands.

"Because they will not come with bombs or guns this time but chemicals or bacteria bombs, maybe even nerve gas. Don't ask me why I know that, but I know that's what they will do. So let's not waste any time arguing, but work to get everyone out."

"Of course," replied the General, showing great respect for David. "I should have known that. Adoni´ doesn't care how he gets us so long as he gets us. Besides, they couldn't win any other way."

Everyone began to scramble when they heard the reason for their exit. Time was so crucial. All the Israeli Air Force had to do was bring the chemical shells out of secret and load them onto their light bombers. Once they dropped the shells, every living thing in the valley would die.

As soon as a goodly number was at the Treasury, they started the exit. David gave the instructions, "All horses will carry two or three of the younger children, depending on size. Fathers or older brothers will lead them through the Siq. The helicopters will load to full capacity and take everyone to our warehouse at the rail. It will be close quarters, but it will have to do. As soon as the women and children are all safe, we will start taking the rest of you in helicopters. But meanwhile, everyone keep moving out of the Siq and out of Wadi Musa as quickly as you can. The helicopters will pick you up where you are. Tell those in Wadi Musa what to expect. They should evacuate too. *B'seder*, let's get moving."

David sent word to the generals and Yigael, "Reserve one helicopter to pack up what we will need in the way of equipment at the warehouse. Make sure you include all the army's tents."

Chapter 56

Two days later the IDF sent just one bomber along with two F-16s. The squadron leader from the former raid advised that they drop the bombs in each canyon as well as the broad valley. They appeared the next morning after the people had evacuated, dropping the bombs from well over the valley floor, the bombs exploding with big puffs of dust and smoke. They were surprised to have no response from the ground guns. The squadron leader supposed it was because they stayed too high and out of range. Well, that was that. "Bye-bye, hijackers."

Having left in such a hurry, they didn't bring out any food. Fortunately, the warehouse had some but not enough to keep the whole population for the remaining thirty days. (Daniel, the prophet, had said that from the time that the daily sacrifice was taken away and the idol set up until the end would be twelve hundred and ninety days. Twelve hundred and sixty days had passed at the death of the two prophets/priests.)

The hijacking planned for the convoy from Al Aqabah would be needed for them as well as the believers in the Judean Desert. Meanwhile the women improvised as best they could with cooking.

They had the basic cooking utensils from their temporary refuges where they waited out the air attack. They were primitive, but they could manage. The biggest problems for such a large crowd was toilet facilities and water. David solved the toilet problem by having his men dig a latrine some distance from the warehouse and put up temporary fences around it made from materials lying around the warehouse.

The Lord continued to take care of the temperature for them. All during the winter months in Petra, he warmed their caves supernaturally just as he warmed those at the temple. Then he had sheltered the secret army under a cloud during the heat wave. During the fall temperatures improved naturally. Fortunately, it was time for the spring rains. Water could be caught from the roof and stored in plastic containers for the remainder of the time. The women were put in charge of that. The Bedouins and Jordanians, under General Shofot's instructions, planned the defense of their new hideout while David planned the hijacking.

David realized that the pressures of caring for the people were taking all of his time, and he was neglecting his obligations to Rachel. He had lost her once; he needed to take steps lest he lose her again. He told Malcomb of his plan to take Rachel to dinner at the hotel in Wadi Musa that evening. "Don't tell anyone where we are unless it's a dire emergency, in which case call my cell phone. I'll put it on vibrate and screen my calls. We haven't had time to really talk, and I want an uninterrupted evening with her. I can't neglect her any longer."

"I won't breathe a word," he swore, smiling as he lifted his hand as if in an oath. He knew his brother was under great stress and needed a break.

"Look, I need to get myself cleaned up a bit. Would you find Rachel and tell her I will meet her at six o'clock in back of the warehouse where we keep the jeeps?"

"Sure. Are you going to finalize your betrothal with an Erusin Qiddushin? That would give her security until we get through these last days to the end."

David nodded. "I'm working on it."

He had already spoken to his mother about borrowing her ring for the ceremony, since he had no valuable assets himself to give Rachel. The Erusin was the first part of the formal Jewish wedding. The groom was required to give his bride a valuable token of his intention to wed, binding her to him. It could be a ring, a deed to property, or some other precious thing that would be a costly loss if he broke the engagement. He had also spoken to one of the priests to perform the ceremony. He had only to gain Rachel's assent, which he hoped to do tonight. Once he had her answer, he would ask his two witnesses unrelated to him to be present at the ceremony to verify the Erusin.

Rachel was all excited. Finally, she would have David all to herself. She carefully bathed with water in a basin and put on the top of the only other clothes she had. Rachel had hurriedly grabbed her entire meager wardrobe when they departed Petra. The lounge top saved from her stay in Adoni"s palace would have to do. Good thing she brought it, because the only other change she had was the outfit Raol had provided for her escape. She still had to wear her jeans of that outfit, because the lounge pants would not be suitable in a public place. At least the colorful lounge top flattered her for such a momentous occasion.

David arrived promptly at six. His eyes sparkled when he saw her.

"Hamoodah, how lovely you look! Even in this austere environment. How do you manage it?"

"Compliments of Adoni´, I'm afraid."

"You mean you wore that while in the palace?"

"Yes. They took away my practical clothes and only allowed me flimsy lounge sets." She took hold of the bottom of the blue paisley silk top and spread it out before her. "You would have thought I was his mistress or something. Isn't that a laugh," she said, screwing up her face in distaste.

"I'm grateful for his sexual orientation. At least he protected you," said David, helping her into one of the army jeeps.

As David climbed into the driver's seat, Rachel said, "Not really, my guard tried to sexually assault me." Then she started laughing.

"What!" said David, greatly alarmed. "What did you do? ... And why are you laughing?" At this point David had turned around in his seat to face Rachel, his arm on the wheel and the other hand on the back of the seat.

"I'm afraid I damaged him permanently."

"I don't understand—you attacked *him*?"

"Not until he reached for me, then I used my martial arts skills, smashing his knee backwards."

After Rachel finished telling him the whole story, David said, "I didn't really believe you when you told me in Washington you could throw men around. Rachel, you are some *superwoman!*"

Rachel answered his praise by shrugging up her shoulders, wrinkling her nose and forming a silly, closed-mouth grin.

David let out a shout of laughter. "*You* are somethun' else."

Rachel wiped her forehead with her sleeve and pushed wisps of hair back out of her eyes. Her hair had grown quite long since she had moved to Israel. She no longer had that chic, classic style that had been her look in America. She hadn't been able to afford expensive trips to the salon. Instead, when it grew long enough, she drew it up into a knot on the back of her head. Now she looked nearly like any other good Jewish girl in their company, except that she was *yafeh m'od* (very beautiful). Everyone knew this was David's intended, for shortly after their escape to the warehouse he had presented her with the *Erusin Qiddushin,* and it had been announced. That made her completely acceptable to them. Especially since she did not hold herself aloft but threw herself into the work along with the rest.

She thought back on that precious night when he had asked her if she would change her mind again and marry him after all. It had totally satisfied her heart when she learned he had been as miserable as she during their separation. *How blessed I am to be bethrothed to such a fine man*, she thought.

As she smiled to herself, Esther noticed. "What are you grinning about?"

"I was just thinking about the night David proposed and our ceremony later."

"I'm glad he went ahead with that," said Esther. "He's so busy these days."

"Tell me about it, but it will be over soon."

She sighed as she handed Esther another platter of pita bread. "When I went to college, I always dreamed that I would do something great for Israel, but I never expected it to be in the kitchen." Then she loaded another platter from one of their makeshift camp stoves.

Esther laughed. "No army can exist without its kitchen. At least we are spared the shopping since it's all right here."

"You mean what's left. If they don't intercept a shipment soon, we will be down to bread and water."

"David said the king provided the goats for the soup. His subjects help us when they can. They are so grateful for the warning about the gas."

"How do they *know* they dropped gas?" asked Rachel.

"I don't know. You'll have to ask David," replied Esther, as she carried the platter inside to a makeshift table.

Ask David, indeed, thought Rachel. *When did she ever see him?* Except for the night he proposed, he had been so busy seeing to their needs, seeing to his men or whatever, that they had time for only a few short words between times. But she refused to complain. At least she caught glimpses of him now and then. That was immeasurably better than before. *When Yeshua comes and ends this time of fire, he will be all mine.*

Behind her she heard a squabble in progress.

"If I just knew how to get out of here, I would go back to the real world where life would be easy," said an angry voice, as she finished folding the family's wash she had gathered from the clothes lines. It was a frequent task, since all had few garments due to their haste in leaving.

"You want to be under a ruler who would kill people with nerve gas or chop off their heads?" asked the other teenage girl named Mary, similarly occupied.

Rachel decided to join them. Maybe if she busied herself helping the young girls as David was with the young men, she could find a place of service among the believers.

"I don't mean to interrupt, but I couldn't help but overhear your conversation. May I join you?"

"Sure," they said in unison.

"I'm Rachel Lieberman," said Rachel. "What are your names?"

"I'm Mary, and she's Judith," said one, pointing to the other.

"We already know who *you* are," said Judith, smiling. The girl seemed honored to have the beautiful Rachel pay attention to them.

"Well, I have been in the so-called 'real world' until quite recently and can tell you, you really wouldn't want to be there. That world is not the same as when you left. People under Adoni´ are beginning to do all kinds of evil things. If you were found out as a believer, you would be sold as a slave, possibly to a wicked man who you would use you as his sex slave. Young girls and boys are priority items for this. Besides that, people are murdering their babies, burning them to a god of fire down in the valley below Silwan. Ra'amon instituted it as a way to worship Mollech and gain wicked spiritual power from him. The New Testament says that the people who worship idols worship demons. Those people who worship Ashtor are all practicing witchcraft now.

Then there's the squabbling over food. Murders are committed over that too."

"But I would simply get a mark, and then they wouldn't bother me," said Judith.

Rachel gasped. "Don't you know that everyone who gets the mark will be cast into hell and burn with fire forever? Is that what you want for a few days of pleasure?"

Judith replied, lifting her chin, "How can you be sure of that?"

Rachel decided to change her direction as she realized either Judith didn't know the Lord *Yeshua*, or else she hadn't had any teaching. How grateful she was for the studies they'd had during her temple stay.

"Do you know that everything is going to change short of thirty days?"

"How do you know that?" asked Judith.

"Because it's all written in the Bible. Have you ever studied the Bible?" she asked.

"My parents must have, or we wouldn't be here." She said frowning like she resented it.

"Tell you what, why don't you two get a group of the young teenage girls together, and we'll start a girls' Bible class and I'll teach you. Would you like that?"

"I would," said Mary, eyes sparkling.

"I guess so," replied Judith.

Rachel was all excited when she left them. Maybe there were others who didn't understand what was going on. She might even lead some to *Yeshua*. She had finally found her place. If she made herself so busy with the girls, she wouldn't miss David so much. She would consult *Yeshua* right away as to where to start.

The next day David conferred with his council of advisors. He said, "I've been thinking it might be time to move back to Petra. The Bedouins have moved back. They confirmed it was gas Adoni´ used from the all the dead animals they found. If they had used bacteria some of them would have still been alive, but sick. I'm sure Adoni´ thinks he obliterated us. It should be safe now. The gas has obviously dissipated. What do you think? We are so crowded here. Besides we don't have much longer 'til *Yeshua* comes."

Malcomb spoke up first. "I think it is imperative! Remember, the sixth trumpet and vial of Revelation speak of a heavenly army attacking from the sky to kill one third of the men who are left on the earth. I saw a dark swirl of something through my telescope after the saints from the temple joined us. It could have been that great army. I think we need the protection of the caves. This warehouse would not save us when fire and brimstone begins to fall."

THE END... AND A NEW BEGINNING

"You're right, but after this last hijack we will have to move, because they would come against Petra again." said David.

"You concentrate on getting the food for our people while Uri and I get the people moved back to Petra," said General Shofat.

"Sounds like a good plan," said David.

Chapter 57

After the darkness lifted from the collision with the asteroid, David had sent Feldman and Gil Shama, Yigael's choice of electronics expert, to watch for the food ship's arrival. The spies had familiarized themselves with the workings of the dock from the time of their arrival. Eventually, Shama joined the dock crew employed as a laborer. Feldman, being more experienced in intelligent work, remained free to roam. The blockade had been destroyed at the Straits of Tiran near Sharma El Sheik, allowing the first food shipment to finally reach Al Aqabah. When the ship approached the port, Feldman called immediately to report it.

Yigael called David to the office as soon as he got the call.

"So, Feldman, how big is the ship?"

"Big enough to hold about thirty-six containers, some refrigerated, so we know it's the food ship. Besides, it came from Iraq."

"Thirty-six, huh. That means they will be sending convoys, more trucks than we usually handle."

"Yes, and since the dock is essentially empty, the unloading began as soon as they moored the ship under the massive cranes. Flatbed trucks are lined up to receive the containers."

"With that many we will have to opt for the last shipment or two to avoid later convoys overtaking our hijack. Besides, we don't want to alert Adoni´. He thinks we have been destroyed. Keep us posted as to their schedules. And Feldman, see if you can figure out their electronic communication system, GPS, etc."

"Be'sedar (Okay), but you know Shama brought several electronic devices sent by Yigeal. We may already have what we need to counter theirs. I know he brought lots of tracker bugs. In fact, we put them on all the armored vehicles. That way Yigael can keep track of them."

"Good thinking, we don't want to worry about them coming upon our hijack on the way back to Al Aqabah. Call us as soon as you determine how much time they take between shipments."

"Will do," said Feldman.

The next day Feldman reported, "They are sending out six trucks per convoy, with three armored troop carriers, one forward, one in the middle, and one behind."

"Six trucks?" said David. "That will mean we need a bigger attack force, or we will have to break the convoy in half."

"And what's more, they do have GPS and a machine gun mounted above the cab of the armored vehicles," said Feldman. "But they don't have GPS in the trucks. They're kinda old."

"Do they have inter-truck communication?"

"No. I guess they are depending upon the guard trucks to communicate with Jerusalem. These are not Israeli trucks but veteran trucks of Jordan's commerce. I'm talking about *old*."

"How much time between convoys?"

"Well, they started the first convoy at 900 hours yesterday. The second followed about three hours later, but they only put two armored vehicles on it. I don't think they have enough guard units to cover all these shipments. Unless they send them back after they reach Jerusalem."

"That could be to our advantage," said David. "Maybe they are waiting to see if the first shipments arrive safely. What happens to the trucks already loaded?"

"They have the other twenty-four parked in a storage yard beyond the docking area."

After they loaded the last container onto a truck, Shama quit his job at the dock, and both he and Feldman watched the trucks in the storage yard. They had been keeping close watch in shifts. Only one more convoy had left, and that with only one guard vehicle, a truckload of Jordanian troops.

After it pulled out of the yard, Feldman said, "That confirms our suspicions about the number of guard vehicles available."

"Yes," replied Shama. "They must be feeling pretty safe with two convoys coming through without a problem."

That evening they observed activity surrounding one of the trucks. "What do you think they are doing?" asked Shama.

"They are working on something on the dashboard," said Feldman, who had the binoculars.

"Equipping the truck with a communicative system and GPS, maybe?"

"Probably. Maybe they think they don't need a guard truck after all. Let's wait and see if they send a convoy without a guard. In any case, we need a tracking device on *that* truck."

The convoy left that evening at eight thirty without a guard truck as they suspected, but they only sent three trucks.

"Looks like they are sure that we are gone. But if these three trucks get through, they may send all the rest of them at once. The hijacking crew couldn't handle a convoy that big."

"Let's call the captain and see what he wants to do," said Feldman.

Chapter 58

After hearing the news, David made his decision. "That late start will make our operation at night. They will be at Masada in less than three hours. That makes it at between 2200 and 2300 hours. Wait ten minutes before you start back up behind them, then catch up and keep them in sight."

"Will do," said Feldman. "We will see you later."

David called the hijack team to report to headquarters immediately. He also dispensed night vision gear to everyone, since they would now be unloading at night without lights to remain undetected. Even the helicopters would lift off from Masada without lights. They had drilled everyone involved on the plan after it was formulated. Only minor changes would be necessary. For instance, since they were dealing with three trucks and no guard trucks, he decided to discard the plan for observers along the road since they had the tracking device on the truck and Feldman and Shama behind it. They would be sitting ducks, once David's men stopped them with a roadblock with soldiers in uniform. As they approached the hijack spot, just short of the turnoff to Masada, Sharma would jam their communication with his jamming device from behind. Once stopped, he would disconnect the communications in the trucks.

Although the roadblock stopped the trucks, David's men, hidden along both sides of the road, would spring up to capture the men in the cabs, bringing them out at gunpoint. After they were tied up, Feldman and two other soldiers would put the six men in a SUV borrowed from the Hever Caves people and take them away before the trucks moved. That was the changed plan.

"Yigael," said David.

"Yes, sir."

"Get Uri on the phone and apprise him of the situation. Make sure he knows we have three trucks to deal with, and we need more help with the unloading. Also, make sure he has his people light the landing places on the mountaintops; outline them with candles if nothing else. We will call from Masada as soon as the helicopter lifts off. No need for lights to be lit before then."

At the last minute David decided to send extra men from Petra for unloading as well. *That way we can bring that extra truck-load back to our warehouse. We need to be quick if we would be undiscovered*, he thought.

No less than a small army loaded into the helicopters and headed toward the hijack point just south of Masada.

―

Adoni´'s army was still mechanized. Iraq, Iran, and Saudi Arabia had their oil production in full swing. Some believed they were spared supernaturally. But in any case, it gave Adoni´ the advantage for his army, which was still pretty much intact.

It was the leverage Adoni´ had over the European countries, having destroyed the Baku oil field in Aszerbaijan with missiles during the Russian invasion. With the US impotent and the Russian fields gone, Europe's source for oil depended on Israel's new fields. Even Venezuela had cut back drastically after being almost destroyed by the invading seas at the overturning. With shipping greatly reduced, it would be foolish to trust their remaining ships to long ocean voyages in recurring catastrophes. The same problem hindered African oil as well. Replacing ships was practically impossible. Thus, the governments of Europe depended on Adoni´'s oil and good graces to keep modern civilization going.

The great oil fields in Indonesia had also been destroyed along with the islands themselves. Because they were located near the juncture of three tectonic plates, volcanic plumes marked their location now. Civilization suffered a reverse in the Far East, but the Middle East remained relatively stable due to Adoni´'s strict regulations.

◆

Taking the route of Genghis Khan north of the mountains and west to Turkestan, a route much more conducive to horses than going across the mountains, Dehuai approached the prize of the Middle East's oil. The rugged horses of northeast China were more than sturdy enough to stand the trek, despite the setback in the great heat. His ruthless reign of terror preceded him as he took village after village supplying his army as he went.

With fresh horses from China where they had been preserved in the many underground facilities, he was ready to take on Babylon, a great prize.

The booming agriculture had made Iraq a rich country. Greedy merchants had ships from the rest of the world docked at Iraq's Persian gulf instead of Rome, unloading treasures for the prosperous.

News began to trickle in of the gigantic army on the move from the east. Fleeing survivors told of seeing vast clouds of dust raised by the galloping armies as they approached their villages. Adoni´ became alarmed. He took Ra'amon with him and knelt before the patched-up image of the dragon. He conferred with Ashtor through deep meditation. Strange words and incantations began to come out of his mouth. It was another language. Ra'amon, seeing his deep concentration and hearing the strange words, dropped to his knees and was also overcome by strong spirits of the occult. He, too, began incantations. After a while they opened their eyes and stared at one another. Out of each of their mouths and the mouth of the one head that remained of the dragon image came wisps of vapor in the shape of a frog. They watched as the frogs dissipated into vapors spreading and rising.

"What happened?" asked Ra'amon.

"We've been communicating with the spirit world. Ashtor is sending out angels to convince the nations to come to our aid."

"You mean against the eastern hordes that are moving toward Iran?"

"Yes, our reporters for CNN say they are out of petroleum. They are after our oil."

"So it's going to come down to a battle between the East and the West," commented Ra'amon.

"We'll win, of course. We have to—otherwise civilization will come to an end. The Chinese have turned into wild men, say the reports from the Far East. They rape and pillage everywhere they go. We will be the battleground. The Chinese can't afford to stop at the oil fields in the Persian Gulf area. They will have to be masters of the whole area first. On the other hand, our newly discovered oil fields are virtually untouched and have a greater potential. We will definitely be the target. I'll call for a meeting between our coalition and Europe immediately. Maybe we can stop them before they reach beyond Iraq. After all, they *are* fighting with horses. We still have a mechanized army."

Chapter 59

Adoni´ dispatched a complete army of tanks and artillery units with a squadron of Cobra attack helicopters to Iraq and penetrated Iran's border, moving beyond the Zagros Mountains to engage the Chinese on the great plateau, better for their tanks and armored troop carriers. The sky turned ominous as the heavenly armies, sighted after the resurrection of the two witnesses, came close to the earth to join the battle. They presented an eerie sight, because the heavenly horses had heads like lions and tails like serpents, both issuing fire and brimstone. It was not the warriors on their backs that were dangerous, but the heavenly horses themselves.

The horse images, which were really small independent comets creating pictures in the sky, traveled each on its own course fighting with the others in their midst as their gravitational and electromagnetic forces clashed. But drawing close to the earth, the earth now attracted them by its greater gravitation. As they neared the earth's surface, their own electro-magnetism and gravity lifted the surface of the earth's crust, causing the land to undulate as they passed over it. Above, they shone like snakes, their sounds like rumbling chariots or like the crackle of fire devouring stubble. They were like a strong people set in battle array, but they were not people. Nothing could stop them, no earthly army! An overwhelming fear fell upon all men. The like had not been seen since the days of Isaiah the prophet.

Isaiah called this army of the most high "the terrible ones."[4] He wrote the Lord's words:

> And I will hiss for them from the end of the earth:
> and, behold, they shall come with speed swiftly:
> None shall be weary or stumble among them;
> None shall slumber nor sleep;
> Neither shall the girdle of their loins be loosed,
> Nor the latchet of their shoes be broken:
> Whose arrows are sharp, and all their bows bent,
> Their horses hoofs shall be counted like flint,
> And their wheels like a whirlwind.
> Their roaring shall be like a lion…
> they shall roar like young lions…
> like the roaring of the sea:
> and if one look unto the land,
> behold darkness and sorrow; and the light is darkened in the heavens thereof.
>
> Isaiah 5:26-30

Each small, individual comet crashed down at random destroying everything near it when it hit. In the end they killed one third of the men left in the whole world, just like Revelation predicted in the sixth trumpet. But those crashing down on Iran's great plateau hit and destroyed Adoni''s army. The Chinese had not yet reached Iran's plateau.

Besides, by this time, the Chinese army had perfected their tortoise-shield defense. But the Chinese Army was saved mostly because they were still in the mountain passes south of Rasht. A few were destroyed by direct hits, but the rest reassembled once the heavenly army passed by. On they came, almost as invincible as the army in the sky. However, the Iranian Army was destroyed as well. They had set up to take out the Chinese when they emerged from the mountains onto the plateau.

When one of the helicopters saw their army being destroyed from above, it headed away from the army on the ground, reporting the damage as it went. Adoni´ ordered it to drop a single bomb on each bridge of the two great rivers of Baghdad. He didn't want to completely destroy the bridges. One span could be repaired. But it would stop an army of horsemen until he could decide what to do.

■

The Chinese, with their two-hundred-million-strong army, matched the heavenly army in the sky. Nothing stopped them, not even the great Euphrates or the Tigris Rivers. By the time they arrived in Baghdad, the rivers were no barrier. The headwaters had been cut off in the same earthquake that flattened Jerusalem and turned the mighty Euphrates River into seven streams, all heading different directions from its source in eastern Turkey. This eventually left the river channel devoid of water.

Chapter 60

The armies gathered for the last great battle—Armageddon. It was the time for the indignation of the Lord to be poured out upon all nations left upon the earth. That which had been predicted was ripe to happen. The European forces landed in Haifa once more. The oft-mentioned final battle of the East and West was finally coming to pass. Miraculously, the newly retrofitted ships from China had escaped the bombardment from the heavens and arrived safely at ports in the Persian Gulf carrying more troops and fresh horses. The great hordes pressed toward Babylon.

When the newly arrived armies joined Dehuai, he gathered all his captains and ordered the whole army through them, "I have read about this city in ancient history. It commanded a great empire in the past, one that Saddam Hussein tried to revive. I want it destroyed forever. Let no future ruler think that its glory can be restored. I want you to destroy it so completely that no one can recognize its location ever again. Let it become the habitation of the wild beasts!"

"China shall replace it in glory once we conquer the new oil fields of Israel. I want your men to tear down every wall and destroy the name of Nebuchadnezzar and Saddam Hussein from every brick."

"We will ship their treasures of antiquity in Baghdad back to China on the ships, but the gold in this city shall be yours."

With gold plentiful in the houses of the rich Iraqis, the armies went wild in their search for treasure. Adoni´'s newly refurbished palace next to the ancient city walls was literally torn apart. When they finished with it, the whole city became uninhabitable because of the destruction. The remains of Nebuchadnezzar's city had become a pile of dirt.

Another Chinese troop ship landed in Al Aqabah, carrying Vietnamese and Cambodians and their horses.

"Captain," reported King Alaham Hassih, king of Jordan, "my scouts in Aqaba report that a troop ship is unloading Asian men and their horses at our port here. (The king had moved his residence to the heights of Al Aqabah when they left Wadi Musa). "I fear that they will shut down this route for food shipments."

"Do your people have enough food to last for thirty days?"

"Oh yes, that last shipment we took is quite adequate for a month."

"Then hunker down and stay out of sight. In less than thirty days, *Yeshua* will have come, and it will be 'the end.' The scriptures say that we here are protected only twelve hundred and sixty days in the wilderness, so we will be moving back into society ourselves. I guess our purpose was to disrupt Adoni´'s food supply and maintain the life of the believers. By marking our foreheads like the temple believers did, we should be able to mingle with the population."

King Hassih, having learned to trust David, said, "Thanks for the encouragement. I'm glad these times are almost over."

The small army's first move toward the final days was to divide up their food supplies. David ordered a thirty-day food supply allotted to each family. That last successful raid on the three trucks had left plenty for all. The women, who had done the cooking, had already learned how to cook for the whole company without wasting what they had. They collectively determined the amounts according to the numbers of each family. The next step was to determine where to go.

David addressed the whole company. "We have been led and graciously supplied with care for almost three-and-a-half years by *Yeshua*, our Lord. We have miraculously escaped Adoni''s death trap. He who has begun a good work in us shall not fail us now. I suggest each family gather together for prayer and let Jehovah's Spirit tell you where to go next. I can't see us moving back into society as a body. As we each know where to go, then we will work out the logistics of how to get there. You soldiers who have no family, meet with your commanding officers—join their families for prayer and relocation."

David enlarged his own family to include the men who had faithfully served on his former intelligence team. So he needed a place to house Matza, Hillman, Feldman, and GG, as well as the five in his regular family counting himself and Rachel. Nine people was quite a large family. Then, of course, they had to consider the horses. They wouldn't want to leave them behind. However, being prime assets to the war, they would need careful consideration, lest they be commandeered by Adoni''s army.

Each group separated for prayer, some outside the warehouse and some in. Not a single person in the whole company was an unbeliever. Their experiences over the three plus years had shown all that *Yeshua* was Lord, and each had individually taken his offer of salvation and joined the family of God.

Adoni´ paced back and forth. "Ashtor!" he screamed. "Where are you? Come out of your hiding place and face me." He had sensed that Ashtor was no longer in his body.

Ra'amon came running when he heard the shouting. "What is it? What's the matter?"

"Our army, sent to stop the Chinese, has been destroyed by the small comets," he said, "*Our army*, not the Chinese.' And on top of that, I just heard that we lost three trucks to hijackers. How can that be? I thought we destroyed them. Is Ashtor in charge or not? And where is he anyway?" he snapped, one question after another. "I just want to know what's going on."

"There must be a reason," offered Ra'amon meekly.

"Reason—REASON?" he shouted. "If he expects us to fight with horses he's crazy. Where would *we* get horses?"

"Maybe he's going to wait until they come to Jerusalem, just like before."

"Maybe. At least we have fortified the hill country with gun emplacements. They've already crossed the Euphrates River. They'll be coming the same route as the Russians. And our allies are waiting for them at Megiddo."

"The reports from up north are bad. The whole area has been devastated," said Ra'amon fearfully. "What's left of Russia seems to be coming, too."

"I know, and the Chinese have already taken the oil fields in Kuwait with the troops coming by ship."

"What are we going to do?"

"We are going to go out there and lead our troops personally and wipe our enemies off the face of the earth," declared Adoni´ with fierce determination. "I will not be denied my destiny—Ashtor," he screamed again and went out in fury because he did not answer.

Chapter 61

David led his big family in their group prayer for the day. They had decided to fast for three days, each individually studying the scriptures as they went before the Lord. Today was the third day. They expected a word to be manifested to someone's spirit in their midst. But so far they had heard nothing. Finally, David in exasperation said, "Has anyone heard anything at all, a scripture, a single word, a place…anything?"

Matza spoke up, hesitant at first, "Well, I keep trying to hear something, but I really don't know what I'm listening for. I tried reading about King David, thinking that might apply somehow, and I did notice a scripture that kinda stood out…and it *was* talking about David of the scriptures, could that refer to you?

David got excited. "God can talk through the scripture in specific needs, and this is a specific need. What was the scripture?'

"I don't remember." He dropped his head into his hands. "I think it had to do with getting away from Saul."

David saw that he hurt Matza with his disappointment. He laid his hand on Matza's shoulder. "It's okay. I keep struggling with a phrase running through my mind, and all it does is frustrate me."

"What's the phrase, David? Maybe we can help you figure it out," said Rachel.

"It's 'ask what I shall give thee'… It doesn't make any sense at all.

"It sounds like King James English…Hey, maybe it's a part of a scripture. How can we find it?"

"Computer," said Malcomb, "There's an online Bible on my computer. I put it on before we left home. It has a concordance." He ran to his quarters to get it.

"Hmm, could it really have been the Lord all along, trying to tell me something?" said David. "I sure have a lot to learn about this 'hearing from the Lord' business."

"Will we be able to find the scripture I read?" asked Matza.

"If you can remember an actual word in the passage, we can. We would only have to search the first book of Samuel," said David, starting to get excited.

Malcomb rushed in, carrying his laptop. "I found it," he cried. "It's in First Kings three, verse five."

The noise of rustling pages filled the room as each hustled to find the passage in his own Bible. David found it first and began reading the whole verse aloud.

> In Gibeon the Lord appeared to Solomon in a dream by night: and God said, Ask what I shall give thee.
>
> 1 Kings 3:5

"Does anyone know where ancient Gibeon was?" asked Rachel.

Everyone looked blank, even David. "Well at least it's a place," said GG. "Read the verse before it."

David read:

> And the king went to Gibeon to sacrifice there; for that *was* the great high place: a thousand burnt offerings did Solomon offer upon that altar.
>
> 1Kings 3:4

THE END... AND A NEW BEGINNING

"Hmm, that does help," said David. "It must be on top of a mountain. It says the 'great' high place. So it's not just any high place."

Malcomb asked Matza. "What was your scripture? Did you think of a word that might be in it?"

"Yes, I believe it said something about 'escape' or maybe 'escaped.'"

Malcomb began his search. He limited it to the book of 1 Samuel, but he came up with only one verse for the word "escape." Matza shook his head. He tried the other word. Several verses came up with the word "escaped" in them. As each one was read, Matza kept shaking his head. Finally, Malcomb read 1 Samuel 19:18:

> So David fled, and escaped, and came to Samuel to Ramah, and told him all that Saul had done to him. And he and Samuel went and dwelt in Naioth.

"That's it." said Matza. "I remember thinking that it couldn't be it, because it has two places in it."

"But the first part of the verse actually applies, because David will actually flee and escape," argued Rachel.

"That's true, so that means we look at Ramah as the place. Is this a mountain?" asked GG.

"Yes!" shouted David as he jumped up. "Yes, yes, yes, it's the tallest mount around Jerusalem. It's where the prophet Samuel is buried. You can see the Mediterranean Sea to the west from there on a clear day and the whole city of Jerusalem below to the east. It's perfect, because it would put the city between us and the advancing army. Now, we must figure out the best way to get there."

Chapter 62

The sky was darkening again. Smoke lingered in the air leftover from the "terrible ones" who ravaged from the sky. That added to the ash already in the upper atmosphere from the volcanos around the world that gave the sky a gray look. But this was different somehow, a prolonged dawn that came after a full night of fighting. As the morning stretched and stretched, all during its hours the battle raged for Jerusalem. The entire Jordan Valley became the battleground as the Europeans' forward armies retreated from the Chinese armies from the east and Russia's forces from the north. The battle reached through it, extending all the way down to the newly formed volcano in Jordan. Armored vehicles had long since been abandoned. The battle was now as primitive as ancient times. The Chinese horsemen, with their skilled swordsmen ruthlessly cutting their way, suddenly turned west to ascend to Jerusalem. Blood flowed like a great river basin with many tributaries, collecting from dozens of separate skirmishes. Adoni´'s army fell back to the outskirts of the city. He still had his gun emplacements. They spoke with the sound of firepower in the dim visibility streaking the air with even more smoke. But they did little to stop the Chinese. On they came, ascending the barren mounts of the Judean Desert just below Jerusalem on their horses, ignoring the road where the guns defended. The Judean wilderness was no obstacle to this army. Unlike the Russian invaders earlier, they climbed the ravines and ascended like an unstoppable tsunami wave flowing over the land to the outskirts of the city. They never hesitated until they had taken the eastern half of the city, when they stopped to pillage and ravish the women.

Then came the first indication of change. The sky brightened and more armies appeared in the sky afar off. Contrary to the former armies, these were not made of celestial matter—comet dust and debris forming weird pictures in the sky—but these were the spiritual armies of *Yeshua*. Defying gravity, they rode on white horses across the distant sky, the clouds under the horse's hooves displayed as the dust of heaven. On they came, visibly announcing the final judgment that descended from God's heaven as long ago predicted.

Earlier that morning the small army that surrounded David was as ready as they would ever be. His small mounted army had not joined the battle yet but had been preparing themselves by forging swords to use with army body armor during these last days. They had occupied much of the time learning how to use the swords. It had been nearly a month since they left Petra. Only one day remained until the end. Two days earlier word came that the Chinese had reached the Mt. of Olives. David sent out a call to collect his army. Most who responded were descendents of Judah, whether they knew it or not. Many former army men still had their conventional firearms. David fasted as he waited for all to gather. He looked to the scripture for a word of encouragement for his troops.

The next morning, Malcomb, who had used his telescope from the top story of the building at Samuel's grave to watch the Chinese take half the city, said to David, "They have stopped fighting, and now they are ravishing the women of the city. I could see them entering the houses, dragging women with them. They seemed to be overcome by strong spirits of lust. It's almost like they're in a frenzy."

"Such passions will distract them. It will give us an advantage. We can't wait any longer," said David.

After the army of barely fifty men assembled, David said, "It will have to be a fight by faith, trusting in our God as ancient King David did. We are not skilled enough as swordsman to stand as a primitive army on our own. The Chinese have had vast experience in primitive warfare by this time. Nevertheless, God used a mere three hundred men with Gideon to rout thousands."

A strange sight they were that morning in the dim light. They brandished handmade swords accompanied by modern Israeli battle helmets and body armor, an ill-equipped army at best.

After leading his men in prayer for the battle ahead, David read the portion the Lord had given him that day before from Psalm 35 for encouragement to his men.

> Plead *my cause*, O Lord, with them that strive with me: fight against them that fight against me.
>
> Take hold of shield and buckler, and stand up for mine help.
>
> Draw out also the spear, and stop *the way* against them that persecute me: say unto my soul, I *am* thy salvation.
>
> Let them be confounded and put to shame that seek after my soul: let them be turned back and brought to confusion that devise my hurt.
>
> Let them be as chaff before the wind: and let the angel of the Lord chase *them*.

Let their way be dark and slippery: and let the angel of the Lord persecute them.

For without cause have they hid for me their net *in* a pit, *which* without cause they have digged for my soul.

Let destruction come upon him at unawares; and let his net that he hath hid catch himself: into that very destruction let him fall.

And my soul shall be joyful in the Lord: it shall rejoice in his salvation.

Psalm 35

After closing his Bible and handing it off to Rachel, David broke out singing in a high praise song in his fine baritone voice; others began to join in. After finishing the song, David said, "Let's mount up."

Chapter 63

A great light flashed across the darkened sky all the way from the east to the west, blinding their eyes.

"All I can see is a blank yellow screen in my eye," cried Feldman. Everyone concurred.

The ground began to quiver under their feet, and their horses staggered sideways.

"Dismount and force your horses to the ground," yelled David, trying to be heard over the clamor of the effects of the earthquake.

"We can't afford any broken legs on our mounts. They're scared and probably as blinded as we are." He pulled down on the bridle, forcing his horse down to the ground.

The wild-eyed beasts deferred to their riders, going down in obedience, probably sensing human protection. Seconds later, when everyone's eyes finally adjusted back to normal and the tremors subsided, they rose carefully to their feet.

"Look at that," Jonathon cried, pointing to the sky. "The sun is going crazy."

They all looked up and gasped. The sun's muted solar disc showed through the haze and zigzagged, lurching first one way and then the other. They all watched in astonishment. The ground was still shaking some. Then they saw it! The dragon had returned to the vicinity of the earth.

"How can that be?" said Hillman.

Then the hills and valleys that made up the city below began to move, undulating like a flag rippling in a breeze. Eventually, the ground leveled out into a plain below them, like flour settles in a sieve when shaken.

"God's destroying our eternal city!" cried out Hillman.

"No!" said David. "Keep your eye on the Mount of Olives."

The mountain shuddered a moment, then ripped apart with suddenness like a rubber band, being stretched to its limits, snaps, sliding the left side of the mountain north and the right side south. It left a wide, gaping valley all the way through the Judean desert. The temple mound, formerly just across the Kidron Valley from it, also separated from Mt. Zion below, lifting up Zion slightly higher than where the unfinished temple had stood.

They were all on the ground again from a quick-following aftershock. David looked around. "Everyone okay?" he asked.

A chorus answered, "Yeah."

"Captain, you knew that would happen, didn't you? Is it in the Bible somewhere?" asked Matza, after rising to his feet again.

"Yes, it's in the Zechariah chapter 14. It tells of the time when the Lord sets his feet on the mountain. Of course, it's rhetorical writing, showing it is God who is making the changes."

"Did he actually put his feet on the mountain?" asked Hillman.

"I don't know, but the mountain split just like Zechariah predicted."

"But what made the sun move like that?" asked Matza.

"The sun didn't move," said Malcomb, matter-of-factly adopting his studious manner. "It would not be possible for us to see the sun move."

"But we saw it move," insisted Matza.

"No, it was the earth that moved. The body in space under the dragon shape must have pulled the earth out of its regular orbit." said Malcomb. "We are the ones that zigzagged."

David spoke up. "I seem to remember a passage in Isaiah 13 that mentions the earth running helter-skelter like an untamed sheep. You may be right, Malcomb. That same passage also says the heavens shall shake, and the earth remove out of her place. It could be that's what we just saw. The heavens would appear to shake if the earth moved erratically."

"Now what?" said Jonathan, pointing to the south. Again, everyone looked in that direction. They saw what looked to be two peaked mountains of glass reflecting rays of the late-rising sun. The mountains were tall, standing many times the height of the normal mountains that rim the Dead Sea valley, which they could barely see from their height. The residual light reflecting off the glass-like mountains made it possible.

"What now?" various ones wondered aloud. They looked first to David and then to Malcomb, who appeared to have all the answers. "Do the scriptures have anything to say about that, Captain?"

"I don't know," said David, pondering the strange sight with a wrinkled brow. "Could it be water?"

"Yes," Malcomb shouted, "It must be water—more likely ocean water—gigantic tides from the seas in the area drawn up by the gravitational pull of the 'dragon-like body' because it is so close to the earth," reasoned Malcomb in awe.

"But…" protested Matza, "those mountains have to be miles high."[5]

The rest listened, waiting for Malcomb to explain further. They already hung on his every word as he knew enough from his studies to explain what was happening.

"So, what do you mean by tides?" Feldman finally asked Malcomb.

"Ginsberg's Legends, quoted from the Jewish Midrashim, tell about the waters of the Red Sea at the exodus standing in heaps piled up to the height of sixteen hundred miles. A great exaggeration, no doubt, but even older traditions say the waters of the Red Sea looked like glass, solid and massive. They may have looked something like that—shiny. A heavenly body influenced the earth in that day too."

Amid stupendous sound, the Lord and his army appeared between the glassy mountains, descending from the clouds above. It sounded like a hundred pipe organs playing all at once as the earth rumbled the deep bass notes, while the comet sent forth trumpeted blasts of high notes. The comet body sang to the earth and vice versa in the music of the spheres, while the glory of the Lord reflected off the mountains, lighting up the whole sky. Suddenly a bolt of lightning shot down the arm of the mighty one of Israel, and *Yeshua's* voice thundered, "The Assyrian shall be beaten down, smote with the rod in my hand." Then meteorites began to fall, some aerolites[5] made of rock rather than metallic objects, and some great chunks of ice weighing a hundred pounds or more.

Chapter 64

Hearing *Yeshua's* words, David and his men stood staring in awe. Then suddenly David and his men felt a dropping sensation of their stomachs, like when they drove over a sharp hill at a fast speed. Their whole mountain dropping caused the feeling. They all laughed as the pleasure of it raised their spirits.

David received a strong impression to go to the Temple Mount. It was like that "word" he received after the battle in Petra, a sure knowledge of direction.

"Mount up," he commanded. "Let's get over to the Temple Mount. *Yeshua* is coming. We don't want to miss his descent."

As they started down their no-longer-so-high hill, they saw the huge armies on white horses drawing closer to Israel. "That's why the Lord wants us to go down now. We may be able to see the battle as his army comes to destroy the nations gathered at Armageddon. He will defeat all the nations at the same time, establishing his dominion over all," said Matza.

"Yes," said David. "As the days of the Beast's rule have drawn to the end, I have been studying the scriptures on the Lord's return. Moses predicted it in Deuteronomy 33. See that fiery flash of red? That's probably evidence of his 'rod of iron,' spoken of as belonging to the child of the woman that we saw in the sign in the sky. Some of you remember studying about that at my father's house three years ago. The rod of iron represents the unbending righteousness of his law. Revelation also tells us that his weapon of destruction is the double-edged sword in his mouth, the 'Word' of God. He will speak the judgment and the armies will die, but the inflexibleness of his righteous law gives him the right to judge them with death, an absolute justice for fighting against the Lord of heaven and earth."

At his bold proclamation, the whole band of soldiers began to praise *Yeshua*. They had escaped this absolute judgment by his grace. As they praised him in a loud voice, the Holy Spirit overshadowed them. Spontaneously they burst forth with song, each singing his own song (a new song never sung before), inspired by the Spirit. Suddenly, they realized they were standing on the Temple Mount. The Holy Spirit, inhabiting their praises, had swept them up in an instant and transported them in the same manner as the Temple Mount faithful had been brought to Petra.

Chapter 65

Lin Yiang Dehuai lost track of his generals; the heavenly bombardment had severed their communications. His army scattered when they thought they had won, and they stopped to pillage and rape as usual. Dehuai, having been informed earlier that the strength of Adoni´ came from his idol god, had determined to take the Temple Mount and destroy the image. He and fifty of his men had made it across the Kidron Valley to the Temple Mount just before the Mt. of Olives split. They were in the process of pounding the dragon image to powder when suddenly a band of horsemen stood barely one hundred feet away. Behind the small army, a great army in the sky grew closer and closer. *Do they not see that we have destroyed the image of their dragon god?* Dehuai thought. However, for the moment he would deal with this paltry band of horsemen. "Mount up!" he commanded.

The leader of the band called out in a loud voice. "We come against you in the name of *Yeshua*, the creator and ruler of the universe."

How could he understand his words? thought Lin Yiang. Then he realized he was not fighting just men. Seated behind each man on horseback was a huge bright creature carrying a sword greater than any he had *ever* seen. His belly began to tremble; his lips quivered; his bones rotted into weakness. He looked at his men and saw that they expressed the same fear. The leader of the horsemen gave a shout, and the small band advanced.

Again the leader shouted. "You have dared to attack God's land that he gave to us Jews. You are doomed." On they came.

Duduai fought back, weak as a woman against an invincible army. His men fell all around him. Finally, he stood alone against the leader, expecting death at any moment. The captain of the army commanded him. "Lay down your weapon! You are captive of the Army of the Lord!" Duduai obeyed, and they bound him up, a captive of their small war.

When the meteorites began to fall, Adoni´ thought that finally Ashtor was coming to their rescue. But then he noticed the heavenly army through the falling stones. Ashtor suddenly appeared at his side and commanded him, saying, "You'd better turn your forces on them, because that is *Yeshua* and his armies, and if they win, the kingdom will not be yours."

"Where is your power?" demanded Adoni´.

"I will help you, but you need the Chinese to help you too. Remember the prayer when we defeated the two prophets?"

"Yes."

"Well, my spiritual forces need you to join with us if we are to win. I have a great army in the sky as well, your fellow Nephilim. We have been waiting for this showdown. Remember, I have angels too." At his words a soldier stepped forward. "He is one of mine. Send him."

Adoni´ sent the messenger to the Chinese. Ashtor's angel appeared to General Peng Lu Zedong in the glorious guise of a mighty one. He addressed the commander in his own Chinese dialect. "We must call a truce between our two armies and join together against a greater threat to the earth. An army from outer space invades us. Come join us and let's thrust these aliens from the earth, else we shall all be slaves."

Zedong ordered his army to turn their weapons heavenward. They turned from fighting Adoni''s army and aimed their remaining missiles (their deadly arrows) toward the sky. In response a great trumpet sounded, and the heavens were laced with crackling lightning and blasts of lighted methane came toward the ground. Thunder rumbled, sounding louder and louder, and then the serious hail began to fall. Lightning shone down the arm of *Yeshua*; again it thundered. It was the voice of the returning King. Men shook their fists at the heavens and blasphemed the Hebrew God.

The Chinese men and horses that were originally fighting against Jerusalem and had turned to fight the heavenly army were suddenly blinded, and men screamed as one by one their flesh ran and consumed away as melting wax. First, their eyes melted and flowed down their cheeks, then the rest of the flesh consumed away from the bones. It was happening exactly as the prophet Zechariah had predicted:

> And this shall be the plague wherewith the LORD will smite all the people that have fought *against* Jerusalem; Their flesh shall consume away while they stand upon their feet, and their eyes shall consume away in their holes, and their tongue shall consume away in their mouth.
>
> And it shall come to pass in that day, *that* a great tumult from the LORD shall be among them; and they shall lay hold every one on the hand of his neighbour, and his hand shall rise up against the hand of his neighbour.
>
> Zechariah 14:12,13 KJV Emphasis added

Terror gripped Adoni''s army who watched the Chinese army destroy each other, and they fled. In their haste, many fell into small sand pits created by the loose surface earth and its movement. As they scrambled out, some were covered by falling sheets of very thin semi-molten metal—like metal in smelting furnaces—fiery streams falling from the sky which enveloped them. In the confusion their armies began to fight one another just as the Russians and Chinese had done.

After about an hour the hail stopped. The spectacle in the sky, seen from the ground, grew even more ominous. The heavens themselves continued back and forth as stars seemed to zigzag; the smoke and ashes suspended in space temporarily cleared by the erratic movement of the earth out of its orbit. Suddenly, out of the swirling darkness came a very bright cloud illuminated by a gigantic fireball that seemed to pulsate. As it came closer, a chariot appeared carrying the throne of heaven. It descended, a large expanse of blue, like a crystal of sapphire formed the floor. Under the crystal at each of its square corners stood four cherubim flanked by special wheels (a wheel within a wheel, situated perpendicularly to each other). The wheels emitted a gentle light the color of aquamarine beryl, and these were ringed with eyes; the wheels themselves did not turn but rather floated downward. The figure seated on the throne was enveloped in the amber of flames.

Every eye saw him and began to wail. It was not unexpected. They had known for centuries that the religious people expected it *someday*. Because of all the catastrophes, they even conceded it might be possible, but now—*now* it was actually happening. The Hebrew God was coming to his earth.

They continued to wail until the thunderous roar of the King had slain every remaining soldier who was still fighting, and invited fowls to his supper. Shortly his feet would touch the soil.

David and his men watched in awe as the sky drew dark from great flocks of birds descending upon the battlefields. His men had cleared the area on Zion of the enemy and were watching the chariot descend toward earth when a flock of eagles and vultures descended upon the men they had slain. Then the final earthquake hit. The land around them moved exceedingly again and lifted. From the Kidron Valley west the whole city was leveled. Valleys and vales lifted—the Hinnon Valley and the Tyropean Valley—plus every valley south almost to Bethlehem, making a wide plain filled with rubble as the rest of the city fell. North of the Temple Mount the city divided, probably weakened as a result of the movement of the Mount of Olives. But the land on the north side of the divide also lifted up to the same level as the Temple Mount as far as Geba.[5]

Chapter 66

With all that was happening close by, the people hadn't noticed that the "heavenly rod" (God's instrument for judging the earth), the body in space, had come close to the earth again closer than ever before.

It appeared just north of Jerusalem, about fourteen miles away. An appendage of dragon body dropped down and connected to the earth with a giant Birkland current of plasma. Actually, the connection joining the two bodies in a tremendous display of lightning was a stationary thunderbolt.

At first, before the earthquake, David's men heard a loud sizzling, crackling kind of noise. Looking to the source, they saw the thunderbolt attached to the ground further north. Then they all tumbled to the ground.

Yeshua's great rod of judgment brought against the earth during the Day of the Lord, the body forming the dragon image in the sky, shot one last parting shot to the earth. A great thunderbolt struck the earth at Bethel. It shimmered brightly for over twenty minutes before yanking a portion of the ground—straight up—forming a flat-topped mountain several hundreds of dunums across that stood erect a thousand or so feet above the surrounding hills. It looked like one of the giant *tipuis* of Venezuela,[6] particularly like La Gran

Saban where Angel Falls, the highest waterfall on the earth, cascades from its heights. The new mountain also had a great falls, forming a river flowing toward the Jordan Valley from the bottom of the mountain and another flowing to Jerusalem. But the men on Zion could not see that detail. What they did see was water flowing from the north onto the plain that the city had become. When it reached what was now the center of the plain, it split and half went east into the old Jordan Valley, and the other half went west toward a smaller Mediterranean Sea. Thus, Jerusalem became "unto the Lord a city of broad rivers upon which no ship could sail," as Isaiah had said. The sound of them rippled over the rubble they covered.

Amazed by the sight, they all began to exclaim over the glorious view. Matza, curious to know what he saw and confident that David would know, said, "David what is that?" pointing to the new mountain. "And where did all this water come from?"

"It must be the new Temple Mount. It's so majestic and unique. Isaiah speaks of it standing erect. Ezekiel describes the temple that *Yeshua* will build on its top. According to him, the river of life will flow from it to all the earth." But before they could absorb David's words, a new spectacle occurred.

The chariot of fire had stopped midair, not directly overhead, but at a distance, so that myriads of angels could be seen standing round about the throne, serving the Lord.

At the brightness of the spectacle, Duduai collapsed to the ground as a dead man, unnoticed as the other men bowed themselves to the ground, unable to bear the sight because of its brightness. David, however, was so absorbed with what he saw, his eyes never wavered from the glory.

He saw a figure on the throne. He wore a pure white garment, and his hair was white like wool. Now in close proximity to the earth, judgment fire issued forth from the chariot all around him.

But the light-blue-green-colored chariot wheels were now hidden under flames of fire. Shortly the whole plain of the heavenly scene filled with angelic beings. An angel touched David's shoulder and said, "Look, your Messiah returns."

David looked above the scene, seeing a single bright spot descending in bright clouds. As soon as the spot reached the plain of the throne, the shimmering light encasing the throngs of angelic beings parted and made a path that led to the chariot throne. Though the throne and the rest of the chariot still leaped with flames, David could see the figure there clearly now. He was clothed in a dazzling white garment, and his hair was like an English judge's wig, white and as wool. *Yeshua* presented a vast contrast to the one on the throne. He also wore a robe of white but the whole lower portion of his garment was stained red like one who treads the winepress at harvest time. His hair was black as a raven. He approached the flaming throne.

"The writer of Hebrews was right when he said, 'Our God *is* a consuming fire,'" said David to himself. "How privileged I am to see this sight!" *Is the one on the throne God the Father?* he puzzled to himself.

An angel nearby said to him, "The one on the throne is the Ancient of Days. *Yeshua* and he are one."

Yeshua stood before the throne. Several angels came forth, carrying huge scrolls. Then the Ancient of Days reached out his hand to *Yeshua* and said, "Unto you I give all my dominion over the earth, all glory, and you shall reign in righteousness as the man that you have become. All nations, peoples, and languages shall serve you. Behold, I give you a kingdom that shall never end. Therefore, the judgment of the wicked is now in your hands, and here are the records of their deeds. You will perform this judgment for a thousand years until all who will ever oppose me are born. After the resurrection and judgment of all men who have rejected me, you will rule for eternity."

With those words the Ancient of Days reached out and touched *Yeshua*, and immediately they became one in the sight of those present. The chariot disappeared, and the hair of *Yeshua* took on the appearance of judge, white like the Ancient of Days. In the place of the chariot throne was a white, marble-like platform with a throne upon it and twenty-four seats, set in a semi-circle, around it. *Yeshua's* first command was to the angels. "Sound the trumpet and gather my own from the four winds and every part of heaven." Then he jangled some keys in his possession.

David gasped as he saw his own father stand before the temporary throne along with thousands of others that had been martyred by the "Beast." *Were those the keys of death and hell spoken of in the Revelation? Was he seeing his father after resurrection just as he had seen Jesse? If so, it was miraculous indeed to see his father singled out of thousands.* Then David heard the words, "The time for judgment has come." At that the heavenly vision disappeared.

For the first time David realized that his men and Duduai were lying on the ground unconscious. *Did they not see what I saw?* he wondered. The angel standing by him touched his arm. "Look up, David, your Messiah comes to earth."

David shouted to the others, "Get up. *Yeshua* is coming!"

"Where?" asked Matza.

"Up there," replied David. "See, in those clouds."

Sure enough, they could see a man descending in white clouds that stood out against the dismal sky surrounding him.

"But what happened to the armies and his horse? He was on a horse before," said Hillman.

"I don't know," said David. "Maybe he doesn't need a horse now that the war is over. Horses in scripture speak of war. Here he comes, just like the book of Acts tells us. He left the earth before by ascending into the clouds.[7] Now he's returning the same way."

THE END... AND A NEW BEGINNING

The second *Yeshua* touched Mt. Zion, the throne reappeared not in vision as before, but in actuality. Another order went out to the angels. "Take prisoners of all living who opposed me and shut them up until the judgment. Shut up the rest of the wicked left in Israel in prisons as well. Fill up all the caves, cisterns, or places of confinement and set guards. Then serve food to my weary ones who are scattered abroad by this war." He continued to give orders to his angels including the order to finish leveling the plain that was now Jerusalem.

Then the angels began to round up the living remnant, those of the people who had opposed God. An angel approached David's band. He reached for Duduai's arm and said, "I'll just take this fellow off your hands."

"What will you do with him?" asked David, out of curiosity.

"Put him in the bundle of the kings," said the angel.

"Bundle?"

"Are you familiar with the parable of the wheat and the tares?"

"Yes," David's eyes flickered with understanding. "You're saying he will be put with all the other kings of the earth?"

"Yes, and then carried to the fire after his judgment, along with the rest."

Duduai stood trembling. From the confusion registered on his face, he clearly couldn't understand Hebrew. Apparently astonished by the awesome display of God's power, he had not even tried to escape. Then the angel stripped off the gold on Duduai's armor and adornment and handed it to David. "Your spoils for conquering this mighty warrior," he said to David.

"But..." stammered David, "it was the power of the Lord."

"You were his instrument," he replied. "It is written that your people will spoil their enemies at this time."[8]

"The rest of you may take the spoil from the dead. Whatever you find of value you may keep, but remember, whenever *Yeshua* builds his temple, you will be expected to give freely of your gold for its adornment. Search the Chinese army first. For they have plundered all the way across their journey. They are rich with gold." That said, he took Duduai, started to rise, and promptly disappeared.

Then King *Yeshua* called David Solomon to come before him. David approached with awe and trepidation through the parting crowd. He knelt at the throne. "My son, I am well pleased with your service to my people. But now you must return to them and tell them what you have seen. My angels will serve them food, and my Spirit will heal their wounds. I will call for you before the judgment of the wicked begins." And with that he dismissed David, who returned to his brothers and his men.

After the throne disappeared, David said to his men, "Time for you to gather your share of the spoils. It won't be fun since the birds have been at them, but the rewards should compensate. May the Lord grant that we all go back to Mt. Samuel with riches for our future."

Chapter 67

Adoni´ escaped the battle without a scratch. Ra'amon did not fare so well. A sword had slashed his right side, blinding his right eye and cutting off his right arm just below the elbow. He was carried to Hadassah Hospital, which had escaped destruction, to be treated.

Adoni´ saw the chariot of fire coming. *Finally Ashtor is coming to set things right. It's about time too. At least the enemy armies had been destroyed. What is left will surely be subject to me, and we can rebuild the world.*

The men he led stood near him also watching, but they did not look confident that Ashtor rode the chariot. Fear registered on their faces, and they began to cry in disappointment.

"What are you afraid of?" demanded Adoni´, troubled that they should doubt his control of the situation.

"That's not Ashtor. That's Jehovah, the God of the Jewish scriptures."

"Why do you say that?"

"Because he's the one with the chariot of fire." And with that they abandoned him and fled.

Adoni´ frowned. *Is it possible?* he said to himself as he watched them go. But before they got out of sight, fire dropped from heaven and engulfed them. *What was going on here? Where were his fellow Nephilim he had been promised?*

Then strong hands grasped him and bound him with strong chains.

"Who are you? What are you doing?" he cried, struggling. "Don't you know who *I* am?"

"We know. The end has come. Your time is up. The Lord God Almighty of Israel allotted you twelve hundred and ninety days to rule. It's over."

His mouth was shut; he couldn't even stammer. He was led to a dry cistern and shut up along with the rest of his rulers over districts and government departments. Shortly, Ra'amon was incarcerated in the same prison. *Yeshua* had healed his wounds. He also was speechless, at least at first.

Rachel saw them coming. She stuck her head in the doorway to the cave and called to Esther and Sarah, "They're back. But for some reason they are not riding their horses, and they are all carrying duffle bags." Then she ran down the slight slope that was left of the great high place as fast as she could go. When David saw her coming, he set down his bag and broke from the others, running to meet her.

"*Hamoodah*," he cried as he picked her up and whirled her around.

"Is it over, David?" she asked.

"It's over," he said with finality. Then he added excitedly, "I saw the Lord, Rachel."

"Really? All we could see from here was a ball of fire descend, but then the ground began to shake so violently, we fell down. After that we didn't see it anymore. Was that *Yeshua*?" Rachel asked.

"I don't know quite how to explain it. The fireball you saw was his chariot, which stopped midair above Zion where we were."

Yes," said Jonathon, interrupting. "We all fell because of the power of God. We fell on our faces."

"No, I didn't fall. Only the rest of you," said David. "I saw two figures, one on the throne, which was in the middle of the chariot, and one coming down in clouds."

"Which was *Yeshua*?"

"I'm not sure, both maybe, because as soon as the one on the throne spoke to the one coming in the clouds, they became one. An angel told me that the one on the throne was the Ancient of Days. I guess I saw what the prophet Daniel saw."

"Did you see the Messiah, David? What did he look like?" interrupted Sarah, all out of breath from running down the grade.

"Yes, do tell us," cried Rachel.

"Oh, he didn't look the same at all. When we saw him the first time, he was in his humiliation. But when he returned, he was in his glory. Even so, his garment was stained with blood below the waist down until he united with the Ancient of Days."

"From his treading the wine press alone," commented Rachel thoughtfully.

"From *Yesha'yahu*?"[9]

"Yes, and the wine press was the whole Jordan valley."

"Wait a minute, David!" exclaimed Malcomb. "Are you saying you saw a *vision*?"

David stopped talking for a minute. "I guess I did…What were you saying Rachel?"

"Have you seen what happen to the Jordan Valley since the earthquake?"

"No, we've been too busy dealing with the army on Mt. Zion."

"Well, we watched from the upper story of Samuel's tomb. The southern valley is full of water. The Arabah must have sunk and let the sea in from Eilat. Come see."

The whole group climbed the stairs to see the new spectacle. The first men up crowded around the windows, expressing surprise over the change. The dry, barren canyon east of Jerusalem, that held the former Dead Sea, shimmered with water.

"I wonder what other changes were made to the earth's surface?" David gazed in wonder at the large blue sea that now entered the *wadis* of the Judean Desert and covered all of the desert below sea level.

By this time the rest of the men had climbed upstairs. They pressed to the windows. "Hey, look what happened to the Dead Sea Valley! It's a sea," said Jonathan. "But look, the upper valley must have been raised. It used to be under sea level all the way to the Sea of Galilee."

"Our cities on the plateau could become ports. Who would ever have believed it?" exclaimed Matza.

"How did you fare here at Mt. Samuel, Rachel?" asked Hillman.

"David's mother and I didn't have any trouble, but Sarah fell hard in that last earthquake and broke her wrist."

David frowned. "A bad break?" he asked.

"It was at the time, and she was in a great deal of pain. But then later it healed up completely. I suppose *Yeshua* must have healed all his people after his return. Isn't there a scripture that says that somewhere?"

"I'm not familiar with it if there is."

"I'm sure I read it somewhere in the Psalms. I used to read them a lot when I was separated from everyone. It was the only comfort I could find."

"Rachel, *Yeshua* called David up and spoke to him," said Malcomb.

"Dav-id! We've been talking all this time and you didn't tell me?"

He laughed at her reaction and said, "Usually you read my thoughts. But then you were full of questions."

"Well, what did he say to you?"

"He just thanked me for taking care of his people and told me to tell the rest of you what I saw. He also said he would call me back later. Oh, and something else I forgot to tell you."

"What now?"

"I saw my abba, standing before the throne along with the others who were beheaded by Adoni´ just like I saw Jesse that other day."

"Did you get to talk to him?"

"No. It was in the vision I saw in the sky."

"Guess what else," said Malcomb, his eyes twinkling. "We are all *rich!*"

"What?" asked Rachel, puzzled.

"Spoil!" shouted Jonathon.

"We brought all we could carry," said Malcomb

Matza chipped in. "Yes, and our poor horses could hardly walk we have such a load."

"Load of what?" asked Rachel.

"Gold!" they all shouted.

GG laughed as he said, "The Chinese collected gold all the way from China just to bring it to us Jews. We are rich as Croesus!"

"Come, let's go tell Esther everything," said Rachel. *Hmm, with all that gold will David be able to build me a nest now so we can get married?* she thought.

Chapter 68

The heavens were still darkly veiled even though the Lord had returned to earth. The rearranging of the earth's crust had touched off many more volcanoes. Their ash had filled the skies. It was depressing, this gloom. It matched the mood of those imprisoned.

That evening Adoni´ paced back and forth in his cistern cell. A fury had taken hold of him. *Where was Ashtor? And why didn't he come to my rescue when those strong men appeared?* Suddenly, he had company. Ra'amon stood before him whole, his eyes full of contempt. "You are *not* the Messiah. *You* are an impostor," he accused.

"What *are* you talking about?" asked Adoni´.

"I have seen the real Messiah. He is the one who healed me and delivered me from all your demons."

"Well, if you are *all that* close to him, how come *you* are in *here*?" he asked with a caustic tone.

"I don't know," he said puzzled. "Perhaps to confront you. One minute I was in the hospital where he had just healed me, and the next I am here."

"If what you say is true, *which I doubt* because *you* are so easily deceived. So how can *I* believe *you*? Nevertheless, if we did anything wrong, you are just as guilty as I am. We did everything together. So don't go painting yourself lily white."

"No, no, you gave all the orders. Besides, you deceived me into thinking *you* were the Messiah."

"Well, if I'm not the Messiah, then who is Ashtor?"

"*Goo-od* question."

In the night David was awakened by a touch to his shoulder. A shining creature stood by his side. He said, "David, the Lord requires your presence at Mt. Zion first thing in the morning. Half asleep, David nodded his assent. Then he drifted off to sleep again.

The next morning he told Rachel, "I had a wonderful dream last night. An angel told me to go up to Zion to see *Yeshua*."

"Oh, can I go with you?"

"Not this time, *Hamoodah*. We'd better not presume upon the Lord. I'm sure you will see him soon," he said with compassion, knowing how much she longed to see him.

David left in high spirits on his horse. On the way he saw how the people were coping with the loss of shelter. Fortunately, the disaster had happened in the early fall, so living outside was not that difficult yet. He was grateful that the faithful at Mt. Samuel had taken them in, finding a place for them all in the caves under the mount.

When he arrived, Mount Zion was empty except for a small crowd of people milling around. Had they been called too? Presently *Yeshua* materialized at the temporary throne and beckoned for everyone to come close. Angels moved through the crowd and separated them into even smaller groups.

That finished, *Yeshua* spoke. "I called you here today to get started on building an arena in which to hold a judgment. I want my people to see the judgment of the guilty in person, therefore the blessed living will view the damned living, judged. I want them to see that wickedness has its just reward. I want everyone to see how righteousness rules and begin to understand justice."

"This will also be an exercise of learning how to work together. Instead of each family struggling alone, in this vast devastation, you will join together in purpose and direction, fellowshipping as you work on this project first. By this exercise you will learn how to build your own communities when the time comes. I will supply your needs for living. I will also generate moderate weather. You will learn to trust my direction through the leaders I have chosen. We will rebuild everything on the earth eventually, but first we have to take care of the unfinished business of the old world before we rebuild the new.

"No one who is rebellious or defiled will enter my kingdom. I have rearranged the surface of the earth—made a new earth as I promised. Now I will renew the inhabitants by purging out the wicked from among you through what the apostle Peter called the judgment of the quick."

David thought in his heart, *How wise he is to let the people of this new earth know his justice and power to execute it. They will know from the beginning how important it is to obey.*

Yeshua motioned to an angel, who in turn brought forth a stack of large envelopes and placed them on a small table in front of him. "I have chosen each of you because of your abilities," he continued. "These packets show where all the materials you will need may be found. Angels will assist you in your tasks. Now, those of you in transportation come forth and receive your written orders. Included in the orders are maps of where to find the vehicles and the fuel, which I have reserved for this operation."

"But won't they belong to someone?" asked one of the transportation committee.

"If anyone asked what you are doing, just tell them the Lord has need of it. Most of the owners of these vehicles are dead, or as in the case the army equipment, it has been abandoned."

Next, he called up workmen in the construction trade and to them he said, "You who have men in your former companies, gather them, plus anyone else who is able to work, and be ready to build as soon as lumber men find the timber I have reserved for this purpose."

On they came, each trade necessary to erect the temporary structure. Even communications experts were ordered to supply short-wave radios for the projects, to coordinate between craftsmen who were out of the city gathering materials and those inside applying their various skills.

David began to wonder what he had to do with all this. He was not a construction man or a craftsman in any field. Surely, *Yeshua* did not need security with all the angels around. Last of all, David was called up.

"David, you have proven yourself an able leader with a real heart for the people. I am putting you in charge of this project. You will coordinate the crafts and get everyone organized to work. I will send you men from the surrounding countryside. After you finish the structure, the excess lumber will be used to build a new city. Even the lumber in the structure can be torn down later and reused. There is plenty of building stone available, but we will need wood to finish the interiors."

"But I know nothing of construction, my Lord," he protested.

"You know how to direct people. The craftsmen know their crafts, and they will help you with their expertise. We will set you up a temporary office right here. Transportation already has orders to provide you with a vehicle with which to travel back and forth. I want this structure built in three weeks. While you are getting the arena built, the angels will be gathering the guilty to be judged."

THE END... AND A NEW BEGINNING

Three weeks! How can we do this in three weeks? But of course if the Lord says it can be done, it can be done, thought David to himself. Then he saw *Yeshua* smile and realized the thoughts of his heart were open to the Lord. David blushed. At this *Yeshua* nodded. David was used to communicating with the Lord by his spirit through prayer. Being able to see Him and talk on a visible plane seemed strange. Yet spiritually speaking, nothing had changed, except faith was turned to sight.

After handing out orders to all the men present, along with maps and blueprints, he addressed the whole crowd. "I will finish the judgment of the living forty-five days from yesterday as has been prophesied,[10] after you have completed the structure." Following that, he disappeared.

Chapter 69

After *Yeshua* left, David conferred with the leader of each craft to know what he could expect from him. Each man handed him a duplicate of his orders that had been marked with his name on them.

Looking over the blueprint, David determined that it was a simple structure consisting mainly of bleachers. The plans called for it to be nearly circular, extending from each side of the temporary throne. Loudspeakers would be placed evenly around the whole area of Zion where formerly the tent had stood with the ark. It was not dissimilar to a baseball park or an ancient amphitheater, except it did not rise to their heights as it was made of wood and temporary. Besides, the area in front of the throne was not as large as a playing field. A giant screen, such as those used for replays in ball parks, would be situated far above the judgment seat for all to see and hear the judgment rendered up close. The same would be broadcast to where such technologies still existed. The communications committee was in charge of that.

David marveled at the precise plans of the Lord, Not so much the architecture but the preservation of what was needed to build the structure. Here in Jerusalem lay power tools, which according to the plans had escaped harm under the rubble. Further north in

Lebanon were whole forests that somehow escaped the fires. The power plant that supplied Jerusalem with electricity was still intact. Of course, all the wires were down, but the plans called for logs and finished lumber to be cut at the power plant itself and hauled to the site as a prefab. Coordinated properly, the whole structure, even at such an enormous size, would go up quickly if they had the manpower.

He could see the biggest problem would be getting started. He met with the transportation crew first. While the vehicles were being rounded up, he advised the construction crews to locate their tools and have them ready to be taken to the power plant. Electricians were called upon to wire up work stations for power saws and planers. Regular sawmills were also set up at the site. Although they didn't need electric power, since they ran on gasoline, which was still available in Israel because of their recent oil discoveries. They saved extra transportation and time by having them close.

David realized that with the lumber being cut and prepared by professionals, anyone who could drive a nail could help erect the structure so long as they had competent supervision. Thus he had all the craftsmen enlist their neighbors, and every hammer left in Israel was commandeered for the erection. Having made a start, David returned home in his assigned vehicle, an army jeep. He called to his horse in Yiddish, saying, "Come on big fellow. Let's go home."

—

Rachel had been anxiously watching for David's return. *Why was he not back? What had the Lord wanted?* The hours dragged by. She had expected just a brief meeting, but it took all day. Finally, at dusk she saw an army jeep crawling up the torn-up road like an old-fashioned buggy, dipping and careening in the ruts with David's horse coming behind. *Now what?* she wondered. But all at once she recognized the horse.

As soon as he parked the jeep in the parking lot below, she ran down. She said. "I thought you were never coming. What took so long? What did he say to you?"

"Whoa, Rachel, one question at a time."

"Well?"

"He put me in charge of building a judgment arena. I am to direct the workmen. But he wants the whole arena built in three weeks. So I had to get them started right away."

"*Three weeks*! How is that possible in all this ruin?"

"It's possible. He showed us how. Would you believe that in all this mess he has preserved everything we need?"

"Well, after all he is God, the perfect planner. All you and the men have to do is obey."

"Exactly."

"He must have a lot of confidence in you, David, to put you in charge of such a big project. It makes you the leader of the people in a way." "No, no, I'm just in charge of a building project. He's totally in charge of everything." Then he added thoughtfully, "What a different world we will live in from now on with *Yeshua* in charge. Just think of it, Rachel, peace…at last! And perfect order. I think I am really going to enjoy this job. I will be working very close to the people through all this."

"It's no wonder he put you in charge. You are always thinking of the people. Oh, David," she sighed. "Is there ever going to be any time for just us?"

"Of course, *Hamoodah*, but since we've waited all these years, surely we can wait three more weeks."

"I suppose so."

"Besides, I'm going to put you and my mother in charge of the women for feeding the workmen on the job to save time. We will have to work in shifts to complete it anyway."

"Kitchen duty again—the Lord must be preparing me to run a soup kitchen." She thought about it for a second, then laughed. "I think *Yeshua* is working on my pride, because it has become a joy to serve him anywhere. He taught me that when he let me teach the young girls. Besides, I always wanted to be where the action is, and that's where it will be for the next three weeks! Oh David, forgive me for being selfish."

He smiled at her and said, "*Yeshua* is changing us all, making us aware of our sinful natures."

The three weeks passed quickly as everyone worked in harmony. Each man worked as unto the Lord. It was like an act of worship. It was true among the women as well. They cooked on the site amidst gaiety and laughter. No one knew where the food supplies came from. They just seemed to be there when they needed them. They were grateful, and continuously blessed and thanked the Lord for his provision. Everyone learned to trust the Lord for the smallest need.

The structure went up in sections. After laying out the position of each section, David divided the men into four teams. Starting at the throne and working out in both directions, they began their construction. Eventually they would meet in the middle of the three-quarter circle. All the workers started on laying foundations and such while more materials were being cut. Then, as the materials for both end sections became available, they divided into two groups of teams. The first group on either side finished the first section, and the second group started the second.

By that time, materials were ready for the third sections. The teams leap-frogged—the finishers of the first section began the third. They worked in this manner until all seven sections were complete. Once they had completed one section, they moved with greater speed, having worked out all the problems on the first section. Finally, it was done on the evening of the last day of the third week.

Chapter 70

The next day in Jerusalem, the arena filled with several thousand people. The angels had transported the surviving faithful to witness the Judgment of the Quick. They came from everywhere. Some were believers who received *Yeshua* when he appeared to Israel on Yom Kippur and then went home to lead others to salvation. Others were believers who had fled Adoni's evil to other countries and won converts in those lands.

The communications people were testing their equipment when the Lord materialized on the temporary throne, which now became the judgment seat. His flowing, white robes shone gloriously with the *Sh'khinah*.

The crowd dropped to their knees, starting at the ground level, with the people on the second row kneeling on the first row's seat, the third row kneeling on the second, and so on up. The Lord spoke. The loudspeakers and cameras brought his person up close and personal on the huge screen behind his seat.

"You may sit down," said the King kindly. He nodded to the angels on his right.

Rachel leaned over and whispered in David's ear, "I don't see any of the marks on his face that you saw, not even in the blow-up on the screen."

"Of course not, what we saw on Yom Kippur was his body as the sacrifice. Now he shows the glorified body of resurrection, which apparently he can display in many different guises."

Then, as if to confirm David's words, the King took on the look of a judge. His eyes shot out leaping flames, his head was like wool, white and soft. A pure-white robe extended down to his feet that were bare and glowing like ore smelting in a furnace.

The crowd let out a collective gasp at the sight. It was time for him to stand in judgment!

The judge spoke, "Before we begin this judgment, I will put all people on the same level of communication. The confusion of tongues is at an end. I now restore to the earth a pure language."

Foreigners who had come to the judgment were surprised to find themselves conversing in Hebrew as if born to it. Actually, they had no choice. The words of their native language had been wiped from their minds in an instant, just as the diverse languages were put there at the outset of the confusion of tongues.

"Also, I want to state that this judgment, which my word refers to as the judgment of the quick, will only involve those still alive today. This judgment is not a personal judgment of individual lives. That will come later after the thousand-year reign when they stand before the great white throne with *all* the unsaved. At the end of this age the living rebels, which survive until that time, will be killed by fire from heaven and join the rest of the unsaved dead to be judged individually before they enter eternity.

Mostly, we will deal with the sins of groups at this time, showing them a reason for their condemnation and execution. They will not be permitted to enter my new kingdom.

The angels with the books appeared. Taking the top book, a glorious angel stepped forth and began to read. "Julius Leucus Adoni´

Danak,[11] step before the judge for the reading of the charges," ordered the angel with the books.

Adoni´ had to be pushed forward before the throne by two angels. The angel with the book began to read: "One. You have robbed God of His place of honor and worship taking these attributes to yourself. Will you yet say before the LORD of heaven and earth, 'I *am* God?' But you shall be only a man, and no God, in the hand of him that slays you.[12]

"I worship another god," he flung back at the judge.

"There is no other God. I Am and there is none else," thundered the judge. Once more the ground shook at his thunder. He, who was no less than King of the Universe, exhibited his power.

"My god is Ashtor, the god of forces," Adoni´ proclaimed belligerently, lifting his head in defiance.

"No, not even *that* is true. You worship yourself. Besides, your so-called god is captive as well."

"I don't believe it," he flung back with full insolence at the judge.

Suddenly Ashtor appeared in chains between two mighty angels. "Is this your god, the image you patterned yourself after?" asked Judge *Yeshua*. "He is the original antichrist spirit, known by many names such as Lucifer, the fallen morning star or son of the morning. Men of the earth call him Satan or the Devil. You have been deceived by your own search for power."

The judge turned to the angel and said, "Proceed with the charges."

Rachel leaned over to David and whispered, "Well, that certainly silenced him. I always knew he was the one in Daniel."

"Shh," said Sarah. "Let's hear the rest."

The angel began to read again before a speechless Adoni´.

"Two. Boasting that you are wiser than Daniel in your knowledge, you have practiced sorcery and trafficked with demons in consolidating your power. This is forbidden in God's word.

"Three. You have led the people into idolatry and taught them to blaspheme God, also forbidden.

"Four. You have usurped the authority of the true King. You have enlarged your desire like hell and gathered all nations to yourself.

"Five. You have laden down the people with your burdensome laws and endless regulations carried out by your equally evil administrators.

"Six. You have gone against nature itself in lying with a man and abhorring the natural use of a woman, a thing abominable in God's sight. This has led to a great number of Sodomites in the land. Their very faces declare their sin.

"Seven. Last, and worst of all, you have killed the Lord's saints, sold their wives and children into slavery, and caused family members to betray one another."

Momentarily, a murmuring erupted throughout the crowd. Some with serious faces nodded their heads. Others broke out in clapping. Adoni´ turned an angry face toward the crowd and spit in their direction.

Chapter 71

Finished with Adoni´'s charges, the angel called for Haik Ra'amon to step forward.

"Wait a minute," he protested. "I believe in the real Messiah now. This man fooled me. He told me *he* was the Messiah."

"Your confession is too late. Be silent and receive your charges," commanded the judge sternly.

The angel began to read: "One. You accepted the Beast, yea you worshipped him, and you even became a physical lover of him, an abomination."

"Who are you talking about? I know of no Beast," he burst out, trying to save his skin.

"His coming and deeds were recorded in the scriptures as the evil one who was to come."

"But I never read the scriptures. How was I to know?"

"Exactly true and to your loss," said the judge quietly. "Proceed with the charges."

The angel began again, saying "Two. Not only did you worship this man but led all the people to do the same, pronouncing him to be god, like a prophet would do—a false prophet. You taught the people to commit abominable and impure sex acts as worship. You led them all as a false shepherd in receiving his mark, causing *their* damnation. Their blood is on *your* hands as well as the blood of thousands of innocents which you burned to Mollech, a very evil demon.

"Three. You used occult power to do false miracles and taught the people to do the same.

"Four. You desecrated my holy altar with your filthy ceremonies.

"Five. You actually celebrated the death of the Lord's saints and caused the people to do the same.

"Now both of you kneel before the King and receive your sentence."

The power of God forced them to their knees. It is doubtful if Adoni´ would have bowed otherwise. "Now confess 'You are God' to him who judges you."

"You are God," they confessed jointly. Suddenly the bodies of the two most abhorrent of all living souls began to change. They distorted into indescribable ugliness, with features resembling angry beasts with horns, and armor-plated hides, beasts of no known earthly origin.

The two-horned beast that was formerly Ra'amon pleaded, "But I always heard you were a merciful God."

"The time of mercy is past," replied the Lord. "However, I will grant you your greatest desire. You shall go down in history being known for who you are." He commanded his angels, "Take them to that volcanic lake of fire in Bozrah and cast them in alive, that the scriptures may be fulfilled. Although this is only an earthly representation of the real lake of fire, it will be an entrance that can be seen by the earth's population."

Angels took hold on either side of each beast and lifted them up from the earth, carrying them through the air out of the sight of the arena. Ra'amon, screeching and flailing in protest, began to roar as a great beast in agony. The crowd buzzed at the fairness of the judgment. They began to shout, "Hail to the righteous King! Your judgments are fair and true, O Lord, and righteous altogether!" The tumult kept up as people left their seats to dance and praise *Yeshua* for his righteousness. Finally, the judge bade them to be seated.

Rachel turned to David and asked, "Why did their bodies change to that of beasts?"

"I don't know. You'll have to ask *Yeshua*. I'm just as surprised as you." But just as he said that he looked up and saw *Yeshua* looking straight at him. Then the words formed in his spirit. "Since they do not die but enter the eternal state without a resurrection, they have received a new body fit for their destination, one that will endure their punishment for eternity." David communicated the reason to Rachel, telling her the source.

"Oh David, you have such a close relationship with *Yeshua*. What did you do to have that?"

"I don't know," he replied. "I just studied the scriptures." He was embarrassed by the question. *That's the truth; it's nothing I did. Why am I shown such favor?*

Suddenly the giant screen showed Adoni´ and Ra'amon falling through the air at what was formerly Bozrah in Edom. The angels had dropped them, casting them into a lake of fire, churning with liquid rock. Adoni´ and Ra'amon could be seen briefly, thrashing about in the fiery lake in agony, before the scene on the screen changed. It had become a literal picture of hell on the surface of the earth. The only living creatures that dwelt there were unclean birds and wild creatures. God had given this barren place to them to possess from generation to generation.[13] A camera crew had been sent to Bozrah to film the placing of the victims. The crowd gasped when they saw the scene flash on the big screen. Praise and thankfulness erupted in the arena for the mercy that had been shown to *them*.

Having judged those who led the people astray and who were their visible enemies, he now turned to the spiritual forces from hell that opposed *Yeshua* through their human puppets and had done so since the times of Adam.

It was time for a period of righteousness—*Yeshua's* kingdom on earth, when men on earth would be judged by righteous judgment and given a lush, fertile earth free of destructive forces. If men would turn against God in these perfect conditions without help from the demonic kingdom, God would have proved that the human heart is depraved beyond measure and helpless to be righteous without Christ. Therefore, Satan's spiritual kingdom would be banished for a short while so that man could be tried on his own in this final world age before eternity.

Once again Satan appeared in front of his Creator, God Almighty. Still bound in chains and accompanied by two angels, he stood in front of a multitude of his kingdom of darkness, princes of darkness, demons with wicked powers—even the four angels that had been bound in the Euphrates River next to their capital on the earth, Babylon. Besides these prominent spirits of darkness were little demons barely a foot high, some in the shapes of animals like the frogs that came out of the mouths of Adoni´ and Ra'amon earlier.

But also among those condemned came a special category of hybrid angels called Nephilim (known to modern man as UFO occupants), who had trafficked with the earth before Christ's return, just as in the days before the flood.

Posing as visitors from outer space, they had attracted much attention with their flashy ships and baffling antics, abducting people, manipulating the genes of men and animals, causing many to expect a new age with planetary cooperation. Great and mighty angels of God herded them away from the judgment ground.

Meanwhile, Satan, still standing in front of the throne, received his sentence. "You shall be bound for a thousand years," said the judge. "After that, you shall be released for a little while, because I still have use for you."

"Not likely," he muttered, then retorted, "I will *never* serve you."

At that a powerful angel materialized just before touching the ground. In one hand he held a key and in the other a heavy chain. He bound Satan with the new chain.

"Take them to Babylon and open the bottomless pit for him and his kingdom there. When you have cast them all in, shut it and set a seal upon it reading: 'Not to be opened for a thousand years,'" said the judge, speaking an immutable word. The rest of the angels assisted the mighty one and took Satan's whole kingdom to the pit.

"This afternoon," he announced, "I will begin the judgment of the kings of the earth."

Chapter 72

Rachel and Esther broke out the lunch they had been given when they arrived, and Sarah began to distribute it among her brothers and David's men. The whole crowd was doing the same. This time *Yeshua* fed more than five thousand. It was not hard to guess the conversation of each little group occupying the arena area. David said to his band, "Isn't it satisfying to see the wicked get their just desserts?"

"Yeah, but it makes me shudder to think I could have been among them," replied Hillman.

"That's right," remarked Matza. "If it hadn't been for you, Captain, and your righteous ways, I don't think we would be here today. I know you influenced me."

"Oh, my," said Rachel. "Just think what my judgment would have been. With my hatred of the Lamb of God and his followers...." She shuddered. "I don't even want to think how close I came. What grace he has to forgive us all so much! Just think, they all could have had his mercy if they had just made the right choice in time."

"All except the angels and demons who followed Satan," broke in David. "They knew God from the beginning and trembled at him, yet they loved their unrighteousness. They knew they would be judged, but still they persisted in their evil anyway, refusing to repent. Apparently, they have no conscience."

"How do you know that?" asked Rachel, wondering at his knowledge of spiritual things.

"Because some of the demons he cast out when he was on the earth asked him if he had come to torture them ahead of time."

"Oh, David, you know so much about our God. Will I ever be able to catch up?" she asked.

"I'm sure we will all get to know him, since he plans to live among us for a thousand years."

"Are the kings he mentioned from the whole earth or just around here?" Feldman asked David.

"I don't know. The angels seem to be in charge of the prisoners."

They continued to talk among themselves until it was nearly two. Then the crowd returned to their seats. At exactly two the judge reappeared.

The kings of the earth consisted of heads of state from the entire world. Some were aware of who *Yeshua* was; others seemed to be in daze like they didn't understand what was happening. Most were clothed in western-style dress. The exceptions were those who wore tribal or traditional dress from their countries. It was a sizable number, in the upper seventies, but they easily fit in the space before the throne. Actually, there would have been more, except that many had been killed in the plagues of the earth. The dead were not on trial here. Only the living.

Contemplating the men before them, Rachel began to lose her confidence. She had a disturbing thought. *Will we have to stand before him and be judged as well?*

David saw the frown upon her face. "What's the matter?" he asked.

"Will we have to stand before him too? Will I have to answer for all that vehemence I felt?"

"Noooo!" he said definitively.

"Why not?" she asked, demanding reassurance.

"Because when you accepted *Yeshua* as your savior, your judgment fell upon him when he died. We will never stand before him for judgment of wrongdoing before we were saved. We will have to answer for our deeds *after* we have accepted him but only for unforgiven disobedience. We now have an advocate to forgive all wrongdoing, *Yeshua* our high priest. If we confess it and ask for forgiveness, he is faithful *and just* to forgive because he already paid for the sin."

"Are you sure?"

"Rachel, that was the whole purpose of his death. He died in place of *every* person on earth, paying for *all* their transgressions. All he requires is that you acknowledge your need for salvation, confessing that you are indeed a sinner. Then offer his death in payment for your sins. You received eternal life from him the moment you believed and will never be brought to account for any of those sins."

"Not even if I sin tomorrow?"

"No, because he paid for them all for your whole life."

"Sure," she said sarcastically, "And I can go out and commit murder, and that's forgiven already."

"You are forgetting that when you believed, you received the Holy Spirit into your very body. The Father sent his influence upon you to give you the nature of God, and that nature cannot sin. He grieves within you anytime you fail in the flesh, and it causes conviction in your conscience. The scripture tells us that if we confess our sins, he is faithful *and just* to forgive them and to cleanse us from all righteousness."

"Because he has already died for them?"

"That's right, but if we don't confess our current sins, it destroys our close relationship with him, since he can't live with sin. That does not mean we will be judged for them and sent to hell after we die. The New Testament tells us every man will have to give account of his life. I suppose even the righteous, for the purpose of reward. Therefore, it pays to follow the Spirit within you as closely as you can."

Chapter 73

"Shh, David, it's starting," said his mother.

"First, bring before me the kings and men who ruled under the Beast."

The King began to speak from his own word in Habakkuk:[14]

"Woe to you that coveted gain for your own house, in order to set your nest on high. You destroyed many people to escape disaster yourself. Now you have plotted shame for your own families and guilt for yourself.

"Woe to you who built a town with crime and established a city with infamy.

"Woe to you who made your neighbor drunk in order to gaze upon his nakedness. You shall be sated with shame.

"Woe to you who sold my people to the Greeks or used my children as barter for a harlot or wine. Your children will be given to Israel to sell to the Sabians.[15]

"Now you will drink the cup of wrath that's in my right hand. Bring forth their families," he commanded.

Women and children of those who shed blood were herded before him. The children were separated from the wives and taken away to be sold as slaves. Absolute justice was rendered—an eye for an eye, slavery for slavery, as proclaimed by the prophet Joel.

Turning himself to address the men, the judge said, "Your wives shall die first and you shall watch."

Some of the men flung themselves down before the King crying, "Mercy, mercy!"

"Your judgment is to see the same infliction upon your families as you gave to others."

Each man watched in horror, as he somehow saw his own wicked wife, individually separated from the crowd, suffer at the hands of an unseen captor the same heinous crimes that he had inflicted on others. After the women died, the Judge commanded, "Bow now and confess me as Lord." After they obeyed, *Yeshua* took the lives of the men, commanding, "Die." Once again the angels cleaned the judgment grounds.

Their judgment had taken more than half of the afternoon as they were so many, and it included the judgment on the wives. Knowing that the judgment of these very wicked men must weigh heavily on the spectators, *Yeshua* called for a brief break, while the angels gathered the kings from other countries beyond Adoni´'s kingdom's of the final ten divisions. The people stretched and moved around, calling to one another.

Esther said, "Let's take this time to refresh ourselves and break out the water. Rachel, you hand out the cups, and I'll pour."

"Great idea, although the weather has not been unpleasantly hot with these dark clouds still lingering from the volcanic ash in the upper atmosphere. *Yeshua's* gracious provision, no doubt," said Rachel as she handed out the cups.

"Yes," said David, suddenly made aware of the blessing. He hadn't thought of the blessing it was while they were building the arena. "Let's stop right now and give him thanks for this blessing. Everyone stand up and stretch up your hands and shout your thanksgiving." As they did, those nearby began to repeat their prayers. Soon the whole stadium was standing and giving thanks.

The Judge smiled, then lifted his hands to quiet the crowd. "You have blessed me, my people, oh, how you have blessed me." At his words, the angels brought forth the first group of kings.

Rachel turned to David and said, "Look what you started! All the people followed you. You actually led the whole crowd to bless the Lord. No wonder *Yeshua* loves you so!"

David turned bright red at her words, "I didn't intend to," he stammered. "I only meant to show *our* gratitude."

"Don't be embarrassed. I think people just like to follow you. You are a natural-born leader."

"Shh," said someone close by.

Yeshua began again. "Woe unto them that call evil good and good evil; that put darkness for light, and light for darkness; that put bitter for sweet, and sweet for bitter![16] Woe unto them that are wise in their own eyes, and prudent in their own sight! Woe unto them that are mighty to drink wine, and men of strength to mingle strong drink: which justify the wicked for reward, and take away the righteousness of the righteous from him!

"Therefore, just as this written word has said, as fire devours stubble, and flame consumes chaff, so *your* root shall be as rottenness, and your blossom shall go up as dust: because *you* have cast away the law of the Lord of hosts, and despised the Holy One of Israel.

"The basis of this judgment is the treatment of my people. Those of you who were kind will receive mercy. Those who followed the directions of wicked men, particularly those with religious authority, and killed my saints will find no mercy."

The angels began to separate the kings according to their deeds. "Bring forth the guilty and read the charges," he commanded. "You shall shut your mouths for that which has not been told you, you shall see."¹⁷

The angel with the books came to the King/judge and read aloud:

"One. You have wickedly executed my people whom you called the 'Lamb of Godders' for the supposed crime of heresy. You, not they, were deceived by false religious doctrines. You have been fooled by the vilest system to ever come out of the bowels of Satan: the ancient religion that began in Babylon."

"But Your Honor," protested one of the kings. "It was the *church* that we followed."

"Not *my* church," replied the Lord. "My Church had already been taken to heaven in the darkness before the Lamb of God movement began. Babylon was fashioned after the doctrines of the world, filled with idolatry who gave my worship to a woman, in reality a goddess figure. I am a jealous God. I share *my* glory with *no* other."

"What about all the people in the church. Will they all be judged, too?" asked another.

"I removed from the earth believers from every denomination, both Protestant and Catholic, who had accepted me as their Savior. Those who were left merely followed the teachings of men, Protestant *or* Catholic."

"But how were we to know?" whined another king.

"My word, recorded in the Bible, was available to you all. You didn't bother to read it. You trusted other men to teach you. *Foxes' Book of Martyrs* was available, showing its evil history through the Middle Ages. History itself recorded the cruel persecutions and murderous decrees. It should have revealed the nature of the doctrines you blindly followed. Religion is no excuse for evil. Proceed with the charges."

The angel read: "Two. Both you European kings and you Middle Eastern kings supported the Beast, and in the end you allowed your armies to fight against me at my return. Kneel and confess it is *God* who judges you."

The judge suddenly blazed with the blinding light of the *Sh'khinah*.

The heads of state shuddered and dropped to their knees, confessing his full nature as God Almighty. Then the judge, using a word like a sword in his mouth, slew them. "Die!"

They dropped to the ground and were gathered by the angels and transported to feed the birds and wild beasts in Bozrah.

Next, one lone king stood before the throne, Lin Yiang Duduai. The judge's eyes blazed with fire. He spoke with a fury. "You rejected me in your youth, which was your right and choice. But you went beyond that and persecuted my followers in China when you came to power. Then you proceeded to execute great cruelty upon your conquered peoples and taught your armies to do the same. Countless peoples have suffered under your leadership." *Yeshua* took on the form of his kingship. "Your judgment will be severe when you stand before the final judgment at your resurrection. In the meantime, you shall kneel before me and confess that I am your God who judges you." Duduai knelt and confessed. The last word he heard was 'die'.

Lin Yiang trembled and shook before the great king of Israel, and then he dropped. Angels carried him away.

"Bring the others before me," he commanded, his judge mode back on display.

There were not many. David recognized the king of Jordan among them. Another king wearing the royal emblems of Belgian was also among them.

The judge looked kindly upon them. Some were trembling. He had promised mercy, hadn't he?

"Because you have shown compassion and mercy upon my people, I grant you mercy. You may accept me as your God and live in my kingdom. But first you must acknowledge your transgressions and accept my sacrifice for them, because no man may enter my kingdom *any other way*."

He singled out King Hassih by name. "To you I grant lands on the east of the Jordan river that formerly belonged to Israel. You have served my people beyond just showing mercy."

They all knelt and showed fealty to the King of kings after confessing him as their savior and king. Then they arose shouting for joy!

The crowd responded with excitement. Some shouted out, "Blessings to you!"; others, "Great is God's grace!" It was clear that they accepted the new believers into God's family.

Then the King said, "Today I have judged the leaders of society. Tomorrow we begin the judgment of society at large," dismissing the crowd for the day. The people left, smiling and talking among themselves of the positive results of the last judgment of the day.

Chapter 74

David said, "Let's go by our old house, Mama, and see if it still remains. It would be more convenient if we were in the city. We have prevailed upon the kindly believers of Mt. Samuel long enough." Then he turned to his men, "Take one of the trucks from construction and go on back while we take a look."

"When will we get to see Jesse?" asked Esther.

"We will see Abba all in good time after the judgment is over," said David with more authority than he felt.

They drove along in silence, realizing there was little left at all. The earthquake had nearly leveled the city. Landmarks were gone. Only a few streets were cleared enough for traffic that was mostly on foot.

They traveled northeast on the Jaffe Road in an attempt to cross over to Mea Shearim, the area where many of the Haredi had lived. There they faced a deep gully of exposed subsoil. The road had been broken here during the great earthquake when the Mount of Olives had split in half. This gully was apparently the extension of that crack. A temporary road had been dug from the sides of the ravine, making a crossing barely wide enough for one vehicle. When they came up on the other side, they saw that more of the houses here were spared on the northern side. They began to hope. Finally, they reached within a block of their street. Forced to walk at this point, they approached on their own street, but they still could not tell if the house was standing.

David hurried ahead of the others with anticipation. Climbing over the rubble, he tried to get an orientation of where he was. Then he recognized a neighbor's house. He counted. "There, it should be there," he pointed as the others caught up with him. They all looked to where he pointed. It was a huge pile of rubble, higher than the house itself. Apparently, the upper stories of the three-story *yeshiva* building located behind had fallen toward their house.

"Come on, let's see if anything still stands underneath," said David with optimism.

"Be careful, David," cautioned Esther.

Sarah scampered after him, jumping from pile to pile of stones, followed by Jonathan. When they arrived at what would be the front door, David began to remove stones. "Must be something holding up this mess," he said as he removed the debris as fast as he could, Jonathan and Malcomb working alongside.

"These are just scattered stones thrown across the house from the fall of the *yeshiva* building," said Malcomb. "Maybe the front of the house is still standing."

"It is!" cried Sarah, peering through some timbers. "I can see the door."

After they cleared the door, David approached it cautiously. "Let's see if it will open."

He leaned against it and shoved with his shoulder. It moved slowly, scraping on the floor. "The jam is out of square, but it is coming." Jonathan and Malcomb helped him push it all the way open. It was dark inside except for what light the open door admitted. Jonathan pushed his way past the others and went inside, disappearing into the next room.

THE END... AND A NEW BEGINNING

"It's completely dark toward the back. That means no breaks in the roof." David and Malcomb followed him to the back, Sarah tagging after. After a few minutes they all came back out, Sarah first.

"It's okay except for the back two rooms. They are crushed and filled with stuff. But, Mama, there's no furniture at all."

"Sold, no doubt," said Rachel.

"Yes, I imagine. But at least we can have our own place back," said Esther with a big sigh.

Chapter 75

Today the King would begin to judge the nations who had heard of him and his glory, yet rejected him mainly for Adoni"s god. These were those close to the Middle East or having communications still intact, such as radio and television and had heard Adoni"s message through Ra'amon's preaching. Primitive tribal nations who knew nothing of the happenings in the Middle East would be judged differently.

Those who received the mark of the beast appeared first. They trembled before him. These had seen his power when he resurrected the two witnesses and the earthquake that followed. These were mostly from Israel, since the system had not yet been fully installed in other countries. *Yeshua* stood before them, eyes flashing fire, feet burning as molten metal, wearing a glistening garment. The judge thundered when he spoke. "I have sworn by myself, that the word is gone out of my mouth and shall not return, that unto me every knee shall bow and every tongue shall swear.[18] I am the Lord King of Israel, and his redeemer the Lord of hosts; I am the first, and I am the last; and beside me there is no god.[19] Bow before me *now* and swear!"

White-faced, they dropped to their knees, mumbling the words. The King spoke again. "Behold, my servants shall eat but *you* shall be hungry: behold my servants shall drink, but *you* shall be thirsty: behold, my servants shall sing for joy of heart, but *you* shall cry for sorrow of heart, and shall howl for vexation of spirit [even while you await the last judgment of the dead]. And *you* shall leave your name for a curse unto my chosen: for I, the Lord God, shall slay *you*, and call my servants by another name. He who blesses himself in the earth shall bless himself in the God of truth; and he that swears in the earth shall swear by the God of truth; because former troubles are forgotten, and because they shall be hid from my eyes. For, behold, I have created a new heaven and a new earth: and the former shall not be remembered, nor come into mind."[20]

"*You* have received the mark of the Beast, an impostor. By doing so *you* swore allegiance to him. *You* shall follow him in your judgment. *You* shall drink the wrath of the true God." He commanded the angels, "Take them to the lake of fire and throw them in. However, their bodies did not change like the bodies of the beasts. Being thrown into the earthly lake of fire merely caused their physical death."

After every group in this category received their punishment, the next group came before the judge. These were from all the nations surrounding *Adoni'*'s kingdom and any others where *Yeshua's* Jewish brethren had taken refuge. But here the people were not separated by nations but by labels. The judge Himself gave them the label as they appeared before him individually. To one he said, "Sheep." To another he said, "Goat."

The sheep were commanded to stand to the right of the throne, and the goats to the left. After everyone had received his label and position, the King pronounced his judgment.

Then the King said to those on His right hand, "Come, you blessed of my Father, inherit the kingdom prepared for you from the foundation of the world: For I was hungry, and you gave me meat: I was thirsty and you gave me drink: I was a stranger and you took me in: naked and you clothed me: I was sick and you visited me: in prison and you came to me."[21]

Those at the right hand were astonished, because although they had believed the "Lambers" to be good people, they did not know the Lamb himself.

"But Lord, when did we see you thus?"

He answered kindly, "Truly I say to you, inasmuch as you have done it unto the least of these my brethren, you have done it unto me. You are spared because of your love and compassion. Kneel now before me and confess me as the savior for you sins, for none shall enter my blessed kingdom otherwise."

But to those on His left he said, "Depart from me, you cursed, into everlasting fire, prepared for the devil and his angels: for I was hungry…" and he continued with a negative response of the same words. They, too, questioned the Lord saying, "When did we see you thus?"

But he answered them the same way. "Truly I say to you, inasmuch as you didn't do it to one of the least of these, you did not do it to me." Then he said to the angels, "Take them to the fire."

"But Lord," protested some of the goats. "Those sheep didn't believe in you until now. Why don't we get the same chance?"

"You saw what was happening to my fellow Jewish brothers but you didn't have any compassion. You didn't care, because it was not your problem. By standing by and doing nothing, you assented to the evil. So you sided with the evil ones." After the *goats* died and were carried off, the King turned to the sheep and said, "Bow now and accept me as your savior from your sins, for your compassion has earned you this chance. In exchange for receiving *me*, you shall receive eternal life. They gladly complied and rose up from their knees, rejoicing.

The crowd stood to their feet and began to cheer them; they yelled and whistled and clapped. After the crowd settled down, the judge turned to the angels one last time and said, "Now bring me all that are left." These were they who were the scattered survivors from around the globe who had heard the gospel as it was preached by the 144,000 before they left their own countries to come to Jerusalem. [22]Angels came in from all directions bringing the dazed people. They had been told on the way where they were going and why. Dread registered on their faces, as they stood before the judgment seat.

The angels came forth with the books and read their charges.

"One. You heard my message of peace and forgiveness, when my Lamb of God witnesses preached it all over the world, but you spurned it.

"Two. Some of you persecuted my messengers—even killed some of them.

"Three. I gave you another chance when I sent an angel to preach the everlasting gospel to you from the sky. You ignored it.

"Four. You agreed with those who wore the mark of the beast, when you saw my servants, the prophets, on TV lying dead on the altar. You even joined the celebration by sending gifts to *your* friends as they did.

"You are guilty, condemned by all these charges! Now kneel before me and finally acknowledge me as God!"

The repeat of this judgment took several more days. At the end *Yeshua* said, "I know this has been hard on you, my people. Death is never a pleasant prospect. I take no pleasure in the death of the wicked. And I know you are tired today. However, I want you to come back one more time tomorrow at ten o'clock in the morning to hear an important announcement." At that, *Yeshua's* guise as a judge vanished, and *Yeshua* appeared in his eternal glory shining brighter than the sun. Everyone in the stands dropped to his seat half blinded.

Then the people began to stand and were prompted by the Holy Spirit to sing a "new song, a song never sung before by *anyone*." Each raised his own voice in his own praise, as he was moved by the final appearance of the Lord and his impression of the judgment overall. He also lifted up his words with his own tune. The arena sounded in an ascending melodious rhythm of praise, fresh as the morning dew that moved like a wave through the crowd. The song seemed to lift the whole crowd in the sensation of floating, though they never left the stands.

Finally, the affairs of the old age were over. Forty-five days had passed from the time that Jesus set his feet upon the earth until the last of the condemned living were judged. Tomorrow was the beginning of a new day!

"See how just he is, how righteous and how holy," said Rachel, filled with awe as they filed out after the last judgment. She shuddered, "Just think, he has put off judgment for centuries, acting in mercy and long-suffering. But he did finally punish the wicked. It's so good to know we serve a just God *who keeps his word*."

"Yes," replied David. "If he did not punish the wicked, he would not be righteous himself. Just imagine a government that allowed murder and thievery to go on without restraint. There could be *no* peace for the society or the individual. We are assured of peace in his new kingdom because he will rule with absolute justice. I think that is why he wanted us to build this arena. He wanted the world to know his true nature, see his righteous power, and give him the worship and honor he deserves."

"What's going to happen next?"

"We'll have to wait until he tells us. Meanwhile we have our homes to rebuild."

Chapter 76

The next morning the stands were full. Everyone wondered, "Now what?"

All of David's band looked to him for what might be coming. David shrugged his shoulders. "I'm just as much in the dark as the rest of you," he said.

Promptly at ten, *Yeshua* appeared dressed as he might have looked in the New Testament times, casually in a teacher-like mode. He smiled at his people, showering them with love they could feel. Then he spoke. "I needed to speak to you about our next building steps before you waste needless labor. I know many of you do not know the plans that my Father has for the new kingdom. I do not want you to start building what might have to be torn down. That would discourage you. So, I am going to let you in on what has already been planned."

"First of all, Jerusalem as a city will no longer exist as such. It will even have a new name, Ya'hovah Sham mah', which interpreted means 'the Existing One is there.' That's because *I* will live here. Very few people will be permanent residents compared to the past. That's why I don't want you to build your own personal residences. Ya'hovah Sham mah', along with its suburbs, will be part of a greater complex that includes the new Temple and the properties of the Aaronic Priests and Levites. This will be the new capital city of the world."

"But the city itself will belong to the entire nation of Israel. Each tribe will have their own section to build and serve in rotation. Basically, Ya'hovah Sham mah' will be a bedroom for the world to "overnight in" when they visit my temple to worship or to get judgments from the king. All of you will have your own portion of land given to you according to your tribe. Meanwhile, we will all build Ya'hovah Sham mah' according to my Father's plan. I will put several of you in charge when I call you individually, and I will choose you according to your gifts and abilities. The work will bring great joy and fulfillment to your souls. I personally will be supervising the building of the new temple. Meanwhile make your temporary dwellings as comfortable as possible until after my great wedding celebration to take place shortly. Take a week off for rest. Then we will begin preparations for that."

The next big event after the week of rest was the Wedding Supper of the Lamb. One group of the workers prepared for that while the rest began building Ya'hovah Sham mah' and the temple.

Gradually, the people learned what *Yeshua* meant by the Father's plan. *Yeshua* instructed contractors to lay out a perfectly square outline of five thousand reeds for the world's new capital city, plus an outer suburb of two hundred and fifty reeds. Stone cutters and geologists were sent by ship to specified locations where God had formed great slabs of semi-precious stones by passing the elements through the fiery heat of his plagues. These were quarried and shipped back to Ya'hovah Sham mah' to build the walls and gates. They also laid out the outline of a palace for the King in the center of town with foundation stones of large glistening non-precious opaque, pink sapphires.

A major part of the city would be allocated to hotels and restaurants to serve the visitors who came to worship at the temple. The other buildings were residential homes for the service personnel, who rotated between their homes in their tribal lands and the city. Each would get their turn to serve. For resources, the city, flanked with newly planted agricultural fields, was also stocked with domestic animals. These vast fields, tended by the twelve tribes, would supply fresh meat and vegetables to the city's restaurants for the great numbers of temporary visitors.

While the city served to meet temporal needs of the visitors, the temple met their spiritual and legal concerns. The temple plan was like Solomon's temple in some ways; however, the differences contrasted greatly. For instance, the gates, both to the outer court and to the inner court, towered sixty cubits (110') into the air and could be seen at a great distance away from the awesome mountain where they stood. No one seemed to know why they were so high unless it had something to do with God's heavenly city. Clearly, they followed the plans given to Ezekiel by *Yeshua's* angel.

They learned that although all worship took place in the outer courtyard in front of the eastern gate to the inner court, teaching seminars and major court cases could be held in the large multi-storied western building behind the sanctuary. Thirty different dining chambers surrounded the outer court for worshippers to eat and fellowship around the peace offerings[23] prepared for them in the corner kitchens of the outer court by the priests. Thus, the outer court would serve as both a place of worship and a fellowship hall.

The workers constructed both the palace and the temple from the same type of gleaming white limestone that had graced Herod's temple. Materials began to pour in from around the globe from strangers who wanted to help with building the glorious temple. They brought gold and incense and sheep for sacrifice. They even brought many Jews (whom the angels had returned to their diaspora homes after the judgment) to the temple as an offering to the Lord.

The other workmen made preparations for a great celebration. Tables and chairs were hurriedly being made in recently equipped temporary factories, constructed from the tools gathered for the judgment arena. Therefore, hammers pounded in Jerusalem almost day and night except on *Shabbot*.

At the beginning of the preparations, David received a call from the King to meet him at the arena. David went to the empty arena and waited at the platform. Presently *Yeshua* appeared.

David said, "You wanted to see me?"

"Yes. I know you have been waiting a long time to marry your Rachel. It's my desire that you be married at my wedding supper."

"If it would please you, my Lord," David answered respectfully. "As you know, we have been waiting until I could provide a place for us to live."

"Yes, it would please me well. I want it to be a picture of me and my bride for the people to see."

"Following the Jewish traditional wedding, I have invited all who survived the judgment of the living to my wedding supper. Earlier, while still in the heavenly realms, I presented my bride to myself after it was determined that she was ready.[24] I married my church just before my return to earth. But now, as in the Jewish custom, friends and neighbors will celebrate the event.

"Having missed the actual wedding, the new believers in my kingdom residing on earth will be able to see the enactment of it in your wedding. They will hear the vows and see the fulfillment of a Jewish wedding. Otherwise, many Gentiles who have been joined to my kingdom will not understand my relationship with my Church.

THE END... AND A NEW BEGINNING

"I have commanded seamstresses to prepare Rachel's wedding dress. Since she is to represent my Church, it must be a glorious garment. Here is the address. See that she gets measured right away. Your attire, however, will be prepared by tailors at this address. Take your groomsmen with you so that all your measurements may be taken at once. We will set up your wedding canopy just behind the head table at the supper. Don't worry about a place to live. When you need it, it will be available."

David wondered in astonishment. *To be chosen by the King for such an honor! Wait until Rachel hears this!* He replied as calmly as he could in his mounting excitement, "We will go for measurements this very day."

Rachel was helping Esther hang curtains in their modestly restored home when David burst unexpectedly into the room. "You'll never guess the news I have," he said, exploding with excitement.

Rachel stood stunned, silent on the chair where she was arranging the folds of a curtain, until David suddenly swept her off the chair and whirled her around the room in his arms.

Never had she seen David this excited, not in the whole time she had known him. He finally set her down.

"You've found a place for us to live," replied Rachel, joy registering on her face.

"Better than that!"

Rachel frowned. *How could anything be better than that?* After being so cramped up with David's family where they had little time to themselves, even when they did steal a few moments alone, passions seethed underneath and had to be constantly checked for lack of privacy. And besides that, David insisted that they wait until their wedding day for intimacies. Now that the King had returned, the weight of righteousness and holiness was being felt heavily in the land so recently separated from a wicked society. *So what could possibly be better than their own place so they could marry?*

"Rachel, we shall have such a wedding as this world has *never* seen!"

"What *are* you talking about?" She looked up at him, with her hands on her hips.

"Yes, David," said Esther, who had been silently observing the interplay between David and Rachel. "Stop teasing us and tell us!"

"The King wants us to be married at *his* wedding supper as a picture of him and his bride. He has already ordered clothes made for both of us, and we need to go this very day to have measurements taken."

"A glorious wedding…followed by a place of our own to live? Surely *Yeshua* would not stop with just a wedding?"

"Spoken like a true female, always worrying about her nest. The King says not to worry. It will be provided."

"The King Himself will provide it! David, how can we be so blessed? We are just ordinary people. Why have we been singled out for this honor?"

"I don't know. He didn't elaborate. Come, there's not a minute to lose," David said.

Chapter 77

One week before the wedding supper, David was awakened in the night by an angel.

"Arise, David. The Lord desires you to see the dwelling place of *his* bride. Since you are representing him as bridegroom, he wants you to know something of his glory." Then he took David by the hand of his spirit body, leaving his physical body in the bed. They traveled straight up, passing through the ceiling and roof as if they were not even there. Up and on through the starry heavens they sped at surprising speed. David gaped at the sights around him with astonishment. *How is this possible?* The angel, reading his thought, answered, "Your spiritual body is not hampered by physical limitations."

"Spiritual body? I have a spiritual body, and I am not even dead?"

"Every human being has a spiritual body. There is a natural body and there is a spiritual body. The natural body simply clothes the spiritual body like a glove clothes a hand. When the glove moves, it is not the glove that causes this but the hand inside, because your spirit body is your life force. So it is with the spiritual body and the natural body. You don't need your natural body where we are going."

David noticed a bright star looming up in the distance. They seemed to be approaching it. As they grew closer he began to make out a pyramidal shape to the "star." Shortly, they zoomed in close enough for him to make out the details. Although David had not noticed, they had to be traveling at an enormous speed to approach so fast.

It was a huge city. On second thought, it was more than a single city; it seemed to be three ascending cities with the base of each slightly smaller than the one below, continuing the idea that the overall shape was like a mountain. Between the cities were beautiful wilderness areas similar to earth but pristine, more like gardens. As they descended just outside the lower city, David made out walls of about two hundred feet high and wide that stretched for miles around the whole city. Under these were foundation stones that sparkled with gemstones of various colors. He could see one enormous gate made of a single pearl, no door, just an opening. He estimated that it must also be at least two hundred feet wide and high to match the wall's dimensions. When David's angel brought him to the floor of the gate, an enormous angelic guard motioned for them to enter. Seeing that, David realized that not everyone could enter. He was blessed to be *privileged*, because of his escort.

He was awed to silence by the sheer majesty of it all. He filled his spiritual eyes, taking note of everything, so he could tell Rachel. They walked on a pearly surface, shimmering with light. He looked upward and saw that the gate arched high above them at least ten stories, according to earthly measurements.

Suddenly the angel took his hand again and lifted him up from the floor, and they floated. "Let's go inside the city."

Almost instantly they had traversed through the gate coming out the other side into a golden light that seem to permeate the entire structure, except for the wall. It was less bright, a translucent green. He knew from the description of the city in the book of Revelation that everything was made of gold, yet it was completely transparent. Did the Scripture mean when you saw it from a distance? Everything inside the city seemed to be made of a pure substance. For instance, up close, grass looked like grass, but at a distance it was as transparent as golden glass. Inside David saw a divided street following both sides of a river, with trees on either side hanging with luscious fruit. David puzzled over these because he saw no apparent soil. Even the so-called green sod under the trees appeared lush, healthy green grass up close, but at a distance it too looked like transparent, gold glass.

"Are these plants hydroponically grown?" he asked.

"You might call it that, since that's the only concept on earth related to it. Actually, the river is made of living waters coming from the throne. They permeate the whole city. All life is derived from them. They even extend to the earth, coming out of the holy mountain near Bethel where the new sanctuary is being built. They will physically renew everything they touch, bringing fresh life to all parts of the earth."

As they floated up to the upper cities, David noticed that each city grew more glorious as they ascended. Finally, he asked why they were different.

The angel replied, "The closer you get to the throne, the greater the glory of those saints dwelling there. These are they that built up the church with gold, silver, and precious stones, the worthy works of *overcomers*, who serve the highest places of the government. Those in the lower regions cannot bear to look upon the Son in his full glory. They are not spiritually matured enough to endure it. In the top city are those whose spiritual fruit production was thirty, sixty, and a hundredfold as in the parable of the sower.

They reached the pinnacle of the great mountain (heaven's Mt. Sion) [25]where the throne stood. On it sat the source of all power, God himself manifested in a powerful light shining brighter than a sun. The throne flashed and crackled with lightning, followed with thunder. It stretched out into the far distance, leaving room in front for thousands upon thousands of worshippers. Here, David, feeling himself but a speck in relationship to the size of it, saw the source of the waters. A huge rainbow arched high up over the throne in a cloud. *The water must be condensing from the cloud and forming the river,* he thought. The thundering sounds occasionally gave the impression of a summer shower. It smelled like the freshness after a rain.

The colors surrounding the throne also added to the idea of freshness. Under the rainbow was an aura of green, banded like the rainbow, but the bands moved irregularly, each a different shade of green light, like it was alive, yet the overriding color radiated an emerald shade. The throne sat upon a sea of blue like a sapphire stone. It was all so glorious David was overcome. After accustoming himself to the light, he made out a form sitting upon the throne. He fell down on his face and worshipped before it.

After a while the angel touched him, and he stood to his feet. "Come, it is time to return."

"Was I in the presence of God?"

"No, you were shown the glory of God and the bride's dwelling place. You were never actually in the scene, even if it seemed so. You were but an observer of it."

"So, only resurrected saints are allowed to live there?"

"Yes, they are in residence, but the kings of the earth will come into the city for Kingdom business and bring the glory and honor of nations into it. Also, those whose names are written in the Lamb's book of life may enter on occasion, but no one who defiles or works abominations may enter."

THE END... AND A NEW BEGINNING

"Is there anybody left on earth who falls into that category now that the judgment is finished?" asked David, remembering the recent purging.

"Perhaps a few—those who have not heard of his glory yet. But remember those of you who are on the earth still have your sinful nature. It will be with you until you die or are changed like the Church. Besides that, all children that will be born to you, will still possess their sinful natures. They may choose not to keep the laws and worship the King."

David could have gone on and on asking questions, but his journey ended. Just as suddenly as it had begun, he was back in his bed. What an experience! He could not sleep for thinking of his glorious journey. Why is the King building a palace here in the city of mere limestone when he really lives in a city of pure gold? Then the answer came—*because he desires to dwell among his people on earth as well.*

Chapter 78

Rachel was dressing for the wedding with Sarah and Esther's help. "Never have I seen such a glorious garment," remarked Esther. "You look like a fairy-tale princess."

Rachel viewed herself in the full-length mirror. She had to admit she had never seen such a dress, not in all her past searches through the houses of high fashion. The dress was of the finest white linen, embroidered with white silk thread and delicately fine twined gold around the jewel settings. A pattern of tiny vines with leaves and grapes covered the bodice and continued into a flared skirt in the pattern of a sunburst. She supposed the design spoke of the Church as the branches and fruit of the vine. Occasionally, grapes were embroidered onto the branches, and every several grapes was highlighted with a diamond emulating a dew droplet. The dress had a simple design with a moderate neckline and overlapped appliqués of linen leaves formed the cap sleeves. The effect of the gold thread did not overpower the whiteness of the dress but gave the appearance of light as it shimmered and sparkled with its diamonds.

Rachel had plaited her very long dark hair and wound it into a corona on top of her head, leaving the ends curled in the center. This style accommodated the veil, whose crown-like gold tiara, encrusted with diamonds and pearls, encircled her curls. The veil itself made of very fine silk interwoven with gold threads, fastened to it.

Sarah bowed before Rachel with overstated exuberance. "Your royal highness." Laughing she said, "You really do look like a queen, you know. I wonder what David's suit is like. Do you think it will match your dress in finery?"

"I don't know," replied Rachel thoughtfully. "He would not say, so I didn't tell him about my dress. We will surprise each other." Rachel smiled. David was right. It would be a wedding like no other. If only the sun would come out, it would be perfect. Unfortunately, the gloomy skies had continued since the Lord's return.

They had to depart from the strict Jewish tradition where the bride is brought to the father's house for the wedding, because the bride was already in the father's house, so to speak, living with Esther. So the King provided David with transportation to bring his bride to his wedding supper where their wedding would actually take place.

Sarah, peeking through the curtains, suddenly exclaimed. "They're here!"

She ran outside. Shortly, she came back in.

"Your chariot is here, my lady," said Sarah, "and you should see David. He is as royal looking as you."

Rachel quickly dropped her veil over her face and waited for David to come to the door. Being formal for the occasion, David knocked. Esther opened the door wide to display the waiting bride.

My bridegroom looks glorious, thought Rachel, *although he doesn't look much like Yeshua with his blonde curls.*

He wore a white linen uniform trimmed in gold similar to that of a high-ranking military officer, complete with visor cap trimmed in gold cord. His jacket was decorated with gold buttons and gold cord on the sleeve cuffs. Pinned to his chest were ribbons of distinction for service in the army. Gold cord also hung in loops from the epaulettes on his shoulders, and a gold stripe ran down the side of his pants touching his white patent-leather shoes. With his blonde curls, he *did* look like Prince Charming.

—

David smiled at his beloved. The King had certainly made her glorious. He beamed with pride that he should be so blessed with a bride like Rachel. He spoke finally saying, "You are beautiful beyond words, *Hamoodah*."

"How can you tell under this hazy veil? I can barely see you through it," she replied.

"Ah, but it increases the anticipation, greater for the glorious revelation."

She laughed, "It is the same for me, too. Where is the wedding *cheder* (chamber)? Do you know?"

"Yes, a large tent has been set up and so designated on the grounds at Zion, but I haven't seen the inside."

"It's to be a traditional Jewish wedding then," asked Rachel, "with the friend of the bridegroom listening outside to tell the guests when the marriage is consummated?"

"That's what I understand. Why?"

"I would have preferred the American type of privacy on my wedding night. But the King has arranged everything, so what can I say? His plans can only be perfect. I'll just have to trust him."

David placed her hand on his arm and escorted Rachel to the waiting carriage.

Two white horses stood in front of a gilded, open carriage with gold velvet-covered seats. David helped her into the carriage, carefully arranging her trailing train.

Chapter 79

They started for the mount a whole hour before six, the time for the supper to begin, even though it was not that far away. They needed that much time to break through the crowds. Two trumpeters went before the carriage, clearing a path through the masses of people clogging the street.

David's men, arrayed in white military dress uniforms, rode before and behind the carriage on white horses, with Malcomb and Jonathan at the head of the column along with Matza who was designated the "friend of the bridegroom." Rachel wondered, *Where on earth had they found the carriage and the horses? Were these the white horses that Yeshua and his armies rode from heaven?* It reminded her of the carriages that had taken English royalty from the church in their weddings. Esther drove the Jeep, with Sarah behind them. The crowd filed in behind the wedding procession according to tradition. Every cleared road was filled as the masses converged to the former, but now greatly expanded Mount Zion, from every direction.

When the wedding company reached the mount, they were directed by angels to a table next to the head table. As they sat down, they saw that the angels directed everybody to tables by family. Some tables were filled and some had a few empty seats. Five were empty at the wedding party's table: one between Esther and

David, three on the other side of Rachel, and one across from David next to Matza.

Rachel's eyes were drawn to the *huppa*, a filmy canopy set upon poles on a raised platform behind the head table. *An exalted wedding*, she mused, tingling with excitement. The huppa was a gauzy, silk-like material draping down in graceful swags caught up at the four corners with white roses of Sharon and lilies of the valley. *Amazing*, she thought. *How could it be that they would find such flowers after such destruction?* A still, small voice reminded her that *Yeshua* was the creator. *Of course, how foolish of me.*

The floor and steps leading to it were carpeted with royal purple. *A royal wedding*, she thought? Again she realized: *David and I represent the King and his bride.*

Most of the people were seated, when suddenly a great light broke through the gloom. The lights glowed in various shades of brightness that lit up the whole area surrounding the head table. The glorious Church had arrived.

Out of the light the King appeared at the head table in the center, dressed in a glorious royal purple robe trimmed with gold bands at the neck and also around the bottom. A pure-gold belt circled his waist with a lion head on the buckle. On his head was a crown set with the same twelve jewels that formerly represented Israel on the high priest's ceremonial garment. These were set in a filigree work resembling a crown of thorns. His bushy, black hair pushed out from under it and curled in wisps at the nape of his neck. The black of his hair was in contrast to his light, ruddy face, which showed only a slight scarring on his cheeks and forehead.

But his eyes were the most striking feature about his appearance. Gone were the eyes of flame seen in judgment. In their place were eyes gentle as doves, filled with love and joy. They seemed to peer at everyone in a personal way so that each individual felt himself intimate with their Lord. He had accomplished the task set before him before the world began. Now he was here to enjoy the fruits of his labor, and the pure joy of it shone in his eyes.

His mouth was soft and slightly turned up at the corners in a welcoming smile. His feet, clad in golden sandals, walked solidly upon the earth as he moved among his people, giving the undeniable impression that this was a man mingling among men, albeit a glorious man. So once again he had appeared in a different form. This time he was the bridegroom come to eat the marriage supper with his bride, the Church, from which emanated the glorious glow in the background. Israel, the restored wife of Jehovah, would participate in the supper as an honored guest. The new Gentile believers from around the world, who had remained in Jerusalem to help rebuild the city after the judgment, were guests as well.

Everyone rose from their seats. Camera crews, strategically placed, shot the scene for close-ups. Every table was in sight of a giant, multisided screen, seen from all directions. It was broadcast to the rest of the world, who still had facilities, so everyone could see the proceedings from a front-row perspective. But even so, each individual felt a personal communication with King Jesus/*Yeshua* exclusively.

Behind him the tables for the bride were filled. On and on they stretched, surrounding the wedding canopy. Notables sat at or near the head table with the King, his apostles, and servants having been awarded prizes in the "high calling" of God at the judgment seat of Christ, following their resurrection.

The king opened the wedding supper by reminding Israel that he was fulfilling a promise to them. "Though darkness has covered the earth and gross darkness the people, I have arisen upon you, and my glory shall be seen upon *you*. Now let the veil that covers the earth be removed, that my light may shine upon this city forever. Let the sun be ashamed and the moon blush at the sight of my glory. And let the Gentiles flow to your light. Never again shall you suffer rebuke, but the nations will honor you because you are my people. I will make your officers peace and your exactors righteousness. These resurrected people, my bride, will render exact righteousness when administering my law all during the kingdom, but during eternity, it will become your job.[26]

"Violence shall no longer be heard in your land, wasting nor destruction within thy borders; but you shall call your walls Salvation and your gates Praise. The sun shall be no more your light by day; neither for brightness shall the moon give light to you. But I, The Sun of Righteousness—your Lord, shall be your everlasting light, and your God will be your glory. Your sun shall never set, and the days of your mourning shall be ended."

The light grew brighter and brighter as the clouds of gloom dissipated completely. Every eye was on the sky watching as a star—or was it a sun?—appeared to descend, pulsating with light and sparkling like a precious diamond. It grew larger and larger as it came closer. Finally, it stopped and stood stationary, flooding the whole surface around them with a brilliant light as bright as the former sun at noonday, and yet strangely, there was no excessive heat.

I got my wish for the light, thought Rachel. *Now everything is perfect.*

David leaned over to Rachel and said, "It's the heavenly city I told you about."

"How do you know?"

"Because that is how it looked to me from a great distance."

"Is that what *Yesha'yahu*[27] meant when he said that the sun would no longer be our light, but the Lord himself would be our everlasting light?"

"Yes, he just quoted that passage from Isaiah."

THE END... AND A NEW BEGINNING

"Oh, look!" exclaimed Sarah, "There's the setting sun, *but it does not compare with the light of the Lord!* No wonder he said it would be ashamed. And look at the moon. It's *pink*! Can you believe it, *pink*!"

"He said it would blush," said a laughing Jonathan.

"Yes, he did," replied Sarah, clapping her hands with delight. "Now we will have to sing: 'in the light, of the pinkety moon, instead of the silvery moon." she said of an old, old song.

"Strange," remarked Malcomb. "The red dust from the comet must have coated the silver to make it pink."

The King spoke again, "One of my promises to you concerning the kingdom was to wipe away all tears. I have dealt with your persecutors with judgment, but now I wipe away all tears because of the grief they caused—the end of mourning as I promised." With a wave of his hand, the empty seats were filled, and great rejoicing broke out at every table.

Chapter 80

Jesse, Simon, Dan, Sheila, and Katz suddenly appeared seated in the empty seats at the bridal table. "Are we late?" quipped Katz in his usual mood. Matza stared at him in shock then slapped him on the back.

"No," answered Simon. "How could they start without the father of the bride?"

Rachel gasped, "Papa! Dan! Sheila!" as her papa, her brother, and his wife appeared.

Embracing them with tears of joy, she cried, "Oh Papa, how sorry I am that I didn't understand."

"But you do now. Look at you, Rachel. You look like a queen, my darling."

"I represent *Yeshua's* bride."

"And a better representation he could not find."

Dan and Sheila agreed.

Curiosity compelled Rachel to ask Dan, "Did you perish in the nuclear blast that destroyed America?"

"No, *Yeshua* warned us. We flew to Denver right after you left and escaped the war in Cheyenne Mountain. The US Air Force had abandoned it several years ago, but it was well equipped for survival.

Several hundred Lambers survived with us. *Yeshua* took us off the earth on Yom Kippur when he appeared in Jerusalem."

Jesse squeezed David with an arm around the shoulders and embraced Esther. "*Matek* (sweet), our son has distinguished himself, I see."

"Yes," replied Esther, "you have every right to be proud of him—of all your sons, because they have all done well."

"What about me?" asked Sarah, feeling left out of the conversation.

"You have become a lovely young lady since I went away," said Jesse, giving her a big hug before embracing his other two sons.

Matza took hold of Katz's arm and said, "Is your body real like ours or what?"

"Sure it's real, but it can do things yours can't, since it's a resurrected body."

"Like what?"

"Like walk through doors, materialize and dematerialize at will, and travel to outer space in an instant."

"Ree-aally?" said Matza, his eyes growing large in amazement.

"I did that last week," said David.

"Yeah, but an angel had to take you. You couldn't have done it by yourself," replied Katz.

"Actually, we can't do it either without the permission of the Lord," interrupted Jesse.

Their conversation was suddenly stopped by a loud blast. Seven angels stood behind the head table and blew seven trumpets, commanding the attention of the rejoicing families. The King beckoned to David. "It's time for the wedding," he announced to his spirit, for their table was not close enough to hear the Lord without shouting.

David and his groomsmen arose. Esther and Simon escorted David. Jesse escorted Rachel and started toward the canopy-clad platform with its glorious *huppa*. Women and maidens who knew Rachel from the days at Petra arose and came to her. They followed Rachel, singing her praises and joyfully beating tambourines all the way to the platform, where the groomsmen formed an aisle, standing on both sides leading to the steps.

So Yeshua himself would be their officiating Rabbi, thought Rachel. She had never seen him this close. *He is so fine, so regal, and so young; the dew of youth emphasizing his pre-resurrection thirty-three-year-old former earthly body.* Virtue you could feel literally flowed from his presence. He smiled at her, eyes filled with love. Joy overwhelmed her. Her papa was back, and now she stood together with the two great loves of her life—David and *Yeshua*. Oh, it was worth the wait—all those years and their misery.

The king looked over the vast collections of tables. "Some of you may wonder why we are having an earthly wedding at my wedding supper. I want this ceremony to remind all of you of the intimacy this occasion expresses. First, it shows the first love experience you should all have with me. It will be the beginning of my bride's reign with me, an intimate time for us. It will stand for the joy I have in her by being one, for she has obeyed me, and her glory reflects mine perfectly. Look upon this wedding as a picture of me with all my people."

Rachel and David looked at each other and smiled, eyes sparkling.

Yeshua spread his hands toward them across the small table between them. He spoke the Kiddusuh, reminding them of the betrothal blessing and promises of David to Rachel. Then he handed them two of the four cups of wine sitting on the table. They drank the first of the cups, Rachel having to lift her veil first.

David winked at her, acknowledging the revelation of her beauty unveiled.

Next *Yeshua* spoke to David, "You may now give your vow to Rachel with your ring."

David reached for Rachel's right hand with his left and slipped the ring on her finger with his right hand, saying, "Rachel, with this ring I give you my heart, my body, my time, and my possessions."

Rachel nearly melted under his obvious love. Joy radiated from her face, making it even more beautiful, if that were possible.

Then *Yeshua* lifted a paper to read David his vows. It was the legal document of the Jewish bridegroom's promises, a marriage contract called the *Ketubah*. It began by telling David to take Rachel according to the laws of Moses and of Israel. In it he promised to work for her, to honor and care for her, and keep her as the manner of the good men of Israel. Normally a sum of money would be mentioned to be added to the bride's dowry guaranteed by the groom's possessions. But since Rachel had no dowry and David no possessions, they expected nothing to be written about that.

Both Rachel and David were given pens to sign the document. It was much longer than David expected. He looked at *Yeshua*, questioning. The document contained a lengthy land description of two properties, both extensive. *Yeshua* said, "Just sign it, my son. I'll explain later."

Next, a silver bowl was brought to the bride and groom for the ceremonial washing of hands. After that, *Yeshua* raised the cup containing the wine of the wedding blessing and began the solemn benediction to the ceremony. After reading the Seven Blessings, Rabbi *Yeshua* reminded David. "Remember that at all times in this marriage you are to represent me and love Rachel with the same sacrificial love with which I have loved my Church. "I bless this wedding with a special blessing inasmuch as it shows the relationship between me and my chosen bride. Therefore, David, you must always consult me in matters of direction and for wisdom, so that you may lead and serve your bride well.

Rachel, you must always remember to honor your husband and serve him with respect, even as you would give me respect. Both of you, remember that when children are born to you, they are only on loan until maturity, for all people belong to me. See that you raise them in the nurture and admonition of the Lord according to my Word."

After David and Rachel drank the cup of blessing, David lifted up the cup, looking at *Yeshua* for permission to execute a current tradition in Jewish weddings. *Yeshua* smiled and nodded his assent. David lifted his cup even higher and shouted, "Mazel tov!" Then he dropped the glass to the floor of the platform and stomped it, smashing it to pieces. The surviving Jewish people in the crowd responded their approval, shouting "Mazel tov!" in response.

Again, the traditional wedding order was changed. David and Rachel sat down to be served *their* wedding supper, since it was really Yeshua's wedding supper, before their trip to the nuptial bed.

Angels appeared carrying great trays, piled with food. There were all sorts of sweet meats flavored with marrow, fine wine, and delicacies innumerable mentioned by the prophet Isaiah. The wedding supper of the Lamb had begun. Everyone feasted with rejoicing.

Chapter 81

"Did you notice that the *Ketubah* had two parcels of land descriptions on it?" asked David.

"Yes. What do you think it means? My nest?"

"Probably. It's listed as belonging to me. But what I don't understand is why. I looked at it carefully, Rachel, and it's a lot of land, territories really."

"Maybe because you represent him in our marriage."

"No, he owns the entire earth. I can't represent him in that. And besides, I don't deserve to be so honored. What about all the others who served so faithfully?"

"He said he would explain. It's his blessing. Can't you just accept that? Come on and eat. You will never see food like this from your bride," she said laughing. "I should think you would really be hungry after fasting for two days. I am."

After they had finished their meal, the women and maidens, along with David's groomsmen, the friends of the bridegroom, swept the couple toward the bride's *cheder* (wedding chamber) and the *chuppah* (bed). Matza had magnanimously offered to share his favored post of "friend of the bridegroom" with Katz, so it was they that thrust Rachel and David through the curtained entrance of the *cheder*, laughing uproariously as they pushed them inside.

"I told you I would dance at his wedding," declared Katz emphatically. Then he whirled in circles. "Come, let's start everyone dancing." Gaeity filled the air as the peoples began to sing and dance. Even the King rejoiced over his people, singing in delight. The bride of the Lamb sang a song to her Lord sung at their time on the earth:

"The Lord our God in the midst of us is mighty, is mighty!"

The King replied: "I will rejoice over her with joy, with joy."

The bride: "We will rest in his lo-ve."

The King: "I will joy over you with singing."

The bride: "The Lord, our God, in the midst of us is mighty, is mighty, is mi-ight-ty."

After repeating their chorus several times, the King began to move in and out among his people, drinking wine with them and communing intimately. He had always known their joys and their sorrows. Now he reassured them in person that he cared. He introduced his chosen nation, Israel (his restored Wife), to his bride, the Church, and the two peoples mingled freely. The invited Gentiles (new believers who inhabited the new earth), looked on and learned of his love.

Outside the tent, it was so noisy that Matza and Katz could not tell if the marriage had been consummated or not. Inside, Rachel and David had undressed behind separate screens, after David unfastened the back of Rachel's dress for her, and were preparing to get into the nuptial bed. Rachel stepped from behind her screen dressed in a sheer white silk nightgown that clung to her slender curves. David, suddenly overcome by the sheer beauty of his wife, stood apart looking at her and began to speak in a dramatic flair. "Ah, you are fair, my *hamoodah*, Ah, you are fair. Your eyes are like doves. Your hair is like a flock of goats streaming down Mount Gilead. Your teeth are like a flock of ewes climbing up from the washing pool; all of them bear twins, and not one loses her young.

THE END... AND A NEW BEGINNING

"Your lips are like crimson thread, your mouth is lovely. Your neck is like the tower of David…your breasts like two fawns, twins of a gazelle, browsing among the lilies. Every part of you is fair, my *ḥamoodah*, there is no blemish in you!"

"Oh, David," said Rachel, exasperated as she sat down on the edge of the bed. "Stop quoting me scriptures and come here!"

He didn't answer; he just grinned as he walked over, pushed her down on the bed, and drew her into his arms, whispering, "Mine at last."

Chapter 82

The King commanded that the angels clear away the tables. Then he separated the crowd by sections, according to their companies, those that were resurrected together. The company of the bride, his Church (the first fruits of the resurrection after him), stood at the front, because they were designated to reign at his side in the coming age of the Millennium. Then he began to call up individual categories of this reign and announce to the rest of the world the officers of peace who would rule with him on and over the earth. They had already been appointed after their resurrection at his judgment seat, seven years before his descent to earth. It was just a public announcement to the world. As he called out their positions, those in each group held up both hands, identifying themselves.

Each person had been awarded a position according to his overcoming as outlined in Revelation chapters 2 and 3. So the positions ranged from a lowly judge to members of a high ruling court—exactors of righteousness in the King's Kingdom where he is Lord over Lords and King over kings.

To the nations the King gave this order: "All weapons of war shall be destroyed. Melt down your war machines, as well as your primitive swords, and turn them into instruments of agriculture.

Food production must be our goal until civilization is restored. Most deserts have been banished since the redistributing of the waters. Now the earth will experience a climate change to perfection. With the increased light of the sun due to the new inclination of the earth, the moon also giving greater light, and with the heavenly city situated stationary over Jerusalem at the north pole, agriculture will turn the whole world into a garden."

Suddenly, he climbed up to the top of wedding platform, raised his hands, and proclaimed, "Arise and shine, O Israel, for your light is come! And the glory of the Lord is risen upon you![28] Yes, I quoted this passage of Isaiah earlier when the light came. Now I wish to explain the source of that light. Yes, it is truly my light, but it is because my dwelling place and that of my bride, is directly above you. As far as my light shines it shall never be dark. My glory shall also sit upon the holy mountain where the temple abides.

Next, he turned to those in Israel who survived the judgment and directed the angels to separate the people according to their ancestral tribes. Then he had the TV crew place a map on the screen where the wedding had been displayed for the masses to see up close. It showed the new boundaries of Israel's land. No other nation dare dispute it.

Portions inside the land were divided off for each tribe from east to west. In the center, the map showed a square, approximately forty-seven miles to a side, that was separated out for the Lord. It was apparently the land he had referred to after the judgment. In it portions for the priests of Aaron, the Levites, and the new city for the capital of Israel (that had replaced destroyed Jerusalem), were designated. It occupied the most central part of the nation, allotting land to six tribes before and after. Ephraim and Manassah were given an equal inheritance with other tribes, the double portion as promised to Joseph, Levi having his portion in the forty-seven-mile-square Holy Oblation. This was further split between the Aaronic priesthood and the Levites.

Ya'hovah Sham mah' lay on the border next to the Levites' allotment of the Holy Oblation. It would become the capitol city of the world, because the King would reign from there. It would be filled with worshippers from everywhere. But the Temple Mount was about thirteen-fifteen miles from the center of town to former Beth El and entirely in the Aaronic Priesthood's territory. The land leftover on either side of the square was designated for the Prince of Israel and his posterity.

In explaining this *Yeshua* said, "No more shall the princes oppress my people taking away their land. This is the only land the Prince may give to his children." After this pronouncement he handed out the deeds to the land to the twelve Apostles of Y*eshua*. They had the administrative rule over each tribe as promised by their Lord. They would see to the fair distribution of all the property to the people of each tribe by lots.

The King searched out Katz with his eyes. "The marriage is consummated," he told Katz, speaking directly to his spirit.

Katz yelled out to David through the tent walls, "She's your wife now. You can come out."

Chapter 83

David growled as he turned his head toward the voice, still holding Rachel tenderly. "Did I ever say I was going to miss that guy?"

Rachel laughed, saying, "He's only doing his job as the 'friend of the bridegroom.'"

Matza called this time, "Hey David, get dressed. The King wants to see you."

"You have to go now, but after today you're all mine," she said with a satisfied grin as she pushed him away.

"Daav-iiid," called Katz in a cat call.

"Aw, shut up. I'm coming," said David, as he began to pull on his pants.

"Tell Rachel the King wants to see her too," said Matza.

"Uh-oh," she smiled, "I feel one nest coming up."

"You may just be right!" replied David, and they both hurried to finish dressing.

After they emerged from the *cheder* tent, a roar went up from the crowd. David thought it was nice that everyone could celebrate this wonderful occasion with them, but he longed for the future when he would have Rachel to himself in some privacy. His mind was still back in the tent savoring the past hour. But as he strode through the parting crowd, he continued to hear joyous shouting. When he reached the King, he led him to the steps to where a golden throne whose arms featured lion heads had replaced the wedding *huppa* on the platform. He commanded the designated elders of Israel to bring the royal robes and the crown. Rachel stood trembling by David's side.

"My son, you have inherited the throne of *your father David*," said King *Yeshua*. Ancient King David of Bethlehem stood by smiling. (It was the fulfillment of God's promises to him. Not only was this prince, of his progeny, to ascend his past throne, but he also knew the Holy One of Israel, his greater son, had already received the greater honor of the throne of the whole world. It was a double blessing to King David). "But...," stammered David , completely surprised. He had no idea that he was a literal descendent of the great king David.

"You shall live in the royal palace, which you shall finish building from my plans. Meanwhile, the tent is yours until it is ready. I too shall stay in the palace when I am upon the earth among my people. Remember the innermost room shall be mine alone. You also shall come to the city above on occasion to carry out Israel's business.

The land I have given you is to be shared with all your sons and their son's sons. You must never take away the people's land. Also, this land must be extensive to receive the oblation of the people's flocks to you as their high priest."[29] Then he led David to the platform and said to the people, "Behold your Prince David, prophesied of the prophets of old. I, the greater Son of David, shall enable him with wisdom in judgment for you, my people and his. He shall also lead the worship to me in the temple on feast days in place of a high priest, using the portions you will give to him for the sacrifices, for he is a prince/priest on the throne of Israel just as I am a King/Priest on my throne over the world. So yes, he will still be a picture of me on earth for a thousand years to come."

THE END... AND A NEW BEGINNING

The King placed a royal purple robe over David's shoulders and commanded him to climb the stairs and be seated. He followed with a small flask, which he tipped and poured oil over David's head, anointing him for the office. Then he took a bejeweled crown and placed it upon David's head. Afterward, he beckoned for Rachel to come stand by her husband.

It was a royal sight with David's pure white uniform contrasting to his royal purple cape and Rachel's dazzling dress. Israeli citizens, who had been called to the throne to witness the coronation, approved in loud shouts and whistles.

At this, King *Yeshua* stepped down in front of the throne; he became all shimmering and gloriously lighted in the brilliance of the *Sh'khinah*, his purple robe eclipsed by the light. Then the saints, *his* bride, began to shine as well, each in differing degrees as the riches of *his* glory *in* the saints became evident. The brilliant display proved the fulfillment of Jesus' words concerning the mysteries of the kingdom. He had said that the saints would shine in the kingdom of his Father. *Yeshua* continued to increase in glory until the people, who had temporarily forgotten that he was very God in his fellowship with them, gasped and fell on their faces in awe. It was a reminder that although he had given them a prince to fulfill his word, God, their Messiah, had come and *he* alone was God. He and *he* alone *was* due their worship for *he* and *he* alone was completely holy. Then he and the bride disappeared along with the various other companies of resurrected saints. Patriarchs of old, with other just men made perfect of the Old Testament; and the 144,000 Sealed Company and their multitude of Gentile converts, presumably returned to their home in the glorious city above. The resurrected martyrs of Israel returned with them to serve from above.

Chapter 84

After he was gone, the blessed earthly people who had survived the world's catastrophes and the judgment of the quick, dispersed, seeking their temporary dwelling places in an aura of peace and satisfaction. What a celebration it had been! But it was not over. It promised to extend for a thousand years. Their righteous King had returned to rule in perfect justice. The earth was renewed to flourish like a garden and all wickedness, evil, and harmful hazards had been removed. And the light shined—ah, that beautiful light—his light—would never dim. Utopia at last!

Former General Shobat and General Uri Saguy stood on the fringe of David's friends, crowded around. They gathered to congratulate him.

"I still say you made an excellent choice in choosing David to command your secret Army," General Shofat remarked, laughing at his words.

"It seems our great God of the universe agrees with you, since he chose him to be a prince. And no wonder, because we saw firsthand his wisdom in leadership in Petra. Just imagine, *we* are on a first-name relationship with the ruler of Israel. Can you believe it? We were never that close to Ra'amon or Adoni´ as head generals."

"Yeah! I wonder if he will need an army?" said Shobat.

"If he does I'll volunteer," said Saguy.

"Me, too!"

Up close, his men and family surrounded David. They were all talking at once. Finally, David got a word in. "I wonder if my *abba* knew we were descendents of King David? Our family probably lost track of its genealogy generations ago."

"Hey, David," piped up Matza, "Are you going to make us some high-fallutin' ministers in your kingdom so we lowly soldiers can get us a beautiful bride?"

"Humph," said David, "I think it will take more than that!"

Everybody laughed.

Esther, evidently sensing David's impatience to get back to the nuptial tent, clapped her hands to get everyone's attention and said, "Enough already, we need to let the bride and groom begin their honeymoon. They've waited long enough!"

They all acknowledged the truth of her statement and accompanied Rachel and David to their tent. Then they reluctantly said their final mazel tovs and left.

Once inside, David laid aside his crown and said, "I could have kissed Mama, but I didn't want to be obvious."

Rachel giggled. She was flushed with excitement and the wine from supper. "Yes, bless her. She is a wise and *sensitive* woman."

"Yes, she is."

"Now that we're alone at last, I'm curious as to what *you* think about being a prince? Did you even imagine it?"

"No, but it certainly explains a lot of things, like being singled out by *Yeshua*, and receiving those properties that were written in the *Ketubah*. I never even imagined that I was a descendent of King

THE END... AND A NEW BEGINNING

David." He began undressing for bed, then motioned for Rachel to turn around so he could unfasten the back of her dress.

"Well, I certainly got my nest!"

"Yes, you did!" replied David with finality, "and remember how you always wanted to do something great for Israel."

"What can *I* do now?" she said, dropping her dress to the floor and carefully stepping out of it. "You're the prince?"

David stepped up to her back and gently placed his hands on her shoulders, nuzzling her neck with his lips. Then he turned her around, still holding her shoulders.

"Put some royal chicks in your nest," he said, winking at her as he drew her into his arms…

Appendices

Normally a novel would not require an appendix since its main purpose is to entertain. However, due to the subject matter of this trilogy, some explanation is required. In order to not bog down the reader with overmuch description and teaching mixed into the story, I have put some of the description and explanation here in the appendices for those who want to understand more and why.

Much of what is found here will be controversial. That is to be expected. I do not claim to be a scholar in real sense of the word, but I have tried to follow the Holy Spirit in my searching for answers. Therefore these appendices will not be inexhaustible treatises on the subjects. Real scholars will no doubt find many flaws. Please forgive where I have made faulty judgments. Do not take my words as the final answer to future things, but try to hear the Holy Spirit wherever he may be found. To the common reader, like myself, I only ask that you check the scriptures to understand where I have taken certain aspects of my story.

Appendix A

Concerning David as Prince

Some of you may wonder about my character David being made the prince of Israel. Will a mere man occupy this position in Israel? Have we not been taught all our lives that Jesus is the Prince of Peace and the King of Israel and *he* will reign on his father David's throne? (And he will!) On the other hand, Jesus is the King *over kings* and Lord *over Lords*. Isaiah 32:1 mentions this: "Behold, a king shall rule in righteousness, and princes shall rule in judgment." So it *is* possible that a man may rule over Israel under Jesus the great King, both being the sons of David.

But beyond this, five times the Lord promises Israel that he will raise up from among them a leader to be their prince who is *named* David. That does not mean that the story I have created for him is exactly true as written. I have only tried to portray a character I think would please the Lord for this position. There is not the slightest clue in scripture as to *how* this David was chosen to be the prince. Nor is there any mention of his being married at the wedding supper. That is purely my addition.

Scholars argue over who they think this David is. Some think the scriptures refer exclusively to Jesus. Some think he rules for Jesus as a kind of regent, as I have portrayed him. Still others see him as the ancient David, himself, who has been raised up again to fulfill the promise.

Below are the scriptures that mention this David in Ezekiel:

> And I will set up one shepherd over them, and he shall feed them, even my servant David; he shall feed them, and he shall be their shepherd.
>
> And I the Lord will be their God, and *my servant David a prince among them;* I the Lord have spoken it.
>
> Ezekiel 34:23, 24 (Emphasis added)

> And *David* my servant shall be king over them; and they all shall have one shepherd: they shall also walk in my judgments, and observe my statutes, and do them.
>
> And they shall dwell in the land that I have given unto Jacob my servant, wherein your fathers have dwelt; and they shall dwell therein, even they, and their children, and their children's children for ever: and my servant *David* shall be *their prince forever.*
>
> Ezekiel 37:24, 25

Later Ezekiel mentions the functions of the prince in Israel:

> And it shall be the prince's part to give burnt offerings, and meat offerings, and drink offerings, in the feasts, and in the new moons, and in the sabbaths, in all solemnities of the house of Israel: *he shall prepare the sin offering, and the meat offering, and the burnt offering, and the peace offerings, to make reconciliation for the house of Israel.*
>
> Ezekiel 45:17 (Emphasis added)

> And upon that day shall the prince *prepare for himself* and for all the people of the land a bullock for *a sin offering*.
>
> Ezekiel 45:22 (Emphasis added)

> And the prince shall enter by the way of the porch of that gate without, and shall stand by the post of the gate, and the priests shall prepare his burnt offering and his peace offerings, *and he shall worship* at the threshold of the gate: then he shall go forth; but the gate shall not be shut until the evening.
>
> Ezekiel 46:2 (Emphasis added.)

> Thus saith the Lord GOD; If the prince give a gift unto any *of his sons*, the inheritance thereof shall be his sons'; it shall be their possession by inheritance.
>
> Ezekiel 46:16 (Emphasis added)

From these scriptures we can tell that the prince officiating in the new temple is human. First, he furnishes *and prepares* all the offerings for *himself* and for Israel in their special feasts, new moons and Sabbaths. He is also a teacher, because he is their shepherd feeding them spiritual truths, which is the job of a priest also. Second, *he shall worship*. Jesus does not worship, *he* is the object of worship. And third, this earthly prince has sons to whom he gives of his land for inheritance. The prince of Israel receives land on either side of the holy oblation, which God designates as his. In this holy oblation the final temple of the millennium will be built, as well as the homes of the priesthood and the capital city. Perhaps the prince receives so much land because he must raise the livestock necessary for all those sacrifices he furnishes.

The rest of the scriptures that mention this David follow. But please notice that beyond Ezekiel's expanded picture of the prince of Israel, Jeremiah, Isaiah, and Hosea also mention him.

> But they shall serve the *Lord their God*, and *David their king*, whom I will raise up unto them.
>
> Therefore fear thou not, O my servant Jacob, saith the Lord; neither be dismayed, O Israel: for, lo, I will save thee from afar, and thy seed from the land of their captivity; and Jacob shall return, and shall be in rest, and be quiet, and none shall make him afraid.
>
> Jeremiah 30:9, 10 (Emphasis mine.)

> Incline your ear, and come unto me: hear, and your soul shall live; and I will make an everlasting covenant with you, even the sure mercies of David.
>   Behold, I have given him for a *witness to the people, a leader and commander to the people.*
>   Behold, thou shalt call a nation that thou knowest not, and nations that knew not thee shall run unto thee because of the Lord thy God, and for the Holy One of Israel; *for he hath glorified thee.* [indicates the time is of their final blessing]
>
> Isaiah 55:3-5 (Emphasis mine.)

> Afterward shall the children of Israel return, and seek the *Lord their God*, and *David their king*; and shall fear the Lord and his goodness in the latter days.
>
> Hosea 3:5 (Emphasis mine.)

These last three scriptures cause the argument among scholars. These seem to refer to Jesus or both, although Jesus was never called by the name of David. Rather he is always referred to as the *son* of David. On the other hand, there is no reason why the people should look forward to the ancient David as their king, for what would this man know of the world today? Or why would he want to give up his blessed place in the heavenly city? In Psalm 27:4 his stated heart's desire was to "dwell in the house of the Lord all the days of my life, to behold the beauty of the Lord, and to enquire in his temple."

Also notice in both sets of scriptures, the people look forward to both their God and *their king*, not God and king, which seems to suggest two separate persons.

I have taken the middle road of the argument. I can see a man, David, who is similar in personality to the ancient king David, sitting on his throne, as his literal descendent, a Priest/Prince on the earthly throne in Jerusalem. Meanwhile, Jesus, also the literal son of David, sits on his Father's throne as Priest/King over the whole world. Remember, although Jesus also sits on his throne on earth, in the holy of holies of the temple, the footstool of his throne in the city above, he still cannot live among men on a day-to-day basis, as God, because earthly people are still sinners. That's why glorified men carry out the government among the people, and the prince is a mediator for the people in worship on the sabbaths. Christ is the great priest after the order of Melchezedeck, interceding for all the people before his Father.

The temple also reflects this type of picture. On the wall and posts stand cherubs with two faces between palm trees. One faces the palm on one side with the face of a man, while the other face turns to the palm on the other side as the face of a lion. The man represents Jesus' reign as a priest, while the lion represents his reign as king. David, the man/king, officiates as a priest and a ruler who judges, while King Jesus officiates as a priest before his Father for earth dwellers and passes down judgments to his bride who rules in judgments (Ps. 149:5-9).

Therefore, because of these scriptures I believe God will raise up a special man, a literal descendent of David to fill this role of a prince in Israel.

Appendix B

The Sensual Religious Aspect

The righteousness of Christ in the Church throughout the past two thousand years has been light and salt to the world, preserving it from the complete debauchery of the idol worship of ancient times. However, today's world is heading back toward those times. Science, through the theories of uniformitarianism (more recently called "gradualism" or "actualism") and Evolution, have effectively removed God from modern intellectual thinking, leading to a post-modern era, eliminating responsibility to God and his laws. The Emerging Church leans toward a "feel good" experience in their approach to God. At this time it involves a sense of feeling God's presence in meditation and holiness in their bodies. Visual aids such as candles, beads, etc., help set the atmosphere. Instead of preaching the gospel to the poor, Christian works match the world's—meeting temporal needs in social programs, neglecting the world's spiritual need of avoiding hell.

How long will it be until the Church deteriorates to the conditions spoken of in the epistle of Jude? Some already engage in rebellion, like Cain, turning against the Word, Pastors seeking power and money, like Balaam, or seeking authority not rightly theirs, like Core, but the final step is to separate themselves into complete sensuality of the flesh. This means using sexual practices in worship. When man can justify indulging acts of debauchery through religion (worshipping his god) he releases his restraints of conscience and anything goes. If the Church should descend into this state, what hope would there be for the world, after the Church is gone?

Seeing the world where it is today, I cannot help but see the religious practices of the last days to equal, if not exceed those of the Canaanites, which God hated completely. Prophets speaking of the Lord's final coming seem to agree. See Habakkuk's vision for an appointed time especially 2:15, 16, which shows the moral climate. Isaiah 66:7-17 connects the redeeming of Israel, and the future judgment of those repeating the sins of idol worship, at his return. They sanctify and purify themselves in the gardens, eating swine's flesh, the abomination (some object?), and the mouse (the image made to a heavenly body of Isaiah's day?) shall be consumed together.

The asherah as a word (called *grove* in King James English), was not a planting of several trees. It appeared forty times in the Old Testament, as the name of an object used in worship. It is always associated with Baal (Lord of storm and fertility) worship, with an altar and incense, and sometimes an image of the goddess Ashtoreth. It is described as a pillar (i.e., mastaba, pole,) a pole or a stump made of wood. It is carved and can be burned to destroy it. No one knows exactly what it was, scholars take different views, but all agree that it was *not* a living tree. It was particularly hated by God, as a thing of shame and disgust. It is somehow connected with the goddess Ashtoreth. Perhaps, the person participating becomes a substitute for her in the union with the male Baal.

THE END... AND A NEW BEGINNING

Spewing is known as an act of shame. Jesus spews the Lukewarm Church from his mouth. Her shameful condition in the last days makes him sick. We take him into our body by mouth in communion symbolically as the bread of life, to become one with him. Contrast this with using a pole to become one with a god sexually in worshipping idols. It is a great abomination! To demonstrate it publicly becomes an even greater shame. I created this meaning for the "grove" as the worst abomination I could think of. I believe this will be a demonic seductive act of the future religion, surpassing even harlots and homosexuals, in couple worship. It will probably figure into the reason the people are unwilling to give up their idol worship after God sends the great destructive sixth plague. Demons addict them to the sensual pleasures by enticement, then bring them into deep bondage to the desire, compelling them to indulge in masturbation. This is not much of a step beyond devices shown openly in household catalogs even today, advertised for sensual pleasure.

The Apostles warned that the only remedy for the flesh is death "therefore reckon yourselves dead to sin and alive to God… (Rom.6:11). These will reckon themselves alive unto their god and dead unto decency. Listen to the works of the flesh: *Adultery, fornication, uncleanness, lasciviousness*, idolatry, witchcraft…These top the list. The sins of the Canaanites covered every depravity known to men. Can we expect the end time civilization, who are the wickedest of all, to be any better?

Appendix C

Bombardment from Heaven

Natural Heavenly Missiles

Hail, in the Old Testament scriptures, comes from the Hebrew word "*Barad*," which can mean meteorite as well as ice. Although there is plenty of ice in space, it would be very rare for it not to melt on its descent through the atmosphere. The grievous hail that fell on Egypt, mingled with fire that destroyed trees, was probably not ice, but meteorites. The great stones that fell in the prolonged day of Joshua 10:11 were called hailstones.

There are three main types of meteorites: Iron, stone, and stone/iron. The Bible doesn't distinguish between types, but most are associated with fire as in a burning body falling apart in space and being drawn to the earth by gravity. With the disintegration going on in the conflict in space, meteorites are inevitable. Revelation 6:13 speaks of them as stars like figs falling from a tree in a windstorm. That indicates they are being hurled in groups.

Bolides however, are considerably larger than meteorites. Sometimes called fireballs, at some point in their crashing toward earth they explode above the earth, spreading debris into an elliptical pattern like the one spreading a bloody type of dust over one third of the earth, affecting the waters.

Special Supernatural Heavenly Missiles

The Mighty ones/Terrible ones is a name given to a particular type of menace not seen since Isaiah's day that only draw near to the earth when a heavenly body coming close to the earth has also closely encountered another planet on its way. During that encounter by its electromagnetic and/or gravitational attraction, it tore away chunks of crust from that planet, forming small independent bodies that then followed in the wake of the original intruder. The planet Mars was said to have had swarms following it (supposedly taken from Venus) when it ventured close to the earth in Isaiah's day. Caught in the gravitation influence of both earth and Mars, these small independent comets took on different shapes, sometimes armies, sometimes chariot wheels, sometimes shiny serpents and when the earth's attraction overcame them, they crashed down upon the earth like storms. In fact, the Indian writers (who wrote hymns to the Maruts), and the Greek writers (who wrote about the Erinyes), the Latin writers (who called them Furies) all referred to them as "storm gods." The Bible mentions them in Isaiah 25:4, where God is described as giving protection: "when the blast of the terrible ones *is* as a storm *against* the wall."

In other places the Bible describes them as the terrible ones or heavenly armies:

> A day of darkness and of gloominess, a day of clouds and of thick darkness, as the morning spread upon the mountains: a great people and a strong; there hath not been ever the like,

neither shall be any more after it, *even* to the years of many generations.

A fire devours before them; and behind them a flame burns: the land *is* as the garden of Eden before them, and behind them a desolate wilderness; yea, and nothing shall escape them.

The appearance of them *is* as the appearance of horses; and as horsemen, so shall they run.

Like the noise of chariots on the tops of mountains shall they leap, like the noise of a flame of fire that devours the stubble, as a strong people set in battle array.

Before their face the people shall be much pained: all faces shall gather blackness.

They shall run like mighty men; they shall climb the wall like men of war; and they shall march every one on his ways, and they shall not break their ranks:

Neither shall one thrust another; they shall walk everyone in his path: and when they fall upon the sword, they shall not be wounded.

They shall run to and fro in the city; they shall run upon the wall, they shall climb up upon the houses; they shall enter in at the windows like a thief.

The earth shall quake before them; the heavens shall tremble: the sun and the moon shall be dark, and the stars shall withdraw their shining:

And the Lord shall utter his voice before *his army*: for his camp *is* very great: for *he is* strong that executes his word: for the day of the Lord *is* great and very terrible; and who can abide it?

Joel 2:2-11 Emphasis mine

Revelation includes them in the next to last plague, just before the Lord returns:

> And thus I saw the horses in the vision, and them that sat on them, having breastplates of fire, and of jacinth, and brimstone: and the heads of the horses *were* as the heads of lions; and out of their mouths issued fire and smoke and brimstone.
>
> By these three was the third part of men killed, by the fire, and by the smoke, and by the brimstone, which issued out of their mouths.
>
> For their power is in their mouth, and in their tails: for their tails *were* like unto serpents, and had heads, and with them they do hurt.
>
> And the rest of the men which were not killed by *these plagues* yet repented not of the works of their hands, that they should not worship devils, and idols of gold, and silver, and brass, and stone, and of wood: which neither can see, nor hear, nor walk:
>
> Neither did they repent of their murders, nor of their sorceries, nor of their fornication, nor of their thefts.
>
> Revelation. 9:17-21 Emphasis mine

It is obvious this army is not human because it is called a plague. Also they seem to be connected to the releasing of the four angels bound in the Euphrates River, which might suggest they are used by forces of spiritual darkness.

Immanuel Velikovsky, when writing about a conflict between Mars and Venus during the days of Isaiah, determined that they were small independent comets drawn off of the planet bodies through their close encounters, to form independent existences. They swarmed close to the earth, crashing down, causing great damage, and horrifying the people.

Only twice are they encountered in the present conflict: once when the earth turns upside down, where the description in Joel describes them falling on the Russian Army (by association with Isaiah 34); and once in the sixth trumpet after the two witnesses are killed in Revelation. In both cases we have world-wide earthquakes where every mountain and every island is moved. This would be a time where the dragon body from space would approach closely to the earth, affecting the whole world.

Appendix D

Actions That Changed the Earth's Surface at the Lord's Return

Changes to the Earth's Surface Noted in Scripture

I have presented a scenario of changes to the whole earth. Some are drawn from geological features I already know exist, such as the small tectonic plates in the Indonesia area, or the great volcano underlying Yellowstone Park, or the great rift valley of Africa. These changes can be guessed at. However, the only sure moves of the earth we can know are those affecting the Middle East that the Bible mentions. Among these would be the destruction of the "tongue of the Egyptian Sea, along with widening the opening of the Gulf of Aqaba into the Dead Sea Valley (where fish of the regular ocean can live). This indicates that the Red Sea water now reaches all the way to Jerusalem. Somehow, the consequent splitting apart of the Mt. of Olives is a result. You can surmise that in order to put enough tension on the Mt. of Olives to cause a spread of the split to be as wide as a great valley, something else of magnitude has also happened (more about that later). Other changes mentioned are the flattening of hills to plains around Jerusalem and his drying of the Euphrates River. These are all specified. Others can be reasoned from these, such as how Jerusalem came to have broad rivers. The raising up of the Mountain of the Lord takes a special explanation (See Appendix G).

The Big Picture as I See It

What David's small band of soldiers could not know was the whole earth, which had been tilted on its axis by the drawing of the nearby body, causing the prolonged sunrise, suddenly righted itself. Then it left its earlier changed elliptical orbit, and ran first one way, then the other, being caught in a struggle between the attraction to the sun and the nearer foreign body. After being jerked back and forth between the two bodies, the sun finally won. It had suddenly taken hold of the earth's magnetic field, just as God told Job, "to shake the wicked out of it."

The magnetic power is really connected to the earth's core. The surface crust continued to move through momentum. Again the earth quaked worldwide. Never, since men inhabited the earth, had the earth shook so completely. *Every high* mountain moved, more like sunk, leaving huge plains. The mass of the sinking mountains forced mountains beneath the sea, such as the Mid-Atlantic Ridge to rise becoming enormous land masses. The ancient sunken land masses surrounding north-eastern North America, called by geologists *Appalachia* rose again, as well as *Fennoscandia* north of Europe. In the Pacific region, *Beringia* near the Bering straits rose and the great continent of *Hawaiki,* the claimed original home of the Maori rose in the South Pacific. Antarctica also slid to a new location. Without solid support on its hot, near-liquid base on top of the mantel, the crust equalized.

These words came from my imagination after reading such books as: Donald W. Patten's, *The Biblical Flood and the Ice Epoch*, Immanuel Velikovsky's *Worlds in Collision, Earth in Upheaval* and D.S. Allen and J. B. Delair's *Cataclysm*.

However, scientists say if a body near to the size of the earth came in close, it would cause tremendous effects *inside* the earth. Besides causing great tides of the seas on the surface, inside, the magma would also be drawn up in tides as well. At high temperatures it could be quite liquid and even more susceptible to movement in response to a foreign body. By this method some geologists surmise that the newest mountains formed: the Alps, Rockies and Himalayas may have attained their present elevations by riding laterally on an interior tide. If you look at a topographical map of the Himalayas you will see a radial configuration of the mountains in China suggesting that a huge mass of surface was shoved into them. With such horrible changes rearranging the surface of the earth it's a wonder any men survive.

Changes to the Vicinity of Israel

Looking down upon the earth, the Lord's invading army saw the bigger picture. The ten thousands of saints spoken of by Enoch: the Church, the 144,000, and their converts, and the great congregation of the Old Testament Saints, riding behind Yeshua, had witnessed it all. They saw the abnormal path of the earth running helter-skelter out of its orbit. They saw the heavenly dragon that Adoni´(being deceived) thought was his god, bring destruction. They saw how the earth, being pounded by God's rod of judgment, destroyed the wicked. As it drew nearer to the earth, they heard the deep (ocean) utter his voice and saw it sweep over the trembling mountains, the forward wave lifting, like hands, as waters from the Mediterranean swept over the Jezreel Valley and the western coasts of Israel and points north. Now Yeshua's heavenly army fulfilled the scriptures in Habakkuk 3:15, 16 as they descended: "Thou didst walk *through* the *sea* with thine horses, *through* the heap of great waters…when he comes unto the people he will invade them *with his troops*."

More Details of the Changes to the Earth

During the erratic movement of the earth, Jesus's armies saw the continent of Africa slam into the continent of Europe, putting such tension on the mountains of Israel that the northern block of the mountain range snapped at the fault through the Mt. of Olives and raised the Jordan Valley, while the southern part followed the African plate moving south, closing the Gulf of Suez. A small sea was left along the western coast of Israel and south. We know this because it later became the western boundary of Israel during the millennium. (It was this sea, and the waters of the Red Sea that David's troops saw as glass mountains in my story.) The heavenly armies saw the European tectonic plate split over Eastern Europe, connecting the Adriatic Sea with the Baltic Sea (speculative). The great volcano over Rome erupted anew, spewing thick black smoke and ash that drifted over the battlefield, darkening it until the evening. They watched as most of the water in the Mediterranean relocated by pouring into the Sahara Desert, which had sunk and was now another small sea (also speculative). They understood the scripture that declared Egypt devastated—the Nile no longer a mighty river since its headwaters in eastern Africa were torn away and separated at the Great Rift Valley, causing the Indian Ocean to invade Africa.

THE END... AND A NEW BEGINNING

Now the individual believers understood how the blood in the battlefield could reach the horses bridals, (a scripture that had puzzled many a saint). Earth's armies, which were still in the Dead Sea Valley (called the Valley of Jehoshaphat in the prophecy concerning Armageddon), were in the way of the invading Red Sea.

Waters from the enlarged sea and the Gulf of Aqaba poured into this widened valley of the Dead Sea and rose to sea level all the way to Jerusalem. Blood from the battle curled around the horses' bridles as they were forced to swim in the rising waters, already pink from the ferrous dust falling with the rocky meteorites. A giant lightning bolt had flashed down the arm of the mighty one of Israel releasing the tides, like what happened after the Israelites had crossed the Red Sea. The Lord and his troops descended into the Valley of Jehoshaphat at that moment. As the crack deepened under the Gulf of Aqaba, it put tension on the mountains of Israel, causing them to split open at their weakest point—the Mount of Olives. The whole valley of Jehoshaphat filled with red water, a mixture of dust and men's blood. *Yeshua* pressed out the blood of the wicked of the earth as he tread the grapes of wrath.

Seen from space, the earth now showed a new inclination. Standing upright instead of inclined at its 23°, Jerusalem now registered 0° N on the compass. This brought fulfillment to a prophecy in Amos that said "Behold, the days come, saith the Lord, that the ploughman shall overtake the reaper, and the treader of grapes him that soweth seed…" (Amos 9:13 KJV). New weather patterns emerged, caused by the changed inclination of the earth. A quote from the book *Cataclsym*, by English scientists, Derek S. Allen (Climatologist) and J. Bernard Delair (Geologist), explains why:

> The present plane of the equator to the orbital plane is currently 23° 27′ 8″ and has been calculated to vary between 21° to 24° [in over 40,000 years according to Delair] …if

the plane of the equator and the orbital plane coincided and the rotational axis were vertical, the following effects would dominate:

- Day and night would be of equal length everywhere on earth.
- Environmental conditions would differ profoundly from those of today, with a widening of the temperate zones and a marked narrowing of the cold and torrid zones.
- Milder polar conditions would prevail and the present ice caps would not exist, or would exist only feebly, at the poles.
- The differences in the seasons would diminish with fewer extremes of climate everywhere, with some regions never experiencing a proper winter.

These factors, and…all the world's major mountain ranges were appreciably lower [God's Word says mountains will flow down—same conditions he refers to of the past]… enable us to readily appreciate how such conditions can only have been conducive to vigorous plant growth on almost every land area, that deserts can only have been small or non-existent; and that ocean currents must inevitably been generally warmer.

Cataclysm, D.S. Allen & J.B. Delair, Bear & CO, Santa Fe, New Mexico, 1997, pp.194/5.

Changes in the Waters

Huge oceans were no longer a factor upon the earth either. The whole surface of the earth had cracked and reduced some of the tectonic plates. Some pieces rose and others overrode, or alternately, under-thrusted one another. The earth's surface now separated into many various sized interconnecting seas. It was basically a new earth; few men had survived.

Appendix F

The Making of a New Heaven and a New Earth

As to Peter's words about the destruction of the world by fire, and the making of a new earth, let's look closer.

> But the day of the Lord will come as a thief in the night; in the which the heavens shall pass away with a great noise, and the elements shall melt with fervent heat, the earth also and the works that are therein shall be burned up.
>
> 2 Peter 3:10

Particularly looking at the phrase, "the heavens shall pass away with a great noise," we find Peter talking about a physical event. Yet, in this physical description, the translators have chosen a metaphorical translation for the Greek word "perechomai," translating it "pass away" instead of its literal meaning "to pass by." What's wrong with its literal meaning? The heavens shall pass by with great noise. Put in the context of the judgments, this makes perfect sense. A heavenly body passing close to the earth, dropping debris from its tail in the form of exploding and crashing meteorites certainly would be noisy!

One can easily see how the ancients would use the meaning of "passed by" and "passed away" interchangeably, since the heavens passing by meant inevitable destruction. They saw it as the heavens coming down upon the earth. Believers saw it as God coming down upon the earth. Isaiah says to the Lord:

> Oh, that thou wouldest rend the heavens! That thou wouldest come down! That the mountains might flow down at thy presence,
>
> As when the melting fire burneth, the fire causeth the waters to boil, to make thy name known to thine adversaries, that the nations may tremble at thy presence!
>
> When thou didest terrible things which we looketh not for, thou camest down, the mountains flowed down at thy presence.
>
> Isa 64:1-3(KJV)

David mentions twice that God bowed the heavens and connected it with his displaying great power. He asks him to do it again in Psalm 144:5, 6.

> Man is like to vanity: his days *are* as a shadow that passes away.
>
> Bow thy heavens, O Lord, and come down: touch the mountains, and they shall smoke. Cast forth lightning, and scatter them: shoot out thine arrows, and destroy them.

Great changes took place when God bowed the heavens. The ancients knew about these changes. Our generation *does not*, because we have been conditioned by the theory of uniformitarianism. As Peter said they would say:

> Where is the promise of his coming? for since the fathers fell asleep, *all things continue as they were from the beginning of the creation.*
> For this they willingly are ignorant ... [of the flood].
>
> 2 Peter 3:4, 5

Looking back in our scriptures in Peter, take the phrase "and the elements shall melt with fervent heat." How can this be translated in a more literal manner? The Greek word "stoicherion," translated "elements" in most versions of the Bible, literally means "something orderly in arrangement, i.e. (by imp.) a serial (basal), fundamental, initial) constituent. What are the most basic elements of the structure of the earth? We of this age might think of "elements" as the elements of matter, such as oxygen or hydrogen. But suppose the Spirit meant the elemental arrangement of the tectonic plates. Add to this thought the literal meaning of the word "lui," which can mean loosen as well as dissolve. Putting these together, could not Peter be saying something like: The basic tectonic plates that make up the earth's surface shall loosen or dissolve, not completely but at their juncture? Now the last phrase—"and the earth also and the works that are therein shall be burned up." How can this match the former two phrases? Beginning with the Greek word "ge," we find its primary meaning is soil. But by extension, it may mean "a region," or the solid part or the whole of the terrene globe (including the occupants of each application). Ironically the phrase "burned up" means literally "to burn down to the ground." The Greek word "katakooai comes from "koia," "to set fire to" and "kata" means "*down.*"

By selecting from these meanings what best fits the judgments, we could say, "And the soil also or the region (of said continental plates) and the works of the inhabitants thereon shall be burned down to the ground."

Now look at verse 12. Could we translate it more literally?

> Looking for and hasting unto the coming of the day of God, wherein the heavens being on fire shall be dissolved, and the elements shall melt with fervent heat?
>
> 2 Peter 3:12 KJV

For the words "being on fire." We could put the words "the heavens glowing with fire" because that is the literal meaning.

[4448 puroo (poo-ro'-o); from 4442; to kindle, i.e. (passively) to be ignited, *glow (literally)*, be refined (by implication), or (figuratively) to be inflamed (with anger, grief, lust):] Notice the meaning that was translated "dissolve."

3089 luo (loo'-o); a primary verb; *to "loosen" (literally or figuratively)*: will be loosened or broken apart, and their constituent parts melted down or liquefied *(teko)* in fervent heat. Here the heavens referred to may simply mean the sky.

Because of the way in which this passage of scripture is translated and interpreted, a whole doctrine has been built upon it. The Doctrine: that the whole heavens shall be completely destroyed along with the earth and remade into a new heaven and a new earth. The Bible does *not* say that. In fact, in the description of the changes to Jerusalem when Israel is restored Jeremiah says:

> Behold, the days come, saith the Lord, that the city shall be built to the Lord from the tower of Hananeel unto the gate of the corner.

> And the measuring line shall yet go forth over against it upon the hill Gareb, and shall compass about to Goath.
>
> And the whole valley of the dead bodies, and of the ashes, and all the fields unto the brook of Kidron, unto the corner of the horse gate toward the east, *shall be* holy unto the Lord; *it shall not be plucked up, nor thrown down any more for ever.* Jeremiah 31:38-40

Zechariah says:

> All the land shall be turned as a plain from Geba to Rimmon south of Jerusalem: and it shall be lifted up, and inhabited in her place, from Benjamin's gate unto the place of the first gate, unto the corner gate, and from the tower of Hananeel unto the king's winepresses.
>
> And men shall dwell in it, *and there shall be no more utter destruction;* but Jerusalem shall be safely inhabited.
>
> Zech 14:10-11 (KJV)

See the following scriptures that speak of things that last forever: Isa. 34:10,17; Jeremiah 31:35,36; Psalm 89:36,37; Psalm 104:5; Ezekiel 37:25; 43:7.

Besides that, every time the Scripture mentions the new heaven and the new earth, it is in the context of the beginning of the millennium. Is not this doctrine an attempt to explain Peter because of the ignorance concerning the physical nature of the judgments? Besides, every time God makes an age change there is a new heaven and a new earth, only this time will be the last ... *and there shall be no more utter destruction* ... he hath promised, saying, Yet once more I shake not the earth only, but also heaven.

And this *word*, Yet once more, signifieth the removing of those things that are shaken, *as of things that are made, that those things which cannot be shaken may remain.*

Hebrews 12:26,27

Appendix G

Gigantic Ocean Tides

When the earth goes through great gyrations because of being attracted to a close body, the oceans, being unattached and completely fluid, are subject to gravitational pull much greater than the land. So besides sloshing about due to the earth's movement, they would draw up into the sky as miles high tides attracted by the close body, being nearer and heavier than the moon. Imagine the damage when they let go! Geologists believe it can only be the power of water or wind that can move the giant boulders of several tons, that exist around the earth, miles away from their origin. These same type of massive tides makeup the glass-like mountains I imagine the Lord and his Army to descend between.

The Raising of the Mountain of the Lord

Isaiah tells of this special mountain being literally raised up, but as with the translation in Peter it leaves much to be desired.

And it shall come to pass in the last days, *that* the mountain of the Lord's house *shall be established* in the top of the mountains, and shall be exalted above the hills; and all nations shall flow unto it. Isaiah 2:2 Emphasis mine

Let's look at the original word for "establish" in the Hebrew. What do the dictionaries say?

Strong's 3559 kuwn (koon); a primitive root; *properly, to be erect (i.e. stand perpendicular)*; hence (causatively) to set up, in a great variety of applications, whether literal (establish, fix, prepare, apply), or figurative (appoint, render sure, proper or prosperous):

Now look at Old Testament Word Studies, by William Wilson: וֻכֻן

--- *to stand, to be erect;* to stand firm, to be established; to be prepared ; to be founded

In the Roget's International Thesaurus, here are the words associated with "establish:" confirmed, customary, entrenched, located, made sure, proved, traditional, true. Does this sound like something you would apply to a literal mountain?

What if you made a mountain stand straight up with perpendicular sides, almost perfectly flat on top, that towered over all the other hills around it? Does that sound more like what Isaiah is saying? This mountain has to be big enough to hold a very large temple plus suburbs, plus a park, with a river and a lake, all on its top. Can you imagine the Lord raising up a peaked mountain, that requires the removing of the whole top, to make room for his plan? The temple complex itself according to Ezekiel 42:16 is 500 reeds square. Chapter 40:5 tells the length of a reed as six times a cubit and a handbreadth (18" + 3"). This would be a measure of 21"x 6 (126" divided by 12" =10.5' per reed X 500 =5,250' divided into yards =1750 yards or nearly 18 football fields end to end square. Wow!

The temple buildings enclosed in a wall measure out to be just over three football fields length on one side of the square.

On the border of Venezuela and Bolivia stand several of such mountains called *tepuis*. They stand straight up as huge blocks of solid sandstone or granite, flat on top, some littered with crystals of quartz, which can also be embedded. In fact, hikers are warned to take precaution against the crystalline nature of the rocks causing a braising to the skin should they fall.

"Electric Universe Scientists" believe only a giant thunderbolt, temporarily attached between the earth and another body (a Birkland current of pure plasma) could cause these, because of the evidence of enormous heat in their make up. Several million volts of electricity sent through the ground could solidified everything inside the affected area, create the crystals and in a parting shot, yank the solidified portion up out of the ground hundreds of feet above the surrounding hills.

This is the type of mountain where I see the Lord's house.

Postscript from the Author

I have presented the story of the end-times through the eyes of Jewish characters. Because of this, I have not fully developed what happened to the Church—the bride of Christ. Although I pictured the rapture in Book 1, it was never mentioned. Instead, I have majored on fulfilling the promises made to the Jews, found in the Old Testament.

However glorious, the new earth will be for kingdom dwellers, it cannot compare to the heavenly Jerusalem, in which all the resurrected saints live during the Millennium. They live in the presence of God, which is ever much better than worshiping him through mediators, such as the priest/prince or other priests. Kingdom believers will only see the outer reaches of his glory in a canopy above the Temple Mount (Isaiah 4:5). The gate to the inner court is open on Sabbaths and feast days for worship, but because of the gate being elevated and having depth, they may only be able to see the fire on the altar inside.

The first generation of the kingdom will have seen his awesome power, wrought through the physical judgments, just as the Israelites brought out of Egypt witnessed his awesome power against Pharaoh, at the Red Sea and Mt. Sinai. Those who sought after God because of their parent's witness, followed him, while others rebelled, went after the images in the sky, and worshiped them.

It will be the same with the kingdom generation. The glories of God will fade from their memory after a thousand years, and unbelief will arise in the children when they begin to chafe under the righteous laws that curb the flesh—hence the rebellion at the end, in spite of the perfect world. Up until Satan appears on the scene, they have no power to resist. But God will loose him and allow him to convince the unbelievers they can overthrow the government of God. God destroys them all without a battle, when they surround Ya'hovah Sham ma', God's city.

And finally, I would like to give a word about God using a member of the heaven's host to bring judgment upon the earth. Beyond God's general statement in Psalm 50:1-6, that judgment physically comes down from heaven, I have found two specific references of a heavenly body in God's hand causing the disasters of the past. God told Moses in Exodus 1:17, that he would smite with the "rod" that was *in his hand* upon the waters of the river and it would be turned to blood. Not only the river, but the blood would be "throughout the land of Egypt" (verse 21).

"The Manuscript Quiche' of the Mayas in the Western Hemisphere [says] that ' in the days of great cataclysm, when the earth quaked and the Sun's motion was interrupted, the waters in the river, turned to blood."[30]

The physical earth also gives evidence to the worldwide display of red pigment in the waters.

> An estimated 10^{16} tons of red clay covers about 104 million square kilometres of the ocean floor...[31]

Two sections of the Pacific Ocean--north and south, nearly half of it—contain deposits of very fine red clay.[32]

During the disasters of Isaiah's day (also mentioned by Amos, Micah and Zephaniah), the sun's shadow on the sundial moved back and forth (Isaiah 38:8), an indication of the inclination of the earth changing. God spoke of the cause:

> Behold the Lord hath *a mighty and strong one*, which as a tempest of hail and a destroying storm, as a flood of mighty waters overflowing, *shall cast down to the earth with the hand…*
>
> For the Lord shall rise up as in Perizim, he shall be wroth as in the valley of Gibeon, that he may do his work, his strange work; and bring to pass his act, his strange act…
>
> A consumption determined upon the *whole earth*.
>
> Isaiah 28:21, 22b Emphasis added

In the next chapter he mentions "the terrible ones." See Isaiah 29:5, 6. We have already described their action of "…thunder, and with earthquake, and great noise, with storm and tempest, and with the flame of devouring fire." (I believe if we look behind every major age change in the Bible we will find a catastrophic event caused by the physical heavens. God created all the physical laws we have discovered by study. He uses them to shape the changes to the earth. Our God calls the stars by name and sends them whither he will. What an awesome God he is!

End Notes

1. This happened in the overturning in book 2.
2. A painting of the dragon in the sky was hurriedly mounted for the people to pray to as the Russian Army approached Jerusalem in book 2.
3. A restoration of the fertility goddess of the Canaanites, presented as the consort of Ashtor.
4. See Gigantic tides Appendix VI
5. See Appendix IV Changes to the Vicinity of Israel
6. See Appendix V Temple Mount raised.
7. Acts 1:9-11
8. "they shall spoil them of the east together:" Isaiah 11:14, see also Zechariah 14:14
9. Isaiah
10. Daniel 12:11,12
11. Adoni''s abandoned natural biological name
12. Ezekiel 28:9
13. Isaiah 34:8-17
14. Habakkuk 2:9-20 KJV
15. Joel 3:3, 8
16. Isaiah 5:20 -25 KJV
17. Isaiah 52:15
18. Isaiah 45:23 KJV
19. Isaiah 44:6 KJV

20   Isaiah 65:13-17 KJV
21   Matthew 25:34-40,41 KJV
22   The 144,000 had preached to the whole world before they came to Jerusalem. Book 2.
23   This was a sacrifice in which the priest received a portion and the offerer received the rest that the priest would boil for him in a temple kitchen. When it was ready he would share it with his family and friends. It was offered as a thanksgiving offering thanking Yeshua for salvation. They would eat it in one of the thirty fellowship halls.
24   Ephesians 5:26,27
25   Hebrews 12:22
26   Deuteronomy 15:6
27   Hebrew word for Isaiah
28   Isaiah 60:1
29   Hezekiah set the precedent of the kings providing the burnt offerings for God' feasts (2 Chronicles 31:3.) God continued the ordinance in Ezekiel 45:6-16. The prince requires much land to provide for these gifts and their increase, which would be necessary with the increase of population.
30   Quoted from Immanuel Velikovsky's Worlds in Collision, Doubleday, Garden City, N.Y., p.48 His reference was Brasseur, Historoire des nations civili'ses du Mexique, I,130
31   "Red Clay," Online Encyclopedia Britannica, http://www.britannica.com/EBchecked/topic/494162/red-clay
32   A state of plasma named for Kristian Olaf Birkland, a Swede who first predicted it, Later it was further defined by Hannes Alfvén, another Swede. A **Birkeland current** usually refers to the electric currents in a planet's ionosphere that follows magnetic field lines (ie: field-aligned currents), and sometimes used to described any field-aligned electric current in a space plasma.[3] They are caused by the movement of a plasma perpendicular

to a magnetic field. **Birkeland currents** often show <u>filamentary</u>, or twisted "rope-like" magnetic structure. They are also known as *field-aligned currents*, *magnetic ropes* and *magnetic cables*). Quoted from Anthony Peratt, (who has become the foremost plasma physicist in the world), in his book, Physics and the Plasma Universe.